THE GOLDEN GROVE

Nancy Kress

BLUEJAY BOOKS INC.

A Bluejay Book, published by arrangement witth the
Author

Copyright © 1984 by Nancy Kress

Cover art by Dawn E. Wilson

For information, contact Bluejay Books Inc.,
130 West Forty-second Street, New York, New York
10036

Manufactured in the United States of America

First Bluejay printing: March 1984

Library of Congress Cataloging in Publication Data

Kress, Nancy.
The golden grove.

I. Title.
PS3561.R46G6 1984   813'54   84–430
ISBN 0–312–94180–3

For the Spiderlings,
Kevin and Brian

——Book I——
THE GROVE

Then you will find a breath about your ears
Of music, and a light about your eyes
Most beautiful—like this—and myrtle groves,
And joyous throngs of women and of men—
The Initiated.
                              —ARISTOPHANES, *The Frogs*

1

THE bronze mirror was full of blue-white light. From where the old woman crouched, just beyond the doorway, she could not see the room itself but only its reflection in the mirror. The reflection gave her the bluish light and two backs, Mistress and Master. For a giddy moment the old woman forgot the light and became caught by what the mirror had failed to reflect.

Those stiff and calm backs! And all the while the mirror left out the sound of quarreling, left out the doorway that was release from the chamber, left out the image of the old woman herself. It was a kind of deliberate caprice, a perverse and therefore fascinating filtering of precisely the kind that delighted Suva the most. She chortled and edged forward on her buttocks.

And now what had the mirror chosen to reflect? Mistress Arachne, her brother, the spider in the corner of the room, and that blue-white light: blue from the sea, white from the plastered stone walls. The light shifted over the bronze as the waves shifted beyond the villa window. Water light, sliding in whorls made heavy with shadows from the ceiling. Aqueous light, and suddenly it seemed to Suva that the room itself was underwater.

She choked and began to thrash at the air, flailing with both arms and rocking on her withered hams, until she remembered why it was not necessary: she was not among the drowning images the mirror had chosen.

Suva stopped thrashing and crept closer to the door jamb, to where she could hear individual words. Again she looked into the mirror. The spider still stood in the corner of the watery room; it had not moved. It had not drowned.

"Then there is nothing more to discuss, is there," the Mistress was saying coldly.

"No," Master Jaen said. "There is not."

"When do you sail?"

"When a ship has been built."

"You could have told me sooner, Jaen."

"I knew you would only behave as you are behaving now."

"And how would you have me behave?" Arachne said. "Pour me some wine."

"I didn't hear you," Jaen said. "Did you ask for something?"

Arachne turned toward him, and Suva could see her profile in the mirror. The Master was hurting his sister; at least half her fury was to hold her chin steady, and Master Jaen knew it; in even the lines of his back Suva could see the sticky man-pleasure in uncontested powers. It rose from him like a smell. Suva clapped both hands over her mouth to keep from chortling aloud. Oh, she would comfort Mistress Arachne when he had left! She would bring her fresh figs from the tree, she would fetch cool wine from underground, she would wrap Arachne in her comfort and squeeze until the Mistress squirmed!

"How long will it take to build the ship?" Arachne said. Ostentatiously she poured two goblets of wine and handed one to Jaen, who took it without comment. Arachne's hand trembled, but Jaen's was like his back: straight and watchful. Suva rubbed her hands together and rocked in glee.

"Till full summer. The ship will have to be much larger than any in the fishing fleet."

"Islanders are not seamen. Even the fishing fleet seldom sails out of sight of the villa. And no pleasure ship does so."

"One did."

There was a pause. The last Mistress of Island and her husband, Jaen and Arachne's parents, had drowned in a ship that had sailed out of sight of the villa. Suva had never seen that Mistress, having come to Island just after that—just the next day!—and her first sight had been the child Arachne, looking down at her from frightened, motherless eyes.

The memory blurred and slipped away, as it always did when Suva thought of that first sight of Arachne, and the something else, something horrible, stirred in the back of her mind. Stirred, rustled, lay down again. Suva picked an ant from the bony cliff of her knee and crushed it.

"It would be more reasonable," Arachne said, "to buy passage in one of the traders' boats. They will be here very soon."

"And get no farther, most likely, than Bylia, or one of the islands just beyond that. I am going to Thera, Arachne—to *Thera*—and I will not go cluttering up some trader's boat, sniffing around like a lost dog for word of some other ship to take me one island closer. I will go as master of my own ship."

"And end up at the bottom of the sea! Islanders are not seamen! Who will crew for you on this nonexistent ship?"

"Sec, Nyles, Hipporen, Traylor—"

"*Traylor?*"

"He is among the best fishermen on Island."

"He was. There is no fool like the old. Jaen, *think*—it's a mad idea. What could there be in Thera to make any difference to us here?"

"Libraries. Priestesses. Astronomers. How should I know what will make a difference until I arrive there and see?"

"The Grove has nothing to do with any libraries on Thera. It has only to do with us on Island!"

"You forget that it was a scroll in a library on Thera that originally led Delernos to discover Island."

"And you forget that that was five generations ago and even Delernos, who came from Thera, never looked back to it for anything! Island today should be your concern!"

From its corner of the room the spider began to crawl across the stone floor.

"It's Island I'm thinking of," Jaen said.

"No, it is not. You want an excuse for some childish adventure, so you tell me this trip is a rescue and a great personal sacrifice in hopes I'll praise you for it. It's a wilful and dangerous indulgence, Jaen, no matter what words you dress it in."

Jaen put down his wine and grasped his sister's wrists. Her wine sloshed over her goblet, and a few drops splashed on her silk chiton. In the mirror Suva could see Jaen's face. She thought that it had not changed much since he was a little boy—men's faces never did. They only turned inside out, so their men's feeligs were just under the skin instead of just above it, like corpses floating two inches below a flat sea. Jaen was handsome still. He would be handsome when this expedition to Thera drowned him, and his corpse lay tangled in gods' beards at the bottom of the sea. Suva chortled and rocked harder.

"Now listen to me," Jaen said, "and listen well. I am going to Thera. I'm sorry if you don't like it, but I'm going. Do you think I can stand by and do nothing while the Grove changes the way it has? Don't you *want* to know what's happening to Island? Don't you want to find out if anything can be done to stop it? It's not like you, Arachne, to be so afraid of action."

"I—"

"Don't interrupt me. If I go at least partly from restlessness, then you oppose me at least partly from fear. But I'm not going to bring hordes of Therans to the Grove, or to leave you for years and years to govern Island alone, or even to die of grief without the Grove. Because no one has left Island for five generations, nor wanted to, does not mean that no one *can.*"

"Maybe," Arachne said slowly, "that's why I'm afraid. Because you *can.*"

The spider had reached the middle of the stone floor. Brother and sister, hands and eyes locked, did not see it. It crawled into the blue-white shaft of light from the window, and a small corner of Suva's mirror burst into color. The spider was golden, the sun-gold missing from the shadowed room, with jagged emerald lines on abdomen and carapace. Its eight legs and two long palps were hairy with fine golden fur, and light glinted off the points of fangs tipping its chelicerae. From palps to spinnerets it was large as a child's thumb. It crawled slowly, blind.

"Don't you remember," Jaen said, and it was not a question, "how the Grove was. Before."

"It still is the same. Sometimes."

"Sometimes, yes. And does that content you?"

"Of course not!"

"Then we can't just stand by and let it happen."

"I want to take action about it as much as you do," said Arachne. "But the action must be effective, not mere blind dashing around the sea hoping to come across some magical remedy. The Grove is unique to Island; whatever troubles it here must be remedied here."

Jaen dropped her hands. "How do you know the Grove is unique to Island?"

Arachne stared at him.

"How do you *know,* Arachne? Perhaps that is only family history —family history born from some desire of Delernos's to be unique in all the world. Many men wish for that."

"The foreign scroll he found in the library in Thera—"

"Was destroyed by Delernos himself. Who knows now what it showed? Perhaps the sea is dotted with Islands, each bearing its own Grove. You make a god of Delernos, do you realize that?"

Arachne ignored the question. "If there existed other Groves, we would have heard. Some word—"

"And precious little word about ours gets out, either. To Bylia, yes, and the smaller outer isles where we trade silk. But who else knows of the Grove on Island? No one. Perhaps farther out on the sea there *are* other Groves, and other Households who understand and can alter what is happening to ours. It seems to me to be worth the risk of finding out. Don't you want Amaura and Pholen to experience the Grove the way it was when you and I were children?"

"How can you even question that?" Arachne asked.

"I don't. But how can you claim to already know that the Grove is singular?"

She didn't answer.

"How do *you* know, Arachne?"

"You can never just gain a length without pointing to the ground. You never could."

"True enough. How do you *know* there are no other Groves? It's an immense sea."

"At last we're agreed on something. It is an immense sea. What if you become lost in it?"

"I won't be lost."

Arachne half-turned from him, toward the mirror, and her body blocked the reflection of the spider. It had stopped crawling and stood motionless, not even waving its palps. From minute vibrations in the floor it had sensed a beetle seconds before the beetle sensed it. When the beetle tried to scuttle away, it was already too late; the spider's chelicerae sank easily into the creature's head and bit it off. In a moment the body did not twitch. The spider withdrew its fangs.

"You are not immune to shipwreck," Arachne said, "any more than other mortals."

"You mean I only think I'm a god. That's not true."

Arachne's mouth quirked unpleasantly. "Which is not true—that you think you are or that it's only in your head?"

"Neither. What's not true is that the thought is mine. It's actually Suva's. She thinks I'm a godling of evil."

The quirk became a laugh, amused but unwilling. "Suva thinks all men are gods of evil."

"No—godlings. She doesn't give us enough stature to be gods."

"Oh—Suva. She is mad, you can't listen to what she says."

"I know," Jaen said. He did not glance at the mirror.

"We are far from the subject."

"We are. How can you be so sure you will not be shipwrecked?"

"How can you be so sure there are no other Groves?"

"In the name of the Goddess, Jaen! Some rumors would have reached Island, some trader's tale or slave's story . . . but none! Not even Suva, with all her stories of magic and gods—not even Suva has ever prattled about so much as rumors of another Grove. If there were one, Suva would have heard of it in some land she had been enslaved, and it would have turned up among her stories!"

"Oh—Suva," Jaen said, grinning. "She is mad. You can't listen to what she says."

Suva curled a fist and spat into it. She began to raise the other fist, but in the mirror Arachne shifted and the spider came into view. It had wrapped the beetle in layers of silk and shoved it into a crack between two stones, and now it crawled on, out of the shaft of light from the window and toward Arachne and Jaen. Against the gray stone their feet in thin sandals were smooth and brown. Suva stared into the mirror, her left fist halfway to her mouth, her eyes pale as bones.

"Don't play with me, Jaen."

"Never." He put his arms around her; she leaned her head sideways against the chiton over his chest. She could not see his smile, but Suva could, in the mirror. It was a fat smile, thick with things she hated: triumph, complacency, a confident man-shitted recklessness. Ordinarily she would have reacted to the smile even when no one could see her, if only to make clear to herself what her reactions were. She would have rolled her eyes, spat into her fist, crackled sourly, snorted hugely. Now she saw the smile but did nothing, frozen, as the spider crawled across the mirror's watery blue-white light.

"How long will you be gone?" Arachne said.

"I can't hear you."

She raised her head from his chest. "I said, how long will you be gone from Island?"

"As short a time as I can."

"I suppose it depends on winds and tides."

"And on what I find."

"You will be gone for harvest," Arachne said.

"Yes."

"I can manage."

"I know you will. With Kyles."

"Of course," Arachne said. She added slowly, "I just wish you didn't sound so—eager."

She glanced up. Jaen looked annoyed. She pulled away from him and turned toward the window. "I will see you at dinner. I have tasks to do."

"As do I."

Jaen kissed the top of her head and strode from the room, his tread quick. As he passed Suva, crouching frozen outside the door, he flicked a finger in her dirty gray hair, grinned down at her, and went on, whistling. Suva did not even see him; he was only a shape passing between her and the mirror. In the room a breeze blew from the window, brought by the midafternoon shift in the wind. The breeze smelled of the sea. It ruffled the folds of Arachne's chiton, and although the wind bore spring warmth, she suddenly shivered and wrapped her arms around her body, shifting her feet on the floor.

The vibrations traveled to the spider. It crawled faster, scurrying on thick and hairy legs, its palps waving above its chelicerae. On one fang was a minute fleck of beetle, sticky with blood. The spider reached Arachne's sandal and crawled over the thin leather and onto her foot.

Startled, Arachne glanced down. The sweep of her glance crossed the mirror, in which she saw Suva huddled beyond the doorway, hypnotized by the spider. Lips pressed tightly together, Arachne jerked her body sideways. The spider tumbled off her foot.

She reached down, scooped it up with one hand, and held it close to her cheek, for comfort.

—2—

THE villa, built of plastered stone one story high, stood on the northwest cliffs of Island. Below the cliffs to both north and west lay the sea, reached from the villa only by a winding footpath to a sheltered harbor indenting the northern cliffs. The harbor was small, and gave onto a narrow beach of bright pebbles and small fishing boats. To the south and east the villa, like the rest of Island, sloped downhill to the sea.

At this western half of Island, the slope was gentle, descending through fields of grain and orchards of olives to the Southern Shore. At the eastern half of Island the descent was wild and rocky, broken by hills, ravines, and abrupt narrow falls of water. Few Islanders lived in the East: mainly vintners and goatherds, but not solely because of the wild land. Islanders wanted to live in the villa, where the Grove was. Thus the villa, built first as an exile's fortification, had become a landowner's retreat, then an artisan's center, and finally an entire town in which most of Island tried to spend at least part of the agricultural year.

All of its corridors were roofless, open to the clear direct sunlight, so that it was difficult to tell which were connected rooms belonging to the same house and which were public thoroughfares between. Some corridors were narrow passageways that had come into unplanned existence when two stone additions were constructed with space between them. Some were planned courtyards

bright with flowers and flat shiny pools of water. Some were mar-
ketplaces. Some were mere flights of steps, as shallow or steep as
the tilt of the land toward the South. Trees grew in odd places:
blocking a narrow alley so that people must squeeze past on either
side, rubbing off bark; through the middle of rooms and out holes
in the roof; beside fountainhouses and kitchens and pottery kilns
and storerooms. None of the trees were cut down, or even pruned.
Stone could be used lavishly on Island but wood, with one excep-
tion, grew crops.

The villa, sprawling around its trees, was still growing. The
corridors rang with the sounds of chisel on stone, of slaves grunting
and heaving to hoist blocks of stone with rope and pulleys, of
acrimonious discussions of the placement of a door or wall. When
the discussions became too acrimonious, the small craftsmen or
laborers or farmer's family moved. Another stone room could be
built, with the help of friends and friends' slaves, to the east, or the
south. On the other two sides the sprawl was checked by the unar-
guable sea.

In the five generations since Delernos, a politcal exile from
Thera, had sailed to Island with his vast Household, the villa had
grown unevenly. One generation it grew mainly to the east; the
next it spread south. Its shape changed from roughly rectangular to
square to the pointed outline of a lopsided star.

Given long enough, the shape always evened out, for no one
wanted to move too far from the huge open clearing at the villa's
center, where the Grove stood dreaming under the warm sun. Only
Island's children knew all of the villa's corridors, but the meanest
fisherman on the far Eastern Shore of Island knew the Grove, its
life and heart.

It was to the Grove that Arachne walked, carrying the spider in
the darkness of her cupped hands. She walked unattended by her
women, and knew that would annoy Jaen. Arachne wished she
could do more than annoy him, wished she could infuriate him and
leave him with the same sore, kicked sensation she was feeling just
behind and below her breastbone. As children they had fought
spectacularly—rolling on the ground, screaming, clawing—until
either their anger was spent or Suva, that mad old meddler, threw
cold water over them both. Either way, there had come after those

showy, public fights a peacefulness, a calm, that Arachne would have given much for now.

She walked faster toward the Grove.

The Islanders she passed, craftsmen who might have spoken to her or slaves who would have bowed, noted her scowl and flattened themselves against the corridor walls to let her pass. Scowling, Arachne's square face—handsome on Jaen, overly strong for beauty on her—was formidable enough to remind even the most independent landholder that Island, however benevolently governed, was owned by brother and sister, and he was but a tenant. The craftsmen flattened against the stone walls nodded respectfully. Arachne didn't see them.

How could he go? She let herself feel the rest of her anger and hurt, held back in his presence by—by what? Why should she never let herself feel as furious with him as she did later, away from him? Jaen smiled, Jaen talked convincingly, Jaen played on her fears for the Grove and for her children's knowledge of it, Jaen looked at her from the smiling dark eyes she had known for as long as she had known anything, and she was robbed of her force of will. She, Arachne, who believed will was what mortals made happiness from —in the name of the Goddess.

Her will would not stop Jaen from leaving Island.

Arachne stopped walking. The stone walls of a short, deserted corridor pressed in on either side of her; between them the sun cast her shadow longer than her height. She had not known it was so late. Her children would be expecting her. She must move, she thought, and did not move.

Her shadow lay dark and flat, shifting at the edges where a breeze ruffled her chiton. Arachne felt herself falling slowly, collapsing into the shadow stretched and pegged before her, mindlessly and without will. It was a frightening sensation, not least because she had never had it before. She was falling helplessly.

The Grove was changing.

Jaen was leaving Island.

Then in her hands the spider stirred, and the bad moment passed.

Grateful, Arachne opened her hands and peered at the spider. Now that she thought—now that she *could* think—she was amazed that the spider had crawled as far from the Grove as the Household apartments. The spiders did not like the sea. Sea rhythms interfered with their own, the monotonous low humming as soporific as hot sunshine. The spider waved its palps and stared at Arachne with blind red eyes. Through her hands she felt it begin to hum, a tingling in the soft crevasses of her palm.

The last of her fragile feeling left her. Her shadow lay still, only a shadow, on the sun-warmed corridor. It was one of the oldest corridors of the villa, built out of disgrace and exile by Delernos, the great-great-grandfather of her and Jaen. His banishment, beginning so bitterly, had led to finding the Grove. Now the Grove lay ahead of her. Arachne walked faster.

A child careened around the corner and straight into her, nearly knocking her over. He threw his arms around her waist and began to climb her like a tree.

"Mama! Here we are!"

"Pholen—be careful, I have a spider here! You will crush it!"

Instantly the little boy let go. He looked up at her hands, raised for safety above her head, and shaded his eyes with one palm against the sun behind her. "Let me see!"

"Pholen," Kyles said, not severely. He had come up behind the boy, holding Amaura by the hand. Arachne smiled over Pholen's head at her daughter, and then at her husband.

She recognized the silk of his chiton, but not why he was wearing it. The silk, magenta with a border of blue shells, she had woven herself. For a moment she could feel it again, heavy and cool in her hands. Kyles wore it severely draped, and the silver clasp on his shoulder was plain. Arachne was used to seeing him in the brown wool he wore to work alongside the slaves in his vineyard. He so seldom wore spider silk.

"Let me see the spider!" Pholen cried.

"You shouldn't jump on Mother like that," Amaura said. "Your manners are very bad." She smoothed the front of her chiton and eyed Pholen's, which was crusted with dried sand.

"Pholen, be careful. You may see the spider if you don't alarm it. See—it doesn't like all this noise and movement, it's stamping its feet. Kyles, why are the children with you instead of their nurse?"

"Father took us down to the harbor," Pholen said. "A trader from Bylia is here! He has *wonderful* things."

"A few of them are very pretty," Amaura said, "but much is shoddy." She was nearly grown, a leggy girl with a sulky mouth and pale eyes.

"It's all *wonderful*," Pholen said. He struck out his full lower lip at his sister, who smiled. "Let me see the spider again!"

"It has to go back to the Grove," Arachne told her son. "I'm taking it there."

"Council," Kyles said.

Arachne had forgotten. But that was why Kyles wore the magenta silk—today was first full moon, and sundown of each first full moon was Council. Had Jaen remembered? Kyles had, of course; he forgot as little as he spoke. Now she would have to hurry back to her apartments, change, go to Council instead of to the Grove. Again she felt the magenta silk between her hands as she wove it. She had been eating pomegranate and spitting the seeds clear of the loom. In her mouth the seeds had been as smooth and symmetric and impenetrable as the silk itself, or her husband's face.

"I forgot Council. I must return this spider to the Grove. Somehow it crawled as far as my apartments." She waited for Kyles to ask why at that hour she had been in her apartments rather than weaving in the Grove. Jaen would not yet have told Kyles his plans; Jaen would tell her first. Kyles did not ask. Arachne turned from him to her daughter.

"Amaura, you come with me. We will return this spider, and you may come with me to Council."

"No, thank you, Mother."

"You don't have to go to Council, then. You can stay when I go back to my chambers to dress, after we return the spider."

"No, thank you, Mother."

Arachne looked at her. "Amaura—you don't *want* to go to the Grove?"

"I am going with Father to Council."

"Instead of the Grove?"

"He said I may."

"Then of course you shall," Arachne said quietly.

"Yes," Amaura said, and her pale gaze was intent on her mother.

"I'll take the spider to the Grove! I can do it!" Pholen cried. "Let me!"

"Pholen—"

"I'll be careful not to squash it!"

"It's sundown," Amaura said. At the same moment a musical note from an aulos drifted over the villa, was repeated once a tone lower, and again a tone higher.

"Council," Kyles said.

"In name of the—all right. My women and I will come as soon as I change. Pholen, come with me; Nurse will give you a bath. Kyles, please take the spider to Council and send someone there to return it to the Grove. Pholen, do not argue."

The child heard the tone in her voice and stayed quiet. Kyles took the spider in his powerful hand. At the moment his fingers closed on it, Arachne glanced at her husband's face. No one on Island—except mad old Suva—could touch a spider without a tingle. Even now. But Kyles's head was bent, and Arachne saw only the top of his black hair, still damp from bathing.

The aulos sounded again. Pholen slipped his hand into hers and they hurried through the deserted corridors. From behind high walls came the smells of cooking: fish and warm oil, heavy on the evening air.

"*I'll* go to Council with you," Pholen said. "Not Amaura, me. I'm big enough!"

"You're not quite, Spiderling. Not yet."

"Yes, I am," Pholen said cheerfully, undismayed. His small hand felt sticky in hers, and his upturned face shone earnestly. Pholen, unlike Amaura, had been born buoyant. "I'm very big! Nurse says I'm too heavy for her to lift even. And Council will be interesting."

"No, it will not. I wish it were."

"Why not? What do you do there?"

"I decide quarrels. As when you and Amaura quarrel, and Nurse decides who is in the wrong."

"Usually she decides me."

"And is it usually you who truly is in the wrong?"

"Yes," the child said, grinning. "But that is because I am like Delernos. Suva says so. She says we are both murderous exiles."

Arachne said sharply, "Suva should not tell you such lies."

"But it's not a lie, Mama, is it? She says Delernos killed a royal favorite but the gods still favored him enough to lead his ships to Island, and I kill her patience but she still favors me enough to tell me stories and give me honey cakes. What is a royal favorite?"

Exasperation washed over Arachne. Mad Suva! "Listen to me, Pholen. Delernos was not led to Island by any gods. He found Island because he searched for it and would not give up. He didn't settle on the first uninhabited island his ships came to—he made the ships sail on and on because he had learned about a blessed and unearthly island and he wanted to go somewhere as unearthly as possible, after the earthly injustice of Thera. He had been accused unjustly—do you understand, Pholen? The man Delernos killed was killed in a fair fight, but then the king said it was not fair and punished Delernos. But Delernos would not give up his idea about Island, and so he found it, and he was the first person to ever set foot in the Grove."

Pholen stopped dead in the middle of the corridor. He lifted his face to look at Arachne, and his small features went slack with wonder. "What if he *had* given up? And got exiled someplace else?"

"Then we would not have the Grove." Her chest tightened. To not have the Grove . . .

"No *spiders?*" Pholen said, horrified.

"No spiders."

The child stood still, contemplating this. Finally he said, "Suva says spiders are bad."

"Then you see for yourself how wrong she can be."

"*Yes.* Spiders are the best things in the world!"

Arachne smiled. Encouraged, Pholen added, "I will come to Council with you now."

"No, Spiderling. Not yet. In a few years more."

"Now. I'm big enough. I can decide quarrels, and exile murders, and everything."

"We have no murders on Island, Pholen. People who live with the Grove—we do not kill. Murder is wrong."

"Delernos did it."

"Pholen—"

"Delernos killed a 'royal favorite' and he got the Grove for a reward."

The aulos sounded again, announcing the start of Council. Arachne grimaced at her son's tangled reasoning, but she had no

time to untangle it. Already she was late. She sent Pholen on to his
nurse, hurried to her own chamber, changed her chiton, and strode
to the Council House. She was late, and if Jaen chose not to attend,
her people would be kept waiting.

But soon she would talk with Pholen. "Delernos killed, and he
got the Grove for a reward . . ." Suva's mad stupidities!

The Council House stood just beyond the colonnade that circled
the Grove, and was built of the same white stone. Three sections
of tiered seats—for landholders, free workmen, and slaves—rose
nearly to the ceiling, but still could hold only a fraction of the villa's
population. About half the seats were empty. In front of the tiers
stood a low dais, flanked by stone altars and backed by a magnificent
hanging of spider silk woven by Delernos's daughter seventy years
earlier. The altars had a vaguely underused look; on the one farthest from the door some flowers, incompletely burned, rotted
unnoticed. The silk hanging, in contrast, looked fresh and whole.
The Council building had only three walls; moonlight from the
southeast and torchlight from the opposite wall shone on the clear
colors of the spider silk.

Council sessions were held at night to permit every Islander,
including slaves, the chance to attend. From the dais Arachne and
Jaen, equal rulers, heard complaints, grievances, requests, criminal
accusations, and suggestions. To each they gave a judgment, which
was binding. Kyles, Jaen's wife when he chose one, and someday
Amaura and Pholen, could contribute advice and opinions, but the
advice was not binding, although sometimes it was useful. Kyles,
heir of one of the landholding families on Island, often heard more
about disputes beyond the villa than was spoken in Council, or than
Jaen did. Tonight Jaen was absent, Arachne late. The Islanders,
some come from as far as the Eastern Shore, muttered at the delay.
When Arachne and her women appeared, a little flustered, the
muttering did not die down.

Arachne was tired. Suva had not been in her apartments to help
her bathe and change. The empty chair next to her own revived the
kicked feeling below her breastbone. She considered her people's
petitions important, but she had to will herself to consider them
interesting. She leaned forward, concentrating intently, and wondered why the petitioner, a thin and balding silversmith, stepped

back a pace. Seldom intimidated herself, she did not know that her frown of concentration was intimidating.

It was Jaen whose interest in Council was effortless. His powerful body lounging at ease on the dais, he joked with the slaves and landholders alike, and his easy authority kept the wit from becoming too familiar or too stinging. "What—using weighted scales?" he would say of a voluptuous widow. "You expect me to believe that *she* lacks ample poundage?" He would not smile himself, but his black eyes sparkled, and even the accused would blush, and smile, and accept Jaen's decision without a murmur.

If he were here, Jaen would say—

"I am sorry, I did not hear you," Arachne said to the silversmith. "Please begin again."

The muttering rose briefly in the high tiers. Arachne leaned forward, willing herself to listen, scowling with the effort not to yawn.

Delernos. Her attention kept wandering to Delernos, no doubt from having talked about him with Jaen and with Pholen. A god, Jaen had said, you make of him a god . . . Jaen was ridiculous. Not a god, but a man who had seized the idea of Island, a blessed and uncertain hope, and hung on with both hands against all adversity. "Delernos killed, and he was rewarded with—" Mad Suva! Suva should not fear Jaen so much, when they were both ridiculous. Delernos . . .

What would her ancestor have made of this Council meeting, droning on in the hall he had built?

Arachne considered. His was the founding of the monthly Council, his the direct handing down of binding judgments by the rulers of Island, his the building and altars and dais on which she sat. But Delernos and his Household had come from Thera, where men killed and kings could command armies. What would Delernos have made of the matters before his Council now?

The silversmith before her had not been paid by the landowner Secoles for silver bowls furnished a full three months ago.

Two tenant farmers with adjoining fields disputed the use of a freshwater spring between them.

Someone's goat—unidentified—had eaten a vintner's only spider-silk chiton from off a bush by the river where he had hung it to dry while bathing, and it was a shame to Island that the poor vintner should be required to identify the goat before he could take some-one—anyone—before the Council for judgment.

Fishing, said a fisherman, was more dangerous than farming, and fishermen should be taxed less than farmers.

A slave claimed he had been beaten by his Master. He was indignant.

Farming, said a farmer, was more back-breaking than fishing, and thus farmers should be taxed less than fishermen.

A sister and brother disputed the division of an inheritance.

The pots sold in the main marketplace in the third stall from the fountainhouse cracked too easily; a fine should be levied.

The old priestess, Stydia, withered and nearly blind, made an impassioned oratory against the falling off of sacrifices to the God-dess, in this new and heedless age, for which she trembled.

The fishermen Epithien had a very talented daughter, modest and obedient, who was so clever with her fingers Mistress Arachne would not believe it, and would the Mistress consider taking the girl as one of her women and teaching her to weave?

Listening to this benign trivia, Arachne's eyes grew heavy. She stopped thinking of Delernos; it took all her effort to pass judg-ments, dictate resolutions, dispatch messengers to inform the absent of her decisions. The Council secretary, an ancient slave whose perfect memory had served Arachne's mother and her grandfather, listened wordlessly, a living record. Occasionally he coughed with the light, dry cough of healthy lungs growing old.

The Household treasurer was absent; Arachne assumed he was with Jaen, financing ships. Questions of taxes, paid in wine or fish or goats or olives for the Household storerooms, were deferred until the next time Council met. Disgruntled murmurs rose from fishermen and farmers.

Kyles, sitting behind Arachne with Amaura asleep against his knee, offered no advice. He sat so still, not shifting weight or rustling clothing, that once Arachne, remembering his presence, turned to see if he was still there. He was. She turned back, a tired and short-tempered woman concerned with responsibility.

Waiting petitioners shifted impatiently on the hard stone, or leaned their dark heads against their knees. The torches burned down, flickered, were replaced. Petitioners who had been heard left, surrounded by quiet groups of friends or relatives. The moon moved past the open wall, and in the dimmer light of torches alone the emptying upper tiers looked cold and remote. Arachne folded her arms and concentrated. Voices droned on.

Then at last the mundane considerations of Council were finished, and she was free to go to the Grove.

3

ARACHNE'S women were tired. She dismissed them and walked with Kyles to the Grove. Apprehension gripped her. Sometimes the Grove was just what it had always been, but sometimes it was . . . different. "Different"—that was the word, neutral and cautious, that her mind offered, and she held it almost sardonically, knowing that she was raising it as a shield against all the other words that might describe what the Grove now sometimes was. The apprehension tightened. She was not used to feeling like a coward.

Only the circular colonnade lay between the Council House and the Grove. Under its roof and between its stone columns the moonlight did not penetrate. In the blackness Arachne stumbled against something and cursed softly. She had stubbed her toe against the wooden upright of one of the looms that had, hours ago, been moved out of the Grove and under the colonnade for the night. Wordlessly Kyles took her elbow. They crossed the stone floor of the colonnade and stepped down into the Grove.

Moonlight glistened on the grass, sifted among the trees, slid over gray rocks turned pearly. Arachne entered the moonlight and gasped, almost cried out, with relief.

A figure leaped from behind a column. It picked up Arachne, spun her off the grass, whirled her around. Jaen was laughing, a strong blur of scarlet silk and black beard and the scarlet smell of wine, and Arachne found herself laughing, too.

"Jaen! The Grove is just as before!"

He set her down. His cheeks were flushed, and the hairs in his beard glistened with wine, or dew.

"We have the plans for the ship!"

It could not touch her—not here, in the Grove as it had been. She laughed at his eagerness. "You look like a little boy again!"

"I feel like a little boy. The Goddess has reincarnated me, with new blood and new eyes. Soon I'll grow a new face and no one will recognize me at all. Hello, Kyles. How was Council?"

"As usual," Kyles said.

"I should have gone, Arachne; I know you dislike passing judgments alone. But we had a meeting to discuss the voyage. Kyles, you don't know about that yet, I've decided—"

"To sail to Thera," Kyles said quietly. "I know."

Jaen laughed. "Trust Island! No such thing as a secret! Tonight we drew up plans with the Treasurer. Sorry to have taken the Treasurer from you, Arachne, but we did need him. I'll show you the drawings tomorrow. You will approve, I *know*."

"The wine knows," Arachne said, not severely. Her initial delight and relief were calming, becoming the deeper, surer clarity the Grove brought to senses and mind. For the moment, she did not want to talk.

The Grove covered roughly two acres, circled by the stone colonnade. On the rest of Island olive trees grew low and dusty in the clear light, but the trees in the Grove were tall and full. They produced neither fruit nor flowers, but their leaves were bright green and broad as a man's hand. Between them bushes, flowers, and grasses grew, seeded, died, and grew again. The trees, however, had remained unchanged since the time of Delernos. None had died; no new ones had grown.

In the white moonlight, trees and grass looked pale green. But by day, when Arachne and her women set up their looms around the Grove to weave, the green of the trees would be touched faintly, shimmeringly, with golden haze. Everywhere else on Island, the air was transparent enough to see for great distances and the light fell with straight, direct clarity. Edges looked hard, shadows sharp, colors clear. Even in the hilly ravines of eastern Island, some so deep that sunshine scarcely penetrated them, the light obliquely striking a cliff face sharply illuminated its rocks and scrub. Only in the Grove, of everywhere on Island, lay this other light, shimmering and golden, with a radiance that blurred shadows and tingled over the skin like refreshing water.

And only in the Grove as it had once been, before it began to fade.

Arachne lifted her face for the pleasure of feeling the tingling air blow over it, and closed her eyes. In the darkness thousands of spiders hummed and that too was a pleasure, a calm vibration of the sweet air.

The next stage came suddenly. It seemed to Arachne that she could feel her mind uncramping, stretching, reaching outward. She had been successful, as a child, in the Girl's Races—this stretching of her mind always felt to her like the stretching of her leg muscles before a race. The sense of power was the same, and the pleasure of active use. But for a race there had been only her own power, and what would meet her next in the Grove came from outside herself, from the Grove itself.

But first, came the heightened awareness that was the Grove's special gift. If the air in the Grove was hazier than elsewhere, its effect on the mind was the opposite. Slowly Arachne felt an increased clarity of perception. She noticed the shape of each moonlit bush, felt the dew on the grass brushing her feet, heard the complex rustling of the leaves above her head. Scents on the night air—thyme, myrtle, healthy leaves—were distinguishable separately, delightful blended. Arachne felt the blood in her own veins and the breath in her own lungs. Every nerve tingled. She felt tautly alive.

Then the aliveness abruptly deepened, and she felt flowing through her all the whole loveliness and poignancy of the created world.

"The Grove as it was!" Arachne said. There were tears in her eyes.

Neither Jaen nor Kyles answered her.

The rush of aliveness passed, and another kind of awareness unfolded in her mind: deeper, calmer. Her tears dried. Her mind stretched yet again, to its greatest limit, and brushed something beyond itself.

It was not a vision; it clarified her sight rather than overwhelmed it. It was not a mood; it came, in the Grove, despite any mood. It was not an act of will; strangers ignorant of the Grove glimpsed it if they stood there, though in slight degree.

To Arachne, standing calmly on the grass, it seemed that she felt, in muscles and breath and mind, an unnamed pattern behind the named world. The pattern was a web of glimpsed associations and sensations, and it transformed not the nature of the objects in the world but the way they fit together. It was the difference between hearing one note struck on a lyre and hearing the music from all seven, or between seeing only the warp threads on the loom and seeing the completed tapestry, intricate and whole. In the Grove she, Arachne, sensed the whole pattern, and that she, too, was a part of it. Not isolated, not random, she had been taken up and woven into the fabric of life and time, warp and weft. She was a necessary part of the pattern; without her it would not be the same; she completed the wordless pattern and was completed by it.

The pattern lay all around her, in the trees and grass and sky. It was orderly, balanced. It did not constrain her; it balanced her. If she raised her foot to set it down again on the grass, the pattern of the world rippled to its farthest edge. She breathed in the scent of thyme and myrtle, and life somewhere breathed it out. She was alive, and made whole.

Without the fragility of the dream, without the caprice of memory, the Grove gave to Arachne a clear sense of the flaying aliveness of the world. It did not confuse her senses nor—after the first rush —dazzle her emotions. It was a sensation, but not an agitation. It was a fact, calm as the ground beneath her, through which other facts became joy.

A door opened, and she laid her mind against the beating heart of the sky.

I know you.

I feel you.

You are I.

Belonging. Balance. Aliveness. Joy.

Jaen spoke first. Moonlight made sharp the plane of his cheek. "Do you remember when we were twelve, Spiderling, and sat an entire day and night in the Grove, determined to choose final words that should describe it for all time? We failed."

Arachne smiled. "It was your idea. I didn't think words were wanted."

"You never do. Nonetheless, I would have you try now. What do you feel?"

It was unlike Jaen to ask. Arachne looked at him. In the heightened awareness of the Grove she caught—not his thought, it was not thoughts that shimmered on the night air—but his sudden desire to hold with words what they had of the Grove, now, before it faded again and they no longer could touch it, be it. Arachne felt this desire of Jaen's in her muscles, as a tightening of midriff and forearm. She understood in the same way that he knew she had felt it, and that the knowledge of the wordless exchange lay in the clarified mind of each. Jaen reached for her hand.

"I feel," Arachne said, "as if I stand on the open palm of the Goddess," and was astonished at herself. That was not what she had intended to say at all. The Goddess—what had the Goddess had to do with her? She had had the Grove instead.

The Goddess had even less to do with Jaen. He laughed, and his teeth flashed in his beard. Tossing her hand back to her, he whistled softly between his teeth, some light and careless tune she did not recognize.

"Let me try again," Arachne said. But she found no words. Words seemed too heavy for this singing lightness of body, too slippery for this calm balance of mind. Heavy, slippery—like seaweed on stones. She could find words for the obstacle, but not for the goal. Nonetheless, for Jaen she would try. She took his hand again and twined her fingers firmly into his. He would not toss this grip away.

Finally she said, "The Grove weaves together. I with the world. I with myself. Time with light."

"I should not have thought *you* needed weaving together," Jaen said. "I can't recall ever seeing you untangled."

"It explains nothing. Words are not—I am sorry, Spiderling."

"Don't be sorry," Jaen said lightly, and pulled on her hand. They walked forward, toward the center of the Grove. The spiders' humming grew louder. In the patches of moonlight between the trees Arachne saw that Jaen was smiling, but in the grip of his hand and in the keen air between them she felt some unknown resentment, and she was troubled.

"Kyles," Jaen said abruptly. "What does the Grove feel like to you?"

Arachne turned to look at her husband.

"See that web," Kyles said, and pointed.

The web stretched between a tree trunk and a stone column, placed there precisely to attract insects. In the moonlight the web silk, strong and fine, looked the color of dark wine, but in sunshine it would be as scarlet as Jaen's chiton. The spider had already constructed the bridge line, radials, and foundation lines. It was spinning the temporary spiral, its spinnerets secreting sticky silk in a long, continuous thread around and around and around the radials. When the temporary spiral was finished, the spider would reverse direction and destroy it, rolling it up and at the same time laying down the more numerous and closely spaced threads of the final viscid spiral. That spiral, patiently unwound by Arachne's women, would provide the silk for their looms. As the spider worked, it hummed. It was an old spider, and the jagged emerald lines on its carapace had faded nearly to moss.

Jaen laughed softly. "Is that answer supposed to be an image, Kyles, or an evasion?"

Startled, Arachne turned from the web to look at her husband.

Kyles did not answer. He gazed at the spider, his face cool and closed. Arachne felt that shimmer, faint but clear, in the air between her and Kyles, and found herself saying, "Kyles was not much in the Grove as a child, Jaen. Remember, he is from the Eastern Shore."

"Of course I remember," Jaen said lightly. He bent and touched the scarlet web with one finger. The spider stopped both spinning and humming. It stood still on a radial line, waiting for the strange vibration to recur. A little of the shimmer left the air. "Island does not have so many landholders, nor Arachne so many husbands, that I don't remember where Kyles belongs. Come, let's walk to the Spider Stone."

The three moved closer to the Grove's center, walking slowly to avoid hitting a web. In the moonlit darkness the webs gleamed faintly, blurs of color. Each morning pharmakons were sprinkled on the dew from which the spiders drank. The pharmakons varied the color and texture of the silk, and the webs weaving across the Grove were scarlet, amber, jade, cobalt, ivory, indigo, alizarin.

They hung from trees, rocks, shrubs, slender stone columns. An occasional tall blade of grass or stem of a flower curved under a burden of heavy silk. Around Arachne webs stirred in the warm night breeze, leaves rustled, and the spiders hummed.

Arachne was still troubled. "Where each belongs," Jaen had said —not "where each comes from." Only in the heightened awareness of the Grove would she have noted the difference, and only in the Grove would she have felt that flash of tautness—like a pull on the air itself—as Jaen spoke. But had the tautness come from Jaen, or from Kyles? Jaen did not like his questions to go unanswered. And the web—there had been some disturbing shimmer around the scarlet web, and she had felt it even before Jaen touched it with his finger.

"Watch out," Jaen said. "Another web."

Concentrating so hard, Arachne had almost walked into it. Hastily she stepped back. The web, stretched between two trees, was a wide labyrinth of silk so fine it was practically invisible. The spider must have drunk no pharmakons in several days, for the silk was its natural color, an ashy gray. The web looked like frozen smoke, or like that misty morning haze so seldom seen in the transparent light of Island.

"The web is huge," Arachne said, and stretched out her arms to measure its span. The arms froze and her face went rigid. An intensity of feeling swept through her blood and mind, so unlike anything she had felt even in the Grove that she shuddered and nearly cried out. It all dissolved: web, Grove, herself—no, not dissolved, but merged. She *was* web and Grove, and everything she had said before about balance and light and time was so much dung. There was no clarity of perception nor balance of light—there was only Arachne, and Arachne *was* perception, *was* light, was the tearing intensity of sky-blood that was the only perception that mattered—intensity of blood, here, in the darkness, at this moment. She did not stand in the hand of the Goddess; she *was* the Goddess, and all else was death.

Jaen said something. She did not hear him. He spoke again, and by that time the moment—how brief!—had passed. Shaken, Arachne dropped her arms and stared at the ashy web.

"I said, I don't know how you and your women can weave threads this fine."

"They can't," Arachne said numbly, "I can."

Jaen said something.

"What? I'm sorry—what?" The moment had passed, but she still felt it tingle in the air around her, and she looked at Jaen in bewilderment. He frowned.

"The silk, Arachne—the silk. What will you weave from it?"

"I don't know. I'm not sure. It's so fine."

"It is that." He reached out one finger, and Arachne cried, "Oh —don't!"

The finger stopped. Wordlessly Jaen walked around the web and across the grass, and Arachne followed. She could not see his face. By the time they reached the Spider Stone, Arachne felt herself descend again over herself, and wondered what it was that had happened in the searing moment by the web. The bright calm clarity of the Grove now seemed dimmed.

For a moment, she had been the First Weaver of the world.

Arachne shook her head. Waves of bereavement for the lost moment washed over her, again and again, grief for the unholdable glimpse of—what? She had no answer. For relief, she put out her hand and touched the hard familiarity of the Spider Stone.

It swelled from the ground, breast-high, in a perfect circle. It was faintly golden, a pale translucent amber that seemed to promise vision to a great depth but was actually opaque as marble, and much harder. Even on moonless nights it glowed slightly. The surface felt smooth and slick, and was honeycombed with hundreds of small round holes that disappeared into the Stone as tiny curving tunnels. Into these the pregnant female spiders disappeared, folding themselves smaller than seemed possible, and from them they emerged a few days later exhausted, wrinkled, and hungry, to crawl off in search of food. Always they would be back waiting at the same hole when the newly hatched spiderlings staggered out to clamber onto their mother's back.

Jaen looked remote, the line of his jaw as set as a vase painting. Arachne saw that he hadn't liked her impulsive "Don't!" and she said, out of a need to cross that tiny breach and to anchor herself to where she had always stood with Jaen, "Do you remember when we used to drop sticks and pebbles down the holes, to try to discover where they went?"

"Entirely without known result."

"But with great satisfaction—remember? Now Pholen does the same thing."

Jaen smiled. "Does he also dig around the sides of the Spider Stone?"

"And gets no farther down than the armspan we also dug. That same priestess, old Stydia, made him fill up the hole."

"What—is *she* still alive?"

"She is, and she still observes the rituals at the temple. Pholen tries to count the holes in the Stone just as we did, too."

"You kept losing count," Jaen said.

"And you kept skipping holes to finish sooner."

"Or so you accused me. Does Amaura accuse Pholen of that?"

"She did until a few years ago, when she suddenly became too dignified to count spider holes. One thing they never did—they never drank the pharmakons."

Jaen threw back his head and laughed, the sound sharp in the darkness. "I had forgotten about that! Kyles, you wouldn't believe it—I actually drank some of a pharmakon. I wanted to spin a web. Arachne was horrified."

"You had diarrhea for three days," Arachne said. "I was afraid you were poisoned and I would be blamed."

"And no web. All that, and no web. I was heartbroken."

"You cried for days. I couldn't comfort you at all."

"You didn't tell our nurse, though. I was afraid you would give me away. I should have known better; you never did."

"Of course not."

"You were always there," Jaen said, and his tone had changed a little, "standing between me and the consequences of my own folly."

Kyles looked up at Jaen. Jaen reached out and stroked the Spider Stone, first with his fingertips, absently, and then with his blunt, square nails. Neither made a sound. Jaen turned his hand over and raked across the surface of the Stone with his ring. The muscles on his arm stood out in cords. The ring, bronze set with gems that came on a trading ship, rasped viciously. Sweat broke out on Jaen's forehead. He scraped at the Stone with all of his strength, and the rasping grew louder. When Jaen stopped and looked up, he was smiling coldly.

"See—no mark."

Arachne and Kyles stared at him.

"It is the ring that is scarred," Jaen said with the same strange smile. "It always was."

"Jaen—" Arachne began, and stopped, not having anything to say. She was appalled by Jaen's small violence, but she did not know why. The transcendent moment before the smoke-gray web was still with her, hovering just beyond their three presences. That somehow made Jaen's smile worse, but she did not know why that should be, either.

"No one affects the Spider Stone," Jaen said. "Not yet, anyway. No one so far. Kyles understands that. Don't you, Kyles?"

"Let us go back," Kyles said, and began to move around the gray web and towards the colonnade. Arachne wanted to stay in the Grove—the Grove now, as it had been—but Jaen shrugged and moved forward with Kyles, and she followed the two men. The grass under her sandals rustled softly. The humming darkness was like water, heavy and warm, and she was conscious of parting it like water with her body and of its closing soundlessly behind her. The scented air flowed into her nostrils and mouth, into her ears and between her fingers. She could not tell where the humming air stopped and she started, and she felt that the two were not so different. She gave herself to the sensation and to the Grove as it had been, and let it whisper to her till her mind was calm and clear. Between the trees patches of moonlight dappled the grass, and in translucent webs glinted flashes of gold that were humming spiders.

By the colonnade the old spider had finished the scarlet web. Arachne saw it, and froze.

The temporary spiral had been wound up, and the spider was laying down the hub of the viscid spiral. It toiled industriously, marching round and round, silk streaming from its spinnerets and hardening on contact with the air. But the silk was all wrong. It wavered from thick to thin and back again, and misshapen lumps appeared along its length. Sections had the brittle stiffness of sick bones, while other sections had already torn, tiny tattered remnants flapping between radial lines. The radials were scarlet, but the spiral was the dull color of scabbed blood. The spider, oblivious, spun on.

Jaen gaped at the web. It was shocking, freakish—as fascinating and upsetting as a deformed child.

"The spider is sick," he said. "Or else it's eaten something sick, or drunk something—that's it, Arachne, it has drunk some poisoned water, water some animal died in or—Arachne—"

She wasn't listening. She had darted away from him and was running from web to web, scrutinizing each for a moment and then running to another deeper into the Grove, tripping between them on nothing. Wild, wordless little cries came from her at each web, but her face looked unconnected to the cries: It was immobile with the terrible rigidity of fear. Jaen stood dumbfounded. Kyles caught her and held her, but she kicked him and broke free, choking on her wordless cries, stumbling to another web.

"Arachne!" Jaen said. She didn't hear him.

He caught her and pinned her arms behind her; she yanked one hand free and struggled against him, kicking and clawing. Her nails raked his cheek and drew blood. Jaen cursed and grabbed for her wrist with his free hand. Arachne hit him in the mouth. His head jerked back and she nearly freed the other wrist, but he tripped her off balance and struggled, using his greater strength and leverage but not his fists, until he had gripped both her hands behind her back and had one of her legs pinned between his. She tried to hit at him with her chin, but he held her wrists with one hand and her head immobile with the other, and dragged her across the rest of the Grove to the smoke-gray web near the Spider Stone.

"Look at it, Arachne! Look at the web!"

She started to struggle again. He forced her head toward the web, his grip preventing her from turning away.

"Look at the web!"

The web swayed in a breeze. Each strand of silk rippled, pliant and strong but so fine that through the web the outlines of the Spider Stone were solid and sharp.

"I have never seen such beautiful silk," Jaen said. "The web is perfect. They're all perfect—all the others. *Perfect*, Arachne."

Gradually Arachne quieted. When she moved to turn her head, Jaen released his grip on first her skull and then her wrists. She leaned forward and examined the smoke-gray web, strand by strand, giving her attention to each radial, each segment of spiral between radials. When she had finished, she turned in a slow circle, scanning the rest of the Grove, although its other webs were only blurs of color in the darkness. Overhead the trees rustled, stirring the exotic scents. Spiders hummed. The moon began to slide down the sky.

"Just an ordinary evening," Jaen said dryly. He was watching her intently, and she felt his concern for her, the self-protection of his irony, and his curiosity that she—*Arachne*—should behave so hysterically. The curiosity was sharp, astonished, and, Arachne sensed, more than a little pleased. Why? At what could Jaen be pleased? That she felt enough a part of the Grove to become wild at its change? But he knew that already. Of all things, he knew that.

Arachne was astonished herself by her reaction to the deformed silk.

"It came of measuring this web," she said, "*That* moment. Not only the scarlet silk."

Jaen looked puzzled. Arachne knew she could not explain, and would not try. Blood beaded on Jaen's cheek where she had clawed him. One side of his upper lip had started to swell. On her own arms were bruises, red now and blue by tomorrow, where his fingers had gripped her. Instead of an explanation, she leaned against Jaen's chest and turned her eyes again toward the smoke-gray web. The elaborate jeweled clasp on Jaen's shoulder scratched her cheek, but she didn't move. He smelled of wine, of silk, of his own scent as familiar to her as the smell of the Grove itself.

Perfect. The smoke-gray silk was perfect.

A mosquito flew into the web. It caught on the sticky viscid spiral and began to thrash. The web swayed but the silk, which could make ropes that would hold a block of stone, held without breaking, and brother and sister watched while the spider rushed to paralyze the mosquito, suck some of it, wrap the rest and attach the package securely to a bridge line. When the mosquito was secure, the spider returned to the edge of its web and crouched, motionless.

Neither Arachne nor Jaen spoke. The rich calm of the Grove lapped around them. Time balanced on the edge of the spider's humming, and Arachne gradually lost herself in both, watching the ashy web, sensing around her the infinitely myriad patterns of an infinitely myriad grace. Leaning against Jaen, she touched one wordless pattern, another, another.

The Grove breathed around her, full with sufficient joy.

It was not until the moon finally set that Arachne stirred and shook her head. Hours—they must have been hours before the ash-gray web, Jaen's arms tight around her. In the darkness Jaen shifted position and stamped his feet. Only then did Arachne remember Kyles, and that she had not even noticed at what point he had gone.

—— 4 ——

THE day that Jaen sailed for Thera, Amaura and Pholen stood on the cliff on the west side of Island and looked out to sea. Behind them rose the walls of the villa. Below them lay the water, sparkling in the sunlight, turquoise near the base of the cliff and deep blue farther out. On the horizon swayed the scarlet patch that was the silk of Jaen's sail.

The ledge where they stood was narrow and rocky, and the cliff fell cleanly to the rocks below. Amaura and Pholen had reached the ledge by climbing out the window, which they were forbidden to do, and they stood with their backs tight against the solid stone of the villa wall. Amaura held one of Pholen's hands. With the other he shaded his eyes against both the dazzling light and the cliff edge a few paces ahead; to block out both he had to peer through two fingers not quite long enough to cover both eyes. Hot breezes plastered the children's chitons against their thighs, and then lifted them away.

"Uncle Jaen is gone," Pholen said experimentally. Amaura glanced at him scornfully and said nothing.

"He's sailing far away," Pholen added.

A sea bird flew past them, wheeling and screaming, and dived out of sight beyond the cliff.

"We're here," Pholen said. "We're not going. Mother and Father aren't going. We don't sail."

"Yes, we do," Amaura said. "We're sailing now."

"Where?"

"You're such a baby," Amaura said, not harshly. She felt pleasurably confused by standing in the hot sunshine on the edge of the cliff. From this unfamiliar viewpoint the world seemed mostly empty, mostly sea and sky between which she floated, detached. Island was in full summer. She was dizzied by the unshaded force of sun on stone, by the shifting points of light on the water, and by the heat so dry it seemed weightless. All this gave her a dreamy sense that it was Island, not Jaen's sail, that was moving, sliding into some deeper and untouched summer. She did not want Pholen's prattle to spoil the sensation.

"I'm not a baby," Pholen said. "If we're sailing now, where are we sailing to?"

Another bird, screaming, wheeled past the cliff.

"*Where* are we sailing?"

"Be quiet!"

"Wherever it is, *I'm* not going. I'm going inside now. Amaura? Let me go. I want to go inside."

"You ruined it!"

"What? I didn't do anything. Don't pinch me!"

"I'd like to throw you off the cliff!"

The child started to cry. His arm was red where she had pinched him.

"Stop that," Amaura said. "Stop crying," and her gaze was on the mark on his arm. The color of her eyes was strange: a flat, light gray that gathered no light to itself but reflected it all back to the watcher. Against her unremarkable brown skin and black hair the uninflected light eyes were startling and, to the dark-eyed and emotional Islanders, disturbing.

Pholen cried harder. The sound became slightly forced.

"Stop crying. Someone will catch us here if you don't. Pholen, you stop that now." Pholen cried, rubbing his eyes. Amaura glanced up at the window. "Listen. Listen to me—if you stop crying, I'll take you anywhere you want to go on Island."

The child took his fists out of his eyes and considered. "Anywhere?"

"Yes."

"Then I want to go to the Grove."

"The Grove? You can go to the Grove anytime. You don't want to go there."

"Yes, I do. I want to see Mama weaving. And I want to see the baby spiderlings come out of the Stone. Some are coming out today."

"You're a baby yourself."

"No, I'm not."

"Then if you're not a baby you can just go yourself to the Grove. Besides, no spiderlings are coming out today. No spiderlings," Amaura said cruelly, "will come out again. Ever."

Pholen glanced at her, startled, and began to cry again. This time there was nothing forced about his tears. Amaura knelt next to him and put her arms around him, the backs of her palms brushing the warm stone of the wall.

"No, no, don't cry. There will be more spiderlings, Pholen, of course there will. I didn't mean it."

"Why did you say it then?" Pholen demanded. His nose was running. He swiped at it with the back of his hand.

Amaura sat back on her heels and frowned. The truthful answer bewildered her. She had said there would be no more spiderlings so that Pholen would cry and she could do just what she had done, put her arms around him and make him stop. But she could have put her arms around him anyway, anytime. There was something else to her lie, something she did not understand and suddenly did not want to understand. Her bewilderment made her ashamed, and she scowled at Pholen.

"I'll take you to find Suva. We'll make her tell us some stories."

"I don't want to find Suva. I want to go to the Grove."

"Then go alone."

"You said you would take me anywhere on Island if I would stop crying."

"You haven't. You're getting set to start again this very minute. If you cry, I don't have to take you anywhere."

Pholen stuck out his bottom lip. He was old enough to see that he was being cheated, but now how.

Amaura picked him up, shoved him back through the window, and climbed in herself, one leg after the other. It took a moment

for her eyes to accustom themselves to the dimmer light in the stone
room. When they had, she saw Suva sitting cross-legged on the
floor before a shallow laundry pot and grinning at her with her sly,
broken-toothed gape.

"Young Mistress. You watch too soon."

"For what?" Amaura said, smoothing her chiton after the climb
through the window.

"The ship will not go down so soon."

"It will not go down at all," Amaura said, and eyed Suva with
distaste, partly feigned. Amaura was both wary and intrigued. All
her life she had been told that the old slave was crazy, and all her
life her fastidiousness had been offended by Suva's straggly hair,
Suva's broken teeth, Suva's withered and skinny hands like yel-
lowed claws. The old woman washed, but looked as if she did not,
and Amaura could not bear dirt. Recently, however, Amaura found
herself seeking Suva out, drawn by some accessibility the girl did
not herself understand. Suva said things Amaura would not be
allowed to say—outrageous, wicked things—and no one cared
whether Amaura argued with Suva, or agreed with her, or ignored
her. Suva's madness put her appalling statements beyond adult
consideration, and in this Amaura sensed both a bond and a resented, shameful freedom.

"Once there was a fleet of ships, great war vessels," Suva said
gleefully, stirring the cloth in the laundry pot with a stick. "War
vessels with the speed and deadliness of of lightning. Oh, they were
fine! Each was propelled by tiers of slaves with muscles enough to
lift a small bull. Each ship had proved itself by the destructon of a
city. Each commander was rich with captured gold and captured
women. Each—"

"What's that?" Pholen said, stooping over the pot.

"A lump of soap, child. Each warrior's lust had fathered more
sons among more peoples than the commander could count. When
the fleet fought, the seas turned so red with blood the fish choked
and rose to the surface and died. So sticky with blood were the fish
that they stuck together and made scarlet-colored floating islands,
and the warriors leaped from island to island to land in order to
rape the fallen cities. When they battered open the gates and fell
on the women and children inside, the warriors brought with them

the terrifying stench of bloody fish, and all the children born nine months later had glassy staring eyes and sticky red fins."

Suva smiled at Pholen, drew out a knife, and began carving on the lump of laundry soap. Pholen bent closer to see. He had not been listening at all. Amaura, who had, stared at Suva in frozen fascination. She did not understand all the actions in the story, but her heart had begun to beat in irregular, painful thumps. Suva chortled, and shook her head, and made expert darts with the knife at the laundry soap.

"One day the fleet sailed to battle. Horns sounded, banners snapped, women wept. It was a thrilling sight! The fleet was going to defeat the enemy, just as they had always defeated the enemy before. The commander consulted with the priests to determine the best day to attack. The priests sacrificed a bull, then a slave, then a dog. The dog they cut open—" Amaura paled"—and decided a day. The commander had hoped to attack earlier, but he heeded the priests and waited. On the day of battle a great storm blew up. Winds howled, waves flogged the ships, the sea boiled. The sea boiled and boiled—"

Still holding the knife, Suva began to flail with her arms. Gurgling, choking noises came from her throat, and her eyes rolled and bulged. The knife flashed in shards of light. Her hands clawed at the air. Pholen straightened, gaping, as Amaura grabbed the wrist of Suva's knife hand and thrust her young face nose to nose with Suva's

"Suva! Suva! You're not drowning now! Not now!"

The old woman's eyes focused. Her choking stopped. She stared a long moment at Amaura, and then nodded briskly and returned to carving the soap. Her entire attention seemed absorbed by the task. The children looked at each other.

"What happened to the ships?" Amaura finally said.

"The ships?"

"In the *fleet!*"

"They were all destroyed, of course. Everyone drowned. Commander, priests, soldiers, slaves. The slaves first, at their oars."

Amaura considered. "The soldiers deserved to be drowned. After all that killing."

"It didn't matter."

"Didn't matter! All those children—" she stopped and glanced at Pholen, but the little boy wasn't listening. He was watching Suva carve the soap.

"All those children," Suva chortled. "All those soldiers, all those slaves. Yes. All from a single dog with twisted bowels, sending them down to the bottom of the sea!" Her chortles exploded, becoming sputters of glee. She laughed and laughed, rocking back and forth on skinny haunches, and the knife flashed in the light from the window giving onto the sea.

Suva laughed until tears of mirth shook from her cheeks and flew in droplets into the laundry pot. Amaura looked away. She was appalled at the cruelty of both the story and the laughter, and thought that she probably ought to be embarrassed as well. But something in both story and laughter—a heightened excitement of freedom inseparable from their cruelty—intrigued her. Such things did not happen on Island. They could not. They were only old stories, probably untrue stories, meant to frighten children. Glassy staring eyes and sticky red fins . . . and nothing ever happened on Island. And nothing ever would. Horns sounded, banners snapped —Amaura seemed to see sun glint on steel, dazzling and thrilling, while women wept. She shuddered, and yearned, and lashed out at Suva.

"You're crazy! Everyone knows you're crazy!"

"The twisted bowels of a single dog!" Suva cried, and gave over to more laughter. Amaura grabbed Pholen's hand and tried to pull him from the room, but he had been splashing in the laundry pot and was too slippery to hold.

"Get on with your laundry. You have work to do," Amaura ordered. Suva ignored her, rocking had chortling. In her fit she had dropped the soap; Pholen bent and picked it up.

"It's a *head,*" he said, with pleasure. "You made a head! But you didn't finish it, Suva. Who will it be?"

The old woman stopped laughing and looked at him. The edges of her nostrils flared.

"Is it me, Suva? Are you making me?"

"No, child. Not you."

"Who is it, then?" Pholen said. No one answered. Suva took the soap from him and began again to carve it, working as quickly and soberly as if the mad laughter had never happened. Her face was calm, her black eyes downcast over the soap, and in all her movements was the industrious earnestness of the obedient slave. Amaura blinked.

"Mama's making something, too," Pholen said. "She's weaving it, in the Grove, and it's different from all her other silk. It's special."

"Is it, child?"

"You should come see it, Suva! I'll take you there."

"She's afraid of the spiders," Amaura said brutally. "And of the sea, too. She's afraid of everything—*aren't* you, Suva?"

"Of *spiders?*" Pholen said, astonished, although he had been told it before.

"Of everything. She won't go away from the sea because the spiders are everywhere else, and she won't go near the window because she might fall into the sea. Again."

"I come from the sea," Suva said. Her voice was serene and fond; she might have been mentioning a beloved village for which she felt nostalgia. "I come from the sea full-grown, and before that moment I had no past. No man has ever touched me. I sprang from the sea, and birds flew ahead of me singing, and since my foot touched Island, the land has been protected from famine and pestilence and war."

"Island never had wars! And not famines!"

"I came from the sea singing," Suva continued, imperturbable, "and the clouds of sea birds, at that one moment and never before or since, lost their screeching and sang with me sweetly as doves. A white owl flew to my shoulders, and in its beak was a white flower, and even holding the flower it too was singing and singing."

"You were shipwrecked, and my mother found you washed up onto the beach, and you were covered with blood and half dead!" Amaura said. "My mother told me so!"

"Singing and singing," Suva said dreamily. The knife flew over the soap. "Singing at the moment my life began. Straight from the sea."

"Then how did you know the story about the war fleet? Tell me *that*—if you had no other life, how do you know all those other stories?"

"Singing and singing. Straight from the sea."

"I like the sea," Pholen said. "I like the stones at the harbor. But I like the Grove better."

"Young Mistress doesn't like it better," Suva said. She glanced up slyly from the soap. Her black eyes were gleeful. "No, no—Young Mistress surely does not."

"Yes," Pholen said simply. "She likes the Grove best. Everybody does. The spiders are there, and I pet them. Mama says not to pet them when they're spinning her silk, though, because if you pet them, they stop. They hum, Suva."

"Do they, child?"

"But they won't hum near the sea. They don't like the sea."

"Singing and singing," Suva said.

Amaura flounced around, turning her back on both of them. Pholen was a baby and Suva was mad. Mad, mad, mad. Mad and wicked. All those children . . .

"Once," Suva said, "the Mother Goddess ate a fig. Inside she found two tiny baby boys, smaller than your thumb, Pholen. They were ugly as toads. She held them on her palm and laughed because they were so small and ugly. But she was a Mother Goddess, and their helplessness moved her, so she gave them to a mortal woman and told her to raise the ugly tiny things. The woman agreed. But when the Goddess left, the woman thought that two babies smaller than thumbs would be a great burden. Still, she was afraid of the Goddess as well."

Amaura kept her back turned. Pholen watched the darting knife. Suva carved on.

"The woman decided to raise only one baby and say the other had died. She looked closely at the babies. They were exactly alike. She closed her eyes and brought her fist down hard, then opened her eyes to see which one she had squashed. Then one on the left was dead.

"The one on the right grew up to be a great hero, as brave as he was just. He made his mother an honored priestess."

Amaura made a sound of disgust. Crossing to the window, she scanned the sea. It lay calm and blue in the transparent light. Jaen's sail had disappeared over the horizon. Close to the cliff, where the water was lighter in color, darted flecks of white: sea birds. She could hear them faintly, screeching and diving, over the monotonous lap of tiny waves on rock. There was no breeze, but she could smell the salt air, warm and lanquid.

"Oh," Pholen said behind her. Amaura turned quickly. Suva, grinning, was holding out her palm, and on it sat the carved laundry-soap head. It was Jaen, with his curls plastered flat to his head. Strands of seaweed and drops of water crusted over his face, and his mouth was open in a wide, choked scream.

—5—

NONE of the women in the Grove would look directly at the silk on Arachne's loom.

Fools, she thought succinctly, but she knew they were not. Standing before her loom, her shuttle flying in and out of the vertical warp threads, Arachne realized that she herself did not like to look at the design growing on her silk. It gave her no pleasure. And if it gave no pleasure to her, why should it to the others? No reason at all—except that, this time, pleasure was not the point.

The slaves had set her loom near the Spider Stone. Her women had all placed theirs a little apart, in various directions. Only Cleis, the fisherman's daughter with clever and obedient fingers who had come to be the newest of the weavers, worked near Arachne. Arachne always taught her new women herself. Cleis's face puckered over her work; until she came to the villa, she had woven only in wool, and she was not yet used to the greater strength and lighter weight of spider silk. Arachne had given her heavy and coarse silk, as close to the texture of wool as she could find, but even so Cleis pulled her shuttle slightly too hard and worked her beater slightly too slowly. Looking at her pretty face peering anxiously at her pattern of flowers and shells, Arachne thought that in time Cleis would become a competent weaver but never a good one, and that the distinction would not hurt the girl because she would never know it existed. Something was hurting Cleis—Arachne could see

the hurt, like a bruise on a dove wing—but it was not her weaving.
Cleis would tell her eventually. There was nothing in Cleis that she
would not tell eventually.

Unlike the rest of the villa in this hot and dusty midsummer, the
Grove was cool and fresh-smelling. Sound lapped softly around the
weaving women. Although there was no breeze at ground level, the
tops of the great trees swayed, a green rustling. The whisper-knock,
whisper-knock of shuttles and reeds blended with the low conversation of the women. At the edge of the Grove, near the colonnade,
craftsmen worked and a group of children played some game in a
circle, laughing often. From shady places spiders hummed softly,
barley audible, their humming more sensation than sound.

Arachne gazed around her, and fought despair.

"The pattern is coming out uneven," Cleis said. "Look, the tip
of that petal bends over."

"You're pulling the shuttle too hard," Arachne said.

"It was easier in wool."

"Only because you were accustomed to wool."

"Sometimes it seems I will never become accustomed to spider
silk."

"You will."

"It doesn't *seem* so."

"Not if you whine instead of working." Arachne said. After a
moment she added, "I am sorry, Cleis."

"I'm not offended," the girl said eagerly.

"You should have been."

"Oh, no—I know it must be very hard to teach a beginner when
you weave as well as you do, Mistress."

"No. You're doing very well."

"It must be a terrible burden."

"No."

"When you sent word to my father that I could become a weaver,
I never expected you yourself to teach me."

"I always supervise the new weavers."

"I never expected it. Not you, personally. It must be a terrible
burden."

"*No.*"

"It's a very kind of you!"

Arachne gritted her teeth. After a pause, Cleis said shyly, "I have admired your weaving for so long. Of course everyone on Island praises it, but I was shown some silks that . . . that everyone doesn't see."

"Yes?"

"By . . . by Master Jaen."

"Ah," Arachne said. She could see the bruise clearly now; the pulse in Cleis's throat fluttered like a trapped bird. A memory came to her: the last Festival of the Goddess, at sowing, and Jaen laughing, dancing with a pretty girl with a smooth, worshipful face. She looked at Cleis more closely. That girl might have been Cleis, or she might not—Jaen danced with every girl, and all of them looked at him like that, and he laughed at all of them.

Had laughed at all of them. For a moment the silk before her on the loom blurred. How far out, by now, were the red sails?

"He showed me the green silk you wove, the one with leaves and trees and spiders," Cleis said hurriedly. "I couldn't tell that they weren't real, Mistress. My hand reached out to pick up a spider!"

"Thank you."

"I told Jaen . . . the Master . . . that none of us would ever equal you as weavers, and should not try."

"You should have told him that you were already far better at it than *he* is."

"Oh, but . . . but men don't weave. I don't understand."

"Challenges rouse his interest," Arachne said, smiling. Cleis looked bewildered and a little frightened. Pretty and stupid, Arachne thought. Cleis would never be a good weaver.

"I hope you don't object that he showed me your silks," Cleis said. "I told him—that is, I suggested that he shouldn't if you might object."

"Of course not. Why do you suppose I weave them?"

Cleis laughed nervously. She had straightened out the tip of the silk flower, which bloomed rather stiffly in shades of blue. Hyacinth, Arachne noted. Hyacinth for sorrow. "I like your silks so very much, Mistress," Cleis said.

"You don't like this one," Arachne said. Cleis bent her head, blushed, and did not answer. Arachne had expected a lie, something clumsy and obvious—*hyacinth for sorrow*—but the girl said nothing. Arachne thought better of her for her silence.

"He may come back," she said gently.

"Of course he will!" Cleis blurted. Her eyes were startled; evidently she had not considered anything else. Arachne grimaced. Unimaginative, pretty, sentimental—no, she would not make a good weaver.

For a time the women worked in silence. The sun slid closer to the top of the western colonnade. How far out now, Arachne thought—over the horizon? Halfway to the uninhabited islands, no bigger than the Grove, where she and Jaen had sailed as children? How far out now?

Shadows lengthened on the grass. The humming of the spiders deepened slightly, blurring the whisper-knock, whisper-knock of the shuttles. A fresh breeze stirred the grass.

Cleis sighed. "It's so wonderful here."

"Here?"

"In . . . in the Grove."

"Do you think so?" Arachne demanded. She had swung sideways on her stool to face Cleis, turning so savagely she dropped her shuttle. At her scowl the girl shrank back. "Now? Is it wonderful now, this moment?"

"This . . . of course!"

Arachne's scowl faded. She searched Cleis's face so intently that Cleis began to look frightened.

"Why is it wonderful?"

"What?"

"Why is the Grove wonderful to you? What do you feel? Here, now?"

Cleis looked around. Her pretty face creased. "The grass is so green, and cool, and the trees and—I love the smell, it's so fresh. And of course the spiders' humming is pleasant."

" 'Pleasant'?"

"Isn't it to you?"

Arachne gripped the girl's shoulder. Cleis winced, and Arachne made herself loosen her grip. "Cleis, listen to me, and don't forget what I tell you. This is not the Grove as it can be, or as it was. Islanders, even you young ones, have to be able to tell the difference. The Grove today is nothing but a pretty strand of trees, cooler and greener than most, in a hot summer. The air is just sweet air. The humming is just a soothing sound. But what it was once—try to remember what it was once—"

She stopped. Cleis had twisted her body away from where Arachne held her shoulder. Her shuttle dangled from her hand. On her face were fright, and embarrassment, and incomprehension. She was too young, Arachne saw, to remember the Grove as it had been. Arachne released her shoulder.

The two women weaved for a time in silence. Cleis bent closely over her work, tugging at the shuttle. She would spoil it that way, Arachne thought, and corrected the girl silently. They weaved again.

Finally, with slow effort, Arachne said, "It was a golden vibration, Cleis, in the Grove. We weavers breathed it in through our nostrils and mouth, and gave it out again through our fingers. We were linked, silk and weavers and spiders and Grove. We weaved, and none of us knew how much time passed while we did it. If no one came to fetch the weavers to a meal, we would weave until nightfall, and never know that we were hungry. But we were never very hungry. For hours afterward we felt a sort of glow in the back and neck, a warm tingling. Sometimes I would spread my fingers out, just to stare at them."

Cleis stared at her now.

"We didn't talk much," Arachne went on. "There seemed no need. The silk was better than words. It was more complete."

Incomprehension lay over Cleis's face. Her eyes were round. Arachne had more to say, but she could not say it to those round eyes. She turned her attention to her loom, and after a moment Cleis, still bewildered, did the same. Arachne's shuttle flew in and out of the shed: whisper-knock, whisper-knock. Cleis turned to her loom, choosing a different color silk from the basket at her feet and rethreading her shuttle. When her head was bent closely over the silk, Arachne said quietly, "A slave was crippled two days ago, on the Southern Shore. He dropped a wine jar and broke it. His master beat him. Both his legs broke. He cannot walk."

Cleis jerked up her head, dropping her shuttle and knocking over the basket of spider silk.

"The master had not come to the Grove in a year," Arachne continued. "He saw no reason to come. The Grove was for women, he said, to sit and weave. He was no woman. The slave was his property."

"How nasty!"

" 'Nasty'?"

"I hope you exile him for life, at Council!"

"I will. But Cleis—"

"I'm glad I don't know any people like that. I'm sure there are no people like that in the villa. People in the villa don't hurt each other, even slaves."

"Why not?"

"Why don't they hurt each other?"

"Yes. Why not?"

Cleis puckered her forehead. "I guess people in the villa don't hurt each other because . . . because they're nice. People are nice. It's not like in the old stories."

"Cleis. *Cleis*—"

"Then I don't know!" The girl cried. "If that's not the answer, I don't know!"

Arachne could see that the girl felt badgered. She herself felt her patience, never strongly woven, unravel rapidly. Looking at Cleis, Arachne suddenly knew that she was trying to force understanding from this simpleminded child for reasons that had little to do with Cleis herself. Because Amaura was too young. Becasue Kyles was so remote. Because her women would not look at the silk on her loom. Because Jaen was gone. Above all, because Jaen was gone. But perhaps he had loved Cleis a little when he was here, and that was a link, of sorts.

I am becoming a beggar, Arachne thought. I, who never begged in my life.

"If you were hungry," Arachne said slowly, with careful deliberation, "would you take food from another house?"

"I don't know," Cleis said. "I might."

"Even rotten food? If you were very hungry?"

"I don't know."

"If you were not hungry, would you take rotten food?"

"Of course not!"

"Look at my tapestry," Arachne said. "No, not merely a glance —*look* at it. Look, Cleis."

Reluctantly, Cleis looked.

The silk on Arachne's loom bore none of the usual Island designs: trees and spiders, flowers and birds, borders of fruit or shells or stylized marine animals or the snakes once—but now less and less

—associated with the Goddess. Nor had Arachne woven her silk in the elaborate weaves, twill and dobby and double gauze, for which her work was famed. This silk was the simplest taftah weave, of muted colors: russet and dun and moss and maroon and a dull gold that looked too heavy for the loom to support. The colors blended in swirling patterns that almost, but not quite, suggested some outline, some disturbing, half-remembered shape, or shapes. It was difficult to be sure because over the dull swirls lay a nearly invisible haze of finest silken threads the color of ash. Above those heavy, dully-glowing colors the ash threads floated cinder-cold; they might have been smoke from fires dead a hundred years. Cleis twisted to peer through the cold ash to see the outline beneath; it was not possible. Her hand moved halfway to the tapestry, to brush away the haze, and stopped. She could not have touched the ash-haze threads for anything. They had no color and almost no texture, and they looked as fragile and persistent as death.

"I saw the web for this tapestry," Arachne said, "on the last night in the Grove when you might have felt why Islanders were not hungry inside, and did not hurt each other. Cleis?"

Cleis jerked her gaze away from the loom. "It's . . . it's a striking silk, Mistress."

Arachne thought, I will not beg for understanding. *I will not.*

But then, despite the thought, she tried once again. "Cleis. Do you know, were you ever taught, what my ancestor Delernos said after he had come ashore on Island and then spent his first night, all alone, in the Grove?"

"Yes, of course, Mistress."

"What was it?"

Cleis folded her hands across her shuttle and recited. " 'This then is what I have been seeking, and never even knew I sought. For this I would have laid down my life, and before this I had no life.' Isn't that right?"

"That is right."

"It's a sort of riddle, isn't it? What did Master Delernos mean?"

Arachne looked at her. Cleis did not know; she truly did not know. Quietly Arachne said, "Thank you, Cleis. That is all. Dismiss the women and send for the slaves to move all the looms except mine. I will weave here a little longer."

"Yes, Mistress."

The Grove emptied of people. The women went quickly, stretching arms and flexing fingers, talking quietly among themselves. Slaves carried the looms, one by one, to the shelter of the colonnade. The sky began to color. Around Arachne, now alone in the Grove, spiders began to emerge, dots of gold on trees and grass and shrubs. Their humming deepened as they began to construct bridge lines and radii. The breeze picked up. Arachne worked on, her shuttle flying over the cinder-cold threads, weaving on and on, in the pretty stand of vacant trees.

That night Arachne lay on her couch in a pool of moonlight, thinking coldly of the dreams she would probably have to endure when sleep finally came. Dishes of cold food sat on tables against the wall where Suva had left them. Arachne had been unable to eat. The smell of the baked tunny had turned her stomach, and Pholen had eaten most of the fish. He had come, bathed for bed, to show her his sums on the abacus, and in his cheerful chatter Arachne had felt, for a moment, her pain about the Grove ease. She had lifted the little boy onto her lap and had buried her face in his black curls, damp from bathing. The nape of his neck still gave off the sweet smell of babyish flesh; she wondered how much longer he would smell like that. He was telling her something, something about a lump of soap, but in the primitive pleasure of hugging the small warm body in her arms, she did not hear what he said. He pulled the wooden pins from her hair and pretended to brush it for her, and then his nurse had come in and led him, protesting, to bed.

Arachne had bathed, brushed her hair, drunk a glass of wine. Then she lay on her couch, listening to the lap of waves at the base of the cliff beyond her window. Hours passed. The sea was calm; the waves sounded subdued and distant. Their lapping became the whisper-knock, whisper-knock of a shuttle, and then the rocking of Jaen's ship, somewhere at sea. The two sounds became one. Jaen's ship was being woven into the sea, held immobile on a warp of hyacinth-blue waves sharp as daggers. She tried to cry out and warn him to dodge the shuttle, to sail away from the whisper-knock, whisper-knock, but she could not force the scream past her throat. The shuttle grew larger and louder, then flew over the daggered waves and slammed into the ship. Arachne sat up wildly. Kyles stood by the slammed door, one hand steadying himself on the doorframe.

Arachne shook her head from side to side, trying to free herself of the dream. Her unbound hair, coarse and black, eddied around her. Kyles crossed the chamber and stood at the foot of her couch, and she realized from the lurch in his gait and the strong smell of wine that he was, incredibly, drunk. With his back to the moonlit window he was a faceless shape, a powerful dark silhouette with one hand outflung to grip a small table for support.

Arachne was startled. Kyles never drank enough to show any effects. In his vineyards he grew grapes and pressed wine, living and working alongside his slaves at sowing and harvest, with her in the villa other times. He sold the wine, trading shrewdly and fairly but with no particular interest, his dark face closed and silent. Arachne had seen him stop in his fields, his chiton soaked with sweat, and tip his impassive face upward toward the hot sun, and it seemed to her that he was deliberately soaking up the heat in the same way the grapes were, without thought but with a primitive, indifferent possession. But never since they had been contracted and then, still boy and girl, marriage-bound, had she seen him drunk on his own wine.

Jaen—yes. Jaen became gay and a little hectic when he drank, words spilling out of him in wild, astonishing, high-colored floods that made his audience gasp and laugh and sputter, but that made Kyles only watch his marriage-brother from over the rim of his own once-filled goblet, his eyes hooded and impassive.

"Kyles," Arachne said softly, and stretched out her hand. All at once she was glad he had come to her. He came less and less often, and she had not really noticed. But now she was glad, drunk or not. She did not want to be alone any longer, on this night. Her dream was still with her, and as she reached her arms to Kyles the memory of the dream made her shudder, and she tried to push it away.

He did not move. Each knuckle of his hand gripping the table rose taut and hard in silhouette. On the ornamental three-legged table were an oil lamp and a bowl of figs, and it occurred to Arachne that their stone outlines were no harder than the set ridges of her husband's hand.

"Kyles?"

"I expected to find you at the window."

"The window?"

"Searching for his sails."

"They crossed the horizon hours ago, Kyles," Arachne said. A sudden breeze from the sea made her shiver, and she wrapped her arms around her bare shoulders, and yawned.

He said nothing. The wine smell was mingled with wool; he must have spilled wine on his chiton, hours ago, early enough for it to have soured. Arachne tried to peer at him in the dim light, but could not make out his face at all. She rubbed her bare shoulders, trying to warm them, and again reached out both arms. His shadow lay across the curve of her breasts, striping them cream and gray. She could not shake off her dream; she felt fuzzy and vulnerable, and she wanted to feel his body against hers.

"Come closer."

He did not move.

"You were not at the harbor to see him sail."

Arachne lowered her arms. "No."

"Where were you?" His voice was quiet, not slurred.

"At the Grove, Kyles. Weaving."

"The Grove."

"Yes."

Without warning, he shoved over the table. The lamp and bowl crashed to the floor, and the scent of lamp oil rose in waves. One leg broke off the table. Figs rolled into the darkness, and stone shards clattered on stone floor and then lay still. Arachne got off her couch and stood up.

She was not frightened. Astonishment left no room for any other feeling. The last of her dream-disorientation fled, and her astonishment was lucid and rational: *How could I have missed this.* She had not known. Her husband stood in her chamber amid the wreckage of a table and said "the Grove" as if it were a curse, and she had not known him capable of anger, let alone of the violence before her now. She had stood with him in the Grove as it had been—*in the Grove*—and had not known, and she did not understand how that could be. Moving closer, her knee rubbing along the side of the couch, Arachne tried to make out his face. In the shadows it seemed to be as closed and set as always.

"Yes, weaving," she said. "I was weaving with my women."

He said nothing. Arachne waited, but the silence went on. She put a hand on his arm; it was corded with tension, and with a shock Arachne realized that he was holding himself rigid with immense effort, restraining himself from some action with the force of every muscle in his body. Her astonishment grew. Under it an involuntary thrill shot through her, a leap of the blood as if at danger, and she narrowed her eyes.

"What is it, Kyles? What is wrong?"

To her surprise, he laughed, the ugliest sound she had ever heard. He moved to the table against the wall and poured a goblet of wine. Arachne saw Pholen standing at the same spot hours earlier, eating the baked fish, his small mouth rosy with a sip of the same wine.

Speaking with great clarity, she said, "I did not go down to the harbor because I did not want to see Jaen leave. I would have cried, and I did not want to cry. I went with my women to the Grove, and I wove spider silk. I taught Cleis, Ethipien's daughter, my new woman. She is trying to learn to handle silk instead of wool."

"Cleis," Kyles said. "Jaen's last bedding."

"I suppose so. Not that it matters, except that she misses him. Neither is contracted."

"Does it matter to you?"

"Of course not." Arachne reached onto the couch for a silk coverlet and wrapped it around herself. So that was it. She knew now, and suddenly knew, as well, that this had been building between her and Kyles for years. She and Jaen had shared the Grove —the Grove as it had been—as children of the same blood and adults of the same mind. She had known with Jaen what she could never know with Kyles, that vibrating and vivid completeness, that oneness—but she had never realized that to Kyles it had mattered. He had neither welcomed nor refused the greater access to the Grove brought to him by his marriage-rank. He had neither welcomed nor refused the contract itself, and they had lived and bedded in the remote courtesy that characterized all Kyles's actions. Arachne thought he had had of her everything—rank, heirs, bedding—that he had wanted. She had not known he was jealous of her bond, Grove-forged, with Jaen.

Except that, somewhere, she had known.

The thought was not unwelcome. She thought again of that afternoon, of the hopelessness of talking with Cleis. Kyles had never been a fool. Arachne ached with loneliness, and it would be a relief to sit with someone and talk about the Grove, about her dream, about what was happening to Island. Perhaps it would be a relief, too, to Kyles. She had never meant to neglect him.

Arachne crossed the floor toward her husband. He halted her halfway by saying quietly, "You are the blindest woman I have ever known."

She stopped dead. Kyles drank off his wine and poured himself another goblet. He had half-turned toward the window, and she saw in profile one moonlit cheekbone, sharp and gray.

"Why am I so blind?"

For answer, Kyles threw the goblet against the wall. The pottery bowl shattered; shards flew over the table and floor. The silver handle clattered to the stone floor and rolled away into the darkness. The handle had, Arachne remembered numbly, been shaped into the horns of a bull. The goblet had been old—it had come to Island with Delernos. Suddenly she was angry.

"Do you plan to smash anything else? The couch? Another table?"

He said nothing, standing by the window, a powerful dark shape blocking the light.

"Or Jaen? Is it my brother you want to smash? Is that what this is all about, Kyles?"

"Jaen?" Kyles said. For a moment she thought he would laugh again: he threw back his head and opened his mouth, but no sound came out. In the grotesque movement Arachne glimpsed something completely outside her experience. Kyles was not being driven by anger or drunkenness or jealousy but by something else, something unnamed and deadly, something she did not understand at all.

"Jaen," Kyles repeated. "Do you think that Jaen exists? For me? For you?"

"That Jaen—" Arachne echoed. But then she saw that Kyles did not mean that Jaen was dead. She could not imagine what he did mean.

"Jaen," Kyles said. He reached for the goblet and seemed surprised that it was not there. His arm fumbled a moment, then reached for the wine jar. In the swing of his arm Arachne saw again that terrible tension, and involuntarily she braced herself. But he neither threw the jar nor drank from it. He stood looking down at it, his head bent into shadow, and said, "In the wine taverns traders say the Mistress of Island beds her brother."

She could not breathe. Around her the room leaped, faded, steadied again.

"Only I know it is not true," Kyles said. He drank from the wine jar, wiped his hand across his lips, set down the jar. "I know the Mistress of Island does not bed her brother. Or her husband. Arachne beds only the Grove."

She had launched herself at him, already scratching. No, she had not—she stood still immobile, and the floor was rising around her with a whisper-knock, whisper-knock that sent waves of blue daggers, cold and smelling of wine, undulating before her eyes. She could not see Kyles for the blue rising, and she thought, stupidly but without pain, *this is how Suva feels in her drowning fit.* Then the blue was gone and Arachne felt his hand on her shoulder. She brought her knee up hard, missing him completely.

He was behind her. He yanked his arm and they fell onto the floor, Kyles underneath. He rolled a quarter-turn and they lay pressed together on their sides, Arachne pinned against the stone and choking on a mouthful of her own hair. Instantly her mind cleared. She spat out the hair, thought, *he will rape me,* but found that she could not picture it happening.

It did not. His arm lifted from across her body. Both his hands stayed off her for one heartbeat, two, three—deliberately, long enough for her to roll away from him, or rise, or again bring up her knee. Arachne could not see his face. But from the length of his familiar body pressed to hers—legs and groin and chest—came a deadly tension, a willed restraint that was more violent than force would have been. It was not sexual tension, nor checked anger, but some violence wilder and more primitive than either, a gnawing passion Arachne did not understand.

For the first time she felt afraid.

Kyles put one hand on her breast, touching her with a gentleness that shocked her because it was so jerky and so forced. The touch was not a question, but she suddenly saw that whatever she did next would be a kind of answer. Kyles was forcing himself to wait for her response, and the waiting was costing him in ways she did not begin to understand, but was right to be afraid of.

You bed only the Grove.

Fury tore through her fear. She jerked upwards to knock away his hand—but found that her arm had not moved. Kyles's hand tightened on her breast. His other hand moved to her leg, and she felt the brush of his clenched fist the instant before it opened and slid over her thigh with that jerky, terrible gentleness. Arachne knew then that he was not going to hurt her but that she was going to hurt him, sharply and irrevocably, by not matching this terrifying desire.

Kyles wanted her in exactly the same way that she wanted the Grove.

She saw that sudden truth, and it felt as if she saw her husband for the first time. Kyles—remote, wordless, and all the while there lay beneath his wordlessness this violent longing for connection, and she was its object. She, her body, and not the Grove. People could do this, then—could ache for another mortal in the same way she, Arachne, ached for the glory of the Grove, and be as consumed by the desire. Why? She did not know why, could not see why, was both frightened and bewildered by her sudden glimpse of the frenzy that drove Kyles. His face above her was taut with passion. Not passion for her body alone—that she might have understood, although probably not shared. But what she saw on Kyles's face was something else, something more, some driven need to love her enough to end separateness and reach some state of wholeness he could not reach alone.

And along with her bewilderment came a tiny shard of contempt. This ache, for a mortal body? This ache, when he could have had the Grove?

"I love you," Kyles said roughly, and, helplessly, she felt her contempt deepen. She did not love Kyles. Not like this, not with this obsession, this naked need.

I can not love like that.

I do not want to love like that.

Kyles's hands moved over her thighs, belly, breasts. The stone floor beneath her scratched her naked back and shoulders. Kyles's fingers left her body and cupped her face with both hands, but Arachne rolled over onto her side, against his body, and pressed her lips to his shoulder. She could do at least that for him: hide her face, and her recoiling.

Kyles slid his arms under her, lifted her, and carried her to the couch. Arachne noted with detachment that the wine had not affected his strength; he lifted her easily and carried her without faltering. Lowering himself on top of her, he kissed her breasts and neck, and she pushed away her detachment and kissed him in turn.

That too she could do for him: she could try.

Too much emotion too fast gave her movements a kind of fraudulent violence. But when at last Kyles knelt above her and parted her thighs, she saw his eyes clearly. The planes of his face were clenched with a desire closer to pain than to pleasure, and Arachne saw the need in his eyes and closed her own. Instantly she opened them, but it was too late. Kyles had seen. He knew. She did not want him.

I do not want to love like that.

He entered her with an explosive despair that was more frightening than anything else he had said or done. Arachne cried out in pain. Despite the long caresses, she had not been ready for him.

Afterwards, he lay a long time silent, his weight thrown across her body. Against her mouth Arachne felt the skin of his chest, and under her hands the solid mass of his back. Both grew cooler. She could taste his sweat, salty and faintly sweet, on her lips. He smelled of wine, and of both of them. Beyond the window the moon set, leaving the room in complete blackness. The weight of Kyles's body in the dark felt both familiar and utterly foreign. Arachne did not dare move.

I do not want to love like that.

If she said one word of pity or regret, Arachne thought, he would never forgive her. He had exposed a depth of longing and desire, a wild and terrifying landscape within himself. Only if she had consented to inhabit it with him could it have served as a bond, and she had not. She had refused. That landscape repelled her, and she had been afraid—not of the physical penetration, but of the emotional one. Kyles might have forgiven her fear; he would not forgive her contempt. He would not forgive himself, either, for having exposed himself to it.

But I can't help it, she thought reasonably, and knew that didn't matter. Reason had nothing to do with it—any more than it had to do, she thought suddenly, with the ash-haze silk. It floated before her closed eyes, cinder-cold smoke over shifting shapes in colors old and menacing as death.

Kyles pulled his body from hers. The moment skin contact ceased, she could not tell where he was in the blackness. The sky could not have clouded, not at this season, but not even faint starlight showed her where the window was. Arachne heard the door open, and realized that Kyles had said nothing, nothing at all. The thrill of danger shot through her—how much did he resent her for not being what she could not be?

"Kyles—"

The door closed.

Arachne lay in the dark. Even without the useless words of regret, he was not going to forgive her. She thought of the passionate despair with which he had entered her, and shuddered. What response had he wanted from her, that she could not give?

You bed only the Grove.

I do not want to love like that.

Shivering, Arachne pulled the woolen bedclothes off the floor where they had slid and yanked them up over her body. As she moved, her shoulder leaned into the couch where Kyles's head had lain. The pallet was wet. Arachne touched it with her tongue; it tasted of salt, but she could not tell if it was sweat, or tears.

She did not sleep until morning. When she went the next day to seek Kyles, he had left the villa. Gone, a slave said carefully, to his vineyard in the east.

6

"**T**HEY'RE coming out now!" Pholen shrieked. "Look—here one comes!"

"Don't you touch it," his nurse ordered. "Let it come out when it comes out. Don't you try to pull it, Young Master."

"I know *that*," Pholen said scornfully. He sprawled over the Spider Stone on his stomach, his body a plump, silk-clad ball with skinny bare legs. The female spider crouching at one of the Stone's tiny holes ignored him. It stood immobile; not even the golden hairs on its legs stirred in the breeze. Next to the Stone the nurse sat on the grass, mending a wool cloak. Her own cloak was wrapped tightly around her and she sat on a cushion; the autumn rains had not yet started in earnest, but the air was cooler. The mild, beautiful autumn was nearly over.

"Here one comes!" The child cried. "It's coming out right now! It's so little—look how it looks!"

"You look for me," the nurse said, bending over her work. She had poor vision, and a headache.

"It's out!" Pholen shrieked. "Now it's climbing up the mama spider!"

Halfway up the motionless hairy leg, the infant spider fell off. For an instant it lay still, a tiny-dull-gold speck with a spongy carapace that had not yet begun to harden. Then it righted itself, climbed the leg, and crawled over the female spider's abdomen and onto the front of the carapace. With two front legs the female brushed it away from her eyes.

"Look at that!" Pholen said.

"I see it, Spiderling."

"The mama spider is humming now."

"Is it?"

The child looked up in astonishment. "Can't you hear it?"

"If you want me to, Spiderling."

Arachne's son was not contented with this. "But can't you *really* hear it, Nurse? With your ears?"

The nurse stopped mending. "I could once. Even now, it makes my head ache a bit less."

Pholen touched his head, and then his ears. Experimentally he stuck his fingers into his ears and tried to gaze upward at his forehead. This made his eyes cross. He gave it up and turned back to the Spider Stone.

Another tiny, crumpled spider crawled from the Stone. It staggered over the rim of the hole and toward the female spider, which again hummed.

"I'm going to get Mama," Pholen said. *"Mama* will want to look."

"Your Mistress mother isn't in the Grove, Young Master."

"But I know where she is—in the apotheca." He slid off the Stone and trotted across the grass of the Grove, leaving his cloak behind. A few of the younger weavers who had not yet moved their looms indoors for the winter were at work. Pholen smiled at them without slowing his gait. The silks were pretty and the looms enormously interesting, but he wanted to find Arachne and bring her to the Stone before all the baby spiders had emerged and gone. Nothing was as pretty or as interesting as spiders.

The sky above the Grove was low and gray, but Pholen, trotting across the grass, could see it only through breaks between the branches of the great trees. Their leaves were as thick as in the summer, and greener. The leaves stirred constantly. All over Island leaves and saplings and bushes agitated in the cooling wind. Between the Grove trees the clear light had acquired a greater urgency. It seemed to fall in straight, brilliant sheets, trapping the roofline of the colonnade against the sky. In days now the rains would begin in earnest. The rain would be fitful, intermittent—

some days it would not rain at all—building to at least one awe-some, thundering storm before the early spring came to Island's hills and ravines and villa.

Pholen did not think to notice either light or sky; neither was connected in his mind to spiders. He did think that it seemed odd not to see Mama weaving with the women. Since she had finished making that funny-looking silk with the gray threads all over it, she did not weave at all. Her loom was moved into its storeroom, and she spent all her time in the apotheca. It was odd. Still, he was content to have her there. To Pholen the apotheca was a fascinating place, made more so by being forbidden to him.

A small chamber huddling directly behind the colonnade to the east of the Grove, the apotheca was built of stone thickly plastered within and without. It had been built without windows and with a door that could be locked, so that no child or feeble-witted adult could enter and upset its pots and jars. Here were mixed the phar-makons that were sprinkled on the Grove each evening to vary the color and texture of the spiders' webs. Among Delernos's exiled Household had been both a remarkable herbist and a mediocre priestess. Delernos had given the care of the Grove to the herbist. Jaen said this was Delernos's revenge against the Goddess for per-mitting him to be exiled, since in consequence the temple of the Goddess compared to the Grove, lost importance each generation —a subtle and humiliating revenge. Arachne doubted this. Deler-nos had been a bold and direct man; the subtlety of such a revenge sounded to her more like Jaen than like their ancestor.

In the windowless apotheca, oil lamps provided light and braziers heat. Generations of confined smoke streaked the walls. To Pholen, however, the apotheca did not smell smoky or stale. There he could breathe in the herbs and oils, minerals and molds used in boiling the pharmakons, overlaid with the thyme-and-lemon fragrance of the spiders. That alone would have made it a thrilling place, had he been old enough to be allowed in among the vases and pestles and herbs, some of which were poisonous before being transformed by the techniques of Delernos's herbal genius. The herbist's name had not come down among the stories of Delernos's exile: he had been a slave, captured somewhere in the exotic east, beyond the sea.

The door of the apotheca stood open to the damp air. In the lamplit dimness Pholen could see three figures standing bent over table and brazier and that funny row of pots, tilted on their sides on new wooden shelves, where Mama was keeping some spiders to try new pharmakons on. As he approached, Pholen saw that the figures were Mama and Amaura and Mama's woman Cleis. Their voices sounded a little too loud.

"*No*, Amaura," Arachne said. "You must grind it much finer than that, or it will not dissolve in the oil."

"I can't grind it any finer," Amaura said.

"Of course you can. Why can't you?"

"I just can't."

"You mean you won't," Arachne said. Amaura shrugged, and looked at her mother from flat, light eyes.

"I'll grind it, Mistress," Cleis said. She moved toward the pestle, but Arachne stopped her with an uplifted arm.

"No, Cleis. Amaura is the one who must learn to make pharmakons. She is the one who will have the responsibility of the Grove one day, she and Pholen. Amaura, grind the mixture finer."

Amaura picked up the pestle and began to grind. Some of her black hair had come loose from its band and fell forward, hiding her face. Pholen burst into the doorway, calling, "Mama! Come see —some baby spiders are coming right out of the Stone!"

Arachne turned and gazed at Pholen. Her forehead, he saw, was puckered into little lines, and so were the corners of her mouth.

"I can't come now, Pholen—I am working. Where's Nurse?"

"At the Stone. Nurse sent me to get you!" he lied. A lie seemed negligible next to the glory of seeing spiderlings.

"Sent you—why? What's wrong?" Arachne said sharply.

Pholen blinked. "Nothing's *wrong*, Mama. Didn't you hear me? There are baby spiders coming out!"

His mother's lines did not unpucker. But she knelt by him, her silk chiton pooling on the stone, and said softly, "Yes, I know— that's very exciting, Spiderling. But I'm busy now, making some pharmakons."

"Those new pharmakons you told me about the other night?" Pholen said hopefully. He wanted to see those; seeing them might be worth a delay in returning to the Stone. If the delay were brief. "The pharmakons that are medicines for the sick webs?"

"Yes, yes. Now run back to Nurse, Spiderling, and watch the Stone. Amaura! You've spilled it!"

Amaura was holding her mortar tilted sharply; a thin line of blue-and-gray mash had dribbled out the side and onto the stone table. The glazed side of the mortar where the mash had touched was dimpled with tiny holes. The mash on the table was spreading slowly at the edges, dying the stone blue.

"I'm sorry," Amaura said. Pholen frowned; he didn't think Amaura *sounded* sorry. She sounded like she didn't much care. Mama was looking at her in a way that made Pholen feel funny. He turned away and inched over to the rows of new pots on the wall.

"That was deliberate," Arachne said slowly. "You spoiled the mash deliberately."

Amaura didn't answer. Hastily Cleis came over to Pholen and took his hand. "See, Pholen, each spider has its own pot, with this thin silk covering the opening to keep the spider in, and it spins a web in there. We put the pharmakon in here, like this, and the spider drinks it." She glanced over her shoulder at her Mistress, and then away.

"All morning," Arachne said, "you have balked, and delayed, and misdone tasks simple enough for Pholen. No—look at me, Amaura."

"I am looking," Amaura said. Her voice was light and firm, but Pholen thought he heard little prickles in it.

Cleis said quickly, pointing, "Look at that spider, Pholen—here, I'll remove the silk so you can see it. It's drinking the pharmakon now. Your Mistress mother is leaving things out of some pharmakons, and adding things to other pharmakons, so that each spider drinks a different kind."

"Why?" Pholen said. He peered at the spider drinking in its segregated pot.

"So your Mistress mother can find out how each pharmakon changes a . . . a sick web without giving that pharmakon to the whole Grove."

"Oh," Pholen said. "Now I want to go see the new spiderlings. Mama?"

"Amaura," Arachne said, very clearly. "Do you want to learn to mix the pharmakons?"

"I wanted to go with Father to the vineyard," Amaura said. Pholen twisted free of Cleis to look at his sister. Now her voice didn't sound like hers at all. It sounded like the music Suva made on willow pipes: high and tight, with sharp points underneath. Pholen didn't like it.

"I told you, Mother," Amaura said. "I told you that. I wanted to go with Father for the grape harvest."

"You will be Mistress of Island one day," Arachne said. "The Grove will be yours to care for. Yours and Pholen's."

"By then there won't be any Grove. It will have finished dying."

No one said anything. Pholen felt Cleis's hand on his arm; she squeezed it too hard. Amaura stood with her chin up and her light eyes all sparkly, but Pholen could see that she was scared. She wore the face from when they ran away from Nurse to hear Suva's stories. But not exactly the same face—no. Something about this face was different.

"It's *true*," Amaura said. "The Grove is dying. At least the vineyard will always grow the same grapes. And Father left too early this year for harvest—you know he did. He left the day after Uncle Jaen sailed, and that was only midsummer. And he didn't even say good-bye to me. This summer he promised I could go with him for harvest, and instead he left so fast he didn't even say good-bye."

Arachne turned away from her daughter. Pholen saw the skin at his mother's neck beat in and out, and suddenly he was frightened. He broke free of Cleis's grip and ran to Arachne.

"Come see my spiderlings come out, Mama!"

Arachne looked down and put a hand on his head, but Pholen had the paralyzing thought that it was not him she was seeing. "Mama!"

Amaura said, "Why did Father leave so early? *You* know, don't you, Mother? Why did he go before harvest even started?"

At her tone, Arachne turned swiftly. "Go to your chamber, Amaura. Ask Suva to bring you your dinner there until Nurse comes."

Amaura did not move. "Did you send him away?"

"I don't send your father anywhere. He does as he chooses."

Uncertainly, Amaura fingered the clasp of her chiton. Pholen saw that it was made like a bunch of grapes, the kind in Father's vineyard. Amaura opened her mouth to say something, but before she could, Arachne said again, "Go to your chamber," and at her tone Pholen jumped and Amaura went.

"She . . . she didn't mean it, Mistress," Cleis said.

Arachne whirled on her. "Mean *what?*"

"About—about the Grove!" Cleis said. She sounded scared, and hurt, but Pholen didn't understand what anyone had said to hurt Cleis, when it was Amaura who had been sent in disgrace away from the apotheca. He didn't understand what Amaura had done, either, other than spill the pharmakon, or why the skin at his mother's throat beat in and out so fiercely, or why it mattered if Father went early for the harvest. Pholen had scarcely noticed he was gone.

"This is not making a difference," Arachne said quietly. She stared stonily at the rows of tilted pots on their new shelves. "We are discovering nothing."

"Should we—should we stop trying, Mistress?"

"Of course not!" Arachne snapped. "Would you have me do nothing?"

In one of the pots, a spider began to hum, the sound vibrating faintly on the smoky air. Pholen squinted, trying to see which pot held the humming spider.

"At the Temple of the Goddess," Cleis said, "I made a sacrifice for the Grove. Perhaps that will help."

"Sacrifices will not tell us why," Arachne said. She began to walk up and down; her chiton brushed Pholen's cheek as she passed. "Unless we know *why,* how can we make a difference?"

"Perhaps if our sacrifices are pleasing, the Goddess will tell us why. There were more Islanders at the temple, Mistress, than I have ever seen there before."

"Yes," Arachne said quietly. "I know. But goddesses are not pharmakons."

"Mistress!"

Arachne did not seem to have heard. She stopped walking and touched the spoiled mash next to Amaura's pestle. Her voice was slow, and Pholen heard it crack in the middle. "Jaen was the one who discovered wild new pharmakons. He made that deep scarlet he always wears—always wore. It was the first new shade since Delernos's herbist, did you know that, Cleis? He perfected it the same way I'm trying now, with different mixtures to different spiders. This is his system, his idea. It was Jaen who dreamed of the new ideas, only Jaen. He dreamed them, and I worked at them."

"Jaen made that scarlet," Cleis said, with pleasure. "Did he make any others?"

"No. He lost interst. And left me to do the pharmakons alone."

"Mama," Pholen pleaded, "the *spiderlings*. They'll be all gone."

Arachne looked down. Pholen saw that her face was puckered again and he thought, despairingly: *She won't come.* But then she said, "Let's go then," and he seized her hand joyfully.

"Come fast!"

"I'll finish the grinding, Mistress," Cleis said.

"Thank you."

"I like it. It's odd—" she bent her head over the table, fumbling a little—"I always thought I would be good at weaving silk, and I'm not. But I can do this."

"Yes, Cleis," Arachne said gently. "You can do this."

"Mistress, don't . . . don't grieve about what Young Mistress said about the Grove. It isn't dying."

"Yes," Arachne said quietly. "It *is*. Come, Pholen—let's go see your spiderlings."

Nurse had come in search of her charge. Arachne sent her to Amaura's chamber and knelt with Pholen at the Stone. The last of the tiny spiders had climbed from their hole and up the female's legs. The female had not moved. Her young swarmed over her back, a squirming, gold-colored mass. Some of the spiderlings were having difficulty staying on their mother; four or five fell off, struggled up, fell again.

Arachne stared at the falling spiders. One had six legs, one seven. One, that could not stay up at all, had only five, three on one side and two on the other; at the missing legs were short, hair-thin stumps swollen at the ends into knobs. There was a spider with only a shrunken fold of skin in place of its abdomen, and another with a lumpy, misshapen cephalothorax. On the Spider Stone, starting to slide down its slick amber side, lay a tiny dead spider.

"Those spiderlings look funny," Pholen said uncertainly.

"Yes, Small One," Arachne said. Her voice was steady, but something in it made the child draw away. Arachne pulled him back and took him onto her lap.

"You're holding me too hard, Mama." Arachne did not move. "Mama?"

"The baby spiders are sick, Pholen."

"Like the webs?"

"Yes."

The child's eyes searched for the tiny dead spider in the grass at the base of the Stone. "Can you make medicine pharmakons for the spiderlings, too? Not just the webs? I could help. Even if Amaura doesn't like the Grove, *I* could help."

Arachne turned him around on her lap until they faced each other. Pholen felt vaguely surprised to see that her face had finally unpuckered. It looked smooth as stone. She put her hands on his small shoulders.

"Pholen—when you sit in the Grove and watch the spiders, what happens? Do you ever feel good?"

"Course I feel good!"

"What does it feel like? What do you see?"

"I see spiders," he said reasonably. "And grass. And trees. And the Spider Stone."

"When you sit near the Spider Stone, does it make you feel different than you feel when you're in your couch?"

"I feel sleepy in my couch."

"But in the Grove—does everything look shiny? And bright? Does it ever feel like . . . like you're floating inside people? Inside Amaura's head, or Nurse's?"

Pholen frowned. From the corner of his eye he saw the female spider begin to crawl down the Stone. Spiderlings fell from her back.

"Do you ever feel like that in the Grove, Pholen? As if you're almost floating inside Amaura's head?"

"I couldn't float inside Amaura's head, Mama. I wouldn't fit."

Arachne closed her eyes.

"And anyway," Pholen added, "Amaura wouldn't like anyone inside her head. She doesn't like me in her chamber. Open your eyes, Mama—I can't see you when your eyes are closed."

"I'm here, Spiderling."

"It's *her* head," the little boy said.

He slid off her lap and onto all fours, peering into the grass to track the spider. The breeze freshened, and Arachne picked up Pholen's cloak and draped it around him. Her thoughts fell off her mind, struggled up, fell again.

Dying, Amaura had said. Amaura was angry with her, for something. Dying, dying. Trees die, and flowers, and people. Living things from which the life has gone, die. The Grove had been a living thing. She had felt the breath of its life blow through her, and never more strongly than on the night she stood with Jaen before the web of smoky-gray silk. All living things die, when their span is done.

Jaen—

Why, she had said to Cleis. They could not help the Grove unless they knew why. But suppose *why* was as simple as that: all living things die. As simple, as unfathomable, and as relentlessly beyond help. Nothing was called back past the moment of death. Not by all her will and effort, not by Jaen's questing, not by the longing of all Delernos's descendants on Island. Living things die.

No. Only the weak do nothing. Even in the face of death, she would not believe that the Grove was beyond hope, beyond help. She would not let herself believe it.

Living things die. They also breed. If Jaen's speculations were fact, and more than one Grove existed—

Jaen.

But he had sailed. He had stood next to her on the last night of the Grove's completeness, and, touched by that wholeness, he still had gone. The ash-haze silk lay in her chamber, buried in a chest under other weavings of silk and wool. She did not like to look at it. The night wind, and that rush of all the sweet strength the world holds, and behind her Jaen and Kyles—

You bed only the Grove.

The grape harvest would be over soon. The huge pithoi of wine, carried to villa by donkey or slave, would be received by the Treasurer. They would be counted, recorded, stored in the dim underground magazines with the rest of the taxes. The vintners would hold their harvest festivals, if they had not already done so, and then to the late autumn Council, the last before the rains. Those vintners who had anything to say to her, would come. Kyles— would Kyles come?

The ash-haze silk, with its smoke cold as fires dead a hundred years and its struggling shapes underneath. How had she come to weave such a thing? The spider web, on the last night of the rove —she could see it as clearly as if she had never unraveled the silk, never threaded the loom, never woven the ash-haze silk she would not look at now. And since then, her silk loom had been stored in the darkness while she worked in the apotheca, grinding and boiling and stirring against death. All living things die. Her loom, and the ash-haze silk, and Jaen and the Grove and Kyles and the pharmakons and the Goddess and Amaura and the *Grove*—

Arachne shook her head. She hated it when her thoughts skittered like that. She liked clean thought, direct. Tipping her head upward to gaze through the trees at the clear, direct light from the sky, she noticed a slave running toward her across the Grove. No one ran in the Grove; running endangered the spiders. She stood up.

"Look, Mama," Pholen said. He had coaxed a spider off a leaf and onto the back of his hand, where it stood waving its palps and humming. Pholen held it out to her carefully but with triumph, grinning hugely. His black eyes sparkled. The spider was perfect.

"What a beautiful spider!" Arachne had time to say, and then the slave reached them, panting hard.

"Mistress! Ship! Two ships!"

"Master Jaen—"

"One has . . . scarlet sails. The two just cleared the horizon, I was . . . sent to tell you. Two ships!"

Arachne started across the Grove, turned back for Pholen, grabbed his hand. He did not want to leave the spider. She made him deposit the spider on the leaf he had taken it from, and then she picked up Pholen and carried him with her, following the slave to chamber windows from which the ships could be seen. In her arms Pholen wiggled, protesting the loss of his spider. His squirming body felt warm and strong. Alive, Arachne thought. Pholen felt alive.

Jaen was alive.

Alive.

—— 7 ——

S UVA crouched on the floor in front of Arachne's wooden chest, both her skinny arms up to the elbows in silk and fine wool. Something sharp jabbed her palm. From the piles of soft stuff she pulled a gold clasp, meant to hold a chiton on one shoulder. Formed as a coiled sea snake, the clasp was set with red stones for eyes and tail. Suva studied the clasp, grinned derisively, and laid it on the floor. She began pulling out weavings and dumping them by the chest: spider silk worked with lifelike flowers, fruit, shells, spiders, leaves. The pile grew, toppled, sprawled airily across the stones.

Most, though not all, of the weavings had been made by Arachne herself. Occasionally Suva would stop at one weaving and hold it to her cheek, and the lines of her face would slacken a little. Arachne had made these. Arachne, who was the first person Suva had seen when she opened her eyes on Island, whom she had petted and cared for as a little girl, bullied and fought with as a maiden, nagged at and irritated as a woman, and followed around always, whenever she could, as the one person Suva had fastened on to love in this land where she had never wanted to be. Arachne, who went away from Suva every day to that cursed tree-place where Suva could not follow.

At the bottom of the chest she found what she had been looking for, a bundle wrapped in coarse wool and tied with threads stouter than necessary. Biting through the threads with two sharp, un-flanked teeth, Suva opened the package and spilled out the ash-haze spider silk.

"Aaaaaaaahh."

She spread the silk flat over the stone floor, stood up, and walked around it. Dropping to all fours, she lowered her head to a hand's span above the cloth and scrutinized it, section by section. She crawled around it, eyeing the edges, and then crawled over it to examine the middle, her head still lowered and her rump in the air, like a grazing goat. As each bony knee lifted, the depression it had made in the overlying hazy threads sprang back as if it had never been.

"Aaaaaahh."

The sound was half groan. Suva looked from the silk to the window, which from her angle of vision was too high to show the sea. She stared again at the silk, and then again at the window. Her breath came faster. Her arms began to flail, and her eyes to roll. Even though she could not see it, the sea rose around her. Then the door to the room opened and two legs entered.

The legs advanced and stood at the edge of the silky sea. The legs were hairy, heavily muscled, and not clean. They stood rigidly, and the rigidity caught that part of Suva's interest that had not yet fallen into the sea. She stared fiercely at the legs. The sea retreated.

The Mistress's husband stood gazing down at the ash-haze silk. His face was set and impassive, but from the floor Suva could see under the lids of his dark eyes, which had gone flat with something interesting, hatred or anger or pain. Yes—pain, Suva thought, it was pain. She stood, grinning, careful to look neither out the window nor at the ashy silk.

"Arachne's," Kyles said.

"Yes, Master. The Mistress weaved it. Don't you admire it? Don't you think it's beautiful?"

He said nothing.

"It's the last. Her silk loom is stored, no more weaving now. And the spider silk worsening."

She waited for him to react, but he did not. She was disappointed. Kyles embodied the best to be hoped for in a master: He ignored her, he took little of the Mistress's time, he was gone much of the year. Unlike that other goat-dung, Master Jaen. Now, however, she wanted him to show fear or pain about ash-haze silk, because it frightened and pained her. It was wrong, unjust! It was evil. A weaving should not be the sea! It should not have the sea's powerful and destructive despair, should not know those things only one who had come from the sea—singing!—should know. She would tear it to bits. She would trample it in the mud. She would spit on it and burn it, and never breathe the evil and acrid smoke. She would—

She could not look at it.

"Do you like it, Master? Isn't it beautiful, beautiful, awful, beautiful? Isn't it?"

Kyles stooped and picked up the silk. He wrapped it in the coarse wool, tied it, dropped it into the open chest. His face showed nothing, which enraged Suva. She clapped both hands to her own cheeks; they felt sticky and hollow, clammy as sea caves. She! Who had been met on the shore by enchanted birds, with a white owl on her shoulder!

"The last silk, the last silk," she crooned, her hands still on her cheeks.

"Put these away," Kyles said, motioning at the woolens and silks strewn over the floor.

"Was the grape harvest good, Master? Is it over? Is the wine full and sweet? Are you just come from the sweet wine?"

"Yes."

"And the Council meets tomorrow night, or the night after? And the grapes are sweet, sweet, sweet. Did you bring wine for the Mistress, Master? Wine for the Mistress who weaves no more?"

Kyles ignored her babbling. He stared out the window. Suva began to hurl weavings back into the chest, hurrying desperately, pointlessly. There was no reason to hurry—no, there was. The weavings smelled of spiders, they smelled of spiders and the sea. No, it was the sea that smelled of the sea, beyond the window. Spiders on one side, sea on the other—Faaugghh! Kyles smelled of traveling, of wool and dirt and wine. Suva slammed the lid onto the chest and sniffed Kyles appreciatively. But no—there was that other smell under the traveling, that man-scent smell. But no man had ever touched *her*. *She* had come pure from the sea, singing. She expelled the man-smell in a great snort, explosive as a sneeze, that scattered droplets of water over chest and floor and Kyles's legs. Kyles ignored the snort, as he had ignored the babbling. He went on staring out the window.

"Suva. When did the ships come?"

"Ships!"

Suva scrambled up off the floor, craning her neck toward the window, trying to look at the sea while avoiding looking at the sea. On the horizon floated two sets of sails. One was scarlet. Suva stared incredulously at the scarlet sail, and the stern loomed large in the sea until water flooded her throat, choking and suffocating and rising.

Kyles shook her gently. His eyes did not focus on hers. When she had stopped thrashing and gurgling, he let her go. His face showed nothing.

"How long have the ships been here?"

"There are no ships, Master, there can be no ship! Master Jaen is dead, dead—I knew it, I *saw* it. Dead in the sea."

"Does the Mistress know of the ships?"

"I saw it. He is dead." But then Suva's eyes in their sunken sockets grew sly. She saw a way out of having predicted wrong.

She had predicted that Jaen would die; therefore he must be dead. And if he was dead but still sailing his ship, it could only be because he had become a god. That was bad, but it was also good: bad because man-gods were too powerful anyway, but good because if Jaen were a god he would be taken up with god-things and not with his sister. And then not so easily would Arachne escape her, Suva, onto the beach with Jaen, at dinner with Jaen, into the cursed tree-place with Jaen! Jaen the god would not need Arachne. Arachne would be left for Suva.

Suva chortled and eyed Kyles, Arachne's husband, sideways. "Master Jaen has become a god. A god! How will you compete with a god, Master? How?"

There was a noise behind her. Arachne stood in the doorway, holding Pholen.

"Father!"

The little boy wriggled from his mother's grasp and ran to his father. Kyles picked him up. Pholen began to prattle happily of baby spiders, pharmakons, the Stone, his small face beaming at his father's. Over Pholen's head Kyles looked at Arachne, a gaze so impersonal on the surface and so violent underneath that Suva forgot about Jaen's ships and shrank back.

Like the sea—he looked at Arachne like the sea, waiting and craving and vastly patient. And dangerous—unless of course you had come from it, singing.

Suva scowled horribly. That other one not dead, this one suddenly man-dangerous under all his silences and ignorings and absences. And she had not seen either of those things! Something was wrong, the world was tilting, soon it would all be underwater and no one would be able to see anything. Suva looked at Arachne. There too something was happening, something had altered.

"Kyles . . . "

"Arachne."

"It's . . . I'm glad you have returned."

"The vineyard has paid its full tax. My men are placing the wine in your storage rooms right now. Your secretary has the complete records. You can check them when you wish."

Arachne looked as if she had been struck, turning first red and then pale. Interested, Suva watched closely. The Mistress was angry with her husband! Better and better—anger between Arachne and Kyles, godhead between Arachne and Jaen. The less she was theirs, the more she was Suva's.

Arachne said stiffly, "No one doubts the full payment of your tax. Suva, take Pholen to his nurse."

"How long have the ships been on the horizon?" Kyles said evenly. Suva thought his face looked as closed as a fortified city, chancy as a besieged one.

"They have only just come. I haven't seen them myself." She crossed to the window and looked out. On the western horizon the two sails, one scarlet and one blue-striped, rode against the sky. Anger and hope, incompatible, made her brutal, and she talked to Kyles as if he were not there. "A bad time to sail. If they had miscalculated and the rains had come early, they might not have made Island at all. There would have to be a strong reason to set sail now. Something that could not wait."

Kyles did not answer.

"He may have found help for the Grove. The other ship may be bringing learned men, herbists, someone with knowledge Delernos did not bring with him to Island. Something. Or perhaps there *are* other Groves, and this . . . situation has been dealt with before."

"No trader has said so."

"It's not traders that Jaen will bring," Arachne said, with scorn.

Suva led Pholen from the room. The child, subdued, did not protest. In the corridor he reached for Suva's skeletal hand. "Mama and Father sound funny."

"Yes, child."

"But the ships are pretty. I like the one with the red sail, that's Uncle Jaen's ship. But, Suva, you said he got drowned. And you made the soap."

"So he was."

"Then how can he bring his ship back?"

"Perhaps he is not aboard," Suva said, although she didn't believe it. "Or else he is back from the dead, child. Back from the sea."

"Uncle Jaen got undrowned?"

"Back, back from the sea."

Pholen considered, frowning. "That's silly. People don't get undrowned. If he's dead, he has to stay dead."

"He has become a god." Suva threw back her head, an almost silent hissing escaping between her bared teeth. Her shoulders twitched violently. Pholen, used to her outbreaks, continued to trot along quietly, holding her hand. He was thinking.

"But, Suva—you said Uncle Jaen came back from the sea and so he got to be a god. You came back from the sea, too—remember? You told me and Amaura? So then you must get to be a goddess."

The old woman halted in the middle of the corridor. Her shoulders stopped twitching. She sucked in her cheeks, hollowing them with a sudden pop, and stared at Pholen.

"Don't you get to be a goddess, Suva? You came back from the sea."

"A goddess," Suva said experimentally. "A goddess." Apart from and above men, lifted over their power by the greater glorious power of her own. Mother-goddess, who had never been defiled by men (*never,* hissed the horrible black memory at the back of her mind, with desperation—*never*), but nonetheless a mother to daughters who were skilled and clever and fertile as Arachne. A mother-goddess, with a daughter. Arachne would be her daughter.

"Well," Pholen said impatiently, his child's face upturned to hers. "Are you a goddess or aren't you?"

"From the sea *singing,*" Suva said fiercely. "Don't forget that part, child. Not that part. Singing and singing."

All afternoon the two ships did not move any closer to Island. Arachne thought: *if it is not Jaen who is directing, if he is somehow not aboard, if pirates*— and pushed the rest of the thought away. No one else would have reason to sail a pirated ship back to Island. Jaen would wait out the night and land with the morning tide.

She gave orders for watchers to be waiting at first light on the beach at the harbor, which lay below the cliffs on Island's northwest side and was reached from the villa by a single steep path downward. The cooks were ordered to prepare food for a great many people. They were annoyed at not knowing how many "a great many" would be, but Arachne did not know. The ships had halted so far out that she couldn't accurately determine their relative size, although it seemed to her that the sail of the strange ship looked larger than the scarlet sail of Jaen's—she could think of no reason for Jaen to anchor so far from Island; it disturbed her.

Slaves prepared bedchambers, shaking out beautiful and little-used weavings of spider silk, some of them four generations old. Pithoi of wine were brought from the underground magazines. Then, having done all to prepare that she could think of but still far from sleep, Arachne retired to her chamber to wait for morning, and to wait to see if Kyles would come to her.

Each time a noise sounded in a corridor, she tensed. He had been cold this afternoon, but the ships had just come and he might not have planned on all the activity that had created. Also—he was always cold, or at least remote. *Not always,* memory whispered, and for a while Arachne considered yet again the night before he left, turning it over in her mind like some inexplicably-shaped pebble. It still puzzled her. The actual events, the sharp perceptions of his invading desire, had faded a little, as had her instinctive repulsion. The puzzlement remained. She did not see how a bedding could have had such intensity for him. But, then—had she ever seen how bedding could have intensity?

In this, she knew, she differed from many of her women. Before, she had not cared.

By midnight Kyles had not appeared. Arachne knew then that he would not.

Wrapped in a woolen cloak, Arachne stood by her window and listened to the sea. The clouds had lifted slightly, but the patchy starlight was too faint to reveal the ships on the horizon. It seemed to her that she ought to think more about Kyles's not coming to her, or about the way Amaura had thrown herself on her returning father—not hysterically, but as if she were trying to be hysterical

—or about the strange ship accompanying Jaen's, but none of the topics would stay long enough in her mind. They slid out and were lost.

Tomorrow Jaen would land. He would bring help to Island from Thera, the city that had unjustly exiled Delernos.

Had that been the true reason for her opposition to Jaen's voyage? Thera had cast off her ancestor, the most brilliant of her line; his descendants should therefore cast off Thera. Pride demanded it. But was it pride, or arrogance?

She was so tired of fighting for the Grove by herself.

Should she then welcome the help Jaen had brought? He *must* have brought help, she reassured herself fiercely, or he would not have sailed at such a dangerous time of year. And nothing *she* had done, on Island, had succeeded in altering the course of the Grove's dying. Pharmakons, spiders, Cleis's pathetic sacrifices to the Goddess—all futile. She had failed. Perhaps Jaen could do better.

Jaen. Longing to see him swept over her with such strength that she shivered, and pulled her woolen cloak tighter. He had loved the Grove, as she had. She had been wrong to oppose his voyage to Thera. She would tell him so tomorrow.

Unbidden, the memory of that last overpowering moment of the Grove's life, the moment she had stood beside Jaen in front of the ash-gray web, slipped into her mind. She thought of it often, and although usually the memory was pain, tonight it was not. That moment when she had *been* the Grove, been the light, been the Goddess—that could come again, if Jaen had brought help. It had been Jaen who had stood beside her when the moment happened. She would welcome him tomorrow.

Tomorrow.

The breeze from the window freshened. Kyles did not come. Arachne went wearily to bed, and dreamed of scarlet silk luminous as sunlight.

In the morning a clean wind blew inland from the sea. Islanders thronged the harbor beach, backing up onto the long path down the cliff. Most wore their best spider silk; chitons flapped in the breeze in a frenzy of shifting colors.

When, by noon, the two ships had not moved from their positions on the horizon, the crowd began to disperse, a few Islanders at a time. By late afternoon the beach held only the watchers Arachne had posted, weary and a little sullen.

"Have fishing boats sail out to the ships with the next tide," Arachne said to Telnis, her chief of the guard. The position was an honorary one, a tradition brought from Thera. Telnis was a prosperous quarryman, and blocks of stone had been moving all day without him. He frowned.

"Begging your pardon, Mistress, but that might not be the best plan. If Master Jaen isn't aboard his own ship—"

"You mean pirates."

"Traders tell tales, Mistress. Or if he is aboard and captive—" He looked away from her. "Not every place had a Grove."

"Has, Telnis!"

The quarryman did not answer. His honest, stubborn face remained averted. Arachne dismissed him, and did not send fishing boats to the ships.

At sunset, the two ships were still stationary. The gray light drained from the sky into the sea, and the ships with it.

"Why does he *wait?"* Arachne said. "The sea was calm enough all day—what is he waiting for?"

"I don't know, Mistress," Cleis said. The girl crept quietly about the chamber, her movements small but her face swept with a high, hectic color. She had come in the afternoon for the wool spinning, she had said in a tiny voice, although Arachne had sent word to all her women that the usual autumn woolen work would be suspended. Arachne, moved by an irritated pity, had let her stay. There had been no work except waiting, the most onerous, but Cleis had been surprisingly organized about giving orders that, for the second night, bedchambers and watching rotations and feasts were to be prepared. The cooks, she had reported timidly to Arachne, were in a bad temper.

"Then let them be in a bad temper. They can't have that much left in the kitchen—that wretched Suva has been carrying it all up here, hoping to overhear something. Have all this meat and cheese taken away, Cleis. Leave only the fruit. I can't stand the smell of the rest."

"Yes, Mistress. Someone else to see you, Mistress."

"Who this time?"

"The priestess, Mistress. She's waiting in the next room."

"The old priestess? Stydia?"

"No—her daughter. Agathelia."

"Tell her Council is tomorrow night, and I will hear then whatever petition she brings."

"I told her, Mistress. She insists on seeing you tonight. She says she has an urgent message for you."

A float, Arachne thought—a float rowed ashore last night, under cover of darkness, to land not on the beach but on an inlet somewhere on the north shore. Dangerous, but it could be done—but why? And why to a priestess, not directly to her? Even if Jaen were somehow not in command of his own ship—

"Bring the priestess here! Quickly!"

Cleis, slower in thought, gaped. "Do you think . . . you don't think—"

"Bring her *in*, Cleis!"

The priestess entered slowly, carrying a libation vase. Agathelia, almost past middle age, large and plain, carried in the lines of her face personal querulousness inadequately disguised as public fervor. When Agathelia assumed, in the spring planting festival, the personification of the Goddess as She gave birth to the Young God of vegetation, Arachne had never been able to stop herself from wincing. And now why would Agathelia be carrying a libation vase to deliver a message? But she was such as would carry it for no reason at all, a badge of office for an office she was not going to perform.

"I give you greetings, Mistress."

"Greetings. You have an urgent message for me, Priestess?"

"I do."

"From whom?"

Agathelia arranged her chiton around herself, smoothing its folds carefully. She was elaborately ornamented with the jewelry of her office: gold and faience worked into owls and snakes and olive trees rode on her hair and shoulders and neck and arms. Delicately she touched a coiled golden snake in her hair, straightening it.

"A message from *whom?*" Arachne repeated.

"From the Goddess, Mistress Arachne. A message of Her displeasure."

Cleis sagged. Arachne turned her back. Disappointment made her voice harsh. "Tomorrow night in Council, Priestess. My woman told you that. Messages and petitions to Island can be presented then."

"This is not a message to Island," Agathelia said, "but to you, Mistress. You rule Island; what you choose for yourself, you choose for Island. And you have chosen neglect of the Goddess, Mistress, for so long that you cannot see that it is Her anger that is destroying your Grove."

Suva had appeared at Arachne's elbow, removing the unwanted meat and cheese. It was amazing, Arachne thought irritably, how unerringly Suva knew where and when conflict would be. Even petty conflict.

"The Goddess is patient," Agathelia continued in her querulous, righteous voice. "For many years you and Master Jaen have given your worship to the Grove and not the sacred cave. That is well-known. Islanders have followed your example, as they followed the example of your parents before you, and the sacred cave has been little visited. The Goddess is patient, but now her patience is exhausted. She seeks to show Her displeasure. Unless you return to Her, the Grove will never flourish again."

Arachne studied the Priestess. A long moment passed. Agathelia lifted her chin, glared resentfully, and fussed with her necklace.

"Priestess," Arachne said finally, "why should the Goddess prefer to be worshipped in the cave instead of the Grove?"

"The cave is sacred."

"But in the Grove I have actually felt the presence of the Goddess—" She made herself push away the memory of the moment before the ashy web, it would not do here "—or what might have been the presence of the Goddess. In the cave I have felt nothing. Why should I believe the cave is sacred against the evidence of my own senses?"

Agathelia began to breathe harder. Her jewelry jingled.

"Why should any Islander believe against the evidence of his senses?"

"The Grove is not the site for the worship of the Goddess! The Grove is for the worship of spider silk and human labor!"

"Priestess—" Arachne said, "Priestess—you are not a weaver. Did you visit the Grove often when it was as it was? What is the evidence of your senses?"

"The sacred cave is where the Goddess is worshipped! Island

must return to the sacred cave!'' She was angry now; the light from the oil lamp danced on her jewelry as she quivered.

"Return to the cave? Or to the power of the priesthood?"

"The sacred cave is where the Goddess is worshipped!"

Agathelia was sincere, Arachne saw. If she wanted more power as priestess, it was a secondary wish. Agathelia believed in the cave, against the evidence of her own senses, because she believed in the cave. It was a kind of belief that Arachne did not understand, and a kind that suddenly bored her. She stood in dismissal, her voice hard.

"I will say three things to you, Priestess. The first is that my brother and I, and all our Household, have never failed to make the correct sacrifices at each season in the cave. We have sent the correct tithe, poured the correct libations, sung to the Goddess the correct paens. All that we should have done, we did. The second is that I have never heard that the Goddess or the Young God practice vengeance. 'Everything they give to man is good and fruit-ful'—isn't that how the paen is sung? The Grove then is a good and fruitful gift. Finally, you are dismissed, Priestess. Anything else you wish to say, you can say tomorrow night at Council."

Agathelia smiled. Arachne, expecting more anger, a whining hysteria, outraged indignation—anything but a smile—was shocked. The smile was complex and unpleasant, a weaving of pity, contempt, and a vengeful superiority. It was the smile of someone who knows something an opponent does not know, and it suddenly came to Arachne that this woman would have disliked the Grove even before it began to die, and would have been afraid of it. She had never seen such an Islander before. All at once she wondered how many there had always been, people in the villa who never walked in the Grove, who sat silent when their families and neighbors discussed what they had felt there, who lived by choice or temperament beyond what she had seen as an all-encompassing circle of truth and light. Kyles's words flashed into her mind: "You are the blindest woman I know."

But he had not meant blind like that.

"Tomorrow night, at Council," Agathelia repeated. Again she smiled. Cleis looked away. "I give you good-night, Mistress. In the name of the Goddess."

"In the name of the Goddess," Arachne said. Cleis led Agathelia to the door. Behind her Arachne heard an odd sound. She turned to see Suva in a corner of the room, her arms wrapped around her concave belly to hold in her laughter, her head bobbing in derisive mirth, her black eyes streaming with silent, suppressed, mad glee.

"Leave the chamber, Suva!" Arachne said. "Cleis, take her away!"

"Yes, Mistress."

"Not vengeful!' " Suva gasped. "A god not . . . practice vengeance . . ." Her laughter broke free, whooping and hooting. She rocked with mirth, doubled over with it, convulsed with it. Glee seemed to have softened her bones; she flopped helplessly, limp with whoops and shrieks. Cleis, with a horrified glance at Arachne, grabbed the end of the cord knotted around the old woman's waist and pulled at her. Suva did not move. When she could talk again, she plunged into a story, still wiping from her eyes the tears of laughter.

"Once the mother Goddess was angry. She sent a drought over a remote island of men. Grain withered, children died. Sacrifices were made, but nothing grew. The people were eating grass, drinking sea water, dying. There was no hope. Finally only one youth and one maiden were left. They had lived in a cave, hoarding food and water, but now they came out to die in the sunshine. As they lay there, the Goddess saw that the boy, despite his starvation and dirt, was beautiful, and finally she was moved to pity. She gave both boy and girl food and water, and they lived. The Goddess made the island bloom again, just for them. A year later the girl died in childbirth, and in his grief the boy threw himself from a cliff and was smashed on the rocks below."

Suva began to chortle. Cleis seized her arm and again tried to pull her from the room. This time Suva went without resistance. Cleis shoved her through the door and closed it.

"I don't see, Mistress, why you have her around you! She should be sold!"

"Who would buy her?" Arachne snapped. "No one purchases a mad slave. And she's afraid of the spiders; there is no place else for her to be except near the sea, and in the villa that means the Household chambers. Suva is one slave about which I have no choice."

Cleis began to gather together the dishes Suva had abandoned.

Cleis heard nothing to question in the Mistress's explanation; neither did Arachne. Yet something prompted Arachne to say, "Thera will not have been like Island."

Cleis picked up a goat cheese and picked crumbs off one end. "Do you think, Mistress, that in Thera . . . in Thera the women are prettier?"

"Prettier? In the name of the Goddess, Cleis, how should I know? The prettiness of Thera's women isn't what I meant."

Cleis did not ask what she had meant. Arachne thought this was probably fortunate; on reflection, she discovered that she didn't know what she had meant, or else had meant so many different things she could not sort them clear.

Neither did she want to sort them clear. The differences between Thera and Island did not concern her, unless they could help the Grove. Only that mattered.

In the morning, the ships still did not land. They remained two sails, one striped and one scarlet, floating on the horizon. Arachne became angry, then fearful with a somber and leashed fear that kept Cleis on the other side of the chamber, then angry all over again. She sent for her women, and for spinning wheels, spindles, and epinetrons. The women all drew, carded, and spun wool, just as if this were any winter afternoon. They looked at each other sideways past their wheels, and did not talk.

The day had dawned warm for the season. By evening the clouds had blown away, and the transparent air taken on a clarity as dazzling as summer's, but softer. Shortly after sunset the full, low moon of autumn Council rose on the opposite side of Island from the villa. The long reflection it cast on the sea pointed toward the ships, a spear of silvery, wavering light.

Arachne and her women walked silently to the Council House. The moon shone whitely on the stone corridors; lamps and torches were not necessary. Arachne, weary from two sleepless nights, thought that it was a beautiful night, and that she was too weary to care. She had not gone to Council for the last two months, working instead in the apotheca on the pharmakons that had accomplished nothing. Her absence was not unusual; in the summer months Council was often held by only the Household secretary. All he could do was report the petitions to her, deciding nothing, but in the summer there were usually neither petitions nor anything to decide, since Island was at work in its fields and vineyards or shepherding on its rugged eastern hills. This autumn Council was thus important, but Arachne thought she would like to have missed it, too. She was so tired.

At the turning to the Council House, her weariness abruptly vanished. She scarcely recognized what she saw, so unlike an Island Council was the scene before her.

Crowds of Islanders milled in the corridors, far too many to fit into the Council House. Their faces were grim, or angry, or fearful. Some carried bundles wrapped in cloth. There were so many they pressed into each other, jammed elbows into each other's faces. They surged noisily, restlessly, unwilling to stand still. Voices, muttered or shrill, rose and fell in angry waves. Telnis, chief of the guard, and some other men were trying to hold the Islanders into orderly lines, but they were largely ignored; Island had no tradition of lines, only of order. Arachne saw at the edges of the crowd faces she knew—a coppersmith, a slave belonging to one of her women, an old woman who sold pots in the marketplace—but against the astonishing and menacing crowd they, too, looked unfamiliar. A puff of wind blew toward her; it smelled of too many bodies in too small a place.

Bewildered, Arachne turned toward her women. In the white moonlight the faces closest to hers looked just as bewildered. Her gaze met that of Aretone, a few years younger than Arachne and as close to a childhood companion as she and Jaen had permitted each other. In Aretone's face Arachne saw fearful comprehension, but before she could ask what was happening, Islanders at the edge of the crowd spotted their Mistress.

The crowd surged toward her, shouting. A few of Arachne's women turned and fled back down the corridors. Telnis, aided by some of the Islanders who began by surging toward Arachne but then stopped when they saw her women flee, held the throng back. Eventually they jostled open a narrow lane into the Council House and through this Arachne and her remaining women pushed and shoved until she reached the stone dais. No one had touched her, no hand had reached out from the shouting mass to pull at chiton or hair, but she felt battered by sound and by the restlessness that pummeled the crowd like fists. Kyles pushed his way from the door and took his place on the dais, behind her chair. Before it, at her feet, sat the Council Secretary; he turned his old face toward her as she sat down, and in his eyes Arachne saw his awareness of the frailty of age. She called over to her a strong youth sitting on the first tier close to the sheltering wall, and told him to give his seat to the Secretary and to stand next to him. The youth complied, but he first stared at her flatly, unsmiling, and this disturbed Arachne more than the rest of the inexplicable crowd. The youth had come close to refusing.

It took a long while to get the crowd quiet enough for Council to begin. Telnis and his self-appointed aides shouted and threatened. When quiet did come, it spread abruptly in waves outward and upward from the dais, unnatural waves that in a few moments transformed the jostling mass into a sea of faces straining to hear, a sea spread throughout the stone tiers, over the floor, and out beyond the open wall into the corridors, all the faces grim and pale in the white light of the enormous harvest moon.

In that strange silence, the Secretary stood in his corner and quavered, "The Household of Delernos will hear the petitions of the people of Island."

One by one, kept orderly by the grim-faced Telnis, Islanders were heard.

A child from a fishing settlement on the Southern Shore had been bitten in a field of olive trees by a wild animal. The animal—no one knew what it was, and the child was unable to talk—had been poisonous. There had never been poisonous animals on Island before. The child was very sick.

A young shepherdess from the central hills, sent to the villa to stay with an aunt for the winter, had been raped in the darkness of the deserted colonnade surrounding the Grove. She had gone there to see the Grove her father talked of so often. The raped girl had not been found until the next morning, huddled against a column, naked and dumb.

The shop of a coppersmith had been robbed through a hole cut in the stone wall. Stolen were a few bracelets, three cooking pots —and twenty daggers intended for trade with the next ship.

The wheat crop on three farms just outside the villa had turned brown and rotted, the stalks growing pulpy and smelling wrong. No one had seen wheat do that before. What was it?

A potter had struck his slave because the slave had built a kiln fire too hot and ruined a batch of pots. He had hit the slave about the head and shoulders with a pot shard, drawing blood. The slave's screams brought the neighbors running; they wanted the Mistress to know that this potter had begun to abuse his slave as they had never seen.

An old farmer from the wild ravines on the Eastern Shore unwrapped from a cloth bundle a dead, deformed goat. He held out to Arachne the baby thing: two heads and three legs. Arachne looked away. Never, said the old man, his voice shaking, had such a thing been born in his herd. He was shamed. How could it be? What did it mean?

Two young men had had an argument in a tavern. The argument had been over a spider crawling over the table. One had drawn a knife and killed the other. The brother of the dead man wanted the murderer burned to death.

Arachne put her head in her hands. Moonlight seeped between the fingers, and in the moonlight she seemed to see Agathelia's contemptuous smile: the smile of someone who knows something an opponent does not know. Arachne took away her hands. The crowd was becoming agitated again; it had heard that others were as angry and hurt, and that added justification to its own grievances and swelled them. Two petitioners pressed toward the dais at the same time; when Telnis chose one to speak, the other began to argue passionately. Arachne could not hear the Islander who was supposed to talk. In the back of the House, on an upper tier, a shoving fight broke out between two women. Somewhere in the crowd a child cried out. Arachne saw the Secretary tremblingly stand, and then sit down again, huddling against his wall. Telnis seized the shouting man who was arguing with him and tried to force him toward the door. He would not go.

The noise rose around her—the muttering mass noise, so different from the individual quarrelsomeness of even a vivid people.

Abruptly Arachne stood up. "This Council is over," she shouted over the noise. Silence fell. Before she could do what she intended next, which was to explain into the silence where and when they could come in small groups to have their petitions heard, the crowd was upon her.

They surged forward, climbing onto the dais, shouting and gesturing. The individual shouts blended into a single smear of sound. Arachne shouted back, not even sure what she was saying. Someone grabbed for her arm and got her chiton; the spider silk did not tear but it yanked sideways, leaving her left shoulder bare and cutting into the right side of her neck. Someone thrust the deformed goat into her arms. The cloth wrapping fell open and the goat's two heads stared up at her from four dead eyes. Arachne snatched back her arms, but the crowd shoved from the back, desperate to be heard, and the kid had no room to fall. It stayed jammed against her, buoyed by the pressing bodies all yelling at her. "I do not know!" Arachne shouted back. "I do not know!" There were tears on her face, or spit. She could not be heard. To her right a woman lost her footing and screamed, sucked down by the surging crowd as by an undertow. More people began to scream.

Arms circled Arachne from behind and lifted her. She kicked backwards, drumming frantically with her heels, until she recognized the arms as Kyles's. He was bearing her backward toward the door, and trying at the same time to turn her around so that his own body would block her from the crowd. Islanders pressed in on them, shouting desperate, unintelligible demands. The shouting pressed in on her too, rushing like liquid into the small spaces between bodies and into the cracks of the room, rising higher and higher. She was drowning in sound. Kyles lunged backwards and turned. A small, brief space opened between Arachne and the crowd; the goat fell into it and was instantly trampled. Islanders rushed the space, filling it with bodies and tearing sound.

And then there was another sound, and then silence—

Islanders' heads jerked up and looked around. Beyond the door of the Council House, riding on the shoulders of another man, towered a stranger holding an instrument no one had seen before, a shining bell-shaped horn on which he had blown the piercing note that silenced them. He put it to his lips and blew twice more; Islanders clapped their hands over their ears. The youth lowered his horn and looked indifferently at the crowd. He was startlingly beautiful, with hair a color none of them had seen before: a warm reddish-brown, like rubbed wood, circled with a band of gold. He was naked except for a gold cloth around his hips and a fur robe. The man he rode was entirely naked, but even the Islanders who could see him clearly hardly noticed: the man-mount measured nearly as high as the adjoining rooftop, and broader than any two Islanders near him. His dull eyes seemed to see nothing.

"To the Council of Island and its Mistress Arachne," the youth called in a voice pitched startlingly high, "greetings from the trader Nikos, the Princess Ikeria, and the Housholder Jaen, Master of Island. Trader Nikos and Master Jaen send to inform Mistress Arachne that their ships are landing now, honored and honoring the autumn Council."

As soon as this announcement had been delivered, the youth and his mount turned and made their way back through the corridor, led by the wide-eyed Islander who had evidently guided them to the Council House. The stranger looked at neither the guide nor the crowd; his beautiful face was bored, and the shining horn hung negligently from his fingers. Islanders began to follow the pair, trailing first in twos and threes, and then as a congested but orderly crowd fanning out into many adjacent corridors. It began to be possible to move within the Council House. A man bent over the woman who had gone down in the mob, picked her up, and carried her out. She moaned loudly. Others walked supported by friends or relatives; the Secretary's arm was held by the boy who had almost refused him his seat. The council House emptied. Finally there remained only Arachne, Kyles, Telnis, and the bloody, trampled body of the deformed baby goat, staring sightlessly in the moonlight.

—8—

S O there was no feast, no attendants, no time to do more than
yank off the chiton stained with goat's blood and pull on
another. Kyles silent beside her, Arachne walked swiftly to
the chamber on the sea where Jaen had taken the Therans and
threw open the door. She gave no thought to how she must look,
standing there with her hair loosened and straggling, her face
streaked, three nights' sleeplessness on her eyelids. Straight from
the ruins of her Council, she stood in the doorway and looked at
Jaen, and did not notice that the lamplit room held anyone else.

In that clear, slow moment, and through the hazy light of her
fatigue, Arachne actually thought the Grove was already restored.
Her gaze met Jaen's and she was aware of him with that heightened
awareness that came usually from the Grove. All at the same time,
her look said *You're back* and *Jaen! Did you find help?* and *Waiting
three days just to land at Council is stupidly gaudy* and *I've longed for you
more than I can say.* His look said *I did return* and *Forgive me my tiny
drama* and *Has it been bad for you?* and *How went Island without me?*

The moment of clarity thinned and widened. There were other
faces in the chamber, and other things in Jaen's eyes, things held
warily away from her. Then the moment collapsed entirely, and
Jaen was crossing the room and embracing her, a separate mind not
woven with hers at all, a familiar body smelling of unfamiliar,
exquisite oils. His beard was gone—he was clean-shaven, as men
of Island never were.

"Arachne!"

"Jaen . . . Jaen—did you find it? Did you find the restorative for the Grove?"

"Always my direct one!" He laughed and kissed her hair, but in the laugh she heard a forced note, a subtle strain. Into her ear he whispered, "Too soon to be sure. I may have. Say little to Nikos," and turned to Kyles. "Kyles! You are looking well. I hope the grape harvest was a good one."

"Jaen," Kyles said, a bare acknowledgment. Jaen gave no sign of noticing. He smiled and led Arachne by the hand to the man and woman seated by a small table holding wine and honey cakes. The man rose.

"My sister Arachne, Mistress of Island, and my marriage-brother, her husband Kyles. Arachne—our guests, the trader Nikos of Nirou, and Princess Ikeria of Thera."

Something complex in the way Jaen pronounced the princess's name might have made Arachne glance at him, but her gaze was already bound to Ikeria.

The foreign princess wore not a chiton, but a dress with a long skirt in ruffled tiers, a tight leather waist, and large ruffled sleeves. The bodice was cut below her breasts, which were oiled and gleaming, the nipples staring at Arachne like blind eyes. Ikeria's black hair was piled in coils and braids, puffs and curls, all threaded with ropes of jewels. At her neck and ears and wrists gleamed jewelry of strange, ornate shapes and subtle workmanship. Her eyebrows had been plucked and her lids darkened with kohl. In the plain, plastered room, holding a pottery goblet of wine, she lounged at ease, smiling and amused. Arachne looked into the Theran princess's slanted, intelligent eyes, felt the glow of her sensual shine and the irony in her smile, and knew that she was not going to understand Ikeria.

"In my sister's name I welcome you both to Island," Jaen said, and now he was laughing and making a mocking little bow, "since she apparently neglects to do so."

"Of course you are welcome to Island," Arachne said. "Jaen—"

"Such as it is," Jaen said, and laughed again.

"You were too hard on your birthplace," Ikeria said. Her voice was husky and musical, accented differently from Islanders. "The settlement has a lovely view."

"You shouldn't flatter the provincials," Jaen said, and something passed from his eyes to hers, some glance that seemed more than a reflection of light.

"We are honored to be here," Nikos said. His voice was very deep.

"Are you a priestess, Princess?" Arachne asked. She did not see how a trader and a noblewoman could help the Grove, or why Jaen had whispered to say little to Nikos. Fatigue and hope struggled in her mind. She tried not to stare at Ikeria's nakedness, and put up one hand to straighten her own hair.

Ikeria laughed. "No, I am not a priestess—I am far too idle! And you must not call me 'princess.' By now Thera has so many minor princesses—we do keep spawning, lesser royalty at least is wonderful at that!—that the title has become a poor joke, useful only to impress the rabble. Call me Ikeria, and I will call you Arachne, as Jaen does." She smiled charmingly.

"Then you, Trader, you bring to sell some elixir . . . some knowledge . . ."

"*Later,* Arachne," Jaen said. He poured more wine for Ikeria and Nikos and handed full goblets to Arachne and Kyles. Wine and goblets seemed to have appeared in midair, carried on trays by unfamiliar slaves so silent and unobtrusive they were nearly invisible. Jaen acknowledged neither trays nor servers, and they vanished.

"Very nice wine," Nikos said.

"But not exactly exportable quality, Trader?" Jaen said, and laughed. The trader smiled, but did not answer.

"You are searching again for compliments," Ikeria said gaily. "A tiresome trait in a man, Jaen, especially when you already receive so many. You must not be greedy. The wine is excellent."

"The compliments should go to Kyles," Jaen said. "His is the vineyard. Here in the provinces, you know, we unsophisticated Householders do not leave the crops to stewards. The compliments are legitimately Kyles's."

"Then he has them," Nikos said in his deep voice. The trader's face was weatherscarred and brown, pointed as the prow of his ship. "But you do not want to export wine. You have exportable goods enough."

"Arachne," Jaen said, "Nikos is interested in exporting spider silk. In exchange for whatever we might need or want from Thera. What that might be, you and I can discuss later."

"But, Jaen—"

"Later." He smiled determinedly, his dark eyes fixed on her in warning. Arachne saw that Nikos did not miss the look. Beside her, Kyles suddenly shifted his weight. There was an awkward silence, and then Ikeria had filled it, gliding in with words polished and light as silk.

"Look, for instance, at the chiton you are wearing, Arachne. We see nothing that fine at Thera, nor even at the palace. Noblewomen and wealthy Householders would be entranced by it, and willing to pay huge prices. Jaen tells us that you and your women do the actual weaving, a sort of family tradition. May I ask if you yourself wove that silk?"

"My grandmother wove it."

"And the color is still unfaded," Nikos said. His eyes were sharp with interest; unlike Ikeria, he did not smile.

"Spider silk does not fade," Jaen said, "nor weaken in folded creases. A paradox for you, Princess—a beautiful doe does not yield the beauty of a hideous spider."

"Just so long as no one forces me to touch the paradox," Ikeria said. It was almost a challenge; again that look flashed between her and Jaen.

"She asked not to be called 'Princess,'" Arachne said to her brother. "Did I misunderstand?"

"You did not. I call her so because I count myself among the rabble beneath her," Jaen said gaily.

"The designs in your chiton are similar to the ones in that tapestry on the wall," Nikos said to Arachne. "Did your grandmother weave that one, too? Is it of the same age?"

"I wove the tapestry."

"Yet the designs are the same. They are traditional to Island?"

"Yes."

"But of course Arachne can weave others," Jaen said quickly.

The trader's gaze searched the room: tapestries, cushions, chitons. His black eyes registered each accurately. Arachne thought of beads on an abacus. It was a relief to dislike him.

"I don't think Trader Nikos admires the traditional designs," she said, and the abacus eyes moved to her, registering.

"No, you misunderstand," Ikeria said. "Nikos, sometimes you are too much the trader, it is very tiresome. Arachne, the traditional

designs are charming. They have a simplicity and a nostalgia that
would cause a sensation at the palace. But what has brought Nikos
all this way—and he doesn't come for nothing, I assure you!—is the
quality of the silk itself, and of its weaving. No one in Thera can
weave like that, and nowhere else produce silk like that. We were
all amazed, and of course to Nikos amazement means wealth! But,
then, where would any of us be without the greed of our traders?''
The slanting eyes tilted up as she smiled at Nikos, a smile that
delicately mocked both him and herself. Arachne, watching, could
not tell what relationship lay between them, or between Ikeria and
Jaen, or Jaen and Nikos. Everything the Therans said seemed to
have layers—not to deceive, especially, but for some obscure pleasure in the layering.

Jaen said, "We can consider it all tomorrow, Nikos, you and I
and Arachne." After a moment he added, "And Kyles, of course."

Nikos's gaze shifted to Kyles. A bead on the abacus changed
position. "Tomorrow, then. I think the Mistress Arachne is fati-
gued. My boy told me your Council session appeared strenuous."

"*Strenuous . . .*" Arachne repeated. She caught a closer glimpse
of Theran layering: large matters were spoken of with small words,
while trivial ones were given mocking emphasis and ornate exag-
geration. Like Ikeria's dress and hair. Like Ikeria herself?

Arachne narrowed her eyes at Jaen. He had been gone most of
a year, and he both was, and was not, himself. *Jaen.*

On sudden impulse she said to the foreign princess, "I would like
to show you the Grove. Jaen must have told you about it. The moon
is bright enough now, and you will see where the silk is made and
weaved."

Ikeria's lashes dropped. Her hands lay motionless on her tiered
skirt. "I thank you, Arachne, but . . . isn't that where the spiders
live? Uncaged?"

"They are harmless."

"I know. Jaen has told me. But still—" She spread her hands
appealingly, laughing a little. "Princesses are cowards. A last de-
generation of a degenerate line! You have discovered my weak-
ness, and I yield."

Arachne looked at her carefully. Ikeria was genuinely afraid, as
afraid as Suva. Her skin had paled, and now Arachne could see the
artificial tint on both her cheeks and her breasts, a rose delicate as

spider silk. Under the paling was something else, or several something elses, that Arachne's tired mind could not sort out: amusement, perhaps, or curiosity. Restlessness. A hard-edged ruthless-
ness. They all slipped beneath the surface of the princess's practiced
charm. Arachne's mind fumbled at an image, lost it, found it again:
the ash-haze silk.

"Arachne, you are staring," Jaen said, smiling. The smile was
tight at the edges. "It is late, perhaps we should all sleep."

Immediately Kyles stood. "Good night," he said, and waited.
Arachne thought first that this was the single word he had spoken
since Jaen's name, and then that what he was waiting for was for
her to rise and accompany him. Startled, she stood and said good
night. Halfway across the room she turned, need overcoming fatigue.

"Jaen—"

"Tomorrow," he said firmly.

He was *reluctant.* Jaen—reluctant to go to the Grove. Something
was wrong, something she should have demanded to know but had
not, in all the silliness about wine and titles and exports, something
about the Grove. But Kyles was holding her arm and leading her
from the room. In the corridor outside her chamber, however, he
abruptly said "Good night," and left her. In the moonlight his face
was cold. Arachne knew there must be some reason why Kyles
wanted Jaen to see them leave together and yet still would not bed
her, but her tired mind could not find it. She stumbled through the
doorway, was undressed and put to bed by a Suva so subdued she
might have been one of Ikeria's slaves, and slept instantly, without
dreams.

In the morning Arachne awoke fierce, demanding answers.

The day was cloudy, and colder. A small wind had sprung up—
not from the sea, for it smelled not of salt but of a vague dustiness,
like rock powder. It must be blowing from the quarry. Blowing
through Island, it was muffled by the walls of the villa but still felt,
a cold wind that gritted slightly against the skin. Arachne, dressed
not in spider silk but in wool, faced Jaen in a chamber where the
mirror reflected white caps on the sea. This morning Jaen, alone,
seemed more himself, with less of self-mockery and more of power.

"I missed you so," Arachne said.

"Of all of Island I missed only two things: you and the Grove."

"What help have you brought? You said last night you may have found something."

"Tell me first how much the Grove has changed."

"It is almost dead."

A shadow fell on his face. "Do the spiders still spin silk?"

She could not believe her ears. "Is that what matters to you, Jaen? The silk was always the least of the Grove!"

"Don't you credit me with remembering that?" Jaen said, with such quiet pain that Arachne felt ashamed. She went to him and laid both hands on his chest, feeling the warmth and heartbeat beneath his chiton. He wore not wool but scarlet spider silk, and she recognized the silk as one she had woven herself.

Briefly she told him of the Grove's changes: the weakening of its effects on the mind, the deformed baby spiders and occasional rotten web, Agathelia's visit, the events reported at Council, and what had happened there. He did not seem as shocked as she had been.

"A murder, a rape, a misshapen birth—why should we ever have had anything else, Arachne? Now that I have seen Thera, I know that these are not rare. It was Island that was rare. Now people here begin to behave as others elsewhere always have."

She said abruptly, "What help have you brought, Jaen? Did you find other Groves?"

"No others. You were right in that; the Grove is singular. No librarian in Thera could tell me of any scroll that mentioned anything like a blessed island or enchanted grove. In fact, the librarians seemed bewildered when Ikeria and I described what we sought. Nor had any of the traders Nikos knew heard of any other Grove."

"How had Delernos heard of it, do you suppose?" Jaen did not answer, and impatiently Arachne seized his arm. "What help have you brought then?"

"That is complicated."

"Tell me! Why are you so evasive? In the name of the Goddess, tell me!"

"I want to see the Grove first."

His reluctance to tell his plan frightened her. Because of her fear, and because she could not deny his need for the Grove—a need that in his circumstances she would have felt as overwhelming—she said nothing. But in his circumstances, the thought came, she would not be going to the Grove only now. She would have been there three days earlier.

They walked through little-used and narrow corridors. He did not, Jaen said, want to be slowed down by greetings and talk from every Islander they met. The tiny, gritty wind blew against them. Jaen talked of Thera. He talked urgently, bending slightly into the wind, turning his head to meet her eyes.

"You cannot imagine Thera, no more than I could until I saw it. I did not visit the palace at Knossos, but I am told it is even grander. Thera trades with the entire world, and she is rich with trade goods Island has never dreamed of: ivory, tin, rubies, spices, papyrus. I have brought you some papyrus, Arachne; you'll marvel at it. The houses are three rooms tall, with painted walls and reflecting pools and water brought in by aqueduct. Even more important, scholars from every civilized country on the Great Sea gather at Thera. The most brilliant minds of the world at one place, learning from each other. The libraries . . . we on Island have spoken so much of what Delernos found, we never questioned what Delernos might have left behind. We should have, Arachne. Delernos was an eccentric, a misfit, even before he was exiled, and for five generations we have been paying for it. Cut off from arts advanced when he left Thera and awesome now. Frescoes, metallurgy, astronomy, navigation, poetry, pottery, building—we are ignorant and backward in all of them. Compared to Thera, we can do nothing."

"Except weave silk," Arachne said dryly.

"Yes. *Yes.* You mock, but it is the truth—all Island has to offer Thera, to be noticed for, is its silk. Ikeria has brought you presents. From their quality you will understand better, although there is no way for you to understand here the quality of the life among the wealthy on Thera. It has so much that we lack—pleasure, and ease, and diversity, and a kind of amusing playfulness."

"I can see that Ikeria is playful."

At her tone, Jaen looked at her carefully.

"Are you going to marry her, Jaen?"

His face changed. "She is already marriage-contracted."

"To Nikos?"

"Nikos? Of course not. He is a trader, whom her family finances. She is a princess."

Arachne was startled. She had never heard anyone say a word as Jaen said "princess": with anger, and longing, and a spitting contempt. Confusion kept her silent. Jaen talked on, describing Thera, and from his fluent descriptions she did catch a glimpse of what he was seeing: a great city at the height of its power, mighty and varied and colorful, its rulers and owners rich enough to take pleasure and luxury as their passions. Arachne frowned. She heard nothing in these praises to account for the way he had said "princess." She did not understand.

Jaen said, "Hipporen chose to stay at Thera, with his two slaves. The others returned with me to Island, but Hipporen stayed."

"He *chose* to stay?"

"Yes."

"Away from the Grove. Why?"

He looked at Arachne sideways. Without the beard, his face looked unfamiliar, but not naked. Armored. "He liked it there. Perhaps that does not make me as singular as you think."

But at the colonnade, Jaen halted for a moment. She took his hand. They crossed the stone floor, their sandals clicking, and entered the Grove.

Jaen stopped cold.

His face, Arachne thought, despairing in his despair, could have been carved of Spider Stone: hard amber with no hint of give. He looked around slowly, walked farther into the Grove, looked around again. Turning over a rock, he picked up the spider underneath, held it a long moment, set it down. The spider crawled away from the light.

"This," Jaen said. "In Thera, in all its richness and pleasure—I dreamed of *this.*"

"Don't—" Arachne said.

"When did the humming stop? When did it all stop?"

"Gradually."

"This."

They walked to the Spider Stone. Jaen rubbed it with his hand; grit from the wind grated under his fingers.

"I tried, Jaen. I did try." She began to tell him about the pharmakons, but saw that he was not listening. In his eyes was pain, yes—but something else as well, something unthinkable. Relief.

Arachne pulled her cloak tighter around her. "Jaen . . . tell me now. What is this plan to restore the Grove?"

He laughed bitterly. "I will not deny that seeing the Grove like this makes it easier to tell you. The scholars in Thera have pharmakons and elixirs we have never dreamed of. They can preserve dead matter—I myself have seen a corpse two hundred years old, looking as if he were simply asleep. They can also make changes in some matter, both unliving and living. I have seen . . ." He halted. A spasm went over his face, and passed. He continued, looking directly at Arachne from his familiar, beloved, changed dark eyes.

"I want to dig up the Spider Stone and take it to Thera for scholars to study there."

She stood speechless.

"I brought Nikos to the Grove last night, after you and Kyles retired. His slaves pushed pointed rods along the base of the Stone. After a few arm spans, it tapers inward sharply. It is not too large to dig up and to float on a barge lashed between the two ships, not for good seamen, and Nikos is that. At Thera both Stone and spiders can be examined—how the spiders breed within the Stone, why the silk is as it is, how the pharmakons change the Stone. When they know, the learned men there may be able to restore the Stone to what it was once. The stone is the center. They must have the Stone.

"Don't look at me like that, Arachne. When the Stone is restored, I can eventually bring it back here, and the Grove may become as it was."

Still she could say nothing. Her throat had constricted too far for even breath. Around her the Grove dizzied, blurred. Through the blur came Jaen's voice, rising higher.

"Do you think I would even propose this if the Grove were as it was when we were children? I would change nothing. I would fight any change as hard as you have fought. But now—do you want Amaura and Pholen to know the Grove as it is now? Like *this?*"

"Think, Arachne. At Thera is the knowledge of a dozen kingdoms. If you had seen Thera, you would know why I think this plan can succeed. They had heard of our silk, there is nothing they have not heard of, but had never seen any. They dismissed the tales as some provincial boasting, or a garbled legend: immortal spiders and local gods. But now Thera has seen our silk. They know we exist. And the silk can bring all the wealth and grace of Thera to us. We can be not backward Islanders but a notable part of *Thera*."

He put his hands on her shoulders, and at his touch Arachne found her voice.

"Never, Jaen. Never."

He did not become angry. His smile said he understood her resistance, said he could be patient. "We have time to discuss it. We stay at Island until the winter rains pass."

"Never. No discussion is necessary."

He continued to smile. "But I like discussion for its own sake. Surely you have not forgotten that?"

"You seemed so changed I no longer know what you like."

Jaen removed his hands. "In the name of the Goddess, Arachne —did you expect me not to? Did you think I could go to a place like Thera and not change?"

"No," she said slowly, "I did not think that."

A gust of cold wind shook the leaves and pulled at Jaen's chiton. It billowed softly, a cloud of scarlet. She had woven the silk.

"I will tell you something, Arachne, so that you may judge how much knowledge Thera has. The messenger whom Nikos sent to Council to announce our landing rode a slave. You saw him— immense, powerful, more than human. He was made that way by their pharmakons."

Arachne recalled her glimpse of the slave's eyes. "Never, Jaen. You will never take the Stone to Thera."

She turned and walked away. Behind her, he said, "The decision is not necessarily yours. We rule Island jointly."

"There is no decision to be made. Mutilation and greed are not ruling."

"Rescue is not mutilation."

"Never."

Jaen hesitated. Then he said, "I could take the Stone by force."

She walked back to him and peered into his face. His gaze met hers steadily. Arachne saw his anger that he had allowed himself to say so much. Under the anger, and the new ambition, and the new intensity of his old restlessness, she saw in his eyes what had not changed and had always been beloved: the Stone-hard conviction of the rightness of his own will. Beloved because it was hers, too. They had shared the Grove and the stubborn will, both, always.

"I could take the Stone," Jaen repeated.

"You would not."

"Are you certain?"

"Yes."

He said no more. Arachne left him there and walked across the cold grass, into the wind, to the apotheca to search for help for the Grove.

9

AMAURA fastened the shoulder clasp onto her chiton and twirled slowly. The chiton fell not to her knees, as her old ones had, but for the first time to the adult length of her ankles. Under the pale green spider silk her small, new breasts curved gently. Amaura ran her hands down her rib cage and circled her waist, squeezing gently, before she remembered Suva's presence and defiantly jerked her head upward.

But Suva was not mocking her. The old woman was carrying away Amaura's bathwater, jarful by jarful, working with such dead-faced quiet that Amaura frowned.

"What is wrong with you, Suva? Are you ill?"

"No, Young Mistress."

"Then are you . . . are you tired? I can tell someone else to do that."

"No, Young Mistress."

"Your face looks like a dried fig. Do you still wish Uncle Jaen hadn't come back?"

Suva set down her slop jar. She might have spoken, but Amaura was twirling again, watching the border of darker green silk flare around her feet. "I am permitted to come to the feast and to talk to the princess. I will sit next to Father, and he'll notice my new chiton. I'm sure he will. Suva, you've seen the princess—is she really so beautiful? Cleis said she is beautiful."

"She is beautiful."

"Cleis doesn't look beautiful, not now. Her eyes are all red and puffy from crying over Uncle Jaen. She looks soggy," Amaura said brutally. "Do you like my chiton? Is it as pretty as the princess's? It would be wonderful to be a princess of Thera and sail all over the sea."

Suva laughed bitterly. Startled, Amaura stopped twirling. Suva hugged the slop jar in her arms, and over its rim her flat mad eyes glittered with what looked to Amaura like fear.

"Why do you look like that, Suva? You're all different since the Therans came. What is wrong with you?"

"They have come back for me."

"Back for you? What do you mean? I thought," said Amaura, her mouth curving slyly, "that you had never seen Therans? Or anyone else? You said you just walked newborn out of the sea. Isn't that what you *said,* Suva?"

"They have come back for me," Suva repeated. In her quietness she looked to Amaura more mad than in her fits. Certainty and fear rose from her like smells. She hugged the slop jar closer, caressing it like a child.

Amaura scented drama, and her lips parted. "Suva. What is it, Suva? *Who* has come back for you?"

"They came in ships," Suva said, her voice flat with despair. "They came in ships, from Thera."

"Came to where, Suva? Sit down, Suva, sit here. You can tell me. Where did the ships from Thera come *to?*"

"To my village. To my island. To Anissos."

Amaura had never heard the name before. "When was this, dear Suva? You can tell me the story—it's a story, isn't it? When did the ships come to you at Anissos?"

"I was a young woman," Suva said and with a jerk her arms tightened again on the slop jar. Then abruptly her preternatural flatness vanished. Her eyes glittered with her old malice and she snorted at Amaura, "You look a pretty child tonight, Young Mistress."

"I am not a child!"

"A child, a child," Suva chanted slyly, and shuffled off with the slop jar.

Amaura frowned and then shrugged. It would be babyish to let herself be intrigued by tales from crazy old Suva, and she was no longer a baby. She was newly, suddenly, a woman. Leaning toward her mirror, she held her hair on top of her head, the way she would wear it in a few more years, and breathed at her reflection, "Princess Amaura."

She let the hair fall. Stepping back a pace, she made a graceful obeisance to a point high in the air, smiling at the spot through her lashes. Silk puddled around her in cool folds.

"King Kyles."

After the feast, the Princess of Thera presented gifts to the Mistress of Island. Slaves, silent and expressionless, carried packages to a table beside Arachne's couch, unwrapped them, and vanished. Ikeria said something about the origin of each gift, something amusing and graceful. Arachne said nothing.

There was a seal ring of gold with an entire sacred ceremony engraved upon it: the Goddess, sacred trees, a tiny libation vase, all with the finished perfection of the miniature. The Goddess wore the same ruffled, bare-breasted dress as Ikeria. There was a vase formed from a single black rock crystal, its neck circled with a crystal ring capped with gold and its handle formed from crystal beads threaded onto wire. There were a jeweled pendant, a drinking cup shaped like a bull's head with golden horns, and an oil lamp of greenish glass, a material unknown on Island. Each gift had an excess to it, a hint of voluptuous shine, that came less from ornamentation or color than from the joyful swooping curves and rich materials.

Then came a carved figure, a female acrobat in a loincloth, caught in a supple back flip of taut muscles and triumphant balance. Palms outstretched and long legs curved back over her head, she was about to land on her hands. The carving was of some white, smooth material that was not stone. Lamplight slid over the curve formed by legs, body, arms.

"That is ivory," Ikeria said. "Amaura, would you believe it comes from the horns of some immense animal larger than three oxen? It is so!"

"The animal lives near Thera?" Kyles asked.

"Oh, no. The ivory is imported. The hunters who kill for it must be very brave. The animal is called an elephant."

"The statuette is called a bull dancer, also very brave," Jaen said. "Can you recognize it as Ikeria?"

"Of course not," Ikeria said, smiling. "It barely has a face."

"They dance on a *bull?*" Amaura blurted.

Jaen answered. "Not dance. The bull charges toward the dancer, the dancer grabs its horns, vaults into a handspring onto its back, and then somersaults off onto the ground. It is a sport for the nobility, and brings a successful dancer roars of applause. Ikeria is one of the best. I have seen her perform."

Amaura felt a slow thrill slide down her body, from the base of her neck down her spine to between her legs. She could see the wicked horns of the charging bull, hear the cheering crowd, feel in her leg muscles the tension of the waiting dancer, poised to spring . . . she stared at Ikeria with greedy enchantment. To bare one's breasts like that, to bring these exotic gifts, to spring half-naked at a charging bull in front of hundreds of people—Ikeria seemed to her scarcely real. She was one of Suva's stories, and she dazzled with the same suggestion of heedless and cruel vitality.

Next to her, Mother looked almost drab. During the feasting Arachne had seldom spoken and never smiled. She did not look beautiful, and for reasons Amaura didn't understand, Mother was not even being mannerly, as Father was. He was quiet, but then he was always that. Kyles had poured Amaura a goblet of wine. She held it constantly, partly to do something with her hands, partly to look at the deep rich color of the wine from Kyles's vineyard.

"And this is for Amaura," Ikeria said.

It was a hair comb of gold, shaped into coiled snakes with jeweled eyes and jointed beaded tails to swing provocatively over the fore-head. Amaura's light eyes lost their usual flatness and sparkled. It was a gift for a grown woman. "Thank you, Princess! Would you . . . would you show me how to do my hair like yours, in those puffs and coils? Then I can wear the comb as you do."

Jaen laughed. Amaura eyed him coldly.

"I haven't any idea how it's done," Ikeria said, smiling. "But I will send my personal slave to you tomorrow to do it for you."

"Thank you," Amaura said. She did not look at Arachne. "The slave can teach me, and I can do it after you sail."

"You will have two months to learn, then, Mistress Amaura," Trader Nikos said in his deep voice.

"Only two months? Then you sail?"

Jaen laughed. "One month is long for a Theran to be away from Thera."

"That is not true," Ikeria said. "I frequently stay away from Thera for longer."

"Only in body," Jaen said. Their eyes met. Amaura watched frankly. She had noticed intimate glances before, but not ones like Jaen's now: angry, yearning, and hot. He does not want to want her, Amaura thought, and again the thrill slipped through her. To be wanted against volition—the idea seemed dark and sweet, and she felt a little breathless about herself for having recognized it. She lifted the wine to her lips and drank.

Kyles said, "The rains last longer than two months."

"Not this year," Nikos said. "Our astronomers foretell a short and mild winter, or I would not still be on the sea."

"Your arts are very exact," Jaen said. He looked pointedly at Arachne. "Are the astronomers ever wrong?"

"I would not trust my ship to them if they were."

"No profit in shipwreck," Ikeria said gaily. "But let us not think of profit tonight."

"Do you ever think of anything else, Nikos?" Jaen said, smiling. Amaura waited to see what the trader would say, but he did not answer. When Jaen had raised his goblet, Amaura saw Nikos glance at Ikeria. The princess made a small motion of her eyes toward Kyles; Nikos shook his head slightly.

The unspoken exchange confused Amaura. She looked down into her wine. Instantly Ikeria reached out to touch the girl's chiton.

"Your dress is very beautiful, Amaura. Do you, too, weave the spider silk?"

"Not very well."

"Ah. But you choose well. The sea-foam green is becoming to your light eyes. Did you know there was a queen of Thera with eyes the color of yours?"

"There was?"

"Yes. It is an amazing legend. She was very beautiful, but she had the most appalling misfortunes." Ikeria began to tell the story. It was satiric, delicately ribald, ridiculous. Amaura could not help smiling. Ikeria told the legend in a serious tone; only a gleam in her tilted black eyes showed her mockery. She lounged on one elbow on her couch, and her naked breasts lay one on the other, a deep scented shadow between.

The three men watched her.

At the end of the story, Amaura laughed delightedly. There was something delicious about the bumblings of the ridiculous queen. The legend excited her in a completely different way than Suva's stories. The queen behaved so stupidly!

"Anyone could be a better queen than that!"

"So the story aids us to believe," Ikeria said, smiling. Amaura did not know what she meant.

Theran slaves poured their princess more wine. Amaura wondered how they knew she desired more; Ikeria had said nothing. It was Amaura's first close look at the Theran slaves. Island slaves talked and grumbled and laughed while they worked. These were so silent and blank that Amaura forgot they were there at all unless one moved. They didn't seem like people at all. They were hands and feet and arms that Ikeria caused to appear or to vanish.

That thought was disquieting—and exciting. Like Suva's stories, like Ikeria's legend. Hands and feets and arms, with no selves attached to them. Amaura sat up straighter and held out her goblet for more wine.

"Please tell another story, Princess!"

"Perhaps another night, Amaura. I'm afraid your father was not amused by my first poor effort."

"Kyles never smiles much," Jaen said, smiling. "You must not assume his silence is directed at you, Princess. It is not, is it, Kyles?"

"No." Kyles's face was calm, his flat eyes unreadable. The trader looked at him closely. Amaura thought that Kyles was the biggest and strongest man present. She inched her stool closer to his couch, and saw how well the brown of his chiton went with her green silk. Sea-form green, Ikeria had called it.

"Nonetheless," Ikeria said in her musical voice, "I would give a gift to Jaen's marriage-brother, as well as his sister. Otherwise, Kyles, you will think our manners in Thera are deplorable. I would not like you to think poorly of us."

A slave appeared, carrying a long, thin bundle. Amaura saw Jaen, his face startled, look from the bundle to Ikeria to Nikos. Amaura could see that her uncle had not known about this last gift; she didn't think he liked it, although why he should dislike it before it was unwrapped puzzled Amaura. Tension sprang into the room— she could feel it on her skin. Jaen got up and poured himself more wine, without waiting for a slave to do it. Ikeria glanced at Nikos, then dropped her gaze and bit her lip. Arachne became very still.

The slave opened the cloth wrappings. On them lay a magnificent sword, the blade forged of some silvery material, the hilt ornately inlaid with ivory and gold in the swooping Theran curves.

No one said anything.

Ikeria moved swiftly, standing to pick up the sword and laughing. "Only ceremonial, of course. But isn't it pretty?" She posed with the sword in two hands, a parody of a warrior. Against her naked breasts and ruffled skirt the sword looked not deadly but provocative. Behind the blade her breasts bobbed gently, gleaming with scented oil. In her hands the gift was not a sword at all; she transformed it into merely a sensual prop, deliberately male only to point up her deliberate, ostentatious femaleness.

The princess smiled charmingly at Arachne. "Isn't it pretty, Arachne? Just the sort of gaudy toys men adore. They are all small boys, are they not?" Her smile drew Arachne into complicity, even while it mocked the audacious transparency of the attempt.

Arachne said abruptly, "I have a gift for you, Princess." She rose and left the room, her sandals clicking on the floor.

Amaura frowned. Her mother should have sent a slave. Ikeria, in her place, would have sent a slave.

The girl's face felt warm, flushed with wine and attention and the tension in the room that prickled over her like summer heat. Picking up the sword that Ikeria had called a pretty toy, Amaura fingered the blade and smiled at her father.

"Suva tells a story about a sword."

Kyles reached for the blade and took it from his daughter. His face was stern, but Amaura didn't stop smiling. She didn't mind that he took the sword from her: it was why she had held it.

"Who is Suva?" Ikeria asked. Amaura saw that the princess welcomed the change of subject, and seeing that gave her a sudden rush of power.

"Suva is a slave. She came to Island a long time ago, half-dead in a shipwreck. My mother's mother drowned at sea, and the next day Suva washed up on the beach. She came from a different wreck, of course—I think from a Theran ship. Mother was just a little girl, and she found Suva on the beach, Suva opened her eyes and saw this girl-child standing above her, and ever since Suva has struck to Mother like pine-pitch. Only Suva's version is that she *walked* new-born out of the sea, wearing flowers and armor and singing birds."

Ikeria laughed. Encouraged, Amaura went on. "Suva is mad, of course. But she tells lots of stories, and foretells what will happen. But she must not be very good at it, because she said Uncle Jaen would drown on his voyage to Thera, but here he is."

Jaen smiled. "Are you sure Suva wasn't wishing rather than foretelling?"

"An enemy, Jaen?" Ikeria said mockingly.

"Palace intrigue at the provincial level. You see what we are fallen to."

"And *now*," Amaura continued, "Suva says the Therans have come back for her."

Jaen threw back his head and laughed. Nikos and Ikeria looked interested, and even Kyles smiled. Amaura was dizzy with success.

"There, Nikos," Jaen said. "Your profit does not lie in silk—it lies in ancient mad slaves with faulty predictive powers. You merely did not see it before."

"Think of the markets you've missed," Ikeria murmured. "Amaura, I would like to see your Suva."

Arachne returned, and with her, tension to the room. She carried a packet wrapped in wool, which she handed wordlessly to Ikeria. A slave moved to fill Arachne's wineglass. Irritably she waved him away.

At the moment Ikeria opened the packet, Amaura finished her wine and lowered the goblet. Looking at them all over the rim, she suddenly had the impression that they had slowed down, had stopped, and that the moment had frozen and come loose and would remain with her always, vivid and unchanged: Arachne's arm chopping the tense air to send away the slave, Ikeria's long ringed hands on the woolen string, Jaen a scarlet figure bent over her chair. Jaen looked at Ikeria, Arachne at Jaen, Kyles at Arachne, Nikos at all of them at once. Amaura knew where each looked, what he saw, how the flickering lamplight struck their eyes and lent the emotions there fire, or depth, or veiled opacity. The tension in the room, which had been an exciting prickling, now burned over her arms and the back of her neck, painful fire. She was inside the fire; she was the fire.

She thought: *That is what they meant by the Grove.*

From the packet Ikeria pulled the ash-haze silk.

Amaura was disappointed: a piece of silk wasn't bright or gaudy or splendid, like the gifts Ikeria had brought. She didn't even like this silk. The colors were dull and heavy, and the hazy overlay blurred them. Why couldn't her mother at least have given them silk that was fiery and dramatic? And why did they all stare at this one so intently, and in such silence?

Ikeria spread the weaving to its full length. It dripped from her fingers and flowed over her skirt onto the stone floor.

"I thought it suited you," Arachne said to Ikeria. Her tone was not gentle.

The eyes of the two women locked. Finally Ikeria, with perfect composure and a hint of amusement, said, "Thank you. I am more honored than perhaps you know. Jaen, you said your sister was a craftsman; you did not tell me she was an artist."

Jaen did not answer. He touched the silk briefly, his head bent. Amaura could not see his face; from the lines of his body she had the sudden impression that that was intentional.

"A magnificent gift indeed," Nikos said. He fingered one edge of the silk. He touched it differently, Amaura thought, than Jaen had. She was irritated—why should all this attention go to the funny-looking silk? It was only a piece of cloth. She glanced at Kyles. His face, as calm as always, reassured her. He must not be impressed. Her irritation lessened.

Nikos said, "A long way from traditional designs, Mistress Arachne. Have you woven more like this one?"

"No."

"But you will."

"That is the only one," Arachne said harshly.

"Then I am doubly honored," Ikeria said.

"Arachne," Jaen said, too quietly, "are you sure you would not prefer to keep the silk?"

Amaura looked at him, surprised. How could he have the bad manners to give away someone else's gift? She expected to see Jaen smiling at Ikeria in mock apology, perhaps teasing her with his offer, but he was not. He looked straight at Arachne, and in both their eyes was such a sharp mix of pain and challenge that Amaura felt the slow burning, gone since the silk was opened, begin to rise again across her arms and shoulders.

"I do not prefer to keep it," Arachne said. "Do you recognize the ashy silk?"

"From the web. The night I told you I would sail," Jaen said.

"I originally intended the silk for you."

"I can see that."

"Can you, Jaen? It's a disturbing pattern. Wrong, somehow. I don't like it much myself."

"I wouldn't expect you to."

"Do you like it?"

Jaen hesitated. His eyes never left his sister's. "Yes. I like it. And it will be appreciated in Thera."

"But not on Island?"

"No, not on Island."

"Why is that?"

"I doubt," Jaen said, "that anyone on Island would truly see the pattern."

"Perhaps we on Island see more than you think."

"In that silk? No. It still belongs to me."

"And to me."

What were they talking about? Amaura thought. The silk belonged now to Ikeria. Amaura felt confused; the wine in her stomach suddenly churned.

Jaen said, "Sometimes, of joint ownership, the wider vision bears the burden of decision."

"Sometimes, what is stretched wide is stretched to tearing."

"Ah," Jaen said, "but you forget—spider silk does not tear. You will find, Princess, that your gift is amazingly durable. It withstands everything. The voyage to Thera will not harm it at all."

"Who knows that?" Arachne said. "So little has ever left Island."

Ikeria said carefully, "I would expect to keep my treasures from harm no matter where they were." Neither Arachne nor Jaen heard her. They saw only each other.

"Yes," Jaen said softly.

"No," Arachne said.

Amaura said, "I feel sick!"

Instantly her mother was there, bending over her, helping her to her feet. A window was opened, and Amaura led over to it. The fresh cold air did not settle her stomach. The room did not stop whirling.

Arachne led Amaura to her room, undressed her, held the basin while she vomited, washed her face, put her to bed. She said little. Amaura, nauseous and disoriented, was hardly aware of her mother until the moment Arachne bent over to blow out the lamp wick, her body bowed forward, her eyes still on her daughter's face. The image stayed with the girl even after the wick was blown out.

The dark was better. Coherent images could form in it, hold, dissolve: the statuette of the bull dancer, Ikeria's dress, the sword Ikeria had called a pretty toy. The way everyone had laughed when she told of Suva's terror. Kyles, silent and watchful. The ash-haze silk dripping like water from Ikeria's hands. And, above all, the strange moment when the tension had risen like fire and she, Amaura, had been as consumed by it as had the others.

She held the moment, turning and tilting it, drawing from it as much of the conflict and tautness and emotion as she could. It was possible, then. Suva's stories were true. People could live feverish hot lives of intense emotion, as burning as bloody swords. That painful and dangerous prickling at the back of the neck could truly be sought, savored, perhaps even created. People did create it— facing charging bulls, challenging each other, mixing sexual passion with anger.

The door opened. At first Amaura thought it was her mother, returning to see her once more before she slept. But Kyles stood there, holding a lamp. Amaura flushed with pleasure.

"Are you still sick, Amaura?"

"No. I feel . . . fine." What had she been going to say instead of "fine"?

"Do not take so much wine." His voice held an intensity unusual for Kyles. "Wine in excess is too frank."

She was too young to understand him, and too much Amaura to be interested in frankness. "Yes, Father. Father! Isn't Princess Ikeria beautiful?"

"Very."

"Much more beautiful than Mother."

Kyles was silent.

"Don't you think she's more beautiful than Mother?"

"Yes," Kyles said quietly. Amaura heard the quietness, and the unquietness beneath it. The wine had made her head light, and her tongue. The lightness felt delicious, as if she were free to say anything at all.

"I'm glad you think she's much more beautiful than Mother. I thought you would say no. You don't come to say good night to Pholen and me any longer, the way you used to do. You haven't done it since before you left for the harvest at the vineyard. You left so early this year, much earlier than usual, and you left me behind. Why did you leave so early for the vineyard?"

"I needed to do so."

"But why?"

Kyles said nothing. After a moment Amaura said, both violently and as if it were part of the same conversation, "Mother didn't behave with very good manners toward the princess and the trader. She didn't behave as a ruler should. She wasn't gracious."

But still Kyles said nothing.

"She was *rude.* She was so rude I was embarrassed by her! And the gift she gave in the name of Island looked poor compared to the gifts that Ikeria gave us. Mother gave nothing but that muddy-colored silk."

Kyles's voice was rough. "You are too young to see the beauty in Arachne's silk."

Arachne was shocked—at Kyles's unaccustomed harshness, at her abrupt demotion to a rebuked child, at the something she heard in the word "Arachne." She sat up angrily.

"Why do you say Mother's name like that, Father? You always say it that way!"

"Good night, Amaura," Kyles said, turning. His lamp flared, sputtered, steadied.

"You say it the same way that Mother says 'the Grove,' " Amaura said, but by that time the door had closed.

Amaura lay down in the darkness. Sitting up had not been a good idea. Her head had begun to whirl again, not so pleasantly as before. Again she relived the evening in her mind, trying to recapture its drama, its prickling tension, its heightening of the way her blood raced in her veins. She could not recapture it with the same intensity. The back of her neck would not prickle. The wine she had drunk had turned from fever to torpor, and no longer helped to heighten anything.

The wine had lasted such a short time!

I wish, Amaura thought for the first time in her life, I *wish* the Grove had lasted longer. Just a little longer. So that we could have all stood there together, Ikeria and Father and me.

——— 10 ———

I T was, as Nikos foretold, a mild and short winter. The rains were soft, hesitant, diffuse. Island hung dripping between sea and sky, and all its edges blurred. From the villa the smoke of hearth fires rose a short way and then fell, gray velvet ash in the gray mist. Sea birds screamed and fought on the cliffs. Their cries, disembodied and softened by mist, became a mournful, distant music.

In the Grove the Spider Stone glistened wetly. The spiders became sluggish, spinning webs to capture prey only every third or fourth night and sleeping the rest of the time beneath rocks or leaves or in cracks in the colonnade. Many crawled, as they did every winter, away from the Grove and into corners in houses and storage magazines. To have a spider winter with you was good luck; no Islander would disturb one, even though its silk belonged still to the Household. Spiders away from the Grove spun grayish webs. Those in the Grove, their pharmakons diluted by rain, spun webs of pale green, light yellow, delicate blue like shadows on wet stone. Most of the silk was sound.

Nikos traded for as much silk as he could find. Islanders, excited by his goods, traded cushion covers, festival chitons, birthing silks, tapestries four generations old. Behind Nikos's head they winked at each other over the value put by this fellow on common spider silk. The other Therans—princess, seamen, personal slaves—kept to the villa chambers closest to the sea, where no spiders crawled or spun. Most Islanders did not see the foreigners at all, except for Nikos.

Nikos was accompanied on his trading by the enormous slave who had been ridden by the messenger to Council. In the plain, lime-plastered chambers of the villa, the giant ducked his head and watched corners. When he saw a spider, there rose from under the dead numbness in his eyes a flicker of rotting, incomplete fear, like debris breaking surface on a cold sea. Islanders, who mostly ridiculed the Therans' fear of spiders, did not ridicule the giant. They looked away, and did not discuss him. They discussed their new luxuries, enchantingly foreign in craftsmanship: hair combs and amulets and shoulder clasps and rings. Tiny boxes made of oiled, sweet-smelling wood. Exotic, inflaming spices. Libation vases with sensuous, swooping designs. All beautiful, all of alien materials, all small enough to be carried in quantity on the immense ship whose galley slaves did not land. Small boats carried supplies to the ship daily. For these supplies the farmers and craftsmen also traded profitably, and discussed the weird fear of spiders that forced Nikos to feed his men aboard a rocking ship in winter, and laughed.

None asked how many men rode the ships, or if they all were slaves.

The Islanders did not discuss the Grove. Younger adults, who had seldom known it as it had been, could not. Older ones did not. The loss was too personal, too private. When at first they had tried to talk about it, stumbling with daily words over what was outside of words, they found that each had perceived the loss so differently a consensus was difficult. Their mourning was for different deaths.

Someone was needed to give the deaths common words, and common action. The priestesses, jealous of the Grove, would not. Arachne, who might have, did not. She did not perceive the necessity, since she refused to admit the death.

The Islander's confusion went underground. Excited by Theran trade goods, rocked by the changes on Island, volatile and a little sullen, Islanders waited for something to step into the empty place where the Grove had been, for some explanation. The next Council was nearly empty. They had seen no direction at Council. They waited for something else.

Arachne was past thinking about them. All day, every day, she worked in the apotheca or in the Grove, mixing and trying and

watching pharmakons. She did not work feverishly, but with a cold
steadiness that frightened Cleis, her only assistant. She slept on a
couch in a corner of the apotheca. Frequently she walked in the
Grove at night, through the cold drizzle, through the cloudy blackness without stars. Sometimes she forgot to eat. Her fingers became
stained with pharmakons, burned from hot oils or acids, rough with
grinding. If she weaved now, she thought, those fingers would snag
on the silk, pull the weft. She did not weave, nor want to. Her hair,
unwashed, hung in greasy coils.

At night, standing in the rain near the Spider Stone and straining
with all her senses to reach what was no longer there, she wondered
if she were going mad. Her wondering was quite detached. Nothing she had discovered in the apotheca, no pharmakon nor variation
of dosage, had made the slightest difference to the spiders or the
Grove. It was mad to keep hacking with the same dull tool. But it
was the only tool she could think of, and even if the pharmakons'
changing the Grove was as mad a delusion as any of old Suva's, she
would try it. There was no other choice, except to do nothing, and
she was not capable of doing nothing.

Once Aretone, one of her women, came to her in the apotheca.
Aretone had a severe, handsome face. She loved her husband, a
farmer, but had borne him no children, and she was very kind to
young Pholen.

"Mistress. It is not my place to speak. Nonetheless, I am concerned for you. You do not look . . . well."

"I am not sick," Arachne said briefly. She mixed dried myrtle
berries, a mild stimulant, into a pharmakon considerably more
potent.

"Mistress—"

"Leave me!" Arachne said, more harshly than she intended. Cleis
would have bit her lip and stayed. But when Arachne again looked
up, Aretone was gone.

Once she visited the room near the colonnade where her loom
sat. It was the only one stored there; her women, whom she had
not summoned since Jaen's arrival, all had had their looms moved
to their dwellings for the winter weavings of wool. Or perhaps they
still wove silk, to sell to Nikos. The Treasurer would know, but
Arachne had not seen the Treasurer for months. She touched the
wooden uprights of her empty loom, and thought of spider silk, and
Jaen, and the way Nikos had looked at the ash-haze silk the night

she had given it to Ikeria. The loom felt cold and heavy under her hand. She did not go to the loom room again.

Walking across the wet winter grass with her cloak wrapped tightly around her, Arachne sometimes caught a brief whiff of an elusive, too-sweet smell. It never stayed long enough to identify. Her nose would wrinkle, and she would walk back to the apotheca, trying not the think of Jaen, of the Therans, of silk. Trying to think only of pharmakons: the inadequate, tangible tool to preserve what had been intangible glory.

Pholen had made a spider house. It was made from a geode, a globular rock with a central cavity lined with crystals. Pholen had found the geode on the beach just that morning, a morning that hinted with patches of bright sky at a too-early spring. The geode, a faint chalky pink, lay in two irregular halves with a chip missing from one half. When Pholen fitted the halves together, there was a hole where the chip had been. Although he had looked carefully, squatting on the beach and sifting through pebbles and sand until his nurse made him come away, he had not been able to find the missing chip. He tried to stuff the hole with a pebble, but the pebble kept falling out. Next he tried wadded leaves, and finally a rolled-up leaf which made a tunnel into the crystal cavity.

A tunnel needed a tunneler. Pholen teased Nurse until she took him to the Grove, where he caught a spider and tried to coax it into the leafy tunnel. The spider balked; it had been asleep under a rock until Pholen found it, and it waved its pedipalps angrily, its shiny blind eyes glittering in the cool sunlight. Pholen prodded its abdomen, very gently, with a blade of grass, and eventually the spider crawled through the tunnel and into its crystal house, where it began to spin.

Pholen wanted to show the house to someone besides Nurse, who had already seen him make it. Carrying the geode in two hands, carefully keeping the halves pressed together, the child walked to the apotheca, first promising Nurse to go no farther.

Cleis met him at the apotheca door. "Look, Cleis—I made a spider house! I'm going to show it to Mama."

"Your Mistress mother is asleep, Pholen. You musn't disturb her."

"Asleep at the apotheca? No, she's not."

"Yes, she *is*," Cleis said wearily. She didn't smile at him the way she always used to, and to Pholen she looked cross. He peered around her into the apotheca. It was very warm; fires burned constantly to simulate summer and keep the captive spiders spinning at their summer levels. On a couch near the spider pots Arachne lay heavily, flushed and unmoving, her tangled hair falling over her face. The child was disturbed by her lack of motion; Mama was always moving, always doing. He held his geode more tightly and sniffed the air.

"Where did the spiders go?"

"What do you mean, where did the spiders go? They're right there in the pots. Don't you hear them humming?"

"I *hear* them, but I don't *smell* them," Pholen said. The absence of spider smell disturbed him more than Arachne's inert sleep. The apotheca was suddenly an undesirable place: hot, motionless, scented wrong. There was something here he didn't understand, something angry and overly moist.

"Go back to Nurse," Cleis said. "Your Mistress mother will awake soon."

Scowling, Pholen pattered back into the colonnade. He would not go back to Nurse; she would only make him release his spider into the Grove and take him to wash off all the sand from the beach. He had made a beautiful spider house, and inside it the spider was spinning a beautiful web, bright red, as red as the silk Uncle Jaen liked to wear. He would show the spider house to Uncle Jaen.

Uncle Jaen wasn't in his chamber. But Pholen, who always knew where to find anything he really wanted, knew where Jaen was. Humming, the little boy skipped through the corridors to where all the strangers stayed. As he neared the sea, the humming inside the geode changed tone, and then stopped.

"I'm sorry," Pholen whispered into the leaf tunnel. "But it's just for a *little* time."

The villa looked different here. Big men with swords stood in front of some doors. Nobody talked, and when the slaves carrying jars and baskets saw Pholen, they flattened themselves against the corridor walls and their faces wiped themselves empty. Pholen didn't like it, but he didn't know what to do about it. He had already learned that if he smiled at the strangers, they did not smile back.

But Uncle Jaen was here, and he would smile. And Princess Ikeria was here, and she would smile. Pholen moved on, trying not to jiggle the already-angry spider.

The princess's chamber had in front of it two of the unsmiling men with swords, and they would not let Pholen in. He was twisting up his face to cry when Uncle Jaen and the princess came out.

"Pholen! What are you doing here? Where is your nurse?" Jaen said. He didn't, Pholen thought, look very happy either. His eyes looked burny, and there were smudges under them. To Ikeria he said, "The child *does* have a nurse. The entire family, contrary to what you see, has ample retainers."

"How tiresome for them," Ikeria murmured. Pholen saw that she thought something was funny; encouraged, he held up his geode.

"Look, Princess! See what I made!"

"Just look at that," Ikeria said, and knelt beside him, a graceful swirl of ruffles. The ruffles were all on the bottom half; her top half seemed to Pholen a little bare, except for bright necklaces and earrings and piles of hair. Like Uncle Jaen's, her eyes also had smudges, but these smudges were on top of the eyes and didn't look so angry. She smelled wonderful, a strong rich smell that made Pholen a little dizzy.

"Aren't you going to show me your creation, Pholen? I'd like to see it."

"You've befuddled him, Princess. Another provincial dazzled by Theran sophistication."

"A lute with one string, Jaen. You really should be more careful of that—it is becoming dreary."

Pholen said, "See, it's made from a hollow rock. I found it on the beach. And something's inside!"

"What?" Ikeria said, smiling.

"Guess!"

"An ocean," she said promptly.

"No, an *ocean* wouldn't fit!"

"A bull."

"No!" Pholen said, giggling. The princess's nail tapped the geode lightly. Her fingers were long and very white, with shiny rings.

"I know. A king."

"No, no, no!" Pholen cried. "It's a spider!"

The tapping nail suddenly stilled. In a different voice Ikeria said, "Is it in there now?"

"Yes! See, I can open its house like—"

But she was gone, vanished in a whorl of ruffles and perfume that left Pholen blinking, astonished, and hurt. Jaen knelt beside him and gently closed the halves of the geode. "The princess doesn't like spiders, Pholen. She is afraid of them."

"Afraid of spiders?"

"Yes. Like Suva." He sounded pleased, and his smudgy eyes burned less. When he smiled at Pholen, the flash of his white teeth looked strong and a little scary. There was something about the glance he sent back over his shoulder to the princess's slammed door that Pholen didn't understand. Uncle Jaen looked the way Amaura looked when she pinched him and then kissed the hurt. Pholen scowled; all his adults had become crazy. It used to be only Suva was.

"When do the strangers sail away again?" he demanded.

"Do you want them to sail away again?"

"Yes! And you, too! It's too crazy around here!"

Jaen straightened. "I agree with you. Take the spider to the Grove, and don't let it out on the way. Then find your nurse. You should not be unattended. Now go."

Pholen stuck out his lip. Jaen stared down at him, stern and tall. Pholen went, but not to Nurse.

He found Amaura with Suva, which was a problem because Pholen didn't want the spider to scare Suva the way it had the princess. Amaura sat on a three-legged stool and drew wool, pulling the tufts straight over her epinetron, a semicylindrical pottery shield that rested over her thigh. She didn't look as if she enjoyed it much. Her hair was piled in those fancy curls like the princess's, and there seemed to be too much of it. Had Amaura had that much hair before? Pholen didn't think so. She also wore a dress like the princess's, bare on top, and Pholen had a vague idea that was why she drew her wool here alone instead of with any of their mother's women. Pholen thought she looked cold.

Keeping his back to Suva, who was scrubbing the stone floor, Pholen sidled over to his sister. "See," he whispered, "I've got a spider house."

Amaura looked disdainfully at the geode. "That's just a rock."

"No. It's hollow inside, and there's a spider in there and a leaf tunnel here. I made it."

"It's very nice," Amaura said, with such superior and deflating tolerance that Pholen hit her with his chubby fist. She didn't become angry, which surprised him.

"You're such a baby, Pholen. Go find Nurse."

Pholen hit her again, harder. His blow didn't hurt Amaura, but it upset her balance and she fell off her stool. The pottery epinetron broke in two. A precarious braid of hair came undone and dangled over Amaura's eyes. Suva stopped scrubbing and stood up. But still Amaura did not become angry. She stood up, tucked in the loose braid, and kicked negligently at a half of epinetron, smiling faintly. Pholen saw at last that she was playing, being someone else than Amaura, and that neither he nor his spider house were going to be allowed to affect her.

"It's broken," Suva said. She gazed, stricken, at the epinetron, as if it had been immensely valuable. Pholen put his geode behind his back. Suva moved closer, and he smelled her. She smelled bad, of dirt and sweat and urine. That surprised him, although it did not offend him—it was just that Suva used to keep herself washed. She had also become even skinnier. To Pholen her knuckles and wrist bone looked as spiky as the crystals of his geode.

"Broken," Suva repeated. Her black eyes glittered. To Pholen she said heavily, "They've come back for me."

"Oh, Suva," Amaura said.

"There was a child," Suva said, staring at Pholen. "In the sea, I think. Yes. A child."

"Singing, I suppose," Amaura said. She sounded like somebody else.

Suva's face wrinkled in tortuous thought. "Wasn't there a child?" she asked Pholen, sounding so uncertain that the little boy tried to help.

"Me? Was the child me, Suva?"

"No. Not you."

"Was it Amaura?"

No," Suva said. "Not her."

"Was it a boy child or a girl child?" Pholen said helpfully. Behind his back the spider began to hum, agitated and low. The sea lapped softly outside.

Suddenly Suva threw herself full length on the floor and began to tremble, not the flailing and thrashing of a drowning fit but a rhythmic trembling that rattled her knees and forehead against the stone. She crawled, howling muffledly, toward Pholen. The crawling was the horrible belly-inching of a severed lizard, and the howls sounded as if her mouth were stuffed with cloth, or as if she were tongueless. Her face twisted in an agony so intense Pholen stepped back. She reached him anyway and clutched at his feet, her arms circling his ankles but her fists staying clenched into tight, jagged knots that could not clasp. She howled, "They've come for me! They've come for me!"

Frightened, unable to either push the howling Suva away or pull her up because both his hands held the geode, Pholen first stood paralyzed and then began to cry. The instant his first wail rose above hers, Suva was on her feet, patting his shoulder, crooning comfort, wholly herself. "There now, there now, child, there now, there."

Pholen, startled into silence and breathless with the speed of her transformation, stared piteously. The old woman gazed back, patting his shoulder. "There now, no one shall take you, no, no, there now. No one, no one at all." She smiled tenderly at the little boy.

"Once," Suva said, "a dove flew to a rich city by the sea. It sat on the roof of the temple and called out that a huge wave would destroy the town the next day at sunset. The dove cried that it had been sent by a god to warn the people to leave. The priests sacrificed to the dove, and everyone marveled and crowded close to see a bird talking. Mothers held up their children as close to the temple as they could. However, no one left the city. This one was too busy, that one had an ill father, another could not abandon a good business. At sunset the next day the bird flew away. No wave came. The sea remained as flat as a pond. The people thought the unknown god had changed his mind, and at the next full moon held a special rite to worship him. At the rite the bull for the sacrifice escaped and charged into the crowd, goring four people to their death before he was slaughtered."

Again Suva smiled at Pholen. Her face was loving, desperate, and mad.

"You shouldn't be afraid of *Suva,*" Amaura said. She watched the old woman greedily, intensely interested.

"I wasn't afraid of Suva," Pholen said, because it was true. His sudden fear had been not of Suva, but of whatever unseen thing could inspire such an agony of fear in *her.*

All of a sudden Pholen was tired of all the wanting. THe villa was full of *wanting.* Mama wanted the Grove to do something it wouldn't do. Amaura wanted to be somebody else. Uncle Jaen wanted everybody to have slaves with them all the time. Suva wanted to remember something about a child and the sea. Or maybe what Suva wanted was not to remember something about a child and the sea. Wanting, wanting, wanting. Nobody would just stop and look at his spider house!

Pholen cradled the house in both hands and ran out to the corridor. Suva called after him, "There now there now there now there," as violently and monotonously as a storm at sea.

Away from the Household quarters, Pholen slowed, checked his spider, and sighed. The only one left to show his geode to was his father. He had not wanted to go to Kyles because, first, where Kyles was, was a long way, and, second, if Kyles sent him back to Nurse, he really would have to go. His father was the one person Pholen obeyed instantly. Also, Kyles might *look* at the spider house, but he wouldn't have much to *say* about it. Pholen liked a fuss made about his creations. Kyles was not a fusser.

But, still, a spider house was special. Kyles might fuss about a spider house.

The bronzesmith's lay clear over on the eastern edge of the villa, where the lime-plastered stone walls gave way to fields of scrub and wildflowers. On the way, it began to drizzle. Pholen walked with the opening of his leaf tunnel angled downward, to avoid wetting the spider. Kyles and the smith were in the yard by the roaring kiln, talking in low voices.

"Twenty more swords."

"Do they understand?"

"Yes," the smith said.

"You trust them?"

"Yes. At dawn, then?"

"Yes."

Pholen thought that bronzesmiths all called his father "Kyles," but called Uncle Jaen "Master Jaen." Why was that? Before he could ask, his father's hand clapped his shoulder. One glance at Kyles's face told Pholen he had made a mistake.

"What are you doing here? Where is your nurse?"

"At the Grove," Pholen faltered. He covered the geode with one corner of his cloak. His father looked stern, with an impassive stillness that made Uncle Jaen's sternness look tiny. This was not the time to show him a spider that, Pholen admitted to himself, should not be this far from the Grove.

Kyles walked Pholen back to the Grove. The child, running to match his father's stride, peeped at Kyles's face. It did not soften. At the colonnade Kyles said, "Now go to Nurse."

"Will you . . . will you take me to her?"

Kyles glanced in the direction of the apotheca. Pholen thought his face hurt. "No. Now go."

But Nurse was gone from the Grove. Pholen knew this was a bad sign; she would be searching for him, and angry. Everyone was angry. He was in large trouble. And still no one had really examined his spider house. Worst of all, his spider was angry at him, too, for all the jostling he had done trying to keep up with Kyles. In the geode it hummed furiously.

Glum and discouraged, Pholen trudged through the wintry Grove, under the colonnade, out again into the drizzle. He steopped into a cold puddle. Mud oozed over his sandal, clammy and cold. Tears blurred his vision.

"What is it you have there, young Pholen?"

A deep voice and two blurry splotches. Pholen blinked; the splotches resolved into the trader Nikos, carrying a packet of silk, and his mute giant.

"I'm not going to Nurse!"

"All right," the trader said, amiably indifferent. "Don't."

"And I'm not putting my spider in the Grove neither!"

"Spider?"

"I suppose you're afraid of it, too."

"No," the trader said, "I'm not." He stepped into the shelter of the colonnade. His hooded dark eyes were bright and kind; Pholen stepped in after him.

"What is your spider doing in there?"

"Being angry at me."

"Suppose you tell me about it. How do you know its angry at you?"

"Can't you tell from the humming?" Pholen said. But apparently the trader could not. He didn't seem to know anything about spiders. Nothing at all, not even things Pholen had known since he could first talk. But the trader asked questions, listening so carefully and watching so intently that Pholen told all he knew. He knew much more than he had been taught, from watching the spiders and playing with them. No one on Island knew as much about spiders as Pholen. Telling Nikos, he felt his discouragement melt away. He told Nikos all about their babies, the silk, the Grove, the Spider Stone—especially the Spider Stone—and about how spiders behaved near the sea, what they ate, how they spun silk, how baby spiders were born. About the pharmakons Mama prepared, the kinds of webs spiders made, the temperatures and places they liked. On and on Pholen talked, wriggling his muddy toes in pleasure at being listened to so closely, at such length, by an adult who seemed to think that everything Pholen said was pure, precious gold.

11

"**WHY?**" Jaen said.

He stood in the doorway of the apotheca. A black wool cloak around his shoulders was flung back over scarlet spider silk. Eddies of sweet air, too warm in this too-early spring, came with him into the pungent dimness of the apotheca.

He caught Arachne by surprise. In all the last two months of argument about the Spider Stone—arguments cold with fury, rotten with longing—Jaen had never come to the apotheca. He had not, since that first morning, come even to the Grove. To see him standing in her doorway disoriented Arachne, and out of her disorientation she answered truthfully:

"Because I can't do otherwise."

A moment later she thought of all the answers she could have given: so that Amaura and Pholen can know the Grove as we knew it. Because it is my duty as Mistress of Island to salvage the Grove, no matter how small the chance of succeeding. For service to the Goddess. Instead, she had answered truthfully and only now recognized it as the truth: because she could not do otherwise. It was true. Let it stand.

Jaen entered the apotheca and gazed around. His gaze missed nothing—he scrutinized the plants and minerals spread on the stone table, the spiders captive in their tilted pots, the web of deformed silk spread on a shelf, the small bowls of pharmakons that had all proved useless. Arachne could see him considering each item, fitting it into this estimates of how much she had accomplished, coming quickly to his own conclusions. The conclusions would be accurate.

"You have found nothing that makes any difference."

"No. Nothing that makes any difference."

"And you won't. The Grove is gone, Arachne, it's dead. You can't change that by any naked force of will. No matter what you try—pharmakons or sacrifices or will—you can not make any difference."

"I don't accept that."

"Of course not," Jaen said. "You never accepted anything you didn't want to."

He began to touch things: a shallow dish of henbane seeds, a pestle, a length of silken fiber unwound from a web but not yet washed of its viscid coating. It stuck to his hand, pale blue tracery on fingers not as brown as Arachne remembered. Jaen scraped off the silk against the table edge, then moved slightly, pointlessly, the position of a small striped bowl. Arachne saw the white ridges on her brother's knuckles. Suddenly and vividly, she remembered Kyles's hand, hurling a wine goblet against a wall. Jaen's tension, she saw, had less self-control; he was not trusting himself to even pick up the striped bowl.

"We sail with tomorrow's tide."

Although she had suspected it, Arachne flinched. Unexpectedly, Jaen came to her and cupped her face in his hands. His palms against her cheek felt warm and gentle.

"Spiderling," he said. "Spiderling—I came to ask you one last time. Let me take the Stone to Thera. For both our sakes. Let me."

His switch to tenderness stunned her. Tenderness—*now?* Tenderness, after the arguments they had hurled at each other, in the face of the mutilation for which he wanted her permission? Arachne could hardly believe it. She thought it was a ploy, shameful to both of them. But, searching his face, she found she was wrong. His tenderness was genuine. And so was his anger, locked into the tenderness like rocks fused together, melted by great heat and suspended together, precariously, from some cliffside over the sea.

"Let me."

She moved away from his hands. "No, Jaen. Never. How can you even still *ask?*"

"Let's discuss instead how you can refuse. Why should you think that you are the only one who might save the Grove? 'Because I can't do otherwise'—is the Grove then a holy endeavor, a sacred trust given only to you? Arachne, and Arachne alone, can make a difference?"

"No one else seems to want to."

"Not so. No one else assumes that his ideas must be the only ones to succeed. But you have always thought so, haven't you? Ever since we were children."

"I always thought it was your ideas that we followed as children."

"Only with your permission."

"Jaen, you don't want to save the Grove. You want to use it as trade goods and exchange it for Thera, and for Ikeria. Can't you admit that? Dishonesty used not to be one of your vices."

"Nor delusion one of yours. Look at what you are doing, Arachne: throwing yourself against the deadness of the Grove, using every measure of will and effort you can summon, to hurt yourself again and again. It hardly even matters to you how bloody you get. You see nothing to the left or right, nothing else on Island, but that barrier in front of you. And why? For something that is dead. That is the heart of it—of all those useless arguments between us all this winter. *The Grove is gone.* It was enchanting, golden, splendid. It was a lovely way to see the world, wrapped in shivering glory. But it is gone. It did not last. You can't make the world look glorious by sheer force of will."

Arachne said nothing.

"Let me take the Stone to Thera."

"No."

"Arachne—to try to do any more here, with the pharmakons, is pitiful. Do you hope any longer to accomplish anything significant juggling drugs neither of us really understands?"

"No. I don't."

"Then why, in the name of the Goddess, keep on doing it?"

"Because I can't do otherwise."

"That's no answer. Has it occurred to you that you are not quite sane?"

"Yes," Arachne said.

He laughed. Jaen laughing, Arachne thought—when I think of Jaen, he is always laughing. But not like this.

"Yes," he said, "it would occur to you. It's amazing how much the blind see. And you, Arachne, are the blindest woman I have ever met."

"She stood very still. The blindest woman I have ever seen . . ."

"Blind. Yes. No one thinks as directly as Arachne, no one acts as competently, no one sees as opaquely. Entire areas of human experience left out of you completely. Tell me something. Do you despise me for wanting to take the Stone?"

"You can't take it, Jaen. I have not changed my mind."

"So you say. What is Kyles so busy with these days?"

"Kyles?" The question caught her off balance; she had hardly seen her husband by day, and not at all by night. His absence hurt her. Clearly she could see Kyles's hand on the wine goblet, and Jaen's on the striped bowl. Jaen's question was not casual; he was watching her intently.

"I don't know what Kyles is doing," she admitted. "Is he doing something unusual?"

Jaen relaxed slightly. "Our guests hardly see him. Or you."

"I don't want to see them."

"Or me?"

"Jaen—"

"Jaen what?"

She didn't answer. What could she say? Jaen—be as you were? Jaen—I don't understand this anger, too large to be about spider silk alone?

He moved toward the tilted pots containing the spiders on which she tried her pharmakons. "You work here alone?"

"Usually."

"Kyles does not help you?"

"No." He caught the bleakness of the one syllable, and gave her a glance of such knowing compassion that he suddenly looked like a much younger Jaen, ally and disciple. Arachne could not stand it. She said harshly, "Sometimes I am helped by Cleis. You remember Cleis, Jaen? Pretty girl you bedded just before you sailed?"

"I remember Cleis. She didn't seem like a girl to give her life to pharmakons. I saw in her nothing of your singlemindedness, or your directness."

"And those are undesirable qualities?"

"To live with, perhaps."

"Jaen. Why are you so angry with me? It's not only for refusing you the Stone. There is something else. Why? What have I done?"

Peeling the thin silk covering from the mouth of one of the jars, Jaen reached inside and drew out the spider. It sat on his palm, facing away from him. Arachne could see its shiny blind eyes, red as blood. Jaen, she knew, was seeing its spinnerets, two pairs of protrusions that last night had spun perfect azure silk.

He said, "There is a leaf from a shrub that grows near Thera. It's called ilo. You boil it and make a powder, the same technique we use for some of the pharmakons. When the powder is mixed with wine and drunk, it produces visions in the mind. Great, glorious visions—all from a few scrubby bushes. Sometimes one bush is enough." He looked at Arachne across the spider. "One scrubby bush, Arachne. One scrubby bush of boiled leaves, and you have the Grove."

She said carefully, "You can't believe that."

"Why not?"

"You can't. You've been in the Grove since we were children. You *felt* it. What the Grove gave wasn't like some drunken dream from excess wine or any leaf of—Jaen, you were *there.* The vision was just as real as the grass or the trees. It wasn't even a vision. It was a way of knowing, a door opening, clear and truthful. You might as well say sunlight isn't real. You stood next to me in the Grove and saw it—I could feel your seeing it!"

"I saw it. But I wasn't consumed by it, as you seem to be. Neither do I spend my life, and the lives of my kin, in futile efforts to save it after it has died."

"I don't believe that hte Grove has completely died."

"Only because you don't want to believe it."

"And you do. You do, Jaen—you *want* to believe the Grove is dead. That's why you're so enraged at my efforts to save it?" Her voice rose, as for a question, but she was not asking a question. "Why would you *want* to believe the Grove is gone?"

"That's your observation, not mine."

"Why?"

"Perhaps," Jaen said, "I have finally surrendered a childish faith in intangible glory."

And then Arachne knew, not from his words but from his tone. He said "intangible glory" in the same tone in which he had, two months earlier, said "princess": with contempt, with longing, with the bitter and mocking rage of one who has been excluded, and knows it. Arachne curled both hands around the thick edge of the stone table and held on tightly.

"You didn't . . . you aren't—you are so angry because you aren't—"

"Aren't what?" he said dangerously.

Arachne closed her eyes.

"Aren't trying to save the Grove yourself. You do know what the Grove was: the truth that quickens life. Nothing less. What stabs you now is that you do know it, did feel it, was part of it—but not enough. It didn't claim you enough to make you work to save it, or to choose it over wealth at Thera, or to change you in any way. And you wish—with all your heart—that it *had*. So you destroy it."

In the apotheca was no sound. Arachne opened her eyes. Jaen stood with the spider still on his open palm, and across it he looked at her. She saw from his face that he had known it all before, as of course he would. It was only to her that his exclusion was a new idea. Jaen had not been given what she had been given. He had not been made joyfully whole, had not been picked up and woven into the fabric of the world. She had not known that, but he had. With his intelligence and perception, and in the heightened awareness that all received in the Grove, he had known his poverty with a clarity few ever knew. He bitterly resented that poverty—and her because she did not share it.

Jaen resented her for the Grove.

Anguished, she cried out, "I thought you had it, too! I would have given it to you myself, if I could have!"

Jaen's face went white; in that whiteness his black eyes blazed. He jerked forward, and for a moment she thought he would hit her. In his voice was such passionate loathing that she flinched; she would have preferred that he strike her. "I do not need to be given your second-hand glory. I am not a beggar, Arachne, not even from you. Especially not from you. Not now, not ever. I do not beg."

He closed his palm. The spider's carapace crunched and shattered. Pulpy bits oozed through his fingers. He opened his fist; the bits fell to the floor.

Jaen walked out into the transparent spring light.

12

A hand touched her in the dark. Arachne had been dreaming; she clutched at the hand and jerked upright on her couch. Starlight from the window showed her Kyles's silhouette, bulky and still. Gladness washed through her, and she drew the back of his hand to rest against her cheek. It had been so long.

"Kyles."

Something hard brushed her face: a band of metal that circled his wrist. Arachne's eyes accustomed themselves to the darkness. Kyles's silhouette looked too bulky, too broad. At first she could not think why, and then she realized that he wore armor.

Kyles wore armor.

"Arachne. Nikos and Jaen have anchored off the Southern Shore. Both ships."

She struggled to throw off sleep, to understand. "The Southern Shore? No—they sailed for Thera two days ago."

"No. The ships circled, out of sight from Island. I think they will land at first light."

"Land? How could you know—"

"Watchers. Bribed slaves."

She gaped at him.

"They thought to take Island by surprise," Kyles said. "They will not."

"Take—"

"The Stone."

"Jaen would not!"

"He will try. He will not succeed."

In the silence Arachne could hear the soft lapping of a calm sea. Stars beyond the window shone large and clear.

Kyles said, "Nikos can't land the men from his ship all at once. He was depending on surprise, and on our believing they were gone. We will meet them on the Southern Shore, in the slow process of landing, and fight there."

"Who?" Arachne cried. "Who will fight them?"

"Islanders. Your army."

Arachne clutched at him. Her fingers struck copper, cool and hard. But there was little armor on Island, only corroded pieces brought with Delernos's Household five generations past. "What army? Fight with *what?*"

"The men I have spent two months gathering and training. The armor and swords our smiths have made."

"You didn't tell me what you were doing!"

"You didn't ask," Kyles said. In his voice, even and hard as a blade, she heard the unknown Kyles who could secretly train peaceful Islanders to fight, and bronzesmiths to copy old armor. No, not "unknown"—she recognized this Kyles. He had been not so much unknown as disregarded. Disregarded, but only by her: *What is Kyles so busy with these days?*

"You should have told me!"

"If I had, you might have forbidden it. You own Island," her husband said.

"You should have told me. To keep the Spider Stone—you don't know that I would have forbidden it, to keep the Stone."

"Bloodshed, Arachne."

"But—"

"Against Jaen?"

She had not seen it. In her bewilderment over the armor, over the ships, over Kyles—she had not seen the thing itself. Bloodshed. Fighting. Death.

"Against Jaen?" Kyles said, relentless.

"Kyles—"

"Forbid me now. Forbid me, and I will let Jaen land. And take the Stone."

He would. She heard in his voice that he would abide by what

she decided, not out of trust but out of a just cruelty. He wanted
the decision to hers: fight the brother she had loved instead of him,
or lose the Grove.

"I can stop him at the Southern Shore, or at the edge of the villa
itself. The fighting will be worse if you let him get as far as the villa.
Or you can let him take the Stone," Kyles said, and this time she
heard not only the cruelty but the bitter relish of it. Yet she knew
in her blood that if the ran to the window and threw herself over
the cliff, Kyles would without hesitation die trying to save her.

"Arachne. Choose."

Shaking, she tried to come to her feet. Kyles stepped back a pace.
Something in his hand glittered: the silvery-metal sword that had
been a gift from Ikeria. With a Theran princess's sword, her husband would try to kill Jaen.

"Choose."

"No! I am not the one to know! Not this!"

"You own Island," Kyles said. "You and Jaen. You have made
that clear often enough. Choose."

Arachne covered her face with her hands.

Kyles said, "Know this. If Jaen takes the Stone, he will never
return it. Nikos would never think it worth the cost. There will
breed no more spiders on Island, no more silk to weave, no more
Grove nor the light it brought."

"She clutched at his arm. "You saw it, Kyles? You did see what
the Grove was?"

"Yes."

"Jaen will not fight! When he sees your men waiting at the
Southern Shore—he doesn't plan on any resistance, any need to
shed blood. When he sees there will be fighting, he will back
away!"

"No. He will not. Choose, Arachne. Do I stop Jaen, or do I let
him take the Stone?"

A spasm shook her body. Kyles remained unmoved. Slowly,
tortured, Arachne finally spoke.

"Stop him."

"Then the women and children and old people from the Southern Shore will be sent to the villa. Find room for them. Send down
to the shore food, wine, blankets, water jars from the magazines,
so that if Nikos decides to wait us out, we will not have to leave.

Find and send women who can nurse, with medicines and cloth for bandages. Don't come yourself. Give me near-grown boys and girls that I can use as messengers—they won't get near the fighting—and the priestess. Tell her to prepare for funeral libations."

"Jaen will not fight!"

"Yes. He will," Kyles said, and strode into the darkness.

The women, older children, and old men worked all night by the light of lamps and torches. Later there was dawn to see by. Barley meal, dried fruit, cheeses, beans, wine from the storage magazines were packed into baskets. The families of the farmers and fishermen of the Southern Shore trudged with children, slaves, belongings up the long, uneven slope to the villa. In the dark their torches bobbed, throwing into sudden relief the curve of a laden arm, a donkey's back, a crying child. At the villa the tired donkeys were taken from the Islanders. The donkeys would be rested, and then loaded in the morning with supplies for the trip back.

Women, frightened or angry or bewildered, came to Arachne as she worked. The older women, who had known the Grove the longest, said little. They asked only for the truth and for any new tidings. Arachne, looking up from her piles of provisions at their creased faces and black eyes, said yes, Kyles and some men of Island were fighting to keep the Spider Stone. She said this one sentence evenly, with no variation of pitch or pacing on even the last words. The women heard in that even tone the ground-down smoothness of perfect pain, and went away without arguing. In the torchlight their eyes looked like deep wells.

Younger women came carrying fretful children who pulled at their chitons or clung to their necks. They came from husbands onto whom they had just strapped armor the women had never seen, husbands who were going to fight a battle the women had not known was going to happen. Too young to have known the Grove well, or often, many of them thought that Arachne had ordered the fighting to keep the silk for which the foreigners were paying so well. The young women, frightened for their husbands, shouted abuse. After the first few, Cleis and Aretone kept them from her. One very young bride, not abusive, slipped past. She had brought Arachne a square of very fine, very soft wool, to illustrate to the Mistress that wool could be just as beautiful as the silk over which

Arachne was going to kill her husband. As soon as the bride had
a clear look at Arachne's face, she stopped talking and backed away.
The scrap of wool fell to the floor. Arachne picked it up and
wrapped in it a jar of oil to be packed in a basket.

The women worked till dawn. Weary Islanders came and went,
carrying away baskets and orders. Once, carrying a filled basket up
from the storage magazine and through a corridor, Arachne saw a
figure standing on a rooftop, motionless, facing south. In the drain-
ing predawn light the cloaked figure might have been man or
woman, young or old. She did not ask.

When they had done all they could, they waited. Arachne,
Amaura, Cleis, Aretone, and one other of Arachne's women, Calthea, stood in a corridor by the entrance to a storage magazine.
They shivered in the dawn cold, and pulled their cloaks tighter.
Reluctant to separate, they had nothing to do together. Silently they
looked at the paling sky. In the distance rose shouts—excited,
young.

"Those are the boys that will run messages between the villa and
the battle," Amaura said. Of them all, only her face had any color.
A hectic flush came and went from chin to cheekbones. Her light,
flat eyes glittered as if with fever. All night she had worked with
a tireless ferocity that had gone unnoticed.

"They let them sleep until now," Cleis said.

"Poor things," said Calthea. She was past middle age, with six
grown daughters. Amaura looked at her in surprise.

"How long to run a message between the villa and the Southern
Shore?" asked Cleis. Her voice had the monotony of forced steadiness.

"Depends on how fast the runner is," said Aretone. "When I was
a girl, I could run it on hard ground in less than an hour, and there
were some, boys and girls both, that were faster. Mistress, you were
faster. You beat me in most races, remember?"

Arachne did not answer. It was obvious she hadn't heard. She
stared upward at the stars fading in the southern sky. Her fierce
remoteness made the others stir, and a little ruffle of resentment
passed through them. It became suddenly important to make the
Mistress answer, to force her inclusion in the fragile net they were
making to support themselves.

"*Remember*, Mistress?" Aretone said. "You won the Girl's Races three years running, and that fool Kaalies complained to your grandfather of favoritism. And each year you won, I came second."

"I didn't know you had been a runner, Mistress," Cleis said loudly.

"That last year," Aretone said, "some girls even beat some of the boys. You. Kaalies. Although none of us ever beat—" she stopped.

"Jaen," Cleis said, too loudly.

Aretone turned to Arachne. "Remember, Mistress? *Remember?*"

"Answer her," the woman with six daughters ordered harshly. "It's the least you owe us for being such a fool."

Cleis gasped. Amaura opened her light eyes wide. Arachne swung her face down from the sky and looked at Aretone. "What's that smell?"

The women began to sniff the air, eager for the distraction, not looking at the woman who had broken through the net.

"I've smelled it before," Aretone said, "but not so strongly. Phew!"

"It smells like something rotting," Cleis said. "Fish or meat."

Amaura said, "It's the Grove."

The breeze shifted. Amaura was right: The stench blew from the Grove. No longer sickly sweet, the smell was not so much unordinary as unthinkable for there, for the Grove.

"It died," Amaura said, "and now it rots."

She did not quite keep the interest from her voice. The events of the night had excited Amaura; they were like Suva's stories, dramatic with the same dark thrill, and that thrill one she had never expected on Island. Some part of her, cruel and artistic, was satisfied by the rotting of the Grove because it completed a pattern. She even pictured the patterns in Arachne's weavings, increasingly satisfying as they grew on the loom. The high color mounted in Amaura's cheeks, and in her voice. She had sounded eager and excited when she said the Grove rotted. She had sound pleased.

Arachne whirled to face her daughter with such ferocity that Cleis's cold hands flew to her cold cheeks. Aretone stepped forward; the woman with six daughters stepped backwards. But before Arachne could speak, the Grove, corridors and buildings away, convulsed in its last and violent death stroke.

Arachne's head jerked backwards and her eyes rolled into her skull. The women gasped until a moment later they felt it too: a wave of agony roiling from the Grove through their minds, terrible and malignant in its resemblance to the Grove's old power. Cleis screamed. The rotting smell intensified to unbearable putrefaction, a sense of decay so physical that the women felt their bones soften and their skin turn pulpy and maggot-ridden. Anguish and death thrashed through the entire villa. Islanders screamed; children jerked from sleep and cried out.

The death rattle lasted only a moment. It left the small group in the corridor gasping for air, leaning weak-legged against the stone walls. Lamps began to gleam in windows. Noise, muffled by the walls, seeped into the corridor. Cleis began to tremble violently enough to chatter her teeth. Aretone abruptly sat down.

Arachne began to run, a zigzagging stagger that bounced her off both walls of the corridor. "It has passed!" Aretone screamed, but Arachne only ran more steadily. Amaura tore after her. The other women drew themselves together and stumbled toward the Grove. In Arachne's face they had all seen some special knowledge, some additional terror she had felt and they, shuddering, had not.

They found her crouching on the withered grass of the Grove. Clinging to her neck and howling was Pholen. Over them stood the nurse, flailing her arms against the lightening sky.

"I didn't know, Mistress! He went when I was asleep, he babbled on all evening about getting one for his rock house but I told him no with all the confusion—I sleep in his very room, I never heard him at all, I sleep in his very room—"

Arachne bent close over her son. Pholen's howls grew softer. Under his tan the little boy's face had gone white. His lips and eyelids looked both swollen and stiff, like the tumescent leaves of waxy plants. On the grass lay a hollow stone split in two and lined with exquisite rosy crystals and one curled leaf. Pholen's forearm was swollen with the same blanched smoothness as his lips and eyelids; the swelling exaggerated the arm's huskiness. On the inside of the wrist, on the vein, was a fresh bruise centered by two red marks close enough to appear as one angry pustule. Next to the beautiful geode the spider lay smashed to a smear of gold.

"He wanted it for his rock house," the nurse sobbed. "I never heard him go, I woke when something didn't feel right, I sleep in his very—at the Grove I found him lying on his stomach the way he does with his face all squinched up at his rock trying to see through the leaf and poking the spider, and I said Pholen come away from the smell, and then he screamed and the whole Grove went sick and I couldn't see! And when I could see the spider was biting—biting!—and it wouldn't let go until I smashed it with the rock—it wouldn't let go! A spider!"

They were transfixed with it. A circle of watchers, growing as more Islanders ran to the Grove, stared at the geode, the smashed spider, the bitten child.

"I scraped it off and smashed it, and Pholen screamed and screamed and he won't stop—"

He had stopped. The thickness had spread to the rest of the child's features; his face looked molded in wax that was still moist, still a little soft. His chest rose and fell and occasionally his eyelids fluttered, but otherwise he lay still. Arachne cradled him, as still as Pholen.

"You should have watched him better!" Amaura cried shrilly at the nurse, but she was looking at Arachne.

"I sleep in his very room—"

"A spider!" Cleis said. "No, it couldn't—a spider!"

A faint shudder which had nothing to do with the ground went through the Grove. The watchers felt it brush past, but not through, them—a thin keening in the tiny spaces between the air, followed by an emptiness so profound the Islanders blinked and glanced around to see if the Grove itself still stood. It did, unchanged. The withered leaves stirred in the dawn wind and the smell of decay lay over the ground. Something else had stopped, something unseen but solid in its absence. Out of that profound absence, Arachne raised her head from her son.

"Tell Kyles to let them take the Stone."

No one moved. Arachne said again, clear and cold, "Let them take the Stone. Tell Kyles." In her arms Pholen whimpered, and she bent her head over him.

"The messenger boys," Amaura said shrilly. "No—no. I am going."

"Amaura," Cleis gasped. "Mistress—"

But Arachne did not look up. Amaura ran from the Grove, her sandals clattering across the stone of the colonnade.

Aretone said suddenly, "There are other spiders."

The circle of watchers started. Their gazes, horrified, darted over the grass, the trees, the low bushes. A woman glimpsed a flash of gold under a leaf, and began to shake. Someone stifled a scream; somone cried loudly, "A web in the children's chamber!" and ran. Cleis noticed, inches from her face, loops of silk. Ivory-colored and fine-fibered, the web was nearly invisible unless specifically looked for. The skin on Cleis's face puckered, and then the skin on her feet. She looked down. Nothing crawled on her feet, but they rested bare between the straps of her sandals on the concealing grass.

Arachne did not move until Cleis and Aretone tried to lift Pholen from her. Her arms tightened around him and she rose. Pholen lay inert, his face waxy over his mother's shoulder and his small feet dangling. Arachne kept her face buried in the back of his neck. When Cleis tugged her forward, she walked.

She didn't speak until they had reached her chamber. Then, in a voice so ordinary that it dazed Cleis and Aretone, Arachne said, "Smell the back of his neck."

"Put him down now," Aretone said gently.

"It always smells so sweet. I had almost forgotten that, the sweet warm smell at the back of his neck."

"Mistress—"

"I should not have forgotten that smell," Arachne said. "Not that one, not that one. That one."

—13—

AMAURA ran down the long slope from the villa to Island's Southern Shore. She ran on goat paths and fields, over brooks swollen with winter rains, past stark outcroppings of rock. The descent was gradual, and Amaura could run until she couldn't breathe and then walk until enough breath returned to run again. Olive trees stood in groves. Wildflowers, arbutus and myrtle and hyacinth, bloomed in their brief spring colors. They brightened as the sun rose, and their fragrance drifted in clouds Amaura burst as she ran. Whenever the land rose slightly in its uneven downward slide, glimpses of the sea flashed blue and flat.

She could not feel the ground under her feet, not even when she stumbled. All else was preternaturally clear and sharp—the scent of flowers and early mint, the sweat cooling on her flushed skin, the piercing notes of birdsong. But still she could not feel her feet. White silk chiton fluttering around her, she skimmed weightless over the ground and marveled to herself at the lack of contact. She felt like a bird, or a free wind.

Something in her spread taut. It was, like the weightlessness, an interesting sensation: fear, but not too much fear. Just as in the storage magazine she had not really believed there would be a battle—and she had been right, there would not be!—now, running weightless over the ground, she did not really believe that Pholen would die. Both events were part of a pattern, darkly gorgeous as

Suva's stories; it was the same pattern as the rotting of the Grove, but more interesting because it led to this tautness stretching from the base of her neck to the base of her spine, to this tingling vitality. Deliberately she made herself think of the exact second the golden spider's chelicerae had fastened on her little brother's wrist and discharged their poison. The moment she tried to picture the scene, she succeeded, and cried out, and noticed that her cry was the same pitch as the birdsong and tingled with the same urgency. That, too, made a dark and satisfying pattern.

Running, Amaura pictured how it would be. She would skim into the camp like a wind, like a white bird. Soldiers would be drawn in two advancing lines, as in Suva's stories. They would be grim-faced, armed, and the armor would dazzle with its brightness. They would already be smelling blood, their nostrils quivering with the scene of what was to come, Nikos's men at the water's edge and Kyles's where the rocky beach turned to field. She would flash between the advancing lines, the only woman there, skimming along without touching the muddy ground. The men would mutter in surprise and wonder, and fall silent. She would cry out that there would be no battle, and the men would lower their arms. Of course, the Islanders would still not like to lose the Stone, but after facing the advancing line of swords and spears, they would have decided that life was to be chosen over death, and they would look at her —all that line of armed men, powerful and dark-faced and danger-ous—with the redemption from death in their dark eyes. At her, Amaura, the only woman on that rocky beach, whose very pebbles tingled with the forbidden exhilaration of violence.

Only there would be no violence—because of her. There would be all the dark thrill of blood, but no blood—because of her. She, Amaura, who did not feel the ground beneath her feet and who felt, in the quickening of this perfect moment, that she never would.

Running up a slight rise, Amaura burst onto a hill above the beach. Jaen's and Nikos's ships rode closer to shore than she had imagined. Kyles's men stood not in the armed line she had pictured but in small, silent knots. They wore unpolished cuirasses on their breasts and plain, unadorned helmets that fit closely around their heads. All, fishermen and potters and farmers and smiths, carried unadorned bronze swords and shields. Amaura first identified Kyles, clad in the same plain armor as the rest, by his sword. The sun flashed on the foreign silvery metal of Ikeria's gift, and Amaura made for that bright flashing at the very edge of the water.

The Islanders stared at her as she ran among them toward her father. Kyles stood flanked by a bronzesmith and a goat farmer, facing not the army Amaura had pictured but only four men: the red-haired youth who was Nikos's messenger and personal slave, and three others. The others stood stiffly behind the youth. They wore polished full armor and crested helmets and carried swords and spears, but the youth wore only a brief chiton, white wool cloak, and gold armbands. His thin, beautiful face curled in contempt—at the lips, at the nostrils, at the curve of his reddish brows. Amaura, with that strange heightened clarity, saw every detail of the group of men and of the small, foreign-shaped boat drawn up beside them on the gray stones.

"Father!"

Kyles turned to her and scowled.

"I bring a message!" She drew herself tall in front of the waiting men. "There will be no battle! Mother says not to fight!"

She heard the red-haired youth snicker. Two of the guards behind him exchanged covert sneers. The smith and the goat farmer glanced at each other, and their faces contorted with sudden anger.

Only Kyles's face looked still.

Amaura repeated, "Mother says not to fight. She says to let . . ." She trailed off. She couldn't continue, not with the Theran boy slave sneering at her and the smith glaring and her father's face like stone. This was not it, this was not the pattern.

"What happened?" the smith demanded. He seized her arm roughly, not releasing it when Amaura tried to pull away. Kyles did not make him release it.

"We have a saying in Thera," the youth said musically. " 'Soldiers ordered at the fancy of queens fight at the fancy of enemies.' "

The smith shook Amaura's arm. "What happened!"

"The Grove! The Grove is—a spider bit Pholen! A spider became poisonous—the Grove rotted, and now the spiders are poisonous!"

"Not possible!" the smith spat. "You're lying!"

The red-haired Theran smiled. "Now you fight at the fancy of insects?"

Kyles said, "Pholen?"

"He'll die!" Amaura cried dramatically, although she did not believe it. "Mother says no one must fight!"

"You can't know the Young Master will die," the smith said. His fingers still dug into Amaura's arm, and he looked at her with disgust. "Kyles—the Grove is *ours.*"

"Has anyone else been bitten?" The farmer demanded of Amaura. He, too, looked at her as if she smelled bad. Other men drew near to listen.

"No—"

"It makes no difference, Kyles," the smith said in a low, passionate voice. "Biting or not, the spiders are ours. Changed or not, the Grove is ours, and the Stone." He tossed Amaura's arm away from him. "Island is ours! And men fight for what is theirs!"

"*Men* do," the Theran youth said musically. He was smiling.

"Kyles—" said the farmer, and stopped. For a moment no one said anything. Kyles stood with his hand on the hilt of the silvery Theran sword, and Amaura was shocked to see that the hilt trembled.

"Kyles," the farmer said again, and it was a demand.

The smith raised his voice. "Island is ours. We did not marry into the Household, we have no great wealth or ownership. But Island is nonetheless ours, we can fight for it alone, if needs be. That has already been said."

"Be quiet," the farmer said sharply.

But the smith would not quiet. "It has been said. The Mistress might put someone else's interest above Island. We do not."

"You're a fool," the farmer told the smith. He turned to face Kyles. "We are men of Island. We follow you. Choose."

Kyles swung his head around to meet the farmer's eyes. A convulsive shudder jerked over his face and left it as rigid as before, except for the eyes. Amaura saw her father's eyes, stopped rubbing her arm, and stood motionless.

"Yes. Choose," the smith said. His hand tightened on his sword, which he had forged himself.

"No!" Amaura cried, without volition. "Mother forbids you to fight!"

The Theran youth laughed. Kyles's fist shot out and smashed into his jaw. The youth dropped, falling half in and half out of the sea. Before Amaura saw them move, the three guards were on Kyles.

He was disarmed, struck, thrown to the beach with a spear poised at his groin. Drawn swords covered the smith and farmer, who had made ineffectual motions, clumsy next to the practiced ease of the Theran fighters.

The youth struggled to his feet, looked down at Kyles, and spat blood onto him. Amaura, numbed, saw that the Theran did not even look angry. Instead he smiled, a smile of mockery and contempt, and made a slight motion of one hand. The guard holding the spear at Kyles's groin jabbed twice. Kyles cried out. A few Islanders leaped forward, but the Theran said calmly, "Attack before he chooses and he dies," and the Islanders halted, confused. They could see that the guard with the sword was not aiming for death, nor perhaps even castration. They could not be sure. The guard smiled slightly, playing, pleasuring himself with the man on the ground's pain and humiliation. Another jab, and Kyles groaned. His face twisted, slick with sweat, and his eyes bulged. Mucus streamed from his nose.

The guard jabbed again. Dark blood stained the chiton between Kyles's legs. The red-haired youth moved his hand, and from above Kyles he said musically, "Do choose."

Amaura's stomach heaved. Fear for Kyles gave way to anger, a glittery anger brilliant as a faceted jewel. She was angry at the Theran youth, she was furious with the guard, she was angry at Kyles. She was angry at herself, because she suddenly saw that she was never going to forget the picture her father made pinned in the mud, under the gazes of a slave he amused and Islanders he was supposed to lead.

Kyles panted and writhed. His hands covered his groin. From between clenched teeth he said, "Take the Stone."

"No!" the smith shouted. And then, "Coward!"

The armed slave moved, leisurely, away from Kyles. Kyles struggled to sit, bent over. Amaura ran to kneel beside him. The other two guards, swords still drawn, backed away from the smith and the farmer and toward the boat. The men on the beach muttered—anger and relief and outrage—but none stepped forward.

"I will tell Nikos of your women's and insects' decision," the youth said, and smiled from his swollen mouth. Gracefully he climbed into the small boat. One of his men pushed it off the stones and into the water; the other two, arms ready, backed after the boat until they were waist high in the sea, then clambered in, one at a time. They began to row toward the large ships.

"Coward," the smith said. He turned to the men on the beach and shouted. "Who will fight with me for Island? Who are still men?"

Men began to move toward the smith—uncertain men, glancing at each other for answers. Some resented that they had come, some that they had to retreat. Their faces were drawn with horror at what might have been done to Kyles, with sleeplessness, with confusion. Laced through their mutterings, tangled with them, was confusion: this was not what they had expected, this accusation and humiliation and sudden choice. The choice frightened them more than Nikos's army would have, because they understood it less. They felt in some way cheated, although they could not have said of what, and in some way violated, although they could not have said how. The ugly scene on the beach had stripped something from not only Kyles but from each of them. Something had been taken, therefore someone must be to blame. They advanced toward the smith, and the smith drew his self-forged bronze sword and turned to face Kyles, who had jerked them all among fighting and not fighting, between the fancy of queens and being spat on with a sword at his genitals.

Kyles, his face gray, staggered to his feet.

Amaura saw the faces of the men and of her father. She didn't delay to think. Darting between Kyles and the smith, she cried, "All the spiders are poisonous! *All!* Your families—your families are in terrible danger!"

The men hesitated. They looked at each other, and then at Amaura: at her white, exhausted face with its strange light eyes. She looked to them like what she had pictured earlier: a weightless feminine presence, superstitiously powerful. But, at the same time, she looked like the Young Mistress, Kyles's child. As such, she forced them to remember Kyles's other child, dying of the unthinkable: a poisonous spider. Some of the men did not believe it. But it, too, confused them. Amaura confused them, and Kyles—leader turned shameful and unmanned coward, shielded by his daughter—confused them. They did not want to have to look directly at Kyles. They were afraid for their families. Their new swords hung awkwardly at their sides. They had no tradition of battlefield honor.

"Island is ours! A girl's lies change nothing!" the smith shouted, but his shouts were not as confident as before. The men heard the difference. They looked again at Amaura, drawn up in front of Kyles as tautly as stretched spider silk, as light as a white bird with strange pale eyes. Men began to turn, by twos and threes, up the rise away from the beach.

Amaura knew how she appeared to the men. It seemed to her, in her moment of power, that she inhabited each of their eyes and gazed upon her own figure from dozens of vantage points. That slim figure stood between her father and violence, and it was violence and the deflection of violence that licked at its white draperies and shimmered around its taut face. The shimmer was dazzling, unearthly, like a crown of dark light on her head. It transformed her from an ordinary girl performing a heroic act into something both more and less: a spinner of her own brightly colored heroism so that she might feed off it later, so that she might bind them all to her with sticky threads that would form a thrilling pattern only she could see.

When half the Islanders had turned, the smith, cursing, followed them. Kyles did not move. Some men remained on the beach, but they stayed a little apart from Kyles and Amaura, waiting to be signaled to come closer. The long slope of land to the north was dotted with climbing men.

Amaura slipped her hand into her father's. He could not stand without pain. Despite her feverish excitement, each of her words came slowly, as if it were a danger to both of them. "You did not know, Father. It was not your fault. You did not know the spider would bite Pholen or those Therans would . . . you did not *know*."

Kyles didn't answer.

"Mother did not know, either. She did not know Pholen would get bitten or the Grove turn not worth fighting for or that when she called you back it would make you . . . like this. Like this."

Still Kyles said nothing. Red bloodlines wavered in the whites of his eyes, radiating from the pupils like webs.

Amaura cried desperately, "I'm sorry!" and looked away over the sea. She couldn't stand to look at her father's face, but not because of the webbed eyes. When she looked at him, she saw standing over him not only the Theran slave, but also Arachne, and herself. A flash of contempt for Kyle shot through her, and she wondered—was the smith right? *Was* it cowardice that had made him say, "Take the Stone"? The part of her that loved her father was horrified at her contempt, and the part of her that fed on the sticky pattern fed also on the contempt. Amaura shivered, and looked out over the sea, reducing her father to a murky patch at the edge of her vision. She could not bear to look at his face, or at where he bled.

The sun on the water hurt her eyes. Jaen's and Nikos's sails bobbed colorfully, making bright patterns on the morning sea.

—— 14 ——

SUVA ladled a pungent herb drink into a cup. The brown stream falling from the ladle reminded her of something, she could not think what. She froze, her face grotesque with the effort to remember, cup and ladle tipped to one side. The cup filled and overflowed. When drops of brown liquid splashed onto Suva's foot, she chortled at the pain. Hot. The memory had not been hot, so this wasn't the memory. This must be someplace else. She carried the cup to the couch where Pholen lay, watched by the Mistress, and remembered the dark place that this was.

The little boy lay naked in the overheated room. He was quiet, and did not seem in pain. Although his eyes were open, they stared without sight, black shiny circles with the top arcs obscured by swollen eyelids. The waxy tumescence still thickened his features, especially the eyelids. Around the bite his arm was red, and a crust had formed over the punctures left by the spider's fangs. His breathing was slow and shallow, lapping against the walls like peaceful waves.

"Child, child, child," Suva crooned. A picture, half-formed and watery, dragged at her: another child, a struggling child, what child? Suva ran screaming through the corridors of memory, arms over her head, away from the watery child. It did not follow.

"Suva," Arachne said, "give him the drink."

"Child, child, child." Suva held out the cup. Arachne raised

Pholen's head and the two women got most of the brown liquid down his throat. It burned his mouth, but he didn't flinch. A few moments later he began to sweat, a strong-smelling sweat too thick for a child.

"Sweat it out, sweat it out, sweat it out," Suva crooned. She turned the small body on its side and gently massaged the skin above the cleft of Pholen's buttocks. A stream of urine trickled from the little boy. When it ceased, Arachne raised him in her arms and poured clear water into his slack mouth. Suva shuffled to the fire to build it higher. Pholen must sweat.

"*He* said I must be a goddess," Suva said aloud, and her face contorted into wrinkles. The man-curse Jaen had come back from the dead, so he was a god. *Then you must be a goddess, Suva. You came out of the sea, too, you told us, remember?* But if she was a goddess, she had only to wave her hand to turn Pholen from death. She had only to nod, to call on the swooping birds, and she and Pholen would skim through the air above the sea, singing and singing. Yes! They flew over the sea, and Pholen threw back his head and cried out—the other child cried out—

No. A goddess could halt death, could—

Singing and singing—

It was so. She was dressed in armor, man-impregnable, flying over the sea and singing. She threw back her head and laughed, flapped her arms, and below her in the sea the other child—

"Suva!"

The young woman Cleis stood in the room, shocked and outraged. Suva lowered her arms and scowled horribly.

"You were *laughing!*" Cleis said.

"You are a stupid girl," Suva said, and threw another log on the fire. Sparks flew up.

Aretone entered behind Cleis, and the two women went to Arachne. Cleis's eyes filled with tears, but Aretone's severe, handsome face closed in on itself and she spoke levelly. "Everyone in the villa has been warned, Mistress. Two more have been bitten, both old women. They went into the Grove to see for themselves one last time, the old . . ."

"Yes," Arachne said. "The old." Her voice was flayed.

"Spiders are crawling from the Grove throughout the villa. One was crushed as far as the eastern wall. None crawl near the sea, though—they still avoid the sea. That at least has not changed," Aretone said grimly, and laid a hand on Pholen's forehead. The child did not stir. "People are fleeing the villa with what they can carry, going to the countryside to relatives or friends. Many are waiting beyond the south wall for their men to return. Some have already come. It is as the runner said: there was no fighting."

"*Everything* happened as the runner said?"

Aretone heard the horrified emphasis in Arachne's voice. "Yes, Mistress. As we were told. Master Kyles . . . has not yet returned. Nor has Amaura. She is with him."

"And your husband, Aretone?"

"Returned. He says that halfway to the villa he turned and saw the first of the Therans land. He climbed an olive tree to see it, Mistress."

"Go with him to your farm. Go with my thanks. And take Cleis with you to her father."

"No," Cleis said. "I will stay. I can be of use."

Suva snorted.

Aretone said, "I will stay as long as necessary."

Suva carried another cup of herb drink to Pholen and began to pour it down him. His lips had begun to blister from the hot fluid. Much of the drink flowed out again and trickled over his cheeks onto the sopping couch. Suva wiped Pholen's face and stared into his open, sightless eyes.

And then, within Suva's mind, something began to happen.

Pholen's eyes were flat and shiny black, like a dark mirror, and in them Suva saw the reflected figures by the bed—Arachne, Aretone, Cleis, herself—begin to shrink and shrivel until they were no more than specks under the curved lowering weight of iris and eyelid. All the light in the room was rushing into Pholen's black eyes, where the light turned dark until the room itself was sucked in and lost in that shiny blackness. Suva groped through the thick dark, in which things happened for no cause and to no end. Cold winds howled by, and the viscid blackness oozed around her. It was not the blue water of the sea drowning her after all, but instead this far worse blackness, this oozing dying sludge that forced itself against the walls of memory and forced them down, until with a shriek the last one gave way and Suva remembered that other dying, that other drowning. Until she remembered it all.

She was rushing knee-deep into muddy water, waist-deep, chest-deep, trying to hide, and her child's arms grasped convulsively at her neck. Suva screamed at the little girl not to choke her, they must hide, but the little girl, terrified by what was happening behind them on the beach, clutched harder and went on crying, her cries whipped away in the salt wind. Seaweed clung to both of them as they waded outward. Suva seized the slimy stuff and tried to drape it over their heads, covering the child's eyes so she would not see the horror on the beach. The little girl felt the cold slippery sea-weed on her neck and clawed it off, screaming louder. Behind them shouts followed, splashes, and then the slavers were on her, drag-ging her backwards to shore. Her child slipped from her grasp.

"She's having a fit!" Cleis cried, and Suva heard the shouts of the men, and the yelling from the beach. Frantically she groped through the water, screaming herself, clutching for the little body through the net of hands dragging at her. Here somewhere, oh here somewhere!

"Grab her, grab her, she has Pholen!" Cleis screamed, and so Suva tried desperately to grab her, and for a moment she had the small arm and saw again the black eyes shiny with terror. Then the child was torn from her fingers, fell back into the dark water, and sank. Men's hands pulled Suva backwards nearly to land, and threw her down. Waves washed over her head, she could not breathe, she was drowning.

"Make her breathe!" Cleis cried, but how could she, she had lost her child's body in the ocean and the hands still gripped her. They slapped and pummeled until she stopped struggling. Then the slaver shoved apart her legs, while the water still washed over her face and, beyond, the great Theran ship rocked in billows of smoke from the burning village. Suva choked and flailed her arms, fighting to breathe, to scream, to forget.

Now, remembering—reliving—her mind did not go black, as it had that first time. She felt what happened next, what she had missed. The muck from the slaver's man-weapon poured into Suva. Muck! And it had been in the muck, in the mud and seaweed and water, that she had lost the child. One muck became the other, and so the child must be pouring into her with the sticky muck, must be flowing into her . . . she had not realized it that first rape, no, had never even realized what had happened! The raping man-curse had shot his sludge inside her, and of course the little girl had slid in with it! Her black-eyed daughter lay safe inside her, because of him! Of him!

"She is quieter now," Aretone said. "Help me get her to another chamber."

Suva struggled to her feet. The last of the viscid blackness had drained inside her, and the room was left in spring sunlight. The Mistress stood against one wall, clutching Pholen in her arms. His arm trickled blood from the marks of fingernails; someone had clutched his arm hard enough to draw blood. Cleis and Aretone gripped Suva's arms; Suva could not think why they thought that could hold her *now.* They were fools. She stood very still so that they would relax their grips, and they did. Suva gazed benignly at where Arachne stood grasping Pholen, and smiled at them.

"I drowned *my* child."

Cleis gasped. Arachne's eyes widened. Fools.

"You don't understand," Suva said, smiling. "I made her safe. From the Theran slavers. Because I drowned her, the child is inside me now. Safe forever."

And she had not seen that before, Suva marveled. How could she have overlooked it? The man-curse, the destroyer, had been the tool by which she made her child safe. Suva threw back her head and laughed, glorying in the perverse justice. And she had not seen it until now, had not heard it either. But now that she knew, she heard it: the small girl with shiny black eyes, inside.

"Do you hear her singing?" Suva asked them. Her face glowed, luminous, with triumph. She laid her hands across her shrunken belly. "Do you hear? Singing and singing!"

Aretone said gently, "Come, Suva. Come with me."

"And Pholen knew," Suva said, marveling yet again. "Young Master Pholen *knew.* He was the first to tell me what I had become."

"Come, Suva."

"He knew even before I," Suva said, and smiled at Arachne: the glorious, tender, omnipotent smile of a goddess.

When Aretone had led Suva from the room, Arachne again laid Pholen on the couch. Aretone returned, her feet soundless on the stone floor.

"I left her in the kitchens. She is sitting there quietly, singing to herself."

Cleis burst out, "She is mad!"

"Yes," Aretone said.

"Do you think she really drowned her own child?"

Aretone glanced at Arachne and bit her lip. "Yes."

"But how could she? How *could* she?"

Aretone said sharply, "How do we know why people off Island do what they do?"

"She tried to hurt Pholen!"

"I think . . . she did not know what she was doing. She looked at Pholen as if she didn't even see him. As if she saw something else instead."

"She is a monster!"

"And so might you be if you had lived her life in her place. Now be quiet."

Cleis subsided. The two women knelt by Pholen's couch, Aretone decisively and Cleis hesitantly; Arachne already crouched there with her arms around Pholen's sweating body. The others could not see her face. Aretone moistened a cloth and wiped the blood from the scratches on the child's arm. Pholen did not stir.

After a while his breathing faltered, caught, faltered again. Aretone rose to her feet, dragging Cleis with her. She drew the younger woman back a few paces, so that only Arachne remained touching the child. That seemed right, just, to Aretone; that was what she, bitterly childless, would have wanted for herself. To be the only one close, with no stranger bodies pressing in, not even a priestess.

And so Arachne knelt alone, the only one, cradling Pholen until he died.

—— 15 ——

ON the Southern Shore Nikos landed his men as soon as the beach had emptied of Islanders. The Theran force consisted of slaves carrying heavy loads of equipment and supplies, mercenaries led by an experienced soldier named Tageas, Nikos, Jaen, and a priest. The priest rode in a curtained litter. The force advanced toward the villa in an armed column. Nikos half-expected an ambush—it would have been an effective tactic, and what he would have done in Kyles's place—but no ambush came. The Islanders glimpsed at farms or groves disappeared into their simple plastered buildings as soon as they saw the Therans. Other Islanders, heavily laden with household goods and children, moved away quickly.

"Refugees," Nikos said, studying one such group. "Why, Jaen?"

"Why do you imagine?" Jaen snapped. He looked moody and drawn; Nikos thought that he would have to be handled carefully. The trader wanted no unpredictable reversals on Jaen's part.

"Are they leaving because they fear we will attack," Nikos said, "or to make more credible to us this tale of the bitten child?"

"It may not be a tale."

"You know your native Island best. However, the poison seems to have appeared rather suddenly, and at a time rather convenient to frighten us off. I have never heard of harmless spiders turning poisonous."

"Wonders and marvels, marvels and wonders."

"A jaded cynicism does not become you, Jaen."

"Nor does the mockery of consulting my opinion become you. That's a flirt's trick. Leave it to Ikeria," Jaen said, and strode away. Nikos looked after him thoughtfully. Yes, he would have to be handled carefully.

Moving with slow caution, the Therans reached the southern wall of the villa by noon. No one intercepted them. The villa seemed deserted. Tageas came to Nikos for orders.

"Unbarricaded, Trader. Could be an ambush. In those narrow streets even untrained natives would have the advantage: barricade forward streets, box us in from the rear, attack from the rooftops. I don't like it."

"No one will attack," Jaen said tightly.

Tageas ignored him. "Your orders, Trader?"

Nikos studied the villa. Before he had decided, a figure appeared in a space between two houses. The Therans raised their weapons.

"Aretone," Jaen said. "Tageas, tell your men to stop that ridiculous position. She will not be armed."

"Who is she?" Nikos said.

"One of my sister's women."

Aretone walked toward them with her head high and her back straight. She addressed Nikos with cold scorn, the planes of her handsome face rigid. Jaen she did not even glance at; it was clear that for her he no longer existed.

"Mistress Arachne sends to tell you that you may take the Spider Stone, if you can. You will not be stopped or attacked. But you must go nowhere in the villa except the Grove and the wide corridor that leads to it from this place. If one man steps elsewhere beyond the colonnade, Master Kyles's soldiers will kill you all."

"I think," Nikos said smoothly, "that I saw two of his soldiers traveling east, carrying children and goats."

Aretone appeared not to have heard him. "The Stone and the Grove are yours. Despoil as you wish. But the spiders have become poisonous, and they have crawled from the Grove throughout the villa. Mistress Arachne would have you know that. I would not have told you."

Tageas smiled.

"One condition more," Aretone said. "Jaen does not come to the Grove. He does not enter the villa."

Jaen jerked his head and flushed. His eyes glittered, but his voice remained low, even pleading. "Aretone—is Pholen dead?"

Not by a muscle flicker did she acknowledge him. "That is all, Trader."

When she had gone, Tageas said, "Clumsy lies. Trader, your orders?"

Nikos considered. "March a preliminary force through the corridors to the Grove and out again. The force should be large enough to spring the trap, if it is one, but should be expendable. Outfit slaves as soldiers; these people will not detect the difference. Put Dalien in charge. Have him note if spiders have indeed moved beyond the Grove, and if the Stone is still intact."

"And if it is not?"

"Take no action. But have it reported at once to me," Nikos said. He added, "And to Master Jaen."

"Yes, Trader."

The expendable force marched into the villa, entered the Grove, and marched out again. They had seen no one. The large round stone, said Dalien, was intact in the middle of the Grove. The whole area stank like a battlefield, although he had seen no carrion. The large stone itself was not the source of the smell; he had sniffed it and found it odorless. Some of the men reported catching glimpses of spiders, but they had not gone close and the vermin had stayed under cover. In the bright sunlight they were difficult to even see.

Nikos was pleased. "Set up camp here, well away from the walls. One-third of the men here under you, Dalien. Full sentry force at all times. Tageas, you and I will take an armed guard, the slaves and other equipment, and the priest. Is he here yet?"

"His litter has just arrived."

"Leave it here; he will have to walk. Guards front and rear."

"On rooftops would be better," Tageas said.

"No. Keep their conditions; no one goes anywhere but the most direct corridor and the Grove."

"Yes, Trader."

"Jaen?" Nikos said, and waited.

"I stay here."

Nikos hid his surprise. He did not believe in wastefully defiant gestures; they consumed resources. That Jaen should share that sense was unexpected. "A prudent decision."

"I don't make it from prudence," Jaen said coldly. His eyes, angry and tormented, were on the tops of trees just visible over the villa's walls. Nikos kept his face neutral. There were many kinds of wastefully defiant gestures.

The Theran force was halfway to the Grove when the smell struck them. Dalien's description was unimaginative, Nikos thought. Mercenaries were usually unimaginative, and hence inaccurate. The stink of a battlefield bore only a superficial resemblance to this smell. This one was both weaker and more malevolent, as if some natural decay were shot through with supernatural resentment at its own rotting. Nikos knew well the impotent anger of the dying at the alive and healthy. He had seen gangrenous soldiers, shaking with helpless rage, spread pus from their rotting limbs over other men's open wounds. This stink was, somehow, equivalent.

At the Grove the priest sacrificed a goat and poured a libation, chanting purification. As many slaves as could fit around the Spider Stone were set to digging carefully along its sides. Others hauled the dirt a short distance away and dumped it on the withered grass. Soldiers stood in an outward-facing circle, motionless.

"I see no spiders," Tageas said, smiling.

Nikos considered him. Unimaginative. "I saw one, Tageas. Under a fallen leaf, as we crossed the colonnade. They dislike light. However many are left in the Grove will come out at dusk, which is when they spin. It is always a mistake to judge before sufficient observation. You should remember that."

Tageas smile disappeared. "Yes, Trader."

"Yes."

Kyles knelt formally by the couch where Pholen lay. He put his big hand over his son's forehead, and then rested his ear on Pholen's chest and listened to the absence of sound. With his fingers Kyles traced each of Pholen's thickened features. He pushed up the swollen eyelids and gazed into the child's black eyes. He turned over Pholen's forearm and looked silently at the crusted punctures. Finally, he held Pholen's wrist and bent, motionless, over the small form.

Amaura saw the blood and dirt in Kyles's hair. He had had to be carried to the villa by slaves, and then had tended his wounds alone. No one knew how much he had been torn by the Theran's spear. That he could stand at all argued for little damage; the searing rigidity of his face argued otherwise. No one dared put out a hand to steady him. No one dared to ask him outright if he had been unmanned.

For a long while, Kyles remained bent over his son.

When Kyles stood, his body stooped over, Arachne knelt by Pholen and repeated the formal movements of the ancient ritual examination. Pholen's body had already been washed and dressed in white spider silk. When Arachne finished, she and Kyles each closed one of their son's eyes and laid on them round circles of bronze. Arachne began the Song of Sorrow. Aretone and Cleis chanted with her, Cleis through sobs, Aretone as pain-dry as the Mistress. Only Amaura could not chant, nor move, not even to bury her little brother with proper dignity.

The sarcophagus stood ready, carried in by Aretone's husband, Akeumis. Unlike a sarcophagus for an adult, it was neither stone nor rectangular, but was made of fired clay with an elongated oval body and a wide-lipped circular opening at the top. It was a flattened version of the man-high pithoi that lined the storage magazines to hold wine or olive oil, lacking the storage vessels' height but sharing their double handles and unpainted exteriors. A tight-fitting lid rested near it on the stone floor. The inside of the lid was painted azure. The lives of small children, that most precious wine of the Goddess, were offered to Her unshrouded in a funeral jar, but the lids of the jars were always painted blue. Familiar things comforted children in strange places. Pholen might become lonely for the sky.

Kyles lifted Pholen and staggered sideways. His face contorted with pain, but each of the others knew better than to help him. Kyles sank to his knees, his face gray, and cradled his son above the funeral jar. Then he lowered Pholen inside, curling the little body against the cool curves of clay. With Pholen, Kyles placed the fresh figs and cheese, the tiny rhyton of new wine, the figurine of the Goddess who would drink his spirit and let him grow again in Her. The women's chant became higher in pitch and more unsteady in rhythm.

When the Song of Sorrow ended, Kyles fitted the lid and sealed it with pitch.

"There won't be a procession to the sacred cave!" Cleis cried. "No priestess, no proper sacrifices—everyone has gone!"

"We will do what we can," Aretone said severely.

When the lid was sealed, Kyles placed his hand on one of the pithoi's handles. Akeumis stepped forward to grasp the other handle, but Kyles waved him away. He tried to lift the jar himself, grimaced with agony, and instead crouched beside it, his arms around the clay curves. He faced Arachne.

"I am taking Pholen to the vineyard, not to the sacred cave. I will entomb him there, in the fields. Alone. You have stripped me of everything else. I will keep my son."

Arachne did not ask what he meant, of what she had stripped him. She knew. She knelt by the sealed jar and laid her cheek against its clay side.

Amaura did not know what her father meant, but his toneless bitterness shocked her. Something dry and hard blocked her throat. She knew what it was: it was the morning on the beach, shriveled and baked hard. Because of the morning, her father would go from the villa and not return. Because of the morning, her mother would not go with him; her presence would have finished what was left of Kyles. Because of the morning and all the other mornings that must have lead to it, Kyles would take the spirit of small dead Pholen away with him. And because of the morning and all the other mornings, Amaura saw, he would have to take her, too. She had bound herself to him by her contempt, by her wondering if he was a coward, by stepping between him and the smith with such joyful denigration. Kyles said Arachne had stripped him of everything. It was not true. Amaura knew that she, too, had stripped him, and then jeered at his nakedness. She felt bound to him by having injured him, and suddenly and fumblingly she sensed what it was that had thrilled her so in Suva's terrible stories: the close and enduring bonds of injury.

She loved her father, but love would not have compelled her so much. It was injury that chained her, injury that she had inflicted herself, injury that both proved her power over another and simultaneously diminished it. She did not love Arachne, because she had never really felt she could injure her mother. She did not have enough weight or sharpness. Arachne could be hurt only by the Grove, by Jaen, by Pholen. Amaura knew that now her mother had been pierced by all three, but as the girl stood over that silent figure with its face pressed against the funeral jar, she felt only an ordinary pity. That frightened her; Arachne was her mother. But the grief she felt for Arachne was small next to the grief she felt for Kyles, and for herself. Yet she knew it was Arachne who had loved Pholen the most.

Amaura looked from her mother to the sarcophagus that held her brother. She remembered the shimmering heat of summer, and the cliff ledge where she had made Pholen cry and then knelt to comfort him. She felt again the small, moist body wriggling against her own, the black curls brushing her shoulder. Pholen's toes, dusty and round, had pushed against her knees. He had stopped wailing when she held him, and, remembering, Amaura gazed at her father's face and began to cry.

As Nikos's slaves dug, they laid bare the sides of the Spider Stone. The sides were as smooth and hard as the surface, although without the same translucent amber. By late afternoon the slaves, digging carefully so that no pick or shovel struck the Stone itself, had cleared away the earth to the depth of a man's height. The Stone lay exposed in a bowl of rich loam, like a swollen jewel on black silk. The exposed sides tapered inward, but only slightly. Nikos estimated the angle to be five degrees.

"No indentations or protuberances," Tageas said. "It's going to be difficult to get a rope around that."

"A little deeper and it tapers more sharply," Nikos said. "I ran in rods with Master Jaen. Priest, what do you think?"

"We have no records of anything like this in the Library. Wonders and marvels—but none like this," the priest said. He was old, and puny. Nikos would have preferred the greater power of a priestess, but the puny priest came from a land where many insects were reputed to have unusual powers. In addition, Ikeria had preferred a male. She liked to be the only female aboard ship.

Nikos said, "Then you can tell us nothing useful?"

"You must remove the Stone before it can be of use to either of us. The Goddess guards Her secrets jealously."

"As do their practitioners," Nikos said dryly. He walked around the Stone, regarding it from all sides. "Tageas, keep digging. As many men in the trough as will fit, and the others start cutting and trimming trees. We'll need them for rollers to move the Stone when it's free. Cut the trees into lengths between the width of the

Stone and the width of the corridor. I've measured the colonnade, and the space between columns is too narrow to accommodate the Stone. Remove two columns; you'll have to take down part of the roof as well. Clear the rubble out of the way. Don't remove anything else, Tageas, or permit your men to go anywhere else."

"Yes, Trader."

The work continued smoothly. Axes rang on wood and stone, and at the colonnade the guards shouted orders. At the Stone, however, the slaves worked more quietly. Often they glanced at each other, and at the sun slipping down the sky.

The length of a forearm further down, the sides of the Spider Stone began to slant sharply. The slaves crouched in the trough they had dug and reached under the Stone for the dirt to fill their baskets, which were hauled up by ropes to be emptied. Under the Stone the thinning sunlight turned to shadow. When the Stone had been laid bare for one and half times a man's height, the slanting base was difficult to see from above. The surface seemed to float weightless on shifting shadows. With some of the Grove's trees gone, the Stone reflected the sunset directly. It glowed sullenly, with amber-red fire.

"Circle the Stone with a rope," Nikos said, "and anchor it with guy lines. If the base narrows much more, the Stone will tilt."

"The balance looks perfect," Tageas said.

"Nonetheless, I will not risk its toppling. Is the colonnade clear?"

"Nearly clear."

"Let me see."

Nikos and Tageas walked to the colonnade. Chunks of stone lay broken on the grass. Grunting with the strain, slaves pushed them aside. Nikos inspected the emerging path and nodded.

"Good. Finish it."

"Yes, Trader."

"In the name of the Goddess!" the priest gasped. He gazed at the western sky; Nikos swung his head around to look.

Across the Grove, on the colonnade roof nearly opposite where the slaves worked, a motionless figure stood against the sky. The Therans saw it framed by the withered leaves of the Grove trees, against the bloody red of sunset. One fold of its dark cloak had been drawn over its head, and the curves of the figure had no projections anywhere except for the light radiating from behind it. Its stillness against that bloody sky made it look heavy as stone.

"A sign from the Goddess," the priest breathed.

"No, it is not," Nikos said quickly. "The only thing here of the Goddess's is the Spider Stone. Confine yourself to that, Priest. It is why you were brought."

"Not armed," Tageas said. He revolved to scan the rest of the colonnade roof. "No others. The sentries didn't signal any approaches. There must be passages your native pet didn't bother to tell us about, Trader." He squinted against the sun. Both men shielded their eyes with their arms. "I can not tell if it's soldier or priestess."

"Neither," Nikos said.

"Trader?"

"It is Mistress Arachne."

Tageas squinted again. "Up there? Why?"

"Does it matter?"

"I don't like it," Tageas said. "I never like spies."

"She is not spying," Nikos said quietly. He lowered his arm. "Neither of you will speak of this to Master Jaen."

"No, Trader," Tageas said, and shrugged. The priest did not answer. He stood staring sullenly at the ominous figure in which he was forbidden to find omen. Before Nikos could mollify him, a man screamed.

The three men ran to the Spider Stone, but the scream had come from a little beyond. A slave who had been chopping down a tree lay writhing on the ground, clawing at his face. Other slaves dropped their axes and backed away, terror rising from them palpable as heat. Gripping the screaming man's cheek was half of a spider —cephalothorax, four hairy legs, and the deadly chelicerae. The slave clawed, shrieking, and ripped off the rest. Between his screams came the crunch of the spider's exoskeleton crushing in his hand.

"Another one!" a slave cried, pointing at the grass. He gibbered and ran. One of Tageas's mercenaries caught him with his whip and the man fell to the ground. Another of the guard clubbed the spider, smearing it across the grass.

"Sentries to scan the ground and air," Tageas said. He was breathing rapidly. "We can dig a circular trench to scorch the

ground with fire. It's safe enough, Trader—the area is not dangerously dry."

"Then start," Nikos said. "Get this man carried back to camp.
Punish the one that tried to run. Make an example of him, Tageas,
but later."

"Of course," Tageas said stiffly.

The bitten slave had stopped screaming. His eyes rolled in terror,
but his body grew slowly still. There was almost a languor in the
fall of his hand on the grass, next to the crushed spider. On one
cheek the red fang marks showed sharply against pale skin.

The priest stared at the figure on the colonnade. It had not
moved.

"She did not cause that," Nikos said sharply, loud enough to be
overheard. A note in his voice set the others to working faster, but
the priest did not answer.

The fallen slave was carried away. Tageas had dug a shallow
circular trench surrounding the Stone, the completed rollers, and
some additional trees. When the trench was completed, he ordered
everyone but four slaves out of the circle. The men went nervously.
The red sun bloodied the edge of the colonnade, and darkened the
silhouette of the cloaked figure.

From large pithoi, slaves filled the trench with fluid. Tageas
dribbled the rest over the grass within the circle, dispersing it in a
pattern of thin, crisscrossing lines. The slaves left within the circle
picked up staves and stood the staves' full lengths away from the
trees. Sweat glistened on their backs.

"Now!" Tageas ordered. The men beat the trees. In the silent
Grove the thud of wood on wood sounded thunderous. From the
trees fell dead leaves, bits of bark, and flecks of gold. The flecks
shone fierce in the red light, dull in the trees' shadow. When the
spiders touched ground they scurried for cover. The staves broke
rhythm, hitting the trees in jerky discord. One man screamed.

The slave closest to the Stone dropped his stave and fell to the
ground, still screaming. The others shot him terrified looks, threw
down their own staves, and sprinted across the grass. Spiders scurried around their feet. One man leaped the oil-filled trench and
stood panting by Tageas, head held straight up, fists clenching and
unclenching. He hesitated before raising the fist, but Tageas struck
him for the intent. A second slave jumped the trench and kept on

running, toward the corridor. A guard lashed him with his whip and the man fell. At the same moment, Tageas bent and lit the trench.

Fire raced around the circle. More slowly, flames spread tentatively over the grass, licking at the trails of oil. The flames flickered, dimmed, caught on another sprinkled spot, petered out, flared elsewhere, moving toward the Stone in a crisscross of uneven lines like a deformed web. Black smoke roiled upward, smelling acrid and obscuring sight. Those downwind choked and moved away.

A sound rose above the crackle of twigs and the snap of flames. The sound was not loud, but it made the hairs at the backs of the men's necks prickle: a sizzle, fitful and sibilant, like the singeing of hair.

"The spiders," the priest whispered.

Nikos did not answer. The priest began to chant, raising his arms. Several of the mercenaries inched closer to him.

The creeping fire reached the slave who had fallen within the circle. His loincloth began to smoulder. The man screamed and thrashed on the ground as if he were trying to rise. The smell of charring meat blew through the stinking air. The man screamed louder, his partially-paralyzed limbs jerking in the passing fire.

When the flames reached the rim of earth around the trough of the Spider Stone, they went out. Over the rest of the grass the fire flickered and finally died. Tageas ordered the men back within the scorched circle. They went fearfully, treading over the smoking lines on the grass, starting at charred bits of anything. Tageas drew his sword and plunged it into the half-burned, half-paralyzed slave. The man stopped writhing.

Nikos looked up. From the colonnade roof, the figure watched.

16

BY late dusk, the Spider Stone lay nearly completely exposed. A rope circled it a hand's span below the top, held in place by ropes crisscrossing the surface. From the encircling rope six guy lines ran to stakes driven into the ground.

The fire in the oil-filled trench had been kept burning, and no one else had been bitten. Just before dark Nikos called for an end to the day's work, and Tageas marched the men from the Grove. Beyond the protected circle, one mercenary felt something brush across his eyes: a web, fine and clear. He gasped, yelled, clawed at his face. As soon as he yelled, the men broke and ran, scrambling blindly in the darkness toward the torches at the corridor, the priest and Nikos among them. The mercenary did not fall; he had brushed away a part of the web that did not hold a spider. Men crashed against each other and against the corridor walls. Two-thirds of the way from the Grove to the southeastern wall, a soldier screamed and fell. The others left him, trampling over the thrashing body, stumbling from the villa to the lighted camp beyond the walls.

Slaves and masters stopped running when they reached the camp. Tageas's men began whipping the slaves, in punishment for what the mercenaries had also done. Nikos looked for Jaen; he was not there. He had, Dalien reported, returned to the ship.

On reflection, Nikos thought that this was for the best. Ikeria would deal best with any clumsy qualms on Jaen's part, and there was nothing useful Jaen could have told him about the spiders in their altered state. This poison was just as new to Jaen as to Nikos, and Nikos had the observations of this afternoon to guide him tomorrow. Tomorrow he would lose no men. Today's losses had not been high—two slaves and a relatively untried mercenary. But tomorrow he would lose not even that.

The first slave bitten was not dead. Nikos examined him with interest: the man's features had thickened with a tumescent pale waxiness Nikos had never seen. He could barely move, and clearly could not work. He kept trying to speak, but could manage only "do-de-ne." The priest also examined him, after which Nikos ordered him killed and both slaves' bodies buried with a purification ritual.

Three men was not an unprofitable loss. But tomorrow he would lose none.

In the morning, when the Therans finally took the Stone from the Grove, Arachne stood on top of the colonnade.

She watched the trader climb down a rope ladder into the hole around the Spider Stone. After a measureless time he climbed up again. Arachne saw first the glint of sunlight on his black hair, then one arm emerge from under the edge of the Stone, and finally his body, foreshortened, stand erect and brush the dirt from his chiton. She was too far away to see his expression, but she knew what it would be: the abacus eyes stilled with satisfaction and competence. He spoke to his commander of the guard. The commander nodded, and the two walked between their net of ropes toward the burning trench. Jaen was not in the Grove.

The ruined Grove was all circles: the trench circling the web of ropes circling the dark hole of nothingness circling the Spider Stone. From inside these circles, men glanced up at Arachne, their faces brown blurs flashing toward her and then away. She learned nothing from the distant faces, nor had she expected to. She expected nothing: not to learn, not to influence, not to communicate. When Kyles had left the chamber by the sea with Amaura and with the funeral jar holding Pholen's body, all Arachne's expectations had come to an end. She crouched on top of the colonnade and watched the desecration of the Grove because she had to. She could not do nothing, and she could not think what else to do. So she watched.

The men rigged the ropes from the Stone to pulleys and then to a metal wheel just inside the burning trench. The wheel was anchored by more ropes to several of the columns of the southeastern side of the colonnade. Nikos raised one hand and brought it down sharply. Men began to heave on the metal wheel. The Spider Stone rose slightly. A loud crack split the air; one rope broke. Tageas shouted. The Stone settled back into its trough, and men began to unwind, untie, and replace the broken rope.

On the second attempt, the Stone was pulled from its hole. It came slowly, majestic and cool in the midst of the straining, shouting men. Wool padded both the hole's rim and the waiting rollers made from the felled trees. The Stone was pulled directly onto the rollers, and it did not scratch or break. No spiders poured forth from its upended bottom. The operation went smoothly and without mishap.

The tapering sides of the Stone did not narrow to the point Nikos had expected. The bottom was flat, a circle with the diameter of Nikos's forearm between elbow and wrist. Although it felt like the same material as the rest of the Stone, the bottom was opaque in a disturbing way. Light seemed not so much to vanish into the bottom of the Stone as not to exist near it, not even the direct brilliant light of an Island morning. Absurd as it seemed, the Stone's end was difficult to actually *see*. Nikos could be sure of its dimensions only by reaching into that prelight nothingness and tracing them with his hands. The bottom of the Stone felt cool and rough, but not gritty.

"Did you ever see a piece of amber?" Nikos asked Tageas.

"No, Trader."

"Expensive goods. When you rub it, it gives off an agreeable odor, and when you light it, it burns. This does neither. But pieces of amber are nearly this color, and they too always have one rough, semiextended point where the amber was formed. Like this. Amber oozes from a living thing."

"Yes?" Tageas said indifferently. He looked frankly bored.

Unimaginative, Nikos thought again. He said abruptly, "See if there is anything else buried in that hole, below the Stone. Dig again at least as deep as a man's height."

"Yes, Trader."

Slaves began to pull on the Stone. It moved easily, even gracefully, over the padded rollers until it reached the last one. Tageas
shouted a command. The slaves stopped heaving, the rollers were
moved from the back of the Stone to the front, and the men pulled
again. The Stone glided forward, dazzling in the sunshine, until it
came to the burning trench.

"We can fill it in enough to make a bridge," Tageas said, "or we
can roll the Stone from one set of rollers to another through the
fire. You say it doesn't burn. That way we keep a protected circle,
and finish sooner."

Nikos glanced at the sun, still high in the bright sky. From the
corner of his eye he glimpsed Arachne, a still dark shape atop the
colonnade.

"Fill the trench in. Fire may not harm the Stone, but I want none
of that fluid on it. Don't move the pulleys; the men can haul the
Stone directly now that it's free of the hole."

The Stone rode smoothly across the bridge of tamped earth.
Flames burned fitfully on either side, throwing onto the Stone's
amber translucence swirling patterns of light. A slight breeze blew
up, fanning the flames and blowing the stench of the Grove across
the polished surface of the Stone. In light and stink and flames, the
Stone passed through the Grove, through the colonnade and corridor, and out of the villa.

When no one was left in the Grove, Nikos returned. He climbed
into the hole the slaves had deepened after the removal of the
Stone. That curious lightless bottom of the Stone—like amber,
which oozed only from a living source. Nikos searched carefully,
his deep eyes thoughtful.

But the hole remained empty.

Still, on the whole Nikos was pleased. Later that night, watching
the Spider Stone at the camp outside the villa walls, he anticipated
no further difficulties. Figures swarmed near the Stone: Tageas's
men, guarding against any belated attack; Dalien, measuring the
Stone for exact dimensions; the priest, putting on it varying fluids
and observing the results. Some of the fluids were holy oils. The
greater number were potions that would show whether the material
of the Stone could withstand salt water, fish oils, seaweed, gull
droppings. Nikos knew he had planned well.

In the morning the Stone would be moved to the Southern
Shore. That should present no obstacles: the slope was steep
enough to give the Stone momentum but not steep enough to risk
its breaking away. There was an unobstructed, if not direct, route
over easy terrain that could accommodate rollers. The voyage from
Island to Thera would require care, but it was possible. Nikos had
seen the transporting of huge blocks of marble, as big as the Spider
Stone and much denser, over the sea from quarries on outlying
islands to Thera itself. He had studied the technique, as he studied
everything that could someday prove profitable. The Stone would
be lashed to immense poles—even now his men were felling suit-
able trees on the Southern Shore—and floated from them between
Nikos's ship and Jaen's all the way to Thera. They would lose all
the oars on one side of each ship, of course, but the weight of the
men on the other would balance the Stone. Nikos's navigator was
skillful enough to maneuver both ships as one, and to synchronize
both sets of oarsmen to one rhythm. The load would be bulky and
the voyage slow, but the weather would hold. And there were
contingency plans if it did not. Nikos always prepared contingency
plans; only fools or ascetics would forego the pleasure that resulted
from an operation imaginatively and profitably executed. Planning
and execution—as perfectly balanced as the Stone in its hole—were
almost sensual. Thera herself held no greater beauty, not to the
discerning.

Nikos's planning had included the spiders. They lived already
aboard the ship, captured weeks ago to be sure they would eat and
spin in captivity. They had. Housed in thick-walled metal boxes
which floated always upright in vats of fresh water. the spiders were
protected from the sounds and rhythms of the sea. Once at Thera,
the spiders could be lightly drugged and then defanged. Nikos had
seen that technique performed far to the east, and had studied it
with great interest. It, too, would prove profitable.

The priest finished his work. The Stone started its descent of the
long slope of land to the Southern Shore, hauled by sweating slaves.
Before it passed from sight of the villa, Nikos climbed a high
outcropping of rock and gazed backwards curiously. On the top of
the villa's southern wall stood a figure, a tiny brown speck in the
clear light.

—Book II—
THE LOOM

But we, they say, live a safe life at home,
While they, the men, go forth in arms to war.
Fools! Three times would I rather take my stand
With sword and shield than bring to birth one child.
                                    —EURIPIDES, *Medea*

17

BY full summer the villa lay deserted and dusty under the hot sun. Lizards ran up the stone walls, noiseless. Already a few chinks in the walls had widened, and a few blocks of stone had fallen into the corridors where only the lizards moved. One winter more, and grass would reclaim the walks. The stone baked silently under a motionless sky brilliant with hard blue light. Of all the noise and movement that had thronged the corridors there remained only Arachne and Suva: Arachne bound to the desolation by grief, Suva by triumph.

On Midsummer afternoon Suva stood at the top of the northwest cliff, where the wide footpath began its snaking descent to the harbor below. She wore finely spun white wool fastened with a clasp of coiled gold sea snake. The chiton was too big for her; like the clasp, it had been Arachne's. On her head sat a crude bronze helmet, also too big, to which were tied some white feathers. Sweat trickled from under the helmet and over her cheeks. She carried a shield, partially polished by someone who knew nothing of metals, and a spear. Her bearing was solemn, a regal wizened figure with eyes both shining with excitement and curiously opaque, like polished stones.

She took a deep breath and started down the footpath to the sea.

Her footfalls startled a snake and it slithered into the dry grass. Suva did not notice. Below her lay the sea, the only motion she saw, the only sound she heard.

Halfway down the path, she coughed. The cough became persistent, and then violent. The old woman's body bent nearly double and, bent, jerked from side to side. With one hand she fumbled at her girdle and pulled from it a piece of white silk, pressing it to her mouth. The coughing, chest-deep and swampy, worsened. Suva squatted on the path, yanked off her helmet, and gave all her energy to coughing. Phlegm and mucus spat into the silk. With one last convulsion, the coughing ceased. The phlegm on the white silk was streaked with red.

Blood! Suva was delighted. There was no stronger omen. Always it was blood that marked celebration, and for *this* celebration, sacred and solitary, the blood of the usual sacrificial goat would not have done. Only the blood of a goddess would do.

Carefully Suva tucked the bloody silk back into her girdle, and the helmet onto her head.

No fishing boats were pulled up onto the beach. Suva supposed, without interest, that the Islanders had come by water and claimed their boats months ago. But Arachne had stayed, and that was all that mattered. A mother-goddess must have at least one mortal daughter, as well as her immortal one safe within. And hadn't she, Suva, been the one to mother Arachne when the child's mortal mother had been claimed by the sea? All those years of servitude for them both: Suva as a slave, Arachne with the men-dung of her House. So it often went with the gods: disguise and strife. But now she and Arachne each stood clear, and Suva saw with exultation and triumph what the trust of her godhead would be: to guard and comfort the abandoned Arachne, daughter and handmaiden and the only one left to Suva to love.

And now Arachne was all hers.

Hers, murmured the sea below. *Hers, hers,* and Suva thought that never before had she been so happy.

She finished the descent to the beach. Pebbles cut into her bare feet, but she scarcely noticed. At the water's edge, she halted. Before her lay the sea.

For just a moment, a blackness stirred in her mind—blackness so terrible her face lost its impersonal shining and looked human. The mouth took an individual quirk, the eyes a quick sharpness, the muscles of cheek and jaw a terrified and personal tension. Suva clutched her shield and raised her arms. Then the blackness slid away, and the shield stilled. The old woman's face became again regal and blank, wiped clean of the chortling fear, the perverse gaity, the thrashing and malice that had been the mortal Suva.

The goddess waded into the sea. One hand held shield and spear, the other stroked her belly. Knee-deep in the water, she lay down on her back, head pointed to the sea and feet to land. To keep her head above water, she had to bend her back and flail with her arms. Flailing, she spread her legs wide and took in the sea.

"It is done!" Suva cried, and threw the phlegm-slimed silk high in the air. It arced over the water and fell an arm's length away, a bloody island. Sea birds flashed from the cliff to converge on it, screaming and fighting. Suva laughed, swallowed water, and began to cough. Coughs racked her, and she flailed and thrashed, muddying the water.

Blood and phlegm wrenched from her lungs and stained the sea. Suva struggled, slipped, regained her feet. Finally the coughing passed, and she stood exhausted in the shallows. Around her the gulls screamed; she heard the screams as music, triumphant and sweet. The sun flashed on their white wings and on her helmet and shield. Suva spread her arms and raised them over the birds, the sea, the cliffs, the hot sky.

Hers—they were all hers. Over them she held her power. She was powerful beyond mortal hurting, blameless of mortal error, cleansed and newborn. She could protect Arachne, and in return Arachne would love her, Suva. Suva laughed, and her black eyes shone.

The goddess walked out of the bloody sea to the singing of birds, in the clear and truthful light.

During the day, Arachne grieved coldly, with set face and with driving motions that produced nothing.

It might be that others found rest from their grief in rest for their bodies, Arachne thought. She had seen women who, grieving for husbands dead too young or parents dead at their time, sat at windows and watched grapes ripen or birds peck at their grain. After days or weeks or months, they rose to take another husband or to become parents to their own children. The stillness, Arachne saw, had held the beginning and ending of their anguish together and let it heal. It was not so with her. Stillness was too much like death.

So in the long months since the Spider Stone had been taken from Island, she had worked at everything—except weaving. Her work was mostly unnecessary; the storage magazines were full of harvest for an entire villa. Arachne carried up food and prepared it, performing the unfamiliar tasks neither well nor badly. She drew water, tended fires, baked breads, washed clothing, scrubbed floors. All this, which Suva had once done and did no longer now that she was a goddess, Arachne did coldly and without thought, because it needed to be done and because stillness was intolerable.

The workrooms of potters and sandal makers and wood turners, all deserted now, stood a few corridors away from her sea chambers. Arachne began to go to them. She used the turning of the potter's wheel, the rise and fall of the awl, the endless smoothing of rough wood to give motion to the spring and summer. She made nothing worth keeping, and she made many of them.

If a pot or shoulder clasp or leather work had turned out to be worth its materials, she would have smashed it. So much had been smashed. The mutilated Grove. Pholen, folded in his funeral jar. Kyles, bitter in his distant vineyard. Amaura, gone with her father for some reason Arachne could not name but in which she sensed a dizzying drunkenness. The last of Suva's precarious reason. All smashed, and in her cold daytime grief Arachne would make nothing less broken than they. It was the grief of an active mind and body, for which skill and resolve were so much acts of life that only pointless ineptitude was left for death. So she threw lopsided pots, tooled unwearable sandals, polished wormy wood, and the motions filled the days.

Never did she walk near the mutilated Grove.

Often she thought of Kyles—more often than in the whole of their marriage. In the silence of her days, it came to her that Kyles had used so few words because to him each carried so much weight: entire speeches packed dangerously into small words dense and heavy as stone. He had been reluctant to risk his being to such words, that could sink so fast.

Only to her had he risked that self, and lost. Whether from rank, or love, or some terrible incompleteness of his own, Kyles had given into her judgment his worthiness as husband, bed partner, and warrior. And one by one, she had stopped him from succeeding at each. Jaen would say men should not give such judgments to a woman.

But Jaen himself had given them to a city.

In the first months, Arachne saw spiders along the corridors and in the workrooms. She never broke her stride or altered her time-filling motions. If it happened that a spider bit her, she would die; if no spider bit her, she would not. She thought this clearly, and not even in the most anguished of her grief did she mistake it for bravery. Like the bad pottery, it was a fact, uninteresting and cold.

But at night, grief turned still and hot.

Each time she woke it was in the same position, lying on her back, hands flung above her head and crossed as if pinned. There was no moment of forgetfulness or drowsiness. She woke and it was all before her: the mutilated Grove, Pholen folded in his funeral jar, Kyles bitter in his distant vineyard, Amaura and Jaen gone. Arachne lay rigid in the darkness, seeing it all, and the hot grief slid down her cheeks and burned.

She tried, in the sleepless nights, to think about the responsibility for what had happened to Island, to Pholen, to Kyles. She was not responsible that the spiders, the Grove's creatures, had become poisonous in the Grove's death throes. But, she thought painfully as moonlight traveled ghostly across the stone floor, responsibility was not always direct. Light would not bend around corners, but the ground behind a wall does not lie in total darkness. Responsibility, too, could be reflected, colored, absorbed by the objects that lay in its path.

She realized that the idea was not hers. Jaen had said it once, long ago. She had not seen then what he meant. It had often been so. Blind.

Jaen and Kyles, both, had called her blind.

She didn't dream of Jaen or Kyles. She had expected to dream of Pholen and Amaura, but only one dream ever stayed in her memory, and it held neither of her lost children. In the dream she stood in the Grove and wove the ash-haze silk. It was a vivid dream, far more vivid than anything in her cold and moving days. She felt in her muscles each motion of shuttle and beater, and heard clearly the whisper-knock, whisper-knock of the loom. The colors of the silk were sharp and clear. She saw the grain of the loom's wood, the splinter curling from the left upright, the intricate design of the basket holding the spider fibers. The silk grew like a living thing under her fingers, and when she woke the hands pinned above her head tingled with life.

In all the busy gray death, only the dream of weaving held color and life.

Summer turned to harvest. Arachne saw no one except Suva. She didn't know if Island was having a harvest, or had had a planting. Although she could have left the villa and walked along the coast, she never did. Her grief was not so exclusive that she couldn't wonder how her people fared. It was, rather, that the Islanders were no longer her people. Delernos had led them to exile, and they had been rewarded with the Grove. Arachne and Jaen had led them to the long battles to keep the Grove, and they had been rewarded with poison.

"The Mistress should not fish like any slave or peasant," Suva said. She stood on the harbor beach, wearing helmet and spear, standing guard. From under the helmet her gray hair hung in the braids of a maiden chaste for the priesthood.

"We have no meat," Arachne said, knee-deep in the water. "And I often fished as a child with—do not stand in the sun, Suva. There's shade by the cliff."

"I do not need shade."

"You'll have another attack of dizziness. And that will start you coughing."

"No. I do not need shade."

"As you wish," Arachne said shortly. She had hitched her chiton around her waist and stood trawling with a small net, aware of the picture she presented: the former Mistress of Island, her silks stained with seaweed and her hair over her eyes. But there was no one to see except the sea birds and Suva, who followed Arachne wherever she went. In the early numb weeks Arachne had scarcely noticed the old woman's presence. Afterwards she had been resentful that she could never be alone. Suva was always there! It was intolerable. Nonetheless, she had not ordered Suva away. Watching the old woman polish her pathetic helmet, listening to her prattle of being a goddess, Arachne's resentment had softened to pity. Where could Suva go, if not with Arachne? They were, both of them, exiles. And Suva, too, had once lost a child. In her bitterest moments, Arachne wondered if injury did not forge stronger bonds than joy.

In addition, Arachne doubted that Suva would leave her even if she were ordered. The old woman, freed from the constraints of rank by having become a goddess, used the freedom to behave to Arachne as whatever her wandering mind dictated at the moment: guard, mother, adviser, dependent, nurse, ruler, deity. She was all the departed people of Island in one mad hag. All day she pulled at Arachne, bullying her, smothering her, demanding that Arachne lift her eyes from her own spiritual maiming and instead regard Suva's, which cavorted grotesquely before her, needing to be propped or staunched or answered. Always answered. If Suva's rantings were not answered, she would tremble and cry, and that would lead her to cough and spit blood. So Arachne answered her and, without realizing it, each time she answered she broke for a moment the strangling obsession with her own despair.

Suva's madness kept Arachne sane.

"I protect you," Suva said from the beach. "While I watch over you, you are safe."

"I am not afraid."

"Ignorance is never afraid. Yesterday I found wild pigs within the corridors. One had come as far as the colonnade, and died there of a spider bite."

Arachne stood still. A fish swam into her net, thrashed briefly, and backed out when she did not lift the net. She said slowly, "You go to the colonnade? That far?"

"A goddess goes where she chooses."

"Suva—"

"The pigs might have a boar nearby. You are fortunate to walk under the shield and sword of an immortal."

"Suva—is there anyone else in the villa? Do you ever see signs of another person besides you and me?"

"A goddess needs no one else."

Another fish swam by. Arachne twisted her net, caught it, and carried it to shore. With her knife she severed the head from the body. Fluid gushed onto the stones.

"Blood," Suva said. She held out to Arachne a piece of white silk stained with blood and phlegm, and smiled regally. "Soon I will need a shroud."

Arachne straightened.

"Did you think," Suva said severely, "that I could stay in mortal form to guard you forever? A goddess should not be so constrained. But before I leave you, I will give you this honor: you shall weave my funeral shroud."

"No," Arachne said. *"No."* She saw Pholen, curled in his funeral jar, his eyes shriveling under the azure lid.

Suva said tenderly, "Don't be so distressed, Arachne. Your work will be acceptable. Do you think a goddess of wisdom would ask of her daughter more than she can perform?"

Arachne squatted on the beach and began to clean her fish. "Suva. I no longer weave. Haven't you seen that, following me everywhere?"

"Protecting you."

"Protecting me, then. I do not weave. I will never weave again, not a shroud nor anything else. All that is over." She stared fiercely at Suva, and then again at her fish. Her knife flew over the scales.

"A magnificent shroud," Suva said, "fit offering for a goddess. It should be a tapestry, with scenes of Island from which I sprang."

"No!"

"Do you dare to challenge a goddess?" Suva cried, and thumped her spear on the ground. She began to cough. Arachne held her elbow and the old woman bent and hacked, gasping for a clear breath. She brought blood and phlegm up from her lungs and spat them out. The fish at their feet became marked with flecked slime.

When Suva could speak, she said, "It will be a beautiful tapestry. An offering fit for a goddess. Yes." She straightened her helmet. Arachne helped her up the path to the villa, leaving the fish behind.

In Arachne's chamber, Aretone waited.

Arachne was so startled to see her that she nearly cried out. Aretone looked shocking, bending over some unfired pottery, because her configuration of arms and head and chiton was not Suva's. For months she had seen no one else; anyone else looked foreign.

"Aretone!"

"Mistress! You *are* here! I saw the food and pottery and I thought —" She did not say what she had thought but stood smiling warily, a handsome woman with tired eyes. She wore unbleached wool. Arachne had seldom seen her, like all her women, in anything but spider silk.

"How did you come?"

"Along the sea to the villa, then through corridors as close to the cliffs as I could."

Aretone's eyes flickered over her. Arachne saw how she must look, in her wet chiton hitched to the waist, stained with fish and bloody phlegm. Aretone looked sane, ordinary. Watching her, hunger for the ordinary life she had exiled herself from hit Arachne so suddenly she felt dizzy.

"Tell me. Aretone—tell me."

Aretone understood. "Most people have left Island. The spiders spread out from the villa to the rest of Island. Each day they crawled further east. Farmers and herders left for Bylia or the smaller islands, or they moved to the shore. The spiders still do not come near shore. People who would not move, died."

"Kyles and Amaura?"

"Still at the vineyard. It is close enough to the sea. The higher hills were not planted this year, but the lower ones were planted as usual."

"How—"

"Amaura is . . . Amaura," Aretone said carefully. "Wilful. She is growing very beautiful."

"Kyles?"

Aretone answered steadily. "He drinks wine. Far too much wine, Mistress."

Arachne did not flinch. She saw Kyles standing drunk in her chamber, tasted again her surprise and distaste. Again he held his clenched fist on the small table, and hurled the wine goblet against the wall.

Bluntly, Arachne asked the question. "Is he unmanned?"

"He beds none of the slave women," Aretone said. "For the rest, he does not say. No one knows. Forgive me, Mistress, but I would not take it as a bad sign that he beds no one. He never wanted any but you."

Arachne averted her face. Aretone continued, "Cleis is at the farm with me, as is her father. They are well. Cleis plans to marry Epaka, the potter."

Aretone's voice had changed on the word "marry." Arachne said, "And your husband? Akeumis?"

"Dead," Aretone said quietly. "Bitten at the planting moon."

"I am sorry."

"He died easily," Aretone said firmly, "and now he lives with the Goddess. Mistress, come with me to the farm. You have shut yourself up to grieve alone too long. It is enough."

"I am not alone. Suva is here."

Aretone grinned. Arachne stared; she had not seen anyone grin like that in nearly a year. Aretone's grin was tough: it mocked Arachne's words, and Suva, and the year that had produced them. To Arachne the grin looked obscene—belittling, trivializing—and then it did not. Something stirred in her at Aretone's grin, something resilient that had been frozen under her pain and anger, but lived still. She said, "Suva has become a goddess."

Aretone grimaced, without surprise. "She was always crazy. You cannot stay here with a madwoman."

"I cannot leave."

"In the Name of the Goddess—why *not?*" Aretone spoke to her as she would never have done before the ruin of Island. Arachne heard the difference; Aretone did not.

They had greeted each other so frankly, Arachne thought, and with such relief. But now, already, their talk was looped about with things left unsaid. Arachne knew plainly what Aretone was not saying: I, too, have lost a loved one to the spiders, yet I do not shut myself away in a deserted chamber alone. I do not brood night and day, I do not turn myself away from the living, I do not make of my anguish a grotesque wallow. Why then should you, who are the first among us, Mistress of Island and heir of the House of Delernos, be prowling a deserted harbor in a dirty chiton smelling of fish? But all Aretone said aloud was, "Do you stay here because of Kyles?"

"What has he said?"

"I told you, Kyles says nothing. Even in his wine, he is silent. He says only to leave him alone, and take any grievances to you, the ruler of Island."

Arachne winced.

"You do not have to see him. The vineyard is not near my farm." Arachne did not answer. After a silence Aretone said, her face showing that it was a new thought, "You blame yourself as much as Kyles blames you."

"Mine was the responsibility for Island."

"For Island, yes. But not for the Grove. You did not cause its sickness and death, and you could not have stopped it. The Goddess knows you tried hard enough. No blame is yours for the Grove, or for what happened there."

"The Therans would not have come had they not seen my silk."

"It was not you who showed it to them."

"It was I who weaved it."

Aretone looked around the chamber, studying it. Her gaze took in the lopsided pots, the cooking utensils on the hearth, the fishing net spread to dry over a silken couch. Arachne knew what she sought, and said before Aretone could ask, "No. I do not weave."

"Not even wool?"

"Not even wool."

"You were a better weaver than you are a potter," Aretone said, and again came that tough, shocking grin.

"Yes. I was too good a weaver."

"In the Name of the Goddess—Arachne, forgive me. I speak too bluntly. Islanders said foolish things the night the Grove turned poison. But despite what was said, your weaving is not responsible for the Therans. You are not responsible. Everything important that happened in the Grove would have happened had the Mistress of Island been not a weaver but a fisherwoman. Or a jeweler. Or an idiot. If you stay here from a sense of responsibility violated, it is a wasted gesture. I don't believe in wasted gestures. Come with me to the farm, and bring that worthless Suva, if she cannot be left."

"I don't know if she can be brought."

"She is a slave."

"She insists she is a goddess."

"And you believe her?"

"Oh, Aretone—of course not."

"Then?" Aretone said. She made a quick sound and then tried to look as if she had not. But Arachne heard the sound: exasperation, distaste, impatience. It was a sound Arachne herself had once made often; she did so no longer. Aretone, embarrassed, walked to a table and bent over Arachne's unfired pottery. She touched the careless curves, the uneven thickness of clay that would crack if it were put into the kiln. Aretone stood still and then turned slowly, and Arachne could see from her face that she had a new thought, one that was not welcome.

"It's not responsibility that keep you in this stubborn exile, is it? Or that keeps you from weaving? It's not Suva. It's not grief over Pholen, or Kyles, or . . . or even Jaen. It's the Grove. Still."

Arachne looked out the window, over the sea.

"You are supposed to be the Mistress of Island!"

"I am no longer the Mistress of Island. My last act as Mistress of Island was to send word for its Master to mutilate the Grove. By that act, I ended my right to be Mistress of Island." She saw that Aretone did not understand. Her face said plainly that Arachne and Jaen had been heirs, so Arachne and Jaen were Mistress and Master; all else was nonsense.

"No," Arachne said softly. "It is not nonsense."

"Do you visit the Grove?"

"Never. But sometimes I dream—" She did not finish. There was no way to explain the dream of weaving in the Grove, its bright clarity the only unfinished significance in the finished insignificance Island had become.

Aretone made the sound again, and this time she did not look embarrassed. "You were a rational and bold girl, Arachne, and a rational and bold woman. The best weaver among us, the fearless ruler. But now you cower here with a mad slave because of a dream you cannot describe—it is not right. Kyles is . . . you are the only one who might help him. He behaves like a man who cannot forgive himself some great shame. He is drunk more days than not. Amaura roams the hills, where the spiders are, and takes terrible risks in the sea. I have seen her swim out to sea until she so exhausted that her return rests solely with currents and tides and the whims of the Goddess. I am told she will take a spider on her open palm and hold herself perfectly still, to see what will happen. Kyles does not control her. He cannot."

Arachne listened with her head rigid. *Amaura.* Finally she said, "I could not control her either."

"Come with me, Arachne."

"I *cannot.*"

"You mean you will not. You are not bound here."

"Yes. I am bound here," Arachne said.

Aretone's face closed. She had, Arachne saw, put the Grove and its life behind her, and gone on to another, just as Jaen had. If Aretone could do that, no words would tell her why Arachne could not. She, like Jaen, must have stood only in the edge of the pattern that had been the Grove, must have seen only the reflection, only the diffused golden glow of light behind walls. Aretone had not reached, or been reached, by that golden radiance, the open door, that was the Grove at its height, and so she felt only an intermittent regret for something beautiful, seen but never actually possessed. There was no way to explain loss to one who has never known possession. Aretone did not know that a soul could be bound as tightly by what is not, as by what is.

Arachne said simply, "I am bound. Else it all comes to nothing."

Pity and hardness struggled in Aretone's eyes. Hardness won. "It *has* come to nothing. The Grove is gone. Dreams and fancies, Mistress, are not for me. I am not a priestess, nor a goddess. But if I had a daughter too wild and a husband drinking his manhood to a deliberate death, I would not give myself to dreams and fancies."

"I cannot do otherwise," Arachne said, and remembered when she had said the words before: in the apotheca, to Jaen.

"You *will* not do otherwise."

"Aretone! Do you truly not remember how it was in the Grove? Am I the only one who truly remembers?"

Something—memory, or the denial of memory—flickered behind Aretone's eyes. But she would not give in. "I will not remember. I choose not to remember."

"Like Suva," Arachne said swiftly, and she did not entirely keep contempt from her voice.

Aretone rose angrily. "I am not a slave."

"Suva would say we are all slaves," Arachne said, scowling. The idea was not new to her, and she hated it. "That is what her stories all meant, all those stories of cruelty and suffering—that mortals are slaves of the whims of gods."

"Once the Mistress of Island did not take her wisdom from a mad old woman. Nor her perceptions of the Goddess." Aretone crossed the room, her back rigid. But at the door she hesitated and turned. "Arachne—is that what your dream was? That it is the Goddess who wishes you to remain near the Grove?"

Now Arachne hesitated. She could see how it would be if she answered yes. The dream would become to Aretone the major obstacle, known and thus able to be chipped at it with Island's blend of skepticism for divine particulars and faith in divine generalities. Aretone would argue for other interpretations of the weaving dream, suggest a substitute sacrifice or libation, bring the priestess to be consulted. Aretone would consider Arachne merely misled rather than stubbornly mad. A dream was a common thing, and so there would be between them common words to discuss it. Not until she had seen Aretone bending over the unfired pots did Arachne realize how she had missed common words with a rational speaker. If she agreed that, yes, the Goddess had sent her a dream to remain near the Grove, the cold silence of her isolation would be warmed a little by Aretone's acceptance, and even more by the energy of her response. All Arachne need say is yes, the Goddess sent her the dream.

But no goddess had anything to do with it.

"No," Arachne said fiercely, "my dream was not a wish from the Goddess."

"Then I will leave you now, Mistress," Aretone said, too formally.

Arachne did not detain her. But when Aretone had gone, Arachne found that two things remained behind her: the strength in her tough grin, and the image of Amaura holding on her palm a deadly spider, her strange light eyes moving to follow its crawl.

18

WHEN on the next day Arachne returned from the harbor, her loom stood in the middle of her chamber.

Slowly she circled the loom. It was hers. The wood grain of the beam and uprights was as familiar as the veins on the backs of her hand; the splinter projecting from the left side was exactly as in her dream. The wooden dowels holding uprights to base and beam were loose. The loom had been disassembled to move it and then reassembled in the chamber, not quite tightly, by someone who lacked the strength to twist the dowels closely. Suva, of course. On the floor by the loom sat the shuttle and baskets of silk fibers, more silk than Arachne supposed Nikos had left in all of Island. Her eyes, after months of white plaster rooms and unbleached wool, ached with the colors heaped unsorted in the baskets: emerald, indigo, amber, sable, azure, dove, magenta, gold. And scarlet—Jaen's scarlet. In her fingers Arachne could feel the texture of that scarlet, hear how it slid on her shuttle through the warp, see it shading or not shading into lesser colors of silk. She stared at the scarlet fibers as if at dung.

"I have brought you the stuffs for my shroud," Suva said from the hearth. She wore her helmet and shield. From under the helmet her hair hung in greasy braids. An unwashed smell rose from her whenever she moved. Daily her old body deteriorated more.

"No," Arachne said. "I told you no."

"'The shroud will glow with scenes of the Island that sprang forth a full-grown goddess," Suva said. "And with scenes of the sea. Of the singing birds and the sea."

Arachne stared at her loom. The bright clarity of the dream rose before her, and the ash-haze silk grew under her hands. She could feel her fingers itch with desire for the shuttle, and its whisper-knock, whisper-knock stirred against her ears.

Almost, she told Suva yes, she would weave for her the shroud. But the moment she framed the words, the impulse died. She could not. The last time, she had woven the ash-haze silk, so that later it could hang dripping from Ikeria's fingers while Jaen watched with hungry eyes. She could not. Not again.

And even in weaving the ash-haze silk, even when the Grove was dying, Arachne had known that it was not only she who moved the shuttle. If there hadn't been the lost golden radiance breathed in through dazzled lips and given out again in flying fingers, there had nonetheless been *something.* She had not been completely alone. Some other power had helped form those desperate shapes and cinder-cold haze. Some other, dying order—

Slowly Arachne said, "I have already woven one shroud."

Suva did not ask when. She smiled with patient reason, as if to a child, her black eyes tender. "You shall weave another."

"I no longer weave."

"But I decree that you shall, my Arachne. You shall weave my shroud, and mortals shall marvel at the fineness of the work and the life of the designs."

"No."

Suva breathed harder. "Think again before you challenge a goddess!" She thumped the butt of her spear on the floor. The loose flesh under her arms jiggled.

Irritation swept through Arachne. Suva was ridiculous, exasperating, pathetic. Nothing she said was woven to any reality. Loose gossamer, lost on her own silly winds. Arachne scowled.

Suva looked at Arachne's face, and her own changed. Her brows quirked, and her eyes sparkled with sudden, malicious life. Even her voice changed, losing its sonorous pronouncements and glinting as if sharp inflections were not sound but light.

"Once there was a maiden who cried for the moon. Her father was a powerful nobleman and he ordered slaves to climb the highest mountain and bring the moon down to her. Any man who failed was to be beheaded. Hundreds died, screaming in their blood. Finally a desperate slave found on the mountain a round globe of amber. He brought it down, calling it the moon. The next night happened to be moonless, and the maid believed she held the moon in her arms. She took it to bed with her. In the middle of the night, wishing to look at and fondle the treasure to which she had given her heart, she lit the lamp. Her elbow knocked it over. The bed hangings caught on fire, and in the fire the amber moon was consumed, leaving the maiden weeping and dirty in the ashes."

Arachne, listening warily, assumed this was the end of the simple tale. But Suva continued.

"Once there was a white bull so beautiful a queen fell in love with it. She gave herself to it inside a wooden cow, and became heavy with child. Their child was a monster, half bull and half man, eater of human flesh. Thus was the sacred beginning of the cities of Thera, where your man-curse Jaen has gone. Eater of human flesh."

Suva laid a finger under her nose and worked it obscenely. "Once there was a grove so golden a lady fell in love with it. She declared the grove sacred, and gave herself to it. Their children were golden spiders, who became eaters of human flesh. Thus was the sacred ending of Island."

Suva let out a shriek of laughter and flourished her shield. Whooping and gasping, she thumped her spear on the floor until the stone rang. The wild laughter turned to coughing, and then to spitting blood. Between bouts of forcing phlegm from her swampy lungs, Suva looked up at Aachne and said clearly, "A shroud for a goddess. I trust it to you." She bent double with the coughing, clutching chest and belly, until the fit had passed and she rose shakily, staring at Arachne with old, scared eyes.

The storage magazines, half underground and windowless, smelled of damp earth. Great clay pithoi as tall as a grown man lined one wall; smaller jars ringed the other three. Arachne held her lamp at shoulder height and the light cast wavering circles on smooth clay curves, tightly corked necks, double handles as arched as scimitars. They held oil, wine, grain, dried fruits paid in taxes to the Household of Island.

One such as these held Pholen.

Arachne moved her lamp over the smaller jars, searching for one marked to hold oil. The lamps above were nearly empty of oil. When she found one, against the wall in a far corner, she shifted the lamp to her left hand and hoisted the jar with her right. The handle felt smooth and cool.

On the earthen floor, in the center of the faint circle left by the bottom of the jar, lay a dead spider.

Usually the spiders shriveled rapidly after death, but this one had remained firm and whole. Perhaps, Arachne thought numbly, it had been preserved by the cool darkness under the jar. But no—the earth was too damp. The spider was not at all flattened, and she lifted the jar to shoulder height and ducked her head to see the jar's bottom. The clay formed a rim and then curved slightly upward; the jar had not rested directly on the spider's body. One section of the rim was chipped. The spider had squeezed itself through the opening, crawled under the jar, and died.

Of what?

Carefully, as if both were more fragile than they actually were, Arachne set down the oil jar and the lamp. With two fingers she picked up the spider, set it on the palm of her other hand, and lifted the lamp to hold it close to the corpse. She saw that the spider was young: the markings on its carapace were more chartreuse than jade, and its golden hairs were fine, almost downy. No part of the spider was deformed. Its eight legs formed perfect golden arcs; the fangs on its chelicerae were sharp.

Arachne turned the spider over. The six spinnerets under the abdomen were all perfect. From one dangled a tiny fragment of ashy silk.

It was the first spider she had seen since the summer. Carefully she lowered it back into the circle of damp earth and set the jar of oil above it. Climbing from the storage magazine into the sunlight, hard and cold between shifting clouds, she walked toward the Grove.

Where were the spiders? In the corridors she overturned clumps of plaster fallen from walls, felt with two fingers into cracks in the stone, forced doors and examined the deserted rooms, especially the corners farthest from any window. She found webs, their sticky silk still strong but crusted with dust and with dead, unwrapped insects. Nowhere did she find any spiders. Had they all died?

Or had they returned to the Grove?

Standing at the colonnade, Arachne paused. She had not seen the grove since the day Jaen had taken the Stone. Since the day the Grove had convulsed and turned to poison, and Pholen had died.

Something blew toward her on the cold wind, and at first she thought it was a scent. It tingled the nostrils like a scent, and Arachne breathed deeply and moved through the colonnade. The scent grew stronger, and the tingling did not stop at the nose. It played slowly over her face and then brushed her mind: delicate as a feather, but already with the warmth that comes from the first mouthfuls of new wine.

She stood very still.

The sensation surged, and it seemed to her that the cold sunlight grew warmer and shone on her bare head with a pearly sweetness. Then the sweetness sputtered and sank a little, like a lamp wick not yet fully caught. But the flame was there, and it came from the Grove.

The Grove stretched before her, looking the same as it had in the spring. Standing under the shelter of the colonnade, Arachne forced herself to look at it, though she was as unable to step down into the Grove as if she had been another of the stone columns. It came to her that she stood now under the colonnade at almost the same place she had stood on top of it that last day. In the Grove before her she saw the same scorched grass, the same hacked tree stumps and discarded branches rotting on the ground, the same pile of earth, like a farm yard dungheap, that had been thrown from the hole of the Stone. She could see the earthen lip of the hole although not, from this angle, down into it. Beyond, where the colonnade had been smashed to gape against the sky, the same broken columns sprawled next to the same stone rubble.

She could go no further. The warm tingling in her mind was fading now, and although the tingling had been silent, now Arachne heard Suva's voice, telling the stories of the maiden, the queen, and the lady. She heard, as well, Kyles's voice saying "The Mistress of Island beds only the Grove," and hated herself for remembering that now.

In a moment, however, the voices passed, pushed away by questions. What had caused the tingling warmth? It had had none of the clarity, none of the profound and grave joy of the old Grove. This sensation was uncertain and tentative. Yet—

Moving a few steps into the Grove, Arachne strained again after the sensation of tingling warmth. It did not come. Squatting on the grass, she turned over rocks and dug under weeds, searching at first carefully, then too frantic for care. But there were no spiders. The parts of webs she found were as dusty and filth-laden as the ones in the corridor.

Suddenly she was terribly afraid. But of what? She didn't know, and she realized that therein lay most of the fear. She didn't know what that tantalizing tingling portended, where it had come from, what had happened with all the spiders, what would happen next. But she had never feared things just because they were new; that had struck her as stupid. The completely new had as much chance of being good as of being bad. Or did she not believe that any longer?

No. Not any longer.

Still, she was not as afraid of what might have caused the tingling warmth as she was of the warmth itself, and that because it was *not* new. She recognized it. Pale, weak, tentative as it was—she recognized it. It was the radiance of the Grove, embryonic and faltering, and she found she was afraid of it. She was afraid she was mistaken, or that it would go away, or that it would not go away. Hope and hopelessness seemed equally terrible.

Arachne stood, and walked across the grass to the hole where the Spider Stone had been. Her face was rigid, and she did not feel the ground under her feet. She did not know what she expected to see, but as she leaned over the rim her teeth clenched so tightly that her jaw throbbed with pain.

The hole was empty.

All at once she was furious. The elusive tingle seemed a mockery, an obscene imitation of the radiant rightness that had been the gift of the Grove. A rightness that had led to death and destruction, pain and—yes, even as in Suva's story—the eating of flesh.

Furious still, Arachne strode away from the Grove and through the corridors to her chamber. The loom sat in it still, Beside it Suva sat splay-legged on the floor, playing with the untouched baskets of silk. She had spread them out in smooth, perfect straight skeins, grouping the skeins as a child would—as Pholen often had—by color. Rose shaded to scarlet to wine to russet to bronze to gold to amber. Suva crouched with her chiton over her knees where she had reached to scratch one flaccid thigh. Pink foam had dried at the corners of her mouth. When Arachne strode in, Suva held up a skein of spider silk.

"Blue. This blue for the background. This sea blue, and all the images on my shroud shall float on the sea."

Arachne glared. Fury and desolation were with her still, and so were Suva's stories of maiden, queen, and lady. "Suva. I have told you. I am not going to weave a shroud!"

"You are," Suva said regally, and scratched herself. "A goddess bids you."

Arachne turned her back. Somehow it had become a contest between them, pointless and stupid. A contest of will. Will—the force that she had once thought could, with desire, be the shaper of life. Will, perverted into a futile contest with a dying goddess.

I am as crazy as she is, Arachne thought, and closed her eyes against Suva, the loom, and all the bright skeins of spider silk blue as the sea.

Daily Arachne had carried fresh water from the nearby fountain house to the rooms she and Suva used. But now the spring, which bubbled up between the rocks on which the villa was built, had turned brackish. Last winter's rains had been too light; this winter's, which Arachne watched for daily, had not yet begun. She cleaned the spring, reaching with bare arms as deep into the opening between the rocks as she could, but the brackishness was not caused by any clogging. Even cleaned, the flow of water was sluggish and the water itself discolored and a little thick. Arachne tasted a mouthful and spat it out.

Another fountainhouse, larger and fed by a deeper spring, had supplied most of the villa's fresh water. The one Arachne had just cleaned had been used only by the Household apartments. The other fountainhouse stood near the Grove, behind the colonnade to the northeast. Picking up her jug, Arachne carried it through the corridors. The day was cloudy and cold, and she drew her cloak around her wet arms.

She had expected the spring in this fountain house, neglected nearly a year, to be clogged and dirty. Instead, water gushed cleanly from the spring. The fountainhouse had only two walls, yet the stone floor was free of dust or blowing leaves, and the sand around the spring was clean and raked. *Suva,* Arachne thought—Suva must have cleaned the spring. She roamed freely around the villa now, protected by her godhead, on whatever tasks were demanded of a mad goddess. It must have been Suva. But then Arachne saw the web.

It was large, hung between an overhead beam and the rough stone of one wall so that the web's bottom edge spanned the spring itself. The web was gray, but not the natural ashy gray of webs spun without pharmakons. This gray was pale and reflective; it caught even the dimmed light of a cloudy day under a roof and gave it back, sparkling a little. Arachne's first thought was that it was a new web, since it was free of dust and flies. But that could not be; that gray was a pharmakon color. Nor could the web have hung undisturbed since before the Islanders had fled the villa, or its viscid threads would have been as crusted and filthy as the webs she had seen in deserted rooms.

She stepped closer. Each strand of the web was as clean as the spring itself. Gently Arachne ran a finger over a spiral, and found it was smooth. Someone had washed the stickiness off each thread, strand by strand.

Suva? But Suva did not know what to mix with water to remove the silk's viscid coating—that was a skill left to Arachne and her women. The spiders were gone; it was only a matter of time before people began returning to the villa. Obviously one of her women had, and had washed the gray web. Who? Why?

The web's color reminded her of something, she could not think what. It also brought to mind so many other webs: the ash-haze web on the last night of the Grove, the deformed scarlet web she had seen with Jaen, webs remembered from childhood for their unusual places. Once one had been spun in Jaen's hair. He had fallen asleep stretched on the grass of the Grove, and as Arachne gleefully watched, a spider had spun a blue web from his curls to a thistle. Jaen, when he woke, had grumbled because the web had been blue rather than scarlet. It had made her angry, that he should pay more attention to the color than to the fact of the web itself—it had struck her as refusal of a gift, and she had slapped him. He slapped her back. They had been very young.

Remembering, Arachne smiled painfully. She dipped her hand into the spring and flicked water onto the gray web. It clung in tiny droplets, and a sudden shaft of sunlight from between the clouds made the droplets sparkle.

She filled her jug, balanced it on her head, and turned without looking again at the web. In the entrance to the fountainhouse stood Amaura.

She looked like Jaen. In the first shocked and painful moment of recognition, Arachne stared at nine months' changes in her daughter and saw Jaen in Amaura's height and slimness, in the restless grace of her stance, in the clear, strong lines of cheek and jaw. Beautiful, as Aretone had said—beautiful, and Jaen. Only Amaura's pale eyes were her own, and, looking numbly into them, Arachne realized where she had seen the color of the web above the spring.

"Hello, Mother."

"Amaura. *Amaura*—"

"Give me the water jar." She took it from Arachne's head. In the last year Amaura had grown so much that the two women were nearly the same height. Amaura smiled faintly, secretively, and brushed her hair, which hung loose about her shoulders, back from her face. Arachne put her arms around her. Amaura neither resisted nor embraced her mother back.

"Are you alone, Amaura? How did you come to villa? Are you well? Amaura—"

"The web is mine, Mother. I picked all the prey off the silk and washed it. It took a long time."

"How did you come? Are you alone, Spiderling?"

She had said it without thinking, but Amaura pushed her hair off her face and smiled. "The web is an offering to the Goddess. Picking off the flies, I did feel like a spiderling. I felt like a spider. Yes, a spider."

Chilled, Arachne stepped back a pace and gazed at her daughter. Under her gaze, Amaura grimaced lightly and pushed back her hair. The gesture was as regular and meaningless as a tic, but Arachne saw that Amaura was aware she did it, and also aware of her mother's questions. Amaura ignored the questions not from any confusion of the mind, but because questions did not fit some dramatic purpose of her own. There was about Amaura an air of deliberate drama: not false, but exaggerated. She was, Arachne saw, playing through a part, as if this meeting with her mother were a ritual and she a priestess, privy to a great but secret intensity. Her light eyes glittered.

"Aretone says that Suva has become a goddess."

Arachne gripped her daughter's shoulder. She spoke clearly, each word spaced. "Amaura. Did you come alone across Island from the vineyard?"

"Yes. It took a few days. I wanted to see Suva being a goddess. Did you know that I used not to believe her stories? I thought she invented all those terrible things." She smiled mockingly, and pushed her hair from her face.

Arachne grasped Amaura and led her out of the fountainhouse, away from the gray web. In the cold sunlight Amaura lost some of her assurance. She looked to Arachne more a young girl, less a mannered performer. But her gray eyes kept their hard glint, and in it Arachne sensed something dangerous. Arachne's chest ached; she reached out to hold her daughter, and this time Amaura embraced her back.

"Your father? Kyles?"

"A drunkard," Amaura said brutally, and pulled back a little. *To observe my reaction,* Arachne thought, and again was aware of some unnamed danger.

"Aretone told me," Arachne said. *Kyles—*

"He takes less wine now then he did at first," Amaura said. Before she said it there had been a brief struggle on her face, as if torn between offering her mother this softening fact, and some other desire. She pushed her hair off her face. "Is Suva truly a goddess?"

"Of course not, Amaura."

"I'll get your water jar." She ducked into the fountainhouse and came out with the jar cradled in front of her in her arms, and knelt. Arachne froze. It was exactly Kyles's stance when he had held Pholen's sarcophagus. Amaura watched her carefully, and Arachne saw that the cruel reminder was intentional. Amaura intended her to see the resemblance. She gasped, and instantly Amaura dropped the water jar and darted to her. "I am sorry! Oh, Mother, I am sorry!"

She grasped Arachne around the waist and hung on. Water from the shattered jar splashed the hems of both their chitons. Amaura was strong; Arachne would have had difficulty freeing her arms.

When Amaura did release her, the pale gray eyes held both remorseful tears and a hungering watchfulness.

Arachne thought clearly: She wants me in turmoil. It is why she came.

Quietly she took her daughter's hand. Amaura's face flushed, and her spine stiffened. With her other hand Arachne smoothed the unbound hair, Amaura's own gesture, before the girl herself could make it. The hair was thick and wild, the black curls as unruly as Jaen's. Jaen's, too, that craving for turmoil, for drama, for emotion and adventure. Such ones were happy—if happy it could be called —only when the moment was hectic and uncertain, no matter what the cost of keeping it so, or who paid it.

"Amaura," Arachne said, and stopped. Her throat constricted roughly. She did not know what to say, but realized that she was not much shocked, nor even surprised. Mostly she sorrowed for the wounds her daughter would seek, and cause. It was not like this that she had envisioned Amaura's future. Or had she envisioned it at all? Amaura was to have been Mistress of Island. There had been no need to visualize.

Amaura watched her mother warily. When Arachne did not speak, Amaura said softly, "Uncle Jaen is back on Island."

Arachne turned white. Amaura said, "All the spiders he and Nikos took aboard ship died shortly after they reached Thera. The priestesses and wise men could not discover what the Spider Stone was made of, or how it came to be, or how to make it grow more spiders. So there was no more silk. It all came to nothing." She pushed her hair back, watching Arachne. "With no silk, Uncle Jaen sailed home again. I think he was not important enough in Thera to want to stay. It all came to nothing, all of it. Mother—don't look like that—don't! I'll get you a cup of water!"

She ran into the fountainhouse, returning with the clay cup kept for travelers and holding it to Arachne's lips. The water was clean and cold. Amaura made her drink it all, watching over the rim of the cup with anguished, predatory eyes. When the water was gone, Arachne pushed her away.

"Where is Jaen?"

"At a farm in the high hills. Lyseles' farm."

It rang true; Lyseles and Jaen had been hunting companions. "How do you know?"

"I was climbing in the hills, and I saw him. I talked with him. He was not pleased to see me." She smiled mockingly at some recollection of her own.

"Has he seen Kyles?"

"No. Father does not know Jaen is here. Jaen came less than a month ago, on a ship from Bylia that landed him on the Southern Shore. Not his own ship. Only Lyseles and his household know that Jaen is here." Again that mocking recollection. "And me."

Arachne seized her daughter's arm, not gently. Her nails dug into Amaura's skin. "Do not tell your father that Jaen is on Island. Do not tell him."

Amaura stared at her. Something flickered across her light eyes, but Arachne could not tell if it was resistance or agreement. A cold breeze ruffled Amaura's hair, blowing black tendrils across her mouth.

Scowling, Arachne repeated, "Do not tell him!"

The air shimmered. A rich clarity brushed Arachne's mind; from Amaura's face she saw that the girl had felt it a moment earlier. Arachne closed her eyes. The sensation of heightened clarity was much stronger than the previous time, in the Grove, but it held still that tentative and flickering quality. It was like one pure, truthful note struck on a lyre, but only one, leaving the ear taut for the rest of the melody. Arachne felt to her bones both the clear note and, beneath it, the harmony and order the one note implied. It promised the harmony of vital rightness, of rich and keen feeling, and she could feel her mind reaching eagerly to embrace it until she opened her eyes and saw Amaura.

The girl had thrown back her head and parted her lips, as if the sensation were a sweet wind to which she lifted her face. Her unbound hair swung free. Amaura's face was rapt but unaware, as if she dreamed in a deep sleep. She had given herself entirely to the moment, and when it passed she came back to awareness slowly, and then grimaced at the fountainhouse directly before her. The grimace was disdainful, a quick down-turning of mouth and brows, involuntary but not meaningless. Arachne saw that Amaura was seeing the fountainhouse against the heightened radiance of the sensation just past. The tangible object looked heavy and stolid, the intangible sensation soaring and rich. When Amaura shifted her gaze to her mother, the grimace flashed again.

Slowly Arachne said, "The sensation was not that strong."

"To me it was."

"Have you felt it before?"

"Twice since I came to the villa yesterday. Once last evening, once this morning." When Arachne did not answer, Amaura said eagerly, "Didn't *you* feel it?"

"Not yesterday. Not this morning. Not till now."

"It is the Grove again, isn't it, Mother? The Grove come again."

"Yes. No. The Grove could never be felt beyond the colonnade!"

"It can now," Amaura said. She smiled and pushed back her hair.

"Have you gone into the Grove since you came yesterday?"

"Yes. There is nothing to see."

"Amaura—never before did you respond to the Grove like that. Never before, when you were a child and it was at its full richness."

"It never felt like that before."

"Yes. It did. That, and more," Arachne said, and tried to think. Amaura was young, her mind still not fully formed, as Arachne had been young when she had felt the Grove at its greatest power. Did a person's age make a difference in how one experienced the Grove? But Jaen was younger than she, and what he had been given had been less. And some of her women were older than she. Delernos, too, when he brought his exiled Household to a Grove at its peak, was in the last third of a long life. How long had the Grove existed before Delernos arrived? No one knew; Island had been empty of men. She and Jaen had never asked the question, because they had assumed the Grove to be immortal.

It had not been. But if living things died, they also bred. Did the age of the Grove—*a* Grove—and the age of a person mix, as in some intangible pharmakon, to affect how strongly one felt that clear radiance? Or was it not age that responded to the Grove but temperament? But the Stone was gone, the trees mutilated, the spiders dead. *Nothing* could not breed again.

Then what had she and Amaura felt?

Amaura drew her cloak closer around her, and shivered. Her face was petulant as she stared at the fountainhouse, and then at the shattered water jar at her feet. The wind blew grit and dust over the shards. The clay water cup still dangled from her hand; she let it drop. It did not break, and she kicked at it disconsolately with her foot.

"Do not tell him," Arachne said experimentally, and waited.

Amaura looked at her in puzzlement; she did not recall what they had been discussing. As clearly as if she were inside her daughter's mind, Arachne saw the pieces of memory return to her: first Kyles, then Jaen, her discovery of Jaen's arrival on Island, Arachne's command, and—last—her interest in all these. The possible heat and drama that Amaura could derive from her family was less than the possible heat and drama from whatever had brushed her mind.

She smiled, shrugged, pushed back her hair. "I will not tell him."

"Come with me to my chamber, Amaura."

"Yes. I want to see Suva. She truly believes she has become a goddess?"

"A goddess who scratches vermin and spits blood."

"Still," Amaura said, and her mocking tone was precisely Jaen's.

But the absentness with which she followed her mother was her own. Arachne saw that Amaura was reliving in her mind that pure, radiant note. She walked without speaking or observing. Arachne held tightly to her daughter's hand, and her thumb caressed Amaura's knuckles, over and over. Once she reached for Amaura's chin and gently turned the girl's face toward her own. She wanted to be sure that Amaura still remembered that Arachne was there.

19

AMAURA'S presence changed the villa. Suva, when she first saw the beautiful young girl standing beside Arachne, did not recognize her. The old woman lowered her chin nearly to her chest and looked upward at Amaura from under the rim of her war helmet.

"Who is that?"

"It's Amaura, Suva. You know the Young Mistress."

Suva glared, belligerent and uncertain. "She is not the daughter of a goddess."

"She is my daughter," Arachne said. She said it quietly, without inflection, but Amaura heard something in the quiet tones that made her unexpectedly reach for her mother's hand. Arachne held Amaura's fingers tightly. The fingers were cold.

"Hello, Suva," Amaura said.

Suva went on glaring. Two scanty tears splashed from under the helmet and splashed on the floor.

"Oh, in the name—Suva, listen. This is my daughter. She too needs the protection of a goddess. So I ask you to extend your sacred blessing to include my daughter."

Amaura watched this ridiculous kindness intently. Her fingers curled inward on themselves. Suva considered, then raised her head and smiled. "You will not go away from me."

"I will not go away," Arachne said wearily.

"This is your daughter."

"This is my daughter."

"Then she is daughter of my daughter."

"Yes," Arachne said, in exasperation and pity. She led Amaura toward the warmth of the fire. Behind them Suva suddenly hissed, "You drove your little brother to tears on the day your uncle sailed. On the cliff ledge. You wanted him to he cry. I know you, Amaura."

Both Amaura and Arachne turned. But Suva's flash of sane memory, if it had been that, deserted her. She stood smiling at them from beneath her helmet, crooning softly to herself, playing with the ends of her gray tattered braids.

Later, Arachne said to Amaura, "You must be gentle with Suva. I think she is dying."

"She is old. It's her time."

"Yes. But she and I have been alone here together, and she has been to me . . ."

"What?"

Arachne looked at her daughter. She could not find words to say what Suva had been to her the long months in the villa. The whip by whose lash the prisoner knows he is still alive. The fellow cripple who is consolation because he has lost two legs to your one. The helpless idiot whose helplessness makes it necessary to move, to work, and so to live. The teeth that draw off the poison. All bitter things, and she could not say them to Amaura, who stood eyeing her disdainfully and pushing back her black hair. Instead, more harshly than she had intended, Arachne said, "Do as I say. Be gentle with Suva."

"She was never," Amaura said, "gentle with me."

For the next month, it rained every day. The three women took to gathering in the late afternoon in Arachne's chamber, by the hearth. Talk among them was slow and dry. Instead of talking they drank a goblet of wine and glanced at each other: Suva regally, surveying her worshipers; Amaura measuringly; Arachne with a dread she could not name.

Except for the daily wine by the hearth, Amaura was an elusive presence in the villa, standing in a chamber one moment, silently gone the next. Arachne never followed her. She thought that Amaura probably went to the Grove, to the spring where the gray web hung, to whatever else of the deserted villa pleased, for a moment, her restless mind. Arachne herself went each few days to the Grove. Each time she felt nothing, sensed nothing. To her the Grove showed merely a ruin, dripping with rain. She did not ask what it showed to Amaura.

Amaura left her wild black hair unbound, and wore only white chitons and cloaks. She darkened her eyes with charcoal, in imitation of Ikeria's paints. Once at night Arachne had seen Amaura dancing alone, on the cliff above the sea—a white figure whirling against the dark sky. Remembering her daughter's youth, Arachne found all this easy enough to forgive; it was silly, but unimportant.

However, behind Amaura's posturings of dress and movement, Arachne sensed still that other thing, neither silly nor unimportant, that had troubled her in the fountainhouse. Amaura craved drama that was not woven in her head. The craving itself was youthful; Amaura's intensity about it was not. She sought not simple diversion but something else, some dark center, that Arachne could not imagine.

"Tell me a story," Amaura said to Suva. Suva crouched close to the hearth, her back against the plastered wall and her helmet and empty goblet in her lap. Nearby Amaura sat on a low stool, polishing the goddess's shield with a soft cloth. She had volunteered for the task. Amaura watched Suva with a narrow-eyed stillness that the old woman took for the respect due a goddess. Arachne, watching them both from her seat by the window, saw that it was neither respect nor fear. She thought that Amaura, possibly without knowing it herself, hoped for something with more texture.

Abruptly, Arachne rose. "I'm going to the storage magazine. We need wine."

Amaura repeated, "Tell me a story, Suva. As you used to do."

Behind her, Arachne heard Suva say, "I had no once. I sprang from the sea." She lengthened her stride; the voices faded.

When her mother had gone, Amaura leaned forward on her stool. Her voice was soft and coaxing. "But surely goddesses know marvels that happened even before they sprang from the sea. Tell me those."

Suva pursed her mouth in thought.

"See, you do remember marvels," Amaura said.

"Once," Suva said, and stopped. "Once."

"Once . . ." Amaura coaxed.

Suva straightened her back against the wall. "Once there was a famine in a distant land. Far to the east it was, on the edge of the world. The people there were ignorant of the Goddess and worshipped only lesser and male gods, which is why nothing would grow. Men can not bring forth from their bellies." She stopped and frowned; her eyes flickered, and then again became serene. "But the Goddess took pity on their ignorance, and in Her benevolence ended the famine. The people then lived."

Amaura shifted on her stool.

"Once," Suva said, "There was a barren woman who desired a child. She sacrificed two bulls to the Goddess, white bulls wearing garlands of flowers, and their blood ran red on the earth. The Goddess was pleased, and rewarded the woman with twin sons with white hair. They grew strong and bright-eyed, and prospered all their lives."

Amaura burst out, "Those aren't like your old stories!"

Suva looked surprised, and then a little agitated. She put on her helmet and picked up her spear, clutching its handle.

"Once there was a maiden who cried for the moon. Her father was a powerful nobleman and ordered slaves to climb the highest mountain and bring the moon down to her. Any man who failed was to be beheaded. But no one died. The first man to climb the mountain, a desperate slave, was taken pity on by the Goddess. She gave him a round globe of amber. He brought it down, calling it the moon. The next night the Goddess made moonless, so the maid believed she held the moon in her arms. The slave was rewarded with his freedom, and the girl happy."

Amaura said flatly, "What happened when the real moon finally rose?"

Suva's face sharpened with strain. She fretted at her spear, scratched her groin, and glared at Amaura. "Why do you stare at me!"

"You are a goddess," Amaura said. Her light eyes watched intently, and she smiled.

Suva cried, "You must not mock a goddess!" The cry broke to a quaver between "mock" and "a."

Amaura rose from her stool. She stood over the old woman on the floor. "Are you a goddess, Suva? *Are* you?"

Suva stumbled to her feet. "Go away! Blasphemy! Go away!"

Amaura did not move. She repeated softly, "Are you a goddess, Suva? Are you? Are you?"

Suva seized her spear by the middle of its shaft and began to lay about her with both butt and point. Amaura danced backwards, but not out of range. Suva, her eyes wide with terror, sobbed and lunged, trying to hit Amaura with the butt or pierce her with the tip. Amaura dodged the spear easily. She could have grabbed it, but did not. She flung out one hand, but not to grab the spear nor shield herself; the hand stayed flung upwards, in entreaty or salute, and the girl moaned softly.

"Go away! Go away!" Suva screamed, while Amaura danced by her. Suva stumbled, fell to her knees, and began to cough. The spear dropped to the floor. Amaura made no move to pick it up; she stood still and watched while Suva coughed and sobbed, spitting blood and phlegm onto the floor. Amaura's face twisted. Her pale eyes were shining.

When Suva's coughing had finished, Amaura helped her to her feet. Suva scowled, trembling. Finally Amaura, licking her bottom lip, said "Are you a goddess, Suva? Are you?"

Suva jerked away, seized her spear, and thrust it at Amaura.

The tip passed between Amaura's body and left arm. The girl's eyes widened and she hissed in surprise. Suva had little strength left, but she thrust again and again, screaming incoherently, beyond reason. Amaura evaded the thrusts, and her eyes shone even when Arachne, who had heard the noise, rushed into the room.

"Suva!"

At Arachne's cry, Suva thrust the spear blindly. Her foot came down on the blood on the floor and she lurched forward. The spear slashed the soft flesh on Arachne's left arm. Blood sprang forth.

Arachne staggered, but only for a moment. With her right arm she grabbed the spear, yanked it from Suva's grip, and hurled it across the room. It clattered on the stone floor. Arachne clapped her right hand over her wound. Blood oozed between the fingers. Dizziness and nausea swept through her, receded.

"Amaura! Come here!"

But Amaura made a sudden turn and lifted her face.

"Amaura!"

The girl glanced at her mother, leaning against the wall, and at

Suva, sobbing on the slimed floor. The glance held recognition and also a desperate analysis—how badly Arachne was hurt, how much help Suva would need. A spasm shook Amaura's shoulders. She lifted her head higher, tilting her face backward as if to a sweet wind, and her desperate look faded. Whirling, she ran.

"Amaura!" Arachne cried. Amaura did not falter.

Still holding her arm, Arachne searched for a piece of wool. She tied it around the wound, using her right hand and her teeth. Suva had begun to cough again. Arachne helped her to a couch and forced her to lie on it. Suva flailed with both arms, glaring weakly. "I came from . . . the *sea!*" Arachne held a basin for Suva, looking away as the old woman spat into it.

"Singing," Suva whispered, and began to cry. Her tears were scanty and hot.

"Rest now," Arachne said, pulling a blanket over Suva's legs. Petulantly Suva kicked it off. Lying on her back with her empty palms flung upwards beside her head, her body exhausted with coughing, she looked like a wizened child, desolate and furious.

"Singing and . . . singing. It is not . . . a story!"

"It is a beautiful story."

"Not a lie. Not."

"All right," Arachne said. "Not a lie!"

"I am . . . a goddess." Suva clutched the edge of Arachne's chiton.

"You are a goddess then! Let go!"

Suva released the cloth in her fingers. Her tears had stopped; she looked at Arachne with sly, desperate eyes. "A goddess needs a shroud."

"In the name of the—"

"Yes," Suva whispered. A sudden stench rose from the couch; Suva had soiled herself. In her weak intensity about the shroud, the old woman did not notice. Arachne turned her head.

"A shroud—a shroud—"

Arachne gritted her teeth. "You shall have your shroud."

"With scenes of Island," Suva whispered. "And . . . the sea." She fell to crooning, smiling peacefully to herself, lying in her own dung.

Grimly Arachne cleaned her. Then she unbound her arm and examined it. Blood flow had stopped; the gash was not deep. She washed it, bound it in clean wool, and strode to the Grove. Anger flamed through her. She had forgotten how heartening anger was.

At the fountainhouse by the colonnade she called out, "Amaura!" There was no answer. The gray web above the spring shone cleanly. Fury leaped in Arachne; she grabbed the web and tore it from the roof. The web fed Amaura's posturing rituals, supported the cruel games she played in her head. Let her find something else to weave her crises from—she would not use spider silk!

The web tore easily from its moorings. The silk itself did not tear, but only tangled. Arachne cast the crumpled web into the spring and strode through the colonnade and into the Grove.

She felt it instantly: the lost golden awareness of harmony and vivid life. Although the sensation was weaker than the Grove of her childhood, it was stronger than on her previous visits. Now those seemed mere disturbances of the air. This was not only a change in the air, not only a brushing of her mind, but a triumphant certainty of knowledge: sensation become truth. There was a pattern to the world, shimmered the truth; there existed a rich tapestry of life and light, and she was woven into it as firmly as sea and sky. She was vital. The tapestry would not be the same without her or without this moment, which contained all moments. The force of life she felt flowing in her veins and breathing in her lungs was clear and precious and right, and it was the rightness of all creation that shimmered purely on the keen air. Arachne's head lifted, her eyes widened, and a golden warmth tingled over her body.

She was alive, who before had only moved.

The surge of sensation passed. Arachne stood still, dazed, tears in her eyes. She did not know if the tears were for the sensation's rebirth, or for its passing. She put her hands over her face, and when she took them down again, Amaura stood watching her from a commonplace clump of mutilated trees.

Amaura said hungrily, "What did you feel?"

Arachne heard the hunger, and sobered again to anger. She closed the distance to her daughter in three strides. "You left me when I called for your help."

"I felt the Grove," Amaura said. Something shifted below the surface of her pale eyes.

"You cannot feel the Grove beyond the colonnade!"

"I can," And then, shrewdly, "You did, too. At the fountain-house, the day I came."

It was true.

Amaura said, "The Grove is different this time, isn't it? This time, *I* know it more than you. This time, it is mine."

Arachne seized her daughter's shoulders. "Amaura! You provoked a dying woman to an anger her mind cannot stand! You knew, or at least you suspected, that her mind could not stand it and still you—"

"You weren't there!"

"I don't need to be there. I can see what happened. The results of that scene you provoked were your responsibility, yet you ran off and left Suva gasping for breath and me in my blood."

"The Grove called me."

"I saw it call you. I will accept what you say—that even at that distance the Grove affected you, and . . . strongly. But I saw your face at the moment you felt the Grove, Amaura. You didn't *forget* Suva coughing her lungs out or my bleeding arm. You looked at us both, saw us both, and chose to go. You would have left if we had both been even at the point of death."

Amaura did not deny it. A small wind ruffled her unbound hair. Her light eyes stared directly into her mother's.

"You were to be Mistress of Island," Arachne said bitingly. "A Mistress of Island does not forget responsibility. A Mistress of Island does not run off and leave those in her Household in distress, not even for the Grove."

"*You* did," Amaura said, "For the Grove."

Arachne let go of Amaura's shoulders. Another gust of wind blew past. The rain began again, a cold drizzle. When Arachne did not answer or change expression, Amaura's face grew sulky.

"I know Aretone says otherwise," Amaura said. "She believes the Grove would have died no matter what you did."

"What do you say, Amaura?" Arachne said. "What do you believe?"

The girl said nothing. Arachne saw that Amaura did not believe her mother responsible. Nor did she believe her not responsible. Responsibility did not concern Amaura at all; she had said what she said not because it was true, or because she thought it was true, but because it was interesting. If she, Arachne, had become explosive or pained, Amaura would have tried to soothe her, apologizing with genuine heat and passion. If Arachne did not become explosive, Amaura would continue until she did, observing her mother with careful, hungry eyes.

Arachne had a sudden picture of Suva arranging skeins of silk on the stone floor, color by color, arranging and rearranging until a definite pattern appeared, a clear and strong image. Even if the pattern was for a shroud.

Patterns shimmered in her head, hurting it. Silks for a shroud, dramas for turmoil, the Grove for life and light.

The ash-haze silk, without pattern.

Through the light rain, Amaura watched. With one hand she pushed her wet hair off her face. "Uncle Jaen is in the villa now."

"Is that true? Or is it that you will make it true, Amaura?"

Amaura frowned. She must have hoped, Arachne thought sharply, for the same dramatic reaction Arachne had had when first told Jaen was on Island. But this time Arachne had willed her voice to be calm, and her reaction to Amaura's attack—for it *was* an attack —to be a question, not an emotion, and the question itself a kind of attack. It came to her that Jaen had done that often: answered one attack with another.

Jaen—in the villa. Pain clenched in her chest, but she kept it from her face. Her daughter was watching her closely. Her daughter, with Jaen's restless stance and stubborn, sullen mouth. When had Amaura adopted that expression? Had she always had it, or was it new?

The two women stared at each other through the cold mist.

Amaura lifted one hand in a pointless gesture, let it fall, all at once raised it again and seized her mother's wrist.

"Come look at something!"

"I do not want to look at anything."

"You *must*," Amaura said urgently, and dragged Arachne toward the center of the Grove, to the hole that had held the Spider Stone.

Wet with rain, the earth piled at the lip of the hole and down its sides was dark. It smelled rich and pungent. At first Arachne could see nothing but the dark dirt and dark shadows. Then, kneeling at the lip and peering down, she did.

At the bottom of the hole lay a globular shape the size of a man's head. A color between brown and gold, a streaky bronze, the sphere's surface was shiny and sleek. Beads of rain slid over the surface and disappeared, still clinging, onto the bottom hemisphere.

"Seen close, it is oval, not round," Amaura said. She was not looking at the streaky globe; her gaze never left her mother's face. "An oval standing on end. The color has lightened almost daily. When I found it, it was the same color as the dirt, and half that size. It is growing, Mother. It is *growing.*"

Arachne slid into the hole and down one side. Cold mud pushed up her chiton and stuck to her legs. At the bottom she squatted next to the globe and peered underneath. As Amaura said, it was an oval on end, the last quarter of its length buried in the earth. Arachne circled it; the oval was uniform on all sides. She bent over it; the top surface had no holes and the streaks formed no pattern. Finally, she touched it. The surface felt taut, like a full wineskin, and under her trembling finger it gave slightly.

"It's still soft," Amaura called from above.

"Soft."

"Yes," Amaura said. "Like a baby's head. Like Pholen's once."

After a long time, Arachne stood. She could not climb from the hole; the damp earth slid from under her footholds and the arm injured from Suva's spear would not hold her weight. Amaura brought a rope—it was of spider silk, Arachne noted—and hauled her up, a long and messy task. Her arm began to bleed again through its muddy bandage. When Arachne stood again at the lip of the hole, the two women stared down at the bronze sphere. Both were covered with mud, straggly haired in the rain, panting hard. Amaura's kohl ran down in her cheeks in black smears. They did not look at each other.

"When the Grove comes alive," Amaura said softly, "the globe swells a little, a very little, and lightens in color. I have seen it."

"You think it is a new Spider Stone." It was not a question.

"I don't know."

"When did you find it first?"

"A few days after I came to the villa."

"Each of us had felt the . . . the sensation before that."

"Yes." Amaura hesitated. "I don't understand that. If the . . . the

Stone causes the Grove to stir, alive, how could I feel it before the Stone came? It makes no sense."

Arachne looked at her. Amaura's face was genuinely puzzled, its lines soft and round now that the unspoken contest with her mother had been momentarily put aside. She squinted into the hole, and to Arachne she looked not like Jaen but like Pholen, squinting into his spider house. Young—she must not forget how young her daughter actually was.

"You have not been pregnant," Arachne said quietly. "You have never felt how a baby stirs even before birth."

Amaura looked startled, then speculative. Swiftly she said, "Like Pholen."

Arachne did not flinch. "Or you."

Amaura dropped her eyes and pushed back her hair.

"Amaura. When the Grove stirs, what is it *you* feel?"

The girl licked her lips. She looked suddenly angry, as if Arachne's calm had robbed her, and suddenly less young. Her face shone, like a priestess's at sacrifice, with a bright and holy doom. "I feel alive! I feel as if I had been a prisoner, and then escaped! Escaped from all the dullness, the working and eating and sleeping and talking and working and eating and sleeping and talking again, until Island someday crumbles into the sea or we on it are all dead. When the Grove calls, I leave this stupid place and suddenly see another where I am important, as important as I was born to be, as important as the people in Suva's stories. Her old stories, not the ones she tells now! They were . . . were passionate and real. Thrilling things happened in them, and in the Grove I feel as if they had happened to me. To *me*, Mother. When I touch something, it feels solid and real. When I look at something, it glows with bright colors. When I feel something, it feels passionate and intense, and true, and *right*. It feels the way life should happen. On Island, before—in the name of the Goddess! Nothing has happened the way it should! But now, in the Grove—"

Amaura stopped. Her bright defiance had faded to sulkiness. She pushed her wet hair off her face; drops of rain slid from the tendrils at her forehead and rolled into her eyes. Staring into the hole at the embryonic Spider Stone, she repeated sullenly, "It feels like a sacred escape."

Arachne stood as if being sentenced.

"So?" Amaura said irritably. "Is that how the old Grove felt?"

"No," Arachne said. "Yes."

Amaura looked up swiftly. But her mother's face was bowed, hidden by sodden masses of hair, as she stared into the shadowed hole.

"Have you thought," Arachne said, "that if you take that much feeling from the Grove now, what you will . . . be, when that small Stone has grown full and large?"

Amaura wrapped her arms around her body. Wind dragged at her hair. She answered something else entirely. "Uncle Jaen *is* in the villa. I did not go tell him about the Grove. He came to the villa of himself."

"Why?"

"I don't know."

"Has he seen the new Stone?"

"Yes. Of course."

"Amaura. Has he felt the Grove come alive?"

"Once. He stood here already, where you stand now. I don't know if it has called to him when he is away from the Stone," Amaura said, sulkily enough that Arachne knew Jaen must not have been much interested in his niece's perceptions.

"Listen to what I say," Arachne said, and turned her daughter's face to her own. "Do not tell Suva."

"Do not tell Father, do not tell Suva."

"If you mock me again, Amaura, I will knock you down."

The girl's eyes widened in surprise. Arachne's tone was calm, grim, factual. "If Suva knows Jaen is in the villa, it will unsettle her. You unsettled her once today, and then left her. To you it was a small fracas, barely a diversion. But it is not small to Suva. She won't forget it."

"How do you know what she forgets? Once you never noticed the moods of a crazy slave."

"No. Once I did not."

Arachne stared at her daughter with level eyes. Amaura nodded, but she was not really interested. The scene with Suva, which had intrigued her this morning, now seemed futile and vaguely shameful. A mad slave, no more. Amaura wrapped her arms more tightly across her shoulders and looked sullenly at the mist-blurred, embryonic Stone. Compared to what the Stone could make her feel, the tensions between her mother, uncle, and slave were unimportant. Distractions. Unreal reflections, like moonlight on water, of the bright and flaying feeling of the Grove. *They* were real. They were truth. They were the radiance worthy of her.

Carefully, Arachne watched her daughter's face. Her gaze missed nothing. It was as thorough, and as pitiless, as once Nikos's had been, or as Amaura's own.

Once back in her chamber, Arachne threaded her loom.

20

I T was changed and changeless at the loom.

Despite the months of idleness, Arachne found she could weave as deftly as ever. The skill had not left her. Silk slid as swiftly through her fingers, and the shuttle was thrown as straight. When she reached into the basket at her feet, her hand closed on the needed silk without breaking the smooth flow of shuttle and reed. Each motion felt as familiar to her as the rhythms of her own breathing, and as necessary.

But, when on that first day she had returned from the Grove and strung her warp with the azure silk Suva had chosen, Arachne had found that the silk pulled and snagged. Her fingernails had grown too long for weaving. For a long time Arachne gazed grimly at her hands, spreading them palms down, before paring the nails. It was such a small fact to imply so much.

Suva was childishly delighted. "My shroud!" she cried, clapped her hands, and beat the butt of her spear on the floor. The white feathers on her helmet flopped back and forth.

Amaura said, "Why are you weaving now?" She emphasized the last word so lightly that Arachne could not be sure what her daughter meant. Amaura worked willingly at both the tasks that a daughter of a Household would assume and those that had once been done by the Household slaves, but she never weaved. Arachne had not asked it of her.

"I am weaving a shroud for Suva."

"But why now?"

"Suva has not much more than now," Arachne said.

Amaura frowned. "She is a mad old slave."

"Yes."

"Mistresses of Island do not weave shrouds for slaves."

"Mistresses of Island weave what they wish," Arachne said. She did not take up the challenge in Amaura's voice, although she heard it: what does it mean to be "Mistress of Island" *now?*

Amaura shrugged. "What is the design of the shroud to be?"

"As Suva wishes. Scenes of Island."

Something in her mother's tone, something too carefully controlled, made Amaura glance up sharply. Arachne weaved on: throw the shuttle, lift the beater, move the silk. The whisper-knock, whisper-knock filled the chamber, broken only by sudden, infrequent croonings from Suva. The weaving noises were monotonous, the croonings mad. There was no design to be seen on the tapestry; Arachne wound each day's work around the beam as soon as it was finished. The fire had sunk, and the chamber was cold.

When next Arachne looked up from the loom, Amaura had gone.

Arachne caught her shuttle in one hand and strained to open her mind. She felt nothing. If she went to the Grove, of course, she would feel it—the cutting clarity that had called Amaura.

Still-faced, Arachne turned again to the loom.

"Singing and singing," Suva said. Regally she lowered herself among the ashes on the hearth. She fondled the bits of silk on her lap and smiled at Arachne with infinite love.

Arachne wound her work higher on the loom's beam. She could not bear to look at it.

Hour after hour, day after day, Arachne did nothing but weave. She rose to her loom at daybreak, her fingers already curved to the shape of the shuttle. Sometimes she weaved even past sunset, working by oil lamp and moonlight. The back of her neck hurt, and a constant ache spread in a triangle from the joint of each shoulder to the small of her back.

The pattern on her loom grew as swiftly as the tapestries of the Grove, but with a difference. In every motion of mind, if not of hand, Arachne knew that she stood not in the Grove but in her chamber by the sea. No golden radiance eased her aches or filled her breath to be given out again in her fingers. The pattern of this weaving welled into her fingers from *somewhere*—she could feel it, like water rising from a long way underground to gush from a fountainhouse spring. The image of the well came to her again and again as she worked. Her tapestry rushed forward, unstoppable as cold water from living rock.

But not, she knew, from the streaky embryonic Stone in the Grove. This pattern did not come from the Grove.

Her dreams changed. Now she never had the painfully bright dream of weaving in the Grove. At first, she dreamed of nothing at all. Exhausted, she threw herself onto her couch at the end of hours of weaving, and the silence of the day's work became the silence of dreamless sleep.

But as winter wore on, Arachne began to have vague, half-remembered dreams of a kind new to her. She dreamed Kyles's hands on her breasts and belly, or his hard body pressed full-length against hers. She could feel his breath on her face. When he moved, the hair on his chest brushed her gently.

She woke, in the shivering half-dawn, to find that she, who had felt little but affection when she was bedded, lay with her hand fiercely between her thighs.

What her body felt, her mind would think of. Working still-faced at her loom, Arachne groped through thoughts of men, women, and weapons.

This tapestry before her—she knew that she was weaving it with the same relentless will with which she would have stalked what Island had never known and Arachne herself knew only from old stories: a blood enemy. But a blood enemy would have been hunted with spear and shield. Armies would have howled and blood flowed—everything that might have happened at the Southern Shore had she, Arachne, not stopped it at the last possible moment. But she *had* stopped it, and Kyles, at whatever price, had obeyed her. Her final choice of weapon for that battle had been retreat. Her weapon for this battle—for she knew, however obscurely as yet, that weaving this tapestry was a battle—was a loom. Retreat, a loom. Perhaps, she thought, women had no heart for other weapons. Small skirmishes, with small weapons: a web torn from above a spring, a pharmakon of herb and mineral, a mind already old and abused retreating farther into darkness. The biting or smashing word. The openhanded slap instead of the sword.

The loom.

Was it, then, that women were cowards? Were they afraid, not so much of wounds but of being the one who inflicted wounds? Was it the sheer responsibility that made them recoil from the thrown goblet, the sword jabbing at fallen bodies, the axes on sacred trees?

She thought that Amaura would not recoil from inflicting wounds.

No. It was not that women were cowards. It seemed to her rather that women sensed more quickly how often the large battles began with the small violence. It was like the spinning of a huge and ornate web, flaming scarlet, that begins with the testing of a single bridge line. Like the heavy lid of a chest that turns on a small hinge.

She realized that she had never thought about the weapons of men and women. On Island men grew and harvested crops and worked metals; women grew and harvested children and worked fibers. Both ruled and judged and owned. And none of these activities had anything to do with the Grove, where men and women both had stood in that rich clarity and—

But in Thera, with no Grove?

Jaen had wanted to know what different marvels would flourish in Thera.

Arachne's fingers spun furiously. It seemed to her that images of men crowded not her mind but her fingertips, clustered thick around the loom. She saw Jaen, mocking and restless, risking all he could command on Island for all he could command at Thera.

She saw Kyles's face, bent intently over hers. With his knee he thrust apart her thighs, and in his eyes and in the clenching of his jaw was a longing she had not understood and had not wanted to understand, a burning so rigidly focused it was like hot light brought to a point, able to catch fire and char them both.

She saw Nikos, his sharp eyes missing nothing: not the altering of an expression, the wealth of a tapestry, the calculated profit in the way a man stared at a woman.

Risking, burning, calculating.

She, Arachne, had never risked anything to conquer another, had never burned for another, had never calculated another. Not with Jaen, not with Kyles, not with Amaura, not even with Pholen. Instead, she understood slowly over the days and then the weeks of weaving her tapestry, that the most vital acts of her life had all been done alone, by and for herself.

Alone, she had touched the Grove.

Alone, she had woven the ash-haze silk.

Alone, she had sent word for Kyles not to attack Jaen at the Southern Shore. Her women had crowded around her and her child had lain dying in her arms, but she had made the decision, by and for herself. She had asked for no one's calculations, burned for no one's love, chosen to risk nothing else in the face of what she had already lost. And her decision itself—the bloodless weapon of retreat—had been to disengage people set on violent acts with each other, not to engage them. The men had wanted to risk, calculate, burn. She had stopped them, and in doing had set them all more, not less, apart from each other. She had set them more alone.

As Kyles knew most. Unable to bear the bitter aloneness with her, he had chosen a bitter aloneness without.

Was it, then, Arachne thought, that men wove their lives among other people, using those others like so many strands of boldly colored silk, while women wove theirs alone except for the small entangled bodies of their children?

Not Aretone. Not Cleis. Not even Suva, so badly mangled in the twisted lives of others that the only act she could undertake alone was madness.

But she, Arachne—she had spun her life alone, of small skirmishes and bloodless acts.

She stood before her loom, her back aching, and weaved. Azure, scarlet, gray, emerald, dove. The pattern grew.

How much did Kyles blame her for his humiliation at the Southern Shore, and how much himself? Arachne did not know. Her husband had been a shadowed corner of her life into which she had rarely looked; she did not know what he was capable of feeling, or of understanding. She did not know, if he could see the pattern growing on her loom, whether he would understand it.

Jaen might have understood, once.

It came to Arachne that this weaving, this tapestry that drove her with such savagery day after day, was the central act of her life: the bridge line, the small hinge. She saw this without the heightened awareness of the Grove, without the probings of Jaen's sharp intelligence, without Amaura's fevers and dramas. The knowledge was less in her mind than in her body. She felt it in the curve of the shuttle under her fingers, in the ache along her back, in the whisper-knock, whisper-knock all day long in her ears. It was a fact, as direct and unsentimental as the fall of Island sunlight. Weaving this tapestry was the central act of her life.

A small and bloodless act. No armies, no battles, no bold and highly colored risks. Only a woman weaving fiercely, alone, at a loom.

Arachne thought that it was fitting. Grimly she weaved, all the rainy winter, at the tapestry she could not bear to look on. And at night she dreamed of Kyles's body, which she had not loved.

21

ON the night Arachne finished Suva's shroud, she could not
stop weaving.

It was long past midnight. On the hearth Suva slept where
she had dozed off, a messy fitful bundle smeared with ashes. In
another chamber Amaura, presumably, slept. A warm breeze, a
spring breeze, blew in the window, and it seemed to be carried on
the clean wash of moonlight. Oil lamps burned near the loom, and
in the two lights, one steady and one flickering, the shroud shone
clearly.

If Arachne tried to stop weaving, her hands began to shake and
her heart to stutter in irregular, painful spasms. As soon as she
picked up the shuttle again, her hands steadied and the pounding
in her chest slowed. Once, when she stopped to sip a goblet of wine,
her fingers trembled so much that she spilled nearly all the wine.
She turned again to the loom, thirsty and grim.

As the night wore on, her breathing became deeper and faster.
She forced it to slow, but when it did she took in too much air and
became dizzy. In the dizziness, her breathing accelerated by itself
until again she breathed as fast as the shuttle passed through the
warp, and her heart pounded.

She focused everything in her mind on her breathing. She tried
to slow the shuttle so that her lungs would also slow. The shuttle
faltered, and her fingers trembled so violently she dropped it. She

picked it up and again wove faster. Her breath raced, and the room began to lurch and sway.

She thought, *This is how the Goddess sends fits,* and immediately her breathing became normal.

On the hearth, Suva stirred fitfully.

Later, she saw herself from the outside. Clearly she felt herself separate into two Arachnes, two distinct female figures standing before a loom. One drifted toward the window and observed the other calmly. That figure—she—saw the other figure—also she—in sharp detail: the too wide eyes, rigid jaw, desperate face, competent hands. The Arachne before the loom weaved with a frenzy completely silent except for the whisper-knock of shuttle and reed. Nevertheless, the Arachne by the window heard the air fill with bitter shouts that rang off the walls like stones. One stone struck the other Arachne on the back of the head, and they both vanished.

Dreaming, she thought, and shook herself—*am I dreaming on my feet? Exhaustion. I cannot stop now,* tried to stop, and began to tremble violently. She seized the shuttle and threw it again through the warp.

She wove for another hour, for two. Twice more her breathing hurt her. Once she did fall asleep on her feet, catching herself on an upright just before she fell forward. The moon set and the sky began to pale.

At first the room lightened with only the ordinary light of dawn, but then with another light. There was no sudden keenness or rapt jolt. Only gradually Arachne became aware of the sensation in the air, and then it was a while before she could be sure.

Her fingers tightened on the shuttle.

It was the Grove. The air shimmered with it, but in a different and more subtle way than before. This was not the emotional rapture that had led Amaura to hiss "escape," nor the radiant and transcendent joy of that last night two years ago when Jaen told her he would sail for Thera. Yet it was the Grove. From nowhere else could come into her mind the same sense of being touched by a warm and calm well-being. It made her desperate frenzy feel like resolute purpose, her exhausted body feel tired in healthy use. It transformed even the way she saw the room around her. The cold ashes on the hearth looked soft and furry, shaded with pearly shades of gray, possessing their own subtle beauty. Soothing waves at the base of the cliff sounded louder than Suva's snoring, masking the harsh sound with a gentle one. Dawn light lay silvery on the stone floor. Somewhere a bird sang, a note Arachne would not have noticed in her frenzy of weaving but which she now heard clearly, poignant and sweet. Nothing had changed in the room, and all had changed. All lay gently in the hand of the Goddess, cherished and golden.

Her hatred flared so suddenly it made her dizzy.

She flung herself again on her weaving. Faster and faster, her face contorted with pain, Arachne drove her shuttle against the sweet fact of the Grove. Toward the end of the tapestry her fingers trembled no matter what speed she worked; she could no longer tell if they trembled from fury or fatigue. She weaved until she felt the golden peace again lap at her mind. When she did, she reached up and unrolled the tapestry from the beam until it hung at its full length, so she could see the design entire. Until now no one, including her, had viewed the whole thing. Now she had to crouch on the stone floor to finish off the bottom edge. To be able to throw the shuttle she moved back and forth on her knees, like cornered prey, or a supplicant. Her knees scraped and bled. Above her the shroud billowed in the light breeze.

When the last pass of the shuttle was complete, Arachne struggled to her feet, fell, struggled again. The clear grace from the Grove shimmered the air around her panting figure. Blood from her knees stained the floor. Bracing one hand on a loom upright to keep from falling again, Arachne shook her hair from her eyes and forced herself to look at what she had made.

The weaving was a blasphemy.

In the center of the shroud shone the Grove as it had once been. Arachne had weaved it in brilliant colors and with all her longing visible: the trees seemed so alive they swayed in an unseen breeze, each leaf clear and fresh around the central glory of the Spider Stone. Trees and Stone were overlaid with a thin web of golden threads, a bright radiance. Strands of the web soared to the edges of the tapestry, connecting the Grove to the images on the weaving's border. These border images, circling the Grove, were done in crude, garish, flat colors.

They were images of despair, mocking the living clarity of the Grove. Arachne had woven Pholen, dying, his small body rigid as stone, covered with crawling spiders. Jaen, his arms outstretched as if groping toward the Grove, his feet held fast by strands of scarlet spider silk that became, at the edge of the tapestry, writhing snakes. Amaura, a slim figure in white with a garland in her hair and jeweled swords heaped at her feet. The figure had no face at all, merely a flat white blur. Aretone, bent over a sarcophagus in which lay her dead husband. Kyles, naked, his powerful body mutilated. Both arms had been cut off at the elbow.

At the bottom of the tapestry Arachne had woven herself. She faced the Grove squarely, so close she could see none of the other figures. In one hand she held a shuttle. The golden light from the Grove ran over her in intense, beautiful, solid beams. It was the brightest thing in the tapestry, this light—more solid than the Spider Stone, more a fact than the trees. The light shone directly into the woven Arachne's eye sockets. She was smiling, and blind.

Arachne dropped her shuttle to the floor. From behind her came a slight noise, an improbable echo to the dropped shuttle, and she turned around. In the doorway stood Jaen, in scarlet silk and Theran dagger, returned to the villa—as she had known he someday must.

"Get out," Arachne said. "Get out."

Jaen strolled across the room to the shroud on the loom. She thought she heard him say softly, "In the Name of the Goddess—" but she was too angry to be sure. What she did hear clearly was, "You don't want me near this."

"I don't want you on Island."

"But I am here, Spiderling."

Her head jerked up. It was monstrous. He spoke, stood, entered the room as if he had never left it, with the affectionate ease of ownership. He might have been resuming a conversation broken off yesterday.

He smiled without looking at her. "You never weaved anything so skillful, Arachne. Look at that spider—it could be alive. The hairs on its legs stir in the breeze. The leaves on that tree are rustling."

"Thank you," Arachne said bitterly. Jaen did look at her then, a sudden sharp glance.

"A year ago you would have struck me for saying that."

"It is not a year ago."

"Your weaving shows that."

"Even a year ago I did not strike broken men."

For a moment his black eyes gleamed, and she saw in that moment how much effort his pose of rightful ease was costing him. The ease came not from arrogance, and not—as she had half-feared—from the gentle insistence on peace shimmering in the air, but from effort of will. Jaen wanted something. He wanted calmness between himself and her. He wanted the belief that both of them had lost and the losses balanced, leaving them again equals: two warriors equally maimed and so equally armed. Neither with an advantage over the other, and so agreeing on that basis to forget their quarrel and act as if it had never happened. Like Suva, he wanted to forget the actual past, and to have her forget. "I am here, Spiderling—" Jaen wanted his presence to be the vital point, and not his acts. Like Suva. Like a god.

"If I have been broken," Jaen said, "then so have you, Spiderling." He touched the tapestry on the loom. "But that is over now."

"Is it? There is that weaving still. Don't you want to take it to Thera, Jaen, and hawk it there? You could wrest it from me with no more trouble than you took the Spider Stone." He turned away but not before she glimpsed his face. "Think, Jaen, what a price this might bring in Thera."

"That is over. Stop this, Arachne. I do not mistake reprisal for grief."

"The tapestry is here, Jaen. Don't you want to take it from me by force? I still have one child living. You are not done here yet."

"I did not cause Pholen's death."

"You merely profited from it. Profit from this, too. You have neither pride nor loyalty to stop you."

Jaen's eyes gleamed. "You would not have a husband to stop me. Or do you think Kyles can be propped up and made to race for one more prize before you bestow it elsewhere?"

They tore at each other quietly, in deadly calm.

"But I forget," Jaen added, "you did let Kyles have his one prize. You let him have his dead son."

"What did Ikeria let you keep? Do you leave a son with her, to grow up lying that his father was anyone else but the failed provincial silk merchant who was laughed out of the Theran court?"

She saw by his face that it was true, there was a child, and he could not bear it.

"A son, Jaen? Perhaps he won't be ashamed of you. Perhaps Ikeria will never tell him who his father is—for fear of ridicule."

Jaen's hand dropped to his dagger. In its long slow fall and in the immense time it seemed to take for his fingers to curl on the bull-shaped hilt, Arachne thought clearly: *He would never be able to forget stabbing me.* There was just time to complete the thought, and to see that Jaen's fingers unclenched from the dagger without drawing it, before a shriek split the air and tore at her ears.

Suva had woken on the hearth. Wild-eyed, she stared at the loom, shrieked again, and charged the tapestry.

"Aiiieee! My shroud—my shroud! Blasphemy!"

Jaen drew back from her charging figure. Suva did not see him. Spittle flew from the corners of her lips; ashes from the hearth whirled from her chiton to the floor. Her eyes glared with fury, with despair, with an outrage so terrible her cheek muscles twisted and her shoulders shook. She seized the shuttle and began to beat Arachne around the head, screaming wildly.

"My shroud—a shroud for a goddess! *This*—mockeries, blasphemies!—a goddess . . . you wove misery, you wove misery, you wove misery from the goddess—misery! From—the—Goddess, blasphemy—*mockery!*"

A blow on the side of Arachne's head made her stagger and cry out.

"Misery . . . " Suva's shrieks changed to a wail, piercing and eerie. It was a wail that stirred the hairs at the back of the neck and made the spine turn watery. The old woman's eyes glazed over, and she began to sway. Words mixed with the keening wail, words in an unknown tongue, words that sounded desolate and dangerous as distant howls. Suva's flailings with the shuttle became a weaving dance, some dead ritual surfacing in her drowned mind. Her wizened body swayed grotesquely, breasts and arms thrust toward the loom and then away, toward and away. With each thrust she slashed the shuttle across the tapestry on the loom.

"Aieeeee—ouou—aieeeee—"

Jaen caught her wrist. Suva easily tore free from his grasp. Her kneeing dance gave her a weird and lush power; she wielded the shuttle like a knife, her wrist turning up with each slash, as if she slashed not silk but flesh. It was the movement of a warrior with an enemy, or a priestess with a sacrifice. Suva's face looked tranced; she wailed loss beyond sanity or hope, and in each movement was a warrior's strength.

"Aieeeee—"

Jaen and Arachne fell back before her. Everything recognizable in her face was gone, blurred into one terrible cold light of violent anguish. Suva had gone beyond them, to a place they could not reach. If they so much as touched her, they would burn.

Again and again she slashed, keening, at the shroud. Arachne had not yet tied off the weaving above the reed. The shuttle, driven with that tranced and inhuman power, broke the reed into two pieces, and then into three. Above it the weft began to separate and finally, struck again and again, to tear. The warp threads parted. The tearing silk sounded like singeing hair, audible over Suva's shivering wails.

"Aaieeee—ououou—aieee—" and then, clearly, "Singing—"

The tapestry shredded. The glowing central Spider Stone twisted, tore, unraveled to amber threads. Pholen's face crumpled and caved in, as it must by now have crumpled and caved in his funeral jar. Suva dropped the shuttle and seized her spear. She pierced the figure of Kyles and splintered the trees of the Grove into dangling threads. Amaura's arm parted from her shoulder.

Amaura stood in the doorway, her hands pressed over her mouth.

"The Grove!" Jaen said. "She's drawing strength from the new Grove!"

The air in the room surged and shimmered. Suva wailed, slashing with her spear, severing head from body and silk from silk. Figure from Grove.

When the tapestry fluttered in tatters from the beam of the loom, Suva flung down her spear and stood panting and trembling. Arachne made herself move forward to catch Suva as she collapsed into coughing, but Suva did not collapse. She bent on Arachne a look of such lacerating anger that Arachne stood completely still. Suva's face, contorted and purple, did not look human. Her eyes bulged, but without losing their tranced glaze, and her mouth stretched open without sound. Her head tipped back, like the head of a corpse that has died in gasping violence. Suva's head looked drowned.

"The soap," whispered Amaura, "the head of soap." No one heard her.

"You," Suva said to Arachne, *"you—"* and then, "My daughter . . ." She whined like a child betrayed, but her eyes were not the eyes of a child. From them glowed the preternatural power of the Grove, itself still in infancy, and the three watchers shrank back. In that weird grief, the mad slave looked, for the first time, a goddess. "You—" She did not finish. Whirling, Suva ran from the room.

Arachne felt weak and sick. She reached out for something to hold onto and found she was holding onto Jaen. His arms supported her weight easily, naturally—so naturally that she glanced involuntarily to see if he really wore the Theran dagger he had half-drawn against her. He did.

Amaura said, "It has stopped! The Grove has stopped!"

The pearly shimmer had left the air. Ordinary sunlight lit the stone chamber.

Arachne let go of Jaen, sat on a low stool, and lowered her head to her knees to stop her sickness. Thus bent over, she lost track of how much time had passed. She saw the room from a tilted angle, and with an intense and timeless strangeness. Crouched close to the floor on her stool, she had become compact and the room had become stretched out, an immense and blurry space. Vast expanses of stone floor lay between Amaura, inspecting the tatters on the loom, and Jaen, pouring a goblet of wine. Amaura's hand was steady but her face was a trembly white blur in a mass of black hair. Jaen's hand trembled—one drop of wine fell slowly, slowly to the floor—but his face looked sharp and clear.

In that clarity was impatience. Jaen, Arachne saw, resented Suva's drama as an interruption to his own drama. Before Suva woke, Jaen had been struggling with Arachne, fighting for both his place on Island and with his sister. Both mattered to him. Suva's slashing of Arachne's tapestry had been a distraction. The tapestry itself—another distraction. What was not Jaen's ally was his obstacle.

"Here, Spiderling. Drink this." He handed her the goblet. Arachne straightened, but her odd vision of the room did not go away. She was compact, small, almost invisible; the chamber was blurry and vast, as blurry and vast as the world, without the Grove to give it focus, had become.

Jaen touched her arm tenderly and motioned to her to drink. The wine tasted sweet and cool, and Arachne's sickness receded. Amaura came to kneel on the floor beside her mother, the girl's eyes darting restlessly from Arachne to Jaen, her hands jabbing at her wild hair.

"What happened here, Mother? Mother?"

"Let her drink," Jaen said.

Amaura's eyes flashed. She had missed the meeting of these two. And she had missed some scene, some crisis. "What happened, Mother? What made Suva become like that?"

"Leave us, Amaura," Jaen said harshly.

When she did not go, Jaen grasped her shoulder and pulled her to her feet. Amaura rose, outraged, and kicked his shin. She was barefoot and the kick was weak, but Jaen cursed under his breath and his look blackened. Amaura smiled. In the middle of the smile her lips froze and her eyes widened.

"No," she said softly, and then screamed, "No! No!"

"In the Name of the—"

"The Grove! *No!*"

She kicked again, not weakly. Jaen released her shoulder. Arachne forced every fiber of her mind, but she could sense nothing. One glance at the bewilderment on Jaen's face and Arachne knew that he, too, could not feel the Grove at this distance, and she knew a moment of fierce and petty triumph. She tried again, straining her exhausted mind, and now something came to her. But it was not a sensation of mind.

It was the smell of smoke.

"No!" Amaura screamed. She tore from the room, black hair and white chiton whipping around her. Jaen sniffed, and his startled gaze met Arachne's. He ran for the Grove, she staggering behind him.

The rains had ceased a month ago. The live trees of the Grove were dry, not as dry as they would be at summer's end, but dry enough. Dead wood had been left by Nikos's men, some in heaps and some scattered about the grass. The wood lay directly under the trees: logs, branches, twigs for kindling. The grass was dry. All Suva had had to do was touch coals to the brush.

Flames crackled fiercely over the ground and sputtered up the trunks of trees. In the clear sunlight the flames threw no additional shadows. Wood and grass snapped and popped, like the breaking of bones. A great burning branch crashed to the ground and landed on a withered bush. Blue wood-smoke, thick with ash, blew on the wind.

"Amaura!" Arachne cried. "Amaura!" She could not see her. Arachne ran raggedly through the Grove, circling as close to the flames as she could, searching for a place where the smoke would blow away from her and she could see through the fire. When she found an opening, she darted forward.

"Amaura!"

"Arachne! No!"

Jaen pinned her arms. She struggled against him, but she was too exhausted and frantic to break his grip. Over his shoulder, scarlet as the fire, Arachne saw Suva.

The old woman stood on the flameless dirt heaped at the edge of the hole which held the Spider Stone. Suva wore her helmet and carried her shield; the reflection of the fire played over the curved bronze. With the other arm she held her spear high, poised to hurl down into the hole. Over the snapping of flames Arachne heard her voice, strong and triumphant, shouting words that might have been battle cries in an unknown tongue.

Amaura sprang at Suva from between two heaps of burning brush. She had circled close to the Stone by running in the dirt trench Tageas had dug, once itself used for fire but now slowing the spread of the flames outward from the Grove's center. Her chiton was smeared with soot and her wild black hair frothed around her. Arachne spied that hair and saw it was a net casting about for flames, and she screamed at Jaen and scratched for his eyes.

"Let me go! Let me go to her!"

Amaura had seized the butt of Suva's spear just before Suva hurled it into the hole. Suva and Amaura grappled at the edge, both tugging on the spear, both shouting, two soot-smeared white figures silhouetted against the bright fire. Arachne saw as clearly as if she stood with them the flames shining across the surfaces of their eyes: Suva's black, Amaura's pale, and slick with fear. She could see, as if it had already happened, the flames catching at Amaura's hair, leaping to her chiton, burning her as Nikos's fallen slave had burned but without the spider's poison to deaden the roasting of flesh and the charring of the skull under that long black hair.

"Amaaauuuurraaa!" Arachne's thumb found one of Jaen's eyes, but before she could gouge it enough to make him let her go, he had swatted the thumb away.

"Arachne! Stay here!" He pushed her to the ground and ran toward the fire. She scrambled to her feet and ran after him. He caught her waist with one arm. "I told you to stay!" She fought him; his other arm drew back, his hand clenched, and his fist smashed into her jaw.

Arachne crashed to the ground. The ground was black, and then it was red. When she could see anything beyond the two terrible colors, she raised her head. Jaen had reached the lip of the hole. The hem of Amaura's chiton burst into tiny beautiful flames. Jaen beat them out with his hands, grasped Amaura around the waist, and dragged her backwards. Amaura still gripped the butt of the spear, and Suva the middle. All three yelled, flames of sound consuming each other. Amaura would not relinquish the spear. Arachne saw Jaen reach around her to pry at her hands with one of his, and at the same saw Suva turn and yank the spear sideways. The three figures tottered, hung suspended, and fell together into the hole of the Spider Stone.

Arachne pushed her arms against the ground, struggling to rise. The fire suddenly blazed higher. The inside of Arachne's head exploded into black and red, and then into nothing at all.

—— 22 ——

SHE woke on cold stone, to the sound of weeping.

For a long while, Arachne was aware only of the weeping. It was loud, but without true passion—the crying of disappointment rather than of anguish. Through the pain in her head Arachne struggled to identify the voice weeping. She heard a quaver in the sobs, and then the thickness of swampy lungs.

Suva.

Not Amaura.

Arachne's body went colder than the stone floor beneath her. She opened her eyes and found she lay on the colonnade, her head turned sideways toward the Grove. The trees closest to her stood unburned. Those farther away were unharmed in trunk and closest branches, but scorched on the ends of those wide branches stretching toward the center of the Grove. Through openings between them she could just see the center. All the trees had burned; the branches had toppled and the trunks stood like great charred stakes, still hot. Most of the fire had burned itself out, but patches of flames still flared among the smoldering ashes. Burned and unburned trees were separated by a clear ring of bare dirt: Nikos's trench had contained the fire and saved the rest of the Grove.

In the middle of the ash, something black stirred against the ground.

Arachne lifted her head, and then her shoulders. Amaura, where was Amaura, she must find Amaura.

"Spiderling. Don't move yet."

Jaen. He was behind her, his hand pushing down on her shoulder. When she struggled against the hand, he removed it and helped her to sit up.

"Amaura?" It came out a croak.

"Safe. She is safe, Arachne." At her look he added quietly, "I give you my word."

"Where?"

He pointed toward the charred Grove. "With the . . . Spider Stone. She will not leave it. But she is not harmed. Only dirty and bruised and distraught."

"Fire—"

"No. There was no fire in the hole itself, and she can get to and from the Stone if she picks her way carefully."

She eased her back against a stone column. Blood and soot covered Jaen's face in greasy clots, more blood on the left cheek than on the right. His scarlet chiton was filthy with ash. Ashes smeared the floor of the colonnade and floated in the air around his head, like flies. When he bore her weight on his hands, he winced; the skin on the palms was charred and blistered from beating the flames on Amaura's chiton. One of Suva's arms also was blistered. She sat sobbing, her head bent so far forward that her bony spine humped like the fin of a beached fish and her braids lay on the blackened stone.

Something sharp and slick cut into the underside of Arachne's tongue, and she spat it out. It was one of her teeth.

"What . . . happened?"

"I hit you," Jaen said. "Nothing else would stop you from rushing into the fire."

"But *you* went."

"Yes," Jaen said. He looked at her steadily, with a marked intensity. Arachne saw that he was implying more than simple agreement, and that he intended her to recognize that. Amaura's life was his reparation for the mutilation of the Grove. Had he thought of that even as he struck her, even as he risked the fire? Or had he gone after her daughter because Amaura was of his blood—and Arachne, once and long ago, the other half of himself—and then thought only later to put his risk to use as a claim?

Meeting his gaze, Arachne understood that she would never

know if Jaen had rescued Amaura for love or for profit. If he himself knew, he would not tell her. And if he did tell her, she would not trust his response.

Suva wept, the simple sobbing of a disappointed child.

Slowly Arachne said, "You went. Thank you."

Through the blood and soot, Jaen's eyes gleamed. Sealed, Arachne thought—the trade is sealed. Amaura for the Stone.

Jaen said, "Suva and Amaura both held that spear, and neither would release it. Suva had a . . . a strange strength. She threw us all off balance and down into the Spider Stone hole." He averted his face from Arachne and looked out over the charred Grove. "Suva and I slid down the sides and onto the dirt at the bottom, but Amaura fell onto the new Stone itself. It is soft, Arachne. Her body glanced off one side and hollowed it like a skull staved in at one temple."

Numb, Arachne wondered when he had seen a skull staved in at one temple.

"The fire suddenly flared above us, and we crouched in the hole until the worst had passed. There was enough air, although just barely. Suva finally fainted. Until she did, all my strength could barely keep her from piercing the Stone with her spear. Amaura would not help hold Suva—she cradled the Stone, keening."

Arachne could see it: Suva fighting Jaen with that eerie strength, Jaen trying to hold her arms and twist his face away from the point of the spear, unwilling to strike her when the strength of the Goddess lay on her, and so fighting his fear as well as her. Amaura with her arms thrown around the damaged Stone, pleading with anguished cries that she had not killed it, her life. And, above, the flames and smoke raging across the sky.

"When Suva fainted," Jaen said, "I broke her spear again and again, and threw the pieces up into the fire. It was not the spear that gave her a strength equal to mine. Nonetheless, I threw it."

There was a pause, broken only by Suva's sobbing. "When Suva revived, the strength was gone from her—and memory of it as well, I think. The fire was slowed by—the fire slowed. I pulled Suva from the hole and carried her, and you, to the colonnade. Amaura would not leave the Stone. She is there now, waiting for the Stone to lighten again, if it can. She has to discover if it still can. First she waits inside the hole, then crawls up to the edge, then again down."

Arachne thought of the thing she had glimpsed moving on the lip of the ashy earth: black. Black of soot and hair.

"She is not hurt, Arachne. Or, not in body."

Arachne stretched out her hand to poke Suva. She must see Suva's face. Suva raised her head, and Arachne saw that she was not a raging goddess, not a warrior, not a slave who had drowned her own child trying to escape Theran slavers. Suva was a soot-smeared crone with bewildered eyes, who remembered being nothing else.

"I will weave you a shroud of wool," Arachne said, slowly and distinctly. Her chest ground against her lungs. She remembered the odd feeling—the compacted, hard feeling, as if something within her had both shrunk and become more solid—that had taken her after Suva slashed her tapestry. The feeling was with her still. She, like Suva, had become ordinary. "Of wool, Suva."

Suva gazed at her without understanding.

"A shroud," Arachne repeated. "I will weave you a shroud of wool."

Suva frowned slightly. Arachne saw that what she said meant nothing, brought no pictures to Suva's mind at all. The words were only sounds, variously inflected, like wordless singing.

Arachne stumbled to her feet. She would not permit Jaen to help her. They picked their way through the Grove toward its charred center. Leaves whispered above them like blackened tongues.

Amaura sat at the lip of the hole, her bare legs dangling over the edge. Skin on both feet and one calf blistered. Her upper lip was split and swollen and her hair, singed on one side, frizzed into fantastic and tortured shapes. Against the soot of her face her light eyes looked huge.

"Amaura—" Arachne said. The girl did not answer. She stared fixedly into the hole. Unable to resist, Arachne peered over the edge.

The smallness of the Stone surprised her. She had expected it would grow rapidly, but it did not appear much larger than when Amaura had first shown it to her. The color, however, had changed markedly, from streaky bronze to a dull and even amber. Tiny perforations dotted the surface; Arachne could easily believe that as the Stone matured they would become tunnels. Tunnels—for new spiders?

Arachne closed her eyes briefly, and told herself it was to escape the despair on her daughter's face.

One side of the Stone was crushed inward. Jaen's description had been accurate. But nothing oozed from the staved-in section, and no edges were ragged or torn. The crushed section appeared to be the same color, texture, and composition as the rest of the unborn Stone.

"It was not your fault, Amaura," Arachne said, and heard herself how feeble her reassurance sounded. In a nearby pile of brush an ember caught, flared, crackled briefly.

Amaura was capable of sitting here day and night, unmoving and not eating, until the Grove should stir again. To Arachne it seemed a hopeless vigil: a smashed Stone, a burned Grove. She remembered, too, the death throes of the first Grove, the night Pholen had died. The Grove had had one fatal burst of strength, and that strength had been mindlessly malevolent, shot through with the spreading of decay and putrefaction. Had the spiders been turned poisonous by that malevolent strength? Or were they spiders that would have been naturally poisonous anywhere in the world but Island, and had reverted to deadliness only because the long life-affirming radiance of the Grove was finally withdrawn?

There was no way to know which had happened. But, Arachne thought, if it were the former, and if the new Stone below her was not dead—then when it did stir again, what sensations would radiate from a smashed Stone in a burned Grove? What nature of spiders would one day crawl forth?

Arachne shuddered.

"Amaura. Come away now. *Now.* There is nothing you can do here."

"I can wait." Her voice was flat.

Arachne thought: *This is one drama she does not savor,* and felt wearily ashamed.

"Come away now. Come."

"No. *No.*"

Amaura meant it, and Arachne was too spent to argue. Exhaustion barely let her stand; her jaw ached where Jaen had struck it; she would not ask Jaen's help to move Amaura. Arachne sank onto the dirt next to her daughter, to wait.

After a few moments, she fell in a doze, fitful and gray. She had

been awake all night. Her head drooped forward, snapped up just
before she lost her balance, slid again forward till her chin touched
her breast, over and over. Sometimes she was jerked upright by the
crack of a coal exploding into ash. Sometimes a shard of dream
brought her awake and clutching sideways for Amaura's arm. The
girl was always in the same position, and always rigid as stone.
Arachne did not see where Jaen was. She was too spent to care.

She sat dozing, and then she sat awake. The charred Grove was
overlaid with a golden softness. The light was not radiant, nor even
clear. It was like a gentle mist under veiled sunshine, remarkable
only because the transparent atmosphere of Island so seldom had
mists and the sunlight was so seldom other than direct and clear.
The sensations brushing Arachne's mind were as gentle as the light:
peace, undemanding harmony, a blurred warmth. They might all
have come from drinking a goblet of strong wine. No more.

Arachne looked at her daughter and saw it was not so for
Amaura.

Over Amaura's face lay the golden rapture. Her eyes shone wide
and exalted, oblivious to the ruin around her. She had thrown back
her head to lift her face to the blackened trees and her singed, filthy
hair fell away from her back and into the ashes. Under the tatters
of her chiton, Amaura's shoulders trembled. Arachne touched her
roughly, the roughness coming from fear and relief and envy.
Amaura did not respond. For her nothing existed but the sensation
from the Grove, and Arachne could see that for Amaura the sensation was no gentle mist. Nor was it deformed malevolence.

Through the mist, Arachne peered into the hole. The Stone
glowed, the same faintly shining amber as the first Stone. Against
the glow the perforations looked darker and slightly more in-
dented. No side of the Stone was crushed. The whole vibrated
slightly, like a sapling that has been pulled aside and has then
snapped again upright. As Arachne watched, the vibrations slowed
and ceased. The small Spider Stone curved cleanly, whole, shining
against the ash-smeared earth.

—— 23 ——

IN the early evening Arachne stood by a window in the Household rooms, looking out at the sea. She had slept the entire day; Amaura and Suva slept still. Below her the sea was purple-blue, like a more restless sky. At Arachne's feet lay a sack of rough wool, half-filled. When she heard a noise behind her, she knew without turning that it would be Jaen, and although her mood had been quiet and a little bleak she found now that she was curious to hear what he would say first. Nonetheless, his words surprised her.

"I have removed the tatters from your loom."

Arachne turned around. The bronze mirror on the wall behind him gave back the seamless dusky curve of sea and sky. A dark space in its center was Jaen, washed clean of soot and dressed in dark wool. She smelled the fresh scent of his hair, and thought fleetingly that he would have left his bath water in his chamber, unemptied and cold.

"Thank you," she said. "But there was no need."

"Why no need?"

"There are looms at Kyles's vineyard."

His foot nudged the sack on the floor. "You are going to the vineyard, Spiderling?"

"Jaen. I would ask you to do something for me. Don't call me that."

"I will not," Jaen said quietly. Arachne looked out the window and waited. He had made a concession; she waited for a demand to balance it. But again he startled her.

"The tapestry that Suva slashed surprised me. I did not know that you had come to hate the Grove, Arachne. I did not know you could come to hate the Grove."

"Was that what you thought formed the tapestry? Hatred of the Grove?"

"Was it not?"

"No." She ran her hands over the stone sill. She could feel Jaen waiting. He wanted to know what the destroyed tapestry had meant, and what she had been when she weaved it, but he would not ask. The bitter accusations between them before Suva's slashings had been forgotten by neither. Jaen could no longer claim entitlement to any part of Arachne's life, and what he could not have as claim or gift, he would not beg for.

For the first time Arachne gave thought to the precarious bleakness of Jaen's position on Island. To the people he should rule, he would represent attack on their men, mutilation of their Grove, and —by unearned association—the inexplicable poisonousness of their spiders. From that, she sensed how much bleaker still must have been his position in Thera to nonetheless drive him home. If Jaen must now create pride out of the asking or not asking of questions, he perhaps had been stripped of as much as she had. It was such a pathetic and tiny pride that she told him what he wanted to know.

"I did not weave that tapestry from hatred of the Grove, Jaen. At first it was to be a shroud for Suva. She asked for one, and on it she wanted scenes of Island because it was here on Island that she cast off her previous life and decided she had become a goddess."

"So Amaura told me," Jaen said, and his voice held no amusement. Arachne knew he was remembering Suva's eerie strength during the fire. "But she was not a goddess."

"What was she, Jaen?"

"A woman pushed by madness and death to draw strength from the stirring of the new Stone."

"No one before has ever drawn bodily strength from the Grove."

"No one before has fought in the Grove," Jaen said. "Bodily."

Arachne glanced at him sharply. In the dusk his face was rigid. The blood on his cheek had been washed away, and she could see the shape of the cut: a smooth arc from temple to chin. Had it been slashed there by Suva's spear? Jaen would wear the scar till he died.

She said, "I don't know if Suva became a goddess or not. She spoke about the gods and their whims constantly—do you remember?—in her stories. We heard them since we were children, over and over, and Suva must have lived with them decades before that. I don't know when belief becomes fancy and when will. Do you, Jaen?"

Fancy and will. She saw again the spiders in tilted pots, the pharmakons that had made no difference. Beyond the window one star shone, low over the sea.

"I do know that Suva was dying, and that she wanted a shroud with scenes of Island on it. I intended to weave it for her. What grew on the loom was the tapestry you saw, but it did not grow from hatred of the Grove."

Arachne stopped. Her hands, restlessly rubbing the stone sill, stopped moving. She realized that she had lied to herself: she was telling this to Jaen not from pity on him, but from a need of her own. Her talk gushed now from the same deep well that her weaving had then. She needed to tell her story as she had needed to weave it, and the telling must be to Jaen, whom she did not trust, because of the entire world only Jaen might understand. It seemed bitter to her that trust and understanding could be formed apart, but she recognized that it was so.

Jaen waited quietly.

Theran slaves I watched die as they took the Stone?

Arachne said, "I thought the Grove had failed me. I thought that clear sightedness, that intense awareness of . . . grace, was a promise to Island. We had the Grove. We were valued, we were protected, we were woven into a central golden web of things alive. I was mistaken.

"I thought, too, that I had failed the Grove. If it was a living thing and in my care, mine was the responsibility to keep it from harm. Mine and yours."

Jaen stood rigid in the gloom.

"I was mistaken in that as well. The grove had nothing to do with anyone on Island, neither promise nor responsibility. When Delernos reached it, the Grove was already old. It was a living thing, but not a living thing connected in any way to mortals. That golden aliveness—it was true enough, not fancy nor will, but it was not ours. It was not ours at all. To claim it because we touched it is like claiming the sun because it shines on our heads. Reason will not support the claim.

"Maybe there *is* a reason why my Grove bloomed, died, and rotted, but the time is gone when I expect to have it shown me. Why *should* we expect that? Because enchantment exists does not mean it must exist as our tool."

More stars dotted the sky. The room, its lamps unlit, was shadowy.

"You are saying," Jaen said, "the mortals should not try to understand the gods."

"No," Arachne said patiently. "I am not saying that. I am saying we should not assume understanding as our right. That other golden world—*"real,* her blood insisted, *the real world "*—is not ours.

Jaen said nothing.

I am going now, Jaen. First to Kyles's vineyard, and then away from Island."

Jaen flinched. "To Thera?"

"No. Not to Thera."

"Where?"

"I don't know. But I knew even as I weaved Suva's shroud that it was the last thing I would ever make in spider silk. I weave, from now forward, in wool. You still do not understand, Jaen. All those painful figures in the tapestry Suva ripped—they were not images of what had been destroyed by the Grove, nor even images of what *I* had destroyed. They were images of things I had not seen because, looking only at the Grove, I had not been paying attention."

Arachne's fingers tightened on Jaen's wrist. He moved restlessly, but before he could say anything—challenge or mockery or question—she scowled at him and rushed on.

"Know this, Jaen: to pay attention to each other's lives, carefully and consistently, is the only golden grace mortals can offer. It is not much. It may change nothing. But it is all we can give. The rest is beyond our help, and in that Suva was right, in all her stories. Did you never think what all of them held in common?"

"That it takes but one innocent step to plunge all into ruin," Jaen said promptly. Her head jerked up, and he laughed, not gently.

"Do you imagine that what you say is so new, Spiderling? Or even that it is true? You speak like a child, or at very most, like someone who has never left a provincial backwater like Island. There are many things one person can be given by another besides your 'careful attention.' There are obeisance, and tribute, and profit, and power, and all the pleasures of the senses. What you say is not trivial, but it is sentimental. You do not have to have touched the Grove, as you touched it, to offer such sentimentality. It is the theme of a hundred Theran street ballads."

Arachne smiled. She saw that Jaen expected her to be offended, and that it disconcerted him that she was not. "A hundred ballads, Jaen. But never before a weaving. Never, until Arachne, a weaving."

"A weaving that has been destroyed!"

"If Suva had not destroyed it, I would have done so myself."

Now she had surprised him. Through the gloom he watched her warily, like an adversary. A cool wind blew in the window, smelling of the sea, and Arachne let go of his wrist and wrapped her arms around herself. Her arms felt solid, compact.

"I weave now only in wool. Suva gave me that." She smiled in sharp imitation of Jaen's mockery. "One of your nonattentive gifts."

"Are you sure it is a gift? The world is full of ordinary and insignificant women who weave in wool. Only Arachne weaved tapestries that breathed, alive, in spider silk."

"There are no more spiders."

"You know there may be again."

She did not answer. After a while Jaen said, "When do you go to Kyles's vineyard?"

"Tomorrow at dawn."

"And when do you plan to leave Island?"

"As soon as the first trade ship from Bylia lands on the Southern or Eastern Shore. It should not be very long; the winter winds are well done. When I leave, Jaen, I take half the Household treasury with me."

"Of course."

She turned to cross the room to get her cloak. The mirror behind her startled her; it was full of reflected stars. Arachne lit a lamp, pulled her cloak around her, and returned to Jaen at the window.

A year ago, she thought, she and Jaen had been at war; a day ago they had torn at each other's unscabbed wounds; today they stood talking carefully, at a window. Tomorrow she would be gone. Where was the pattern in all that? There was none.

"What will you do now, Jaen?"

"Guard the Treasury," he said lightly. Then, "Island rumbles with rumors about the new Spider Stone. Now that the spiders have died out, some Islanders will return to the villa. Only the adventurous, at first—I *will* need to put a guard on the Treasury. Later, when nothing horrible befalls the first ones, others will come back. Don't worry about Amaura, Arachne. A settled life will eventually return to the villa, and until then I will watch over her for you."

"She is going with me away from Island."

Jaen laughed with a flash of his old gaiety. "To get her away from the Grove she would have to be tied, gagged, and drugged."

"Then she will be."

"By *you?*"

"By Kyles."

Jaen stopped smiling.

"Amaura can not stay here," Archne said. "The new Stone—she has stayed too close to its conceiving. It blinds her even more than the old Stone blinded me. She uses it not to touch something immortal but factual; she uses it to escape entirely what *is* factual. I did not know until recently the Grove could be so used." She stumbled over the last words, then went on sharply. "Amaura will go with me off Island, and Kyles will make her. Don't turn away like that, Jaen. You are keeping nothing from me. I know what Kyles has become."

"Does he still wish to kill me?"

"I don't know that."

"Had we met face to face, swords in hand, I would not have killed him."

"You had not the same cause. What life I had left after the Grove, I gave to you. What life I needed besides the Grove, I needed from you."

"And now," Jaen said, "you hope to reclaim Kyles by the straight-forward method of choosing him instead of me to help you with Amaura. Isn't that simpleminded?"

"No. I am not choosing him. There *is* no choice. He can take

Amaura away from Island. You cannot, because you cannot go away yourself. Now I need *him.*"

"And you expect Kyles to see this as you do?"

"Yes. He is Amaura's father, no less than Pholen's."

"What if I said *I* would leave Island with you?"

"Ah, Jaen," Arachne said. She added no more, but both heard the unspoken words: *I would not trust you enough.*

Jaen bit off his next sentence. "Amaura is the heir to Island."

"You will marry. Soon, I think. It would make you a little more palatable to those who return to the villa."

She saw from his stillness that he had already thought of that. From bitterness, from amusement, from the bereft compact solidness Suva had left her, Arachne said, "Cleis has already married. A pity, don't you think?"

Jaen smiled, a smile that held such a hard edge in the soft lamplight that Arachne was startled. "Aretone has not."

"Aretone?"

"Do you think an insipid child like Cleis would help my position —or suit my tastes? A pallid and weepy companion to talk with— after you?"

"After Ikeria," Arachne said, and heard that her voice and was steady, and wondered how.

"Ikeria and you," Jaen said. His stillness tested both her distaste and his own pain at the joining of the two names. "Neither of you were insipid."

"Aretone will never forgive you for attacking Island."

"I did not attack Island."

"For intending to attack Island. She will never forgive you."

"You mean she has not forgiven me yet."

"She is not young."

"She is young enough to bear children."

"Children who will live with the new Spider Stone?"

"As I will," Jaen said, and in his voice Arachne heard a mongrel hope, part desperation and part excited interest. Jaen would be here with the new Stone and the new Grove, and without Arachne or Amaura as a constant measure of how deeply he touched, or did not touch, its radiant core. An untested possibility, an unknown challenge. She had been mistaken: Jaen was not among the broken men.

Arachne felt hungry. She had eaten when she woke, but only a few bites. Bread and olives lay on a table, near the lamp. She took a handful of olives and held out the bowl to Jaen, who took it and said abruptly, "In Thera I learned the cause of Delernos's exile."

Arachne turned him. "We know the cause of Delernos's exile. He killed a royal favorite in a fair fight."

"So he told his exiled Household," Jaen said. "You have always admired him, haven't you, Arachne? The man of will. The uncorruptible Delernos, who uncovered the knowledge of a blessed isle in a forgotten scroll and then persevered against all odds until he actually found it."

"It is worthy of being admired."

"But it is not true. No, don't turn away from me, Arachne. On Thera I heard a different story. Delernos did kill a royal favorite, but not in a fair fight. It was a struggle for power, and Delernos had his rival poisoned. Assassination by poison was common enough in Thera. It still is. But Delernos's plot was discovered after it had succeeded, and he was found guilty and exiled by the king."

"I don't believe it!"

"Believe it. His Household was given one day and one night to leave Thera. It was a wild scramble, and Delernos was overheard to cry to his Master of Ships, 'I do not care in what direction we sail! Choose any direction, any cursed point, so long as it is away from here!' The Master of Ships did not want to share the exile, and Delernos's cry to him is remembered even after all this time by the family he left behind—was forced to leave behind. Family history."

"Why are you telling me this, Jaen? Why now?"

"Don't you see? There was no lost scroll, no persevering search, no act of will to reach a legendary refuge. Delernos came to Island and found the Grove by pure chance, blind and undeserved luck. Island happened to be uninhabited, and the Grove happened to be at the peak of its . . . life. If what you say is true and that other golden world has no connection with ours, then that time Delernos just happened to profit by that world's rhythms, and at a later time you happened to lose by them. He deserves no admiration, and you and I no blame."

Arachne said evenly, "I do not class you and me together."

Jaen grinned, his teeth very white in the starlight. "But I do. And so, with persuasion, will Aretone. Eventually. And there is one more detail in Delernos's story that I want to tell you. He is surprisingly well-remembered in Thera: the man who gambled on murder to move closer to the king's ear, and lost his gamble. He is considered quite a dramatic figure. But do you know who betrayed his plot to the soldiers who arrested him?''

Arachne said nothing.

"His own Household priestess. Delernos was stingy with his offerings, inclined to rich enough gifts or honors to the Goddess because he was off pursuing favor at the palace. The priestess bore a grudge. I suppose that as Delernos saw it, he was advancing all of their fortunes, the whole Household's, by pouring his wealth and energy into the palace. But as the priestess saw it, he was neglecting the wealth and energy due *her* position. Somehow she learned of the plot to poison Delernos's rival, and she betrayed it.''

Jaen still held the bowl of olives. He smiled at his sister over them. "You could regard that sordid little story in a number of ways, couldn't you, Arachne? For one, you could say that Delernos was not what you thought him, a man of will and justice. Or, you could say that he was a victim of Suva's one false step that plunges all into ruin. Like you. Like me.

"Or you could say something else, Arachne. You could say that Delernos was exiled for 'not paying attention.' For giving all his attention to the care of his Household, and no attention at all to that golden Presence beyond. You could say that.

"Which would you choose? How do you regard our beloved ancestor now?''

Arachne looked straight out over the sea. "As dead. Dead and passed.''

"Ah," Jaen said, and the sound was a soft desolation; he did not say for what.

24

SUNLIGHT broke over the edge of the sea, over the rocky cliffs of the Eastern Shore, over the rest of Island in a long, direct sweep west. Wherever it touched, the light flung down shadows. Two fell behind the women trudging east on a goatpath worn across Island's long and fertile center.

Arachne noticed Suva's shadow before her own. Carrying nothing, Suva shuffled along the path docilely, and slowly; her gait would more than double the time to reach Kyles's vineyard. But Suva would not be left behind. She had cried, and the childish tears on her mute face had contrasted so much with her former eerie strength as a goddess that Arachne had been irritably moved and had agreed to not leave her alone with Amaura and with Jaen, whom she seemed to fear. Suva's face, like her hands, was empty except for a slight, foolish smile at the warmth of the sunshine on her shoulders and bare head. She looked as if she needed nothing more. She could not talk, but she shuffled between olive trees and spring wildflowers with an unquestioning serenity that Arachne was near; that she, Suva, would be fed and covered; that all was fine.

If I have lost a false sureness, Arachne thought, then Suva has gained one.

Arachne carried the wool sack on her shoulders, a waterskin at her waist, and a shepherd's stick in her hand. The morning sun was in her eyes, and she lowered the wool band around her hair to give some shade to her eyes. But midafternoon, when they were tired, the sun would be behind them. Long before dark they would reach some farmer's house or goatherd's hut: abandoned, reoccupied, never left. Island was cautiously on the move. The Mistress's journey to her husband would not be unpeopled or unremarked.

And it was not. By the second day they had spoken with a goatherd and a farmer's slave. The slave, who at first looked flustered at seeing the mistress of Island dirty and sweating and on foot, looked after them with a sullen frown. But the goatherd scampered away eastward, fleet as his goats, eager to spread the word that the Mistress herself was traveling her depopulated domain.

The morning of their third day of travel dawned hot and clear. Insects droned in the grass. A lizard ran across the path. The leaves of olive trees, dusty even this early in the spring, rustled silver in the morning breeze. From a thicket of white myrtle rose fresh, astringent scent.

Arachne smelled the warm earth around her. She gazed at the land rising ahead, to the east. Seen through the transparent air and against the blue sky, the line of the hills looked severe and pure. Fruitful vines grew there, and good grains.

A figure, small and dark, topped the nearest hill. As Suva trudged forward, Arachne saw the figure start down the hill. She caught her breath. Slowly the figure grew larger, looking darker whenever it descended into the shadow of a dell, hard-edged with sunlight whenever it climbed a rise. The figure followed a goat track that rose, dipped, rose again, and then Kyles stood before her.

"Arachne."

He was sweating hard, too hard for simply walking, and his eyes were bloodshot and weary. Untrimmed beard and hair gave him a dangerous look; Suva, not recognizing him, shuffled backwards and clutched at Arachne's arm. But Arachne saw that his weary eyes. were sober, and the smells of his sweat clean. "I was told you were crossing Island."

"To your vineyard."

"Why?"

"Because I choose to," Arachne said. She could not tell yet if they were still adversaries, and she looked away from him. Around her lay the warm fields, the vines, the olive trees. Sunshine and abundance. *Not enough,* her heart insisted quietly, *not enough, not enough. If only I could hold Pholen in the Grove once more—just once more!*

Dead and passed.

But Kyles was not dead, nor Amaura, nor herself.

Kyles said, in the level voice of too much emotion too much chained, "Is Amaura with you?"

"Yes. But she is not . . . she must leave Island, Kyles. The Grove has . . . come back, and is harming her. She must be made to leave Island."

"And you?"

"I will leave, as well. With your help—if you will give your help."

"Help you to follow Jaen?"

"No. *No.* Jaen is not off Island; he is here."

Kyles threw up his head, and his dark eyes flashed. *"Here."*

"In the villa. Yes. But I am taking Amaura to Bylia, and you . . . Kyles . . ." her voice faltered.

He looked at her quietly, for a long moment. She could not tell from his impassive face what he thought, but she was unprepared for what he said next.

"I am not unmanned, Arachne."

"I know," she said, and knew as she said it that it was somehow true. She had known. And yet neither was it the whole truth, for either of them. She put one hand to his cheek, feeling the rough hollows.

"Nothing could unman you, Kyles. Not you."

He opened his arms and she moved into them, deliberately and steadily, her back to where the villa lay behind her in the clear light.